twice in a
Lifetime

a *love found* novel

RUTHIE HENRICK

twice in a lifetime

© 2014 by Ruthie Henrick

All rights reserved.

Interior Designer: The Write Assistants

ISBN: 978-0-9914164-0-0

For the Big Kahuna
My Once in a Lifetime

Prologue

Alexandra Tate had loved her husband. Then she hated him. But after three years of laying her soul bare, she finally accepted him.

She'd just said good-bye to Doctor Baker for the last time. Pulled away from the therapist's office and drove through town with the woman's words echoing off the block and stucco buildings lining the street. *"You've had quite a journey, Allie. I'm pleased with the progress you've made. I think you're ready to leave the past where it belongs—in the past."* The comfort of her doctor's arms as she offered a final hug was meant to warm her. As was the boost of parting advice. *"Be happy."*

By all rights, triumph should shimmer in her veins. The hard part was over, after all. But instead of the thrilling sensation of accomplishment—the invisible cloak of victory she longed for—the only sensation curling through her right now was the passive lassitude of acquiescence.

On a sigh, she turned her car into a nearby strip mall. She'd put her life on hold to search for answers, and found few. But she could live with that. Eyes bare against the bright morning sun, she scanned the parking lot, whipped into an empty space, and climbed out. Doctor Baker was right: it was time to move on.

An easy slap anchored the hem of her sundress before it caught a gust. The clack of her strappy sandals echoed off the sidewalk as she dashed into the florist. The fragrance—heavy, heady, nearly cloying—assaulted her as she swung open the door.

The beefy woman behind the counter didn't bother to look up, just continued to stuff pale pink roses one after another into a sea of citrus stems and airy fern. "Help you?"

With a quick scan of the displays, Allie spotted what she presumed was her order. This part was easy, she knew what he liked. She cleared her throat to get the woman's attention.

"Excuse me, I called earlier. The name's Tate." She aimed a finger toward the cooler. "Are those mine?"

The woman raised her eyes—just her eyes—and peered over the top of safety orange frames. Fake pearls were barely visible as they hung from one ear to the other across the back of her fleshy neck. The gaudy garland caught the glasses as she slipped them from her nose with fingers stained green. "Tate, you say? Imagine they are."

Allie drummed the counter as the florist shuffled across industrial vinyl in orthopedic shoes, then returned and slid the tissue-wrapped bundle across the counter. In an impatient scrawl Allie signed the charge slip. "Thanks for your help," flew over her shoulder on her way out the door. She'd be on the freeway within minutes.

Her thumbs tapped the rhythm of the bass line pouring through in-dash speakers as her tires whined on the blacktop. The rude glare of morning sun sliced through the windshield, forcing her to dive through her purse for sunglasses. She slipped them on as she cruised the freeway, heading east. Her day—which for three years had been slated as her independence day—in reality fell a little short.

But she was limping from the battlefield whole.

Mirrors checked, she steered her vehicle into the fast lane. After three tumultuous years she would allow herself no more guilt, no more self-doubt. Her breath escaped in a rush of relief as welcome as the cool air blowing into the sedan through vents.

Even mid-morning, it would take a while to get through traffic. Her bare legs stuck to the leather seat as she shuffled to settle comfortably. In the past she needed this time to gird herself. To prime. But after today's visit with Doctor Baker it was merely a trip across town.

At least, she needed it to be that.

Following Ben's accident she'd needed to start a new life—she had no choice. But now, with time as a buffer, she was changed. She was solid, confident. Once again in control.

With a flick of the turn signal she dodged cars one lane at a time until she landed on the off ramp. The route through town was a warren of twisted streets, but she was off the tangle of the interstate, and nearly there. The sign stood just ahead. *Sunnyside.*

Her foot light on the gas, she eased around the corner. Patchy shade spilled through towering jacarandas as she crept along, the respite from the harsh mid-August sun welcome.

The slow breath she drew in through her nose was calming. The air she expelled through pursed lips was no fiercer than a whisper. Gravel crunched beneath her tires as she eased onto the shoulder at the end of the lane and parked her aging car. This sense of peace was new, but she was more than ready for it. Her chest rising and then lowering, she let one more calming breath fade from her lips before she slid out, clutching the bouquet. Sunflowers. Pert, and happy. Not too . . . girly.

She smoothed her cheery blue dress and brushed stray wisps from her face as she strolled to the familiar stone bench and perched on the edge. Warmth seeped through the thin cotton tucked beneath her thighs, a harbinger of the day ahead. Phoenix—a modern city steeped in history and culture—was home. But monsoon season in the desert was no picnic.

She set the blossoms on the seat beside her, rested her palm softly over the stems as if holding her husband's hand. "Hello, Ben." She managed a nostalgic smile. "Happy anniversary."

After a muffled cough she struggled to speak. Tilted her head back and let her eyelids slide shut as words crawled up her throat and were halted by a bitter blockage. The lump appeared with no warning, clotting her throat, unwelcome and impossible to talk around. She swallowed it back, freeing her thoughts. Freeing her emotions which, after her appointment this morning, still rode near the surface. Freeing *her*.

She needed to talk to him—it was the reason she came here. For three years now she visited from time to time. But always on this day.

She lifted the flowers and held them in her hands. In the beginning, in the first months after he was gone—after she *knew*—she found herself overwhelmed. Guilt, shame, anger all swamped her. If only their lives—if only *he*—had turned out differently. But her emotions were tempered by time now and she could at last look back and remember Ben fondly.

She missed him. Missed the hours they spent together. Chatting, catching up at the end of the day. After so many years together, how could she not?

She conjured an image of their son, and a smile stole onto her face. "Trey's ready to leave for college next week." If she had a mirror she'd find a bit of dimple denting her left cheek. She always hoped she would outgrow it, but never did, much to Ben's delight. Memories of their son's childhood filtered through her mind. "We dreamed of this day often as he grew, didn't we? You would be so proud of him.

"You'd be proud of Jake, too." Jake, Ben's best friend, who still ran the company he and her husband built together. "He's there for us whenever we need him." And even though they had a rough beginning, she and Jake, they'd developed a strong familial affection for each other over the years. "As a matter of fact, I've already spoken with him this morning." When the steamy hot shower she'd envisioned following her sunrise run turned out to be nothing more than a tepid spray. Her smile turned rueful. "He's at the house right now, replacing the water heater."

Her heart gave a familiar skip. What would she do without Jake?

With only the slightest breeze to ruffle her hem, the air lay as heavy and uncomfortable as a wet woolen blanket. She lifted her arms, dragged up the weight of hair overdue for a trim, and gained momentary relief from the hot and sticky. She let a smile bloom. "I'll start work on my classroom this afternoon." She lowered her arms back down, let her curls tumble around her shoulders even as her naked left hand lifted to cover her heart. "I'm so excited about the new school year; you know how I always get."

Her students—herds of rambunctious kindergarteners—also helped rescue her over the past few years. The children amused her, and filled an empty part of her soul. It was their fresh-faced enthusiasm that she loved most about her career.

What she wouldn't give for a flock in her own home.

Wrenching heartache shifted inside her, forced her to return to the bench. More than a topic of discussion, their family—or rather, the *size* of their family—was the basis for nearly all the arguments between her and Ben. Trey was their child—and only Trey. But it wasn't supposed to be that way. Ben promised.

Her eyes flooded, and she blinked back the useless tears. On a huff she stood, prowled the area fronting the bench, sunflowers drooping in her fist. After three years she still didn't understand what Ben did, or why. But it was in the past. She couldn't turn back the clock.

She was no longer angry, yet tears trickled down her cheeks. Once again, tears of regret. Regret not only for herself, but for Trey, for Jake, even for *them*. Whoever *they* were.

She stopped, turned. Dropped the limp flowers on the granite headstone and her voice thickened. "Why Ben? Why, when we made plans? So many plans." Today she put them all to rest. Her eyes slid shut, then flicked open to study her clasped hands through the blur of tears."

The question—the demand to know—elicited no answer. She turned back, sank once again onto the bench. She was ready to let go. She *was*. But first she would cry just one last time.

"Damn you, Ben."

Chapter One

Nineteen Years Earlier

Mother Nature was just plain showing off, the black-hearted bitch. A dazzling blue sky painted the backdrop for wispy veins of sheer clouds. The fragrance of springtime wafted in on a breeze. Allie propped her hip against the sill of the open window and stole a moment to wallow in the warmth of the sun. The sun she had no time for today.

In response to her roommate's monologue she turned toward her, folded her hands against her chest and mocked a swoon. "Yes, Reese, I heard it all. He's tall, he's brilliant, he's a stud." Was there any hope of shutting her up?

A sultry sweet aroma tickled her nose, followed closely by the sound of laughter. She dropped her hands, turned back to face the outdoors and let her eyes scan the yard. Virginal white clusters of jasmine lined the manicured lawn, but it was the upstairs neighbors who caught her attention. Shirtless and barefoot even in March, the hunks from 2A were blowing off the brilliant Wednesday afternoon with a Frisbee and a six pack.

Reese continued to rhapsodize.

She pretended to listen.

She lifted her chin and let the warm afternoon breeze tease her skin and ruffle the curls that framed her face. The gods of academia were against her. Why should she be stuck inside writing a term paper when the sun, the warmth, beckoned her outside? She heaved a long, ponderous sigh. The day was lazy, made for lolling. It was the type of day she would normally oil up, catch some rays with the girls. A masculine yell had her darting her eyes, locating the source.

Mmm. Or maybe spend a long, slow afternoon with someone special.

If she had someone special.

It was hopeless. She turned back to her single-girl bed, clambered on and surrounded herself with research books and loose-leaf paper. Pale redheads did not bronze, anyway. And she did not have time—not right now—for someone special. Legs pretzeled, she focused on curriculum development rather than Reese, still chattering about her latest hunk of manflesh.

Wait. *What?* She whipped her head around. "Forget it, Reese! Absolutely not!"

"Come on, Allie." Designer heels stuttered as Reese Fielding spun to a stop in the miniscule room. "What do you have against Ben Tate? He's an awesome looking guy."

Allie curled her lip. "I hear he's a player."

"So, like, *play* for a change."

"And he's a jock."

Reese smirked. "It's not a dirty word."

Allie swept a hand over the clutter surrounding her and let her words snap. "You make goo-goo eyes at Jake all you want. I have a paper due Monday." *And* a stack of graduation announcements to address, *and* lesson plans to prepare. "I have no interest in—her finger jabbed in Reese's direction—a blind date."

As usual, Reese heard only what she chose to hear and merely lifted one shoulder. "What-ever. It's just pizza, you know? And besides, he's like way fun."

Reese pretending she wasn't annoyed was almost comical. But she was annoyed. Oh, Allie knew it for certain. Didn't matter how long she was gone from the coast, Reese's *Valley Girl* emerged a living thing when she was wound up. But a blind date? Oh no, that was a bad idea for many reasons. Allie dug her fists into her hips. "You're a giant pain in my ass."

"Come on Allie, do this for me? We can double. Ben's like Jake's best friend since they were babies."

Allie slapped the frilly pink comforter, which set pages of her term paper flying. "Do I need to remind you I don't know Jake, either?"

"So? I'll be there. What's the worst that can happen?"

She could give her a list—with bullet points—but flipped her off instead. Much more satisfying.

"I bet you'll like him."

With her hands full of papers, Allie paused, cocked her head, narrowed her eyes. "You're putting way too much effort into this. What's in it for you, Reese?"

Reese was unfazed by the glare aimed her way. She merely rolled her eyes and huffed. "Look, you're a nice girl. You're always doing things for me. I just thought I'd do something for you for a change."

Allie studied her thoughtfully. Reese *could* be sweet. If she set her mind to it. "Really? That's all?"

"Sure."

Allie would have gobbled the lie, too. Swallowed it as eagerly as a mama bird with a nice, plump worm, if only Reese made eye contact. Her eyes narrowed again. "Damn it, Reese. Spit it out."

Reese probably would have continued to argue, so she stretched her glower into another outright glare.

"I sort of cut Jake off until you both agreed."

"Crap." It was all so clear now. She let the papers scatter around her. At least Reese seemed embarrassed. "A little extreme, don't you think?"

Reese sank onto the side of the bed. "It seemed like a good idea at the time."

Embarrassed and miserable. Good.

"Guess I forgot one little detail."

"Yeah. Guess so."

Reese held out on her guy once before, during summer break, thank God. Because nothing screamed *edgy* like Reese without regular action between the sheets. And with mid-terms looming, Reese could not afford to be edgy.

Allie collapsed back into the pillows, her arms outstretched. Her mom always told her compassion was a virtue, but not today it wasn't. Today it was a curse. She rolled her head to meet Reese's hopeful stare, her shoulders taking a swift slump into the thick comforter, her chin lowering to her chest. "I don't know if I'm more disgusted with you or myself." She gritted her teeth. "When are we doing this?"

"Saturday." Reese fell back beside Allie, grabbed her hand with a chuckle and squeezed. "Oh Allie, it won't hurt a bit." Reese lifted her free hand and traced the letter X over her heart. "Promise."

Wearing nothing but plaid boxers and a snarl, Jake Taylor leapt from the ancient sofa to pace. "Fucking Michaels!" He prowled the room, fingers tunneling through his hair, leaving it standing on end. "Bottom of the ninth, my first no-hitter of the season, and what does that prick do? He tanks it for me!"

Ben Tate's eyes darted from the game on TV. He hung his head and let it sway. "It bites ass, man. That throw from Taggert whizzed past him like a stray bullet."

"And Jefferson—that jerk couldn't beat his grandfather in a snail crawl, but there he was, safe on first. Sucking wind." Jake snared his roommate with an accusing glare. "*You* would have caught that ball! Damn it!" He dropped back onto the ratty tweed and glowered at his roommate, the sportscaster blabbering in the background.

Ben gave him a *what can you do* shrug and gestured toward his sling. "I'm off the DL next week, dude. I'll have you covered."

He didn't want Ben's platitudes. He wanted him back on the field.

"C'mon, man, forget it. Let's get cleaned up and hit the town."

He had to admit blowing off a little steam might ease the frustration grinding at him. "Yeah, okay. We could—*oh, shit!*"

Ben shot him a quick, quizzical glance, then rolled to his feet and kept up as the conversation took a left turn. "What's up?"

Jake lowered his head into his hands. The hair flopping over his face hid his eyes. *Reese.* He couldn't believe he forgot. He couldn't believe he got roped into this. And if Ben called him a pussy, heads would definitely roll. He plastered his gaze on the television and forced nonchalance into his voice. "Hey, Tate, you got plans Saturday?"

Ben strode into the kitchen, an ice pack strapped to his bum wing. "Aren't we in Lubbock?" The refrigerator opened, then closed.

"Nah, those games aren't until next week."

"Right." Ben reappeared, one can tucked into his sling, another in his free hand. He lobbed it Jake's way.

Jake popped the tab with a muted *pfft* and guzzled half.

Ben made it back to the recliner, then one-handedly popped open his can and sat back without taking a sip. "You need me out of the apartment? I can make plans."

Jake propped his drink between his knees. "Still seeing Vivian?" He didn't see the attraction, but friends ask anyway.

"Nah. She's history."

Jake nodded in understanding. And something like relief. "Bye, bye, prom queen." He waved a flippant farewell to Cheerleader Barbie, the love of Ben's life for two whole months. "Actually, I need you to do me a favor. Reese hatched this plan."

Ben arched an eyebrow. "So? I thought you weren't serious."

Jake lifted an amused eyebrow. "How serious is a blow job?"

"Good point." Ben matched his smirk as the commercials ended and the game resumed. "So what's the deal?"

"She's got this friend. Allie."

Ben's eyes went hot as he dragged them from the tube. "Are you fucking insane? Our first free weekend in a month and you want me to do *what?*"

"Yeah, I know. But she's bugging the shit out of me." And she told him he wasn't getting laid again until her friend did, but he didn't see the need to overshare.

"Jesus, Jake." Ben blew out a breath. "What's she like anyway, this Allie? Is she a dog?"

"Hell if I know. Supposedly she's Reese's best friend, but I've never met her."

"Maybe she's fat."

God, he hoped not. He wanted his hands on Reese's tits. "Reese says she studies all the time. One date then done, all right?"

The glare Ben leveled on him was pure blue flame. "In case you haven't figured it out, genius, the idea sucks."

"C'mon B. Just to get her off my ass?" Fuck, now he was begging.

"This is not a date. It's a favor. And you owe me big time." Ben added a scowl to his glare. The roar of the crowd pulled his attention back to the game.

Damn it, he'd deal if it meant Ben caved. "Sure, anything."

Ben gave him half his attention. "I'm not talking about a case of beer or gas money to Snow Bowl, either."

"Fuck you, dude. We're talking pizza, for chrissake. I'm not asking you to marry the girl."

Chapter Two

Sparky's was having a busy night. The mixture of college students and young families made snaking his way through the pub a challenge. "Over there." Ben used his chin to point toward a relatively clean booth far enough away from the stage. He already had to shout to be heard over the rowdy mob of kids in the arcade. He didn't need his ears bleeding from the band too.

Duct-tape Band-Aids made sliding onto the vinyl seat tricky. He craned his neck to search out a waitress. "Jesus, it's crowded tonight. We'll never get service."

"Don't be a girl. The pizza's hot, and the beer's cold and cheap. She'll get here. Suck it up." Jake turned his head to watch the door. "Oh, good. Here they come."

"All right, let's get this over with." Ben swiveled his head until he could see the entryway. The glass door was just closing behind Reese. She was distracted, jabbering with someone on her far side. The crowd shifted and he bolted upright in his seat. "Oh, shit. Not fat."

From across the table, Jake cleared his throat. "Definitely not ugly."

Ben's eyes were glued to the girl. The tangy aroma of oil and spices drifted from the table behind them. A couple laughed as they strode past on their way to the bar. A waitress finally appeared and took an order across the aisle. As she left, she jabbed her stubby pencil into the nest of hair piled on her head. All of this was distracting, but nowhere near as compelling as the chick crossing the room.

Short curls in some dark shade of red bounced atop the package strolling toward him wrapped in curve-hugging jeans and ankle-breaking heels. Her sudden laugh lit up her light eyes—gray maybe—and exposed a single dimple.

His night was looking up.

His hands actually itched to map the lush curves hidden beneath her fuzzy blue sweater. *What the hell?* He scrambled to stand, and clapped his arms across his chest.

On legs that caused him to imagine wild, wicked acts, she approached the table and abruptly jerked forward. From instinct his hands shot out, caught her by her shoulders to save her from tripping. The urge to draw her closer startled him.

Before he could release her, Reese swept in, swung a finger back and forth in an introduction of sorts. "Ben, this is Allie. Allie, Ben." The amused gleam in her eyes drew a wide-eyed glare from Allie before she darted her eyes downward, her thinned lips silent.

He followed her gaze to the floor. The hardwood was ugly and worn. What did she see down—*Oh, Christ.* His mouth went a little dry at the hot pink toenails peeping out from her stilettos. Maybe it was a good thing she hadn't said anything yet. He couldn't talk if he tried.

With a casual gesture he guided her onto the seat. He needed distance. Her scent—something soft and floral—was lodged in his brain and playing hell on his good intentions. He remained standing at the end of the table. Maybe he was safe there.

Jake reclaimed his side of the booth, leaving Reese to slide in beside him. "At last we meet the mysterious Allie. I'm Jake."

With a quick curve of her lips Allie reached across the table and took

Jake's outstretched hand. Her words, however, were directed at her friend tucked underneath his arm. "So, not a god after all. I'm disappointed."

Jake coughed out a laugh and tugged Reese closer. "Telling stories on me, woman?"

Reese's eyes could only be described as adoring. She patted his forearm. "Just girl talk, sweetie."

Jesus. What had Jake gotten himself into? Whatever it was, he hoped it wasn't catching. He met Reese's gaze. "Something to drink?"

She paused in removing her jacket. "Draft for me."

He raised an eyebrow to Allie.

"The same, thanks."

Her eyes *were* gray. And sparkled with green flecks when she smiled. With a flourish that he hoped didn't look as foolish as it felt, he sketched a bow. "Your wish is my command, ladies."

Across from her, Jake's eyes narrowed and followed Ben as he wove his way across the crowded floor. "Who does he think *he* is? A genie who just had his fucking lamp rubbed?"

Amusement twitched on Allie's lips at the muttered words. And immediately slipped off as her eyes followed Ben as he crossed the room. Why, for all the times she'd heard his name bandied about, did she not realize exactly *why* he had enough ex-girlfriends to form a fan club? He was a blond god, and evidently she was not immune. He made her breath catch. And her shoulders burned where he'd grasped her. She couldn't help but track him—and the glorious way he filled out those faded Levi's—as he made his way to the bar.

Oh, good Lord, she was in trouble.

Ben returned with their beers. Set them on the table and settled in close. The arm he dropped over the back of her seat was all hard muscle and teased her shoulders through her thin cotton blouse. To keep from torturing herself she pulled away but was instantly eased back.

This was getting complicated. Her heart skipped an uneven beat and she put a quick damper on it. Ben's shaggy sun-bleached hair and bright blue eyes were complemented perfectly by his bronzed skin. But she didn't have time for . . . what? A relationship?

Don't even think about it.

Besides, this wasn't a date. This was a favor for Reese. She didn't even want a guy. She dragged in a long breath and squared her shoulders. Tonight was all about letting Reese off the hook.

Jake's eyes swept her way, his elbow planted on the tabletop, his chin on his fist. "So, Allie, we all know Reese is a spoiled trust fund baby from LA. What's your story?"

The organ beating overtime in her chest proved she wasn't immune to his dark intensity. In desperation her gaze flew to Reese, who didn't seem to notice she'd gone from celibate to slut in one fell swoop. A quick jab with the toe of her pump thankfully got her friend's attention. "He's sure got your number, Reese."

Reese turned her gaze back to the table. "Her ice scraper broke. She took it as a sign." Reese snickered at her own joke.

Allie merely shook her head. "I'm from Chicago. Got tired of the snow so I thought I'd learn to educate young minds in a warmer climate. Now I wear shorts in February." She lifted her frosted mug, took a sip. "My parents are teachers too. They love it here so they moved to Arizona a year after I did."

Ben rested against the seat back, let his hand trail along her shoulders. "How'd you meet Reese?"

"We were assigned the same room freshman year." She winked at Reese and got a toothy grin in response. Those memories were epic. "I'd never been to the beach before I went home with Reese."

Jake could easily picture Allie in one of those skin-baring string bikinis and held in a whimper. Or maybe he didn't, because both Ben and Reese were staring daggers at him.

"What about you guys? Reese tells me you've been friends a long time."

The dim lighting had her eyes smoky. Ben's palm swept across her shoulder and Jake's shoulders stiffened in response. "Best friends since age five, don't ask me why." He forced himself to relax and as an apology tossed a half-hearted grin to Ben.

"Wow, you have known each other a while."

Ben removed his arm and wrapped his hands around his mug, which was almost empty. "We played football and baseball together in high school, took State."

Good times, but he'd jab at him anyway. "Traffic jam on Memory Lane, Ben?"

Seeming embarrassed, Ben jerked a shrug. When he looked away his attention was caught by Allie's finger, idly tracing figure eights in the condensation on her mug.

A guy had to know when to take advantage of a situation. Jake snatched up the conversational fumble and ran with it through the sounds of the band tuning up in the background. "Our parents are friends. We spent lots of weekends and vacations together over the years."

Recovered, Ben fought back for position. "We hit the lake in the summer, my dad has a great boat. You should come along some time."

He was *hitting* on her? Unbelievable. He shot a hot stare towards Ben, who was still talking. "When we were sixteen we got jobs digging ditches for Old Man Billings. Been with him ever since."

"But this was always our plan, the university." For the love of *God*, why did he have this sudden need to one-up Ben? And why did Reese seem so amused by their pissing contest? Still, he was more than a jock who knew the business end of a shovel—and for some reason it was important Allie understand that. Like a bulldog, he muscled back into the conversation. "Then our own company, T-Squared Construction."

Allie furrowed her brow, her questioning gaze landing on Reese.

Reese snapped her fingers with a grin. "I get it. It's a play on your names and a T-square ruler.

Ben grinned and nodded approvingly. "Ding. Ding. Give the girl a prize."

Ben's hand unwrapped from his mug, slid off the table and landed . . . where? The idea of what it might be doing down there out of sight had Jake's nerves thrumming. Best to turn his attention back to Allie. "How about you? Have you always wanted to teach?" Not his worry where Ben's hands were. Not with Reese sitting right beside him. He hitched his arm across the back of the seat.

"I love to teach. I guess it's in my genes. Every day is different, and I love the kids. It's like opening a classroom full of presents." Her mischievous grin told him there was a worm on that hook.

Okay, he'd bite. "How's that?" And where *the fuck* were Ben's hands?

"Well, you can see what's on the outside, but the inside is still a mystery."

A pair of towheaded boys chose that moment to race, howling, past the table. Allie rolled her eyes. "Kids like that I'd like to regift."

With a chuckle at her jest Ben glanced down at the hand he'd slid onto Allie's lap. She had it trapped against the dark denim encasing those legs. Those legs that he could practically *feel* wrapped around his waist.

Screeching feedback came through the speakers as the lead guitar announced their first set. Ah, next best thing. Flipping his palm up, he linked their fingers, cocked his head toward the dance floor. "Wanna dance?" She nodded with a quick smile.

Wordlessly he followed her onto the parquet floor. He let his palms ride on her hips as the aching ballad began, then pulled her in to him. He caught a whiff of her scent—sweet, light, intoxicating. He was getting a buzz from a chick. *What the hell?*

Where was his tongue? He held off the panic and drew her closer. It must be there somewhere. Allie would surely expect conversation. Girls liked to talk, right? But damned if he could find his tongue. Relying on habit, he lifted her hands to his shoulders and held them there.

Like butter on hot toast she melted right into him. He liked girls with a little length on them. Preferred their headlights to hit him a little higher than his stomach. Her fingertips swept along the ends of the hair along his collar, and it tickled. He allowed his arms to loosen as she leaned back with a reckless smile.

"You didn't mention what position you play. Baseball." She answered the pursing of his lips before he had a chance to ask what she meant.

There it was, found it! He rejoiced as his tongue unglued itself and words finally came. "Number three on the score sheet." She had that *I have no idea what you're talking* about look again, but he could forgive her for not being a baseball groupie. Preferred it, actually. "First base." He almost kept the wolfish grin in check.

As he led her around the dance floor he got another whiff of springtime. Mindful of her stilts, he gave her a slow spin and pulled her in tight. The slow notes from the band filled the air.

"Really? Oh. Um. Well."

Hah! Had her flustered. Did her head spin like his did, now that they were plastered together? *Maybe.* Her breath took a sharp hitch before she spoke.

"You dance well for a . . . a guy."

"For a *guy?*" He mocked her, then tweaked her chin and laughed. "You started to say jock, didn't you?"

She fit comfortably in his arms, and it surprised him. Slow dancing was really not his thing, but somehow this was right. He gave her another twirl.

"Busted."

Her laugh was breathy. *How about that?*

"Did your mom make you take dance lessons when you were a kid?"

"My dad." In some misguided effort to be a mom too. "What's your excuse?"

"Dance classes. Ballet, tap, jazz."

Yeah, he could picture her in a tight little leotard. *Jesus.*

The song ended and another began. The music drifted, seeped through him. He let his hands glide across her back, and closed his eyes when her hands caressed his shoulders as the notes caressed them. He opened his eyes and lowered his chin to meet her gaze. Let his hands drift down her sides, settle low on her back. And damn if his heart didn't trip.

Yeah, not his usual *hey, baby, let's blow this joint.*

Which was ridiculous, really, considering this wasn't even a date.

Jake led Reese off the dance floor to rejoin Allie and Ben, seated at their table. His gut clenched tight with what he recognized as shameful remorse. Along with a healthy dose of envy. Oh, Reese's friend wasn't beautiful with runway-model good looks, but she was certainly cute. Hell, he knew as much about saccharine prom queens as Ben did. This girl was the real deal.

Her grin, those changeable eyes and the dimple in her cheek—other parts of his anatomy clenched at the image. But she was with Ben tonight. He scowled and cursed fate, and wished he was with her instead.

She wasn't Ben's type, even though he'd spent the evening stuck to her like a rash. Ben liked them blonde and eager, then gone. He blew out a slow breath. Damn if Ben wouldn't break this girl's heart.

Ben led Allie back to the table through the low light, hands clasped together, laughing and bouncing off nearby patrons as the pub got more and more crowded and the music throbbed. She was flush with excitement and the heat of the crowd and Jake found himself fidgeting nervously in his seat.

Shoving aside the remains of her pizza, she picked up her beer and drained it, soft mewls of satisfaction vibrating in her throat.

Jake sucked in his breath and slid his eyelids shut.

Her empty mug hit the table. "It's almost midnight, folks. Time for my carriage to turn into a pumpkin." Her smile, though apologetic, had her dimple peeking through.

"So early?" He wanted to beg her to stay. To dance with him. To ditch Ben and—Crazy. It was all crazy. But so was the pressure in his chest.

Reese sidled up to him, looped her arm through his elbow. Probably kept him from saying something really stupid. "Sure you can't stay, Allie?"

Allie wrapped her in a quick hug. "Not tonight, thanks. Got church in the morning. I'll see you tomorrow afternoon." She turned to face Ben, who stood beside her with his jaw tight, his hands shoved into his pockets. Her smile faltered. "I had a nice time. Thank you."

The jerk didn't say a word. No *you're welcome*. No *later, baby*. No *take a hike, I'm just not into you*. Just stood there with his hands stuffed in his jeans and a dumbass look on his face.

Even with Reese hovering beside him, Jake kept his eyes on her as she dashed through the crowded restaurant, hugging her sweater with her head held high, glorious curls bobbing across her shoulders. Christ, was she *crying*? His feet had already moved, taken a step to follow her, and he halted in his tracks. What the hell was he doing? He shot a glance at Ben, whose eyes also followed her as she shot through the exit. Good old fashioned lust and something like—oh, Jesus, *longing*—pouring from his baby blues.

His buddy was a moron.

Chapter Three

Allie grabbed her purse and sweater and ran. Stumbled her way back through the crowded restaurant, shoved open the door and escaped into the cool night air. She was embarrassed enough. He didn't get to witness her tears.

Couldn't she even recognize when a guy wasn't interested? God, she was out of practice. Hours of talking, laughing, dancing—it was all for show.

Crossing the dimly lit parking lot, she wrapped her arms around her stomach, let the salty droplets fall. She was such a fool. There she was with her heart in her throat—probably in her eyes, damn it—and all along Ben was counting the minutes until he could cut her loose.

She sniffed as she approached her car. Loosened the death grip on her midsection and dug through her purse for a tissue.

Well, all right then. That settled the matter, even if the hot flash of anger did still simmer. The voice of reason taunted a reminder in the background:

She didn't even want a boyfriend. That's right. Didn't have time to date until after graduation, anyway.

She should have listened to it from the beginning.

Unlocking her car, she climbed in. It all washed over her—her stupidity, her irritation, her indecision. Annoyed, she buckled her seatbelt. She'd just forget the whole night. But—she released a pent up sigh—she really did have a good time.

With a snap of her wrist she turned the key and started the engine. Then slumped back in the idling vehicle. Visions of Ben invaded her musings and she sighed again. Yeah, Adonis in a Henley pullover. And wasn't it humiliating that his hot looks had her melting like a Popsicle on a summer sidewalk. She needed to sit herself down for a stern talking-to if that's how she acted on a first date.

No, non-date.

Even though he was acting, even though thirty days was probably a long-term relationship in his book, Ben made her laugh. She'd never met anyone she enjoyed so much, but he didn't even say good-bye. The evening left her overwhelmed, mortified. And now, even with cold, hard sanity again taking charge, bereft.

His stupid tongue had deserted him again. Ben cursed that useless flap of tissue as he sat with his back to the door. He didn't need words—actually needed only his imagination to remember the feel of her as she pressed against him on the dance floor. The sway of her hips as she strode across the floor in her heels tempted him as no bribe Jake promised ever could. But words—he was certain as he scraped a hand across the back of his head—would have worked better as good-bye than a thick-tongued stare.

No, she wasn't the blonde A-lister he was usually attracted to. And wasn't it odd that the idea didn't bother him at all. He didn't even need to see her again. The sight of her was tattooed on his brain. Through the heavy aromas of oregano and stale beer he could still catch the light scent of her perfume. Through the denim of his jeans he could still feel her as she brushed against him, dancing. No, he didn't need to see her again, but the persistent tug around his heart told him he would. And soon.

Pulling from the parking lot, Allie kicked off her heels as she entered traffic. Her head was clearer now, no longer clouded with what she could only assume were pheromones. She was two months shy of graduation and busy with classes, student teaching, and lining up a job for the next school year. All valid excuses—no, *reasons*—why she didn't date.

She always considered there would be time for dating when she was done with the craziness of college. Too many of her girlfriends lost focus on school once a boyfriend was in the picture. No, thank you very much. She was patient. First things first. But the events of the evening were stuck in her mind—the four of them talking, laughing, wolfing down pizza. Telling stories on each other like they were all old friends. And like quicksand, the harder she tried to escape them, the more the memories sucked her in.

Allie dropped her books on the sofa and yelled through the apartment. "Hey, Reese, you cooked? It actually smells good!" The growling of her stomach punctuated the lateness of the hour.

A quick toss landed her purse on the kitchen counter and she opened the oven. Knowing Reese, it was only marginally edible, but it mostly resembled a bubbling lasagna so she pulled it out. Because her shoes pinched her toes she peeled them off, dropped them near her purse. A scrap of paper in Reese's neat block writing rested nearby. Reaching out a hand, she—

"Ben called yesterday."

The palm that slapped against her chest would have knocked the breath from her if she hadn't just let it all out in a scream.

Reese threw back her head and laughed. "Jeez, anybody ever tell you, you shriek like a girl?"

"And I'll cuss like a sailor if you scare me like that again." Her heart was ready to jump out of her chest. From the fright—probably.

And just how long did Reese plan to chortle?

Holding her still-shaking midsection with one hand, Reese waved the note with the other. "I forgot to tell you about this. He said he'd call back."

"I told you I wasn't interested. And quit chuckling"

To her credit, she toned it down to a grin. "That was when you missed his call on Tuesday. Today's Thursday. I thought maybe you'd reconsidered." Reese waved a dismissing hand. "You know what they say about absence and the heart and all that."

Allie deliberately shook her head no, and hoped it was true. Her eye caught the flashing green light of the answering machine. "Who called while I was at the library?"

"Dunno." In no hurry, Reese pressed the button to check the message. "Maybe it was Jake. I was studying."

Ben again. Call you later.

Reese smirked. "He's either in love or he wants in your pants."

Trust Reese to call a spade a spade. "I told you a blind date was a bad idea." And yet, laughing blue eyes had invaded her dreams for the past several nights. Miserable, she dropped into a chair.

Monday morning, she awoke to the insistent clamoring of the telephone. Through bleary eyes she checked the time before dragging the receiver to her ear.

"It's six o'clock in the freaking morning. What do you want?"

"Oh, I'll hear that raspy voice in my dreams tonight."

Like a rocket Allie shot out of bed, untangled herself from the sheet, tripped over her slippers in the dark. She slapped at the switch and the room flooded with light. "Ben?" Oh, God, that loud squeak was *not* her voice.

"You've been hard to get hold of."

Oh, she remembered that voice—low and throaty. *Sexy Ben.* The mattress caught her when she sat. She was fully awake now. And curious. "How *did* you get me? You didn't ask for my number." *And where have you been since Thursday, by the way?*

"From Jake, who got it from Reese."

A regular Sherlock Holmes, wasn't he?

"Sorry about the weekend. We played a double header in Texas."

"Oh?" Did he mention they'd be out of town? Did Reese? With her brain so fuddled, it was all she could think to say. Hopefully he didn't notice.

"We got in late last night—early this morning, actually."

She opened her mouth, but he cut her off.

"Let's do something."

"Now? It's the middle of the night."

He chuckled. "Not quite. What's your schedule?"

She needed to shower, do her hair, iron a blouse . . . *Stop!* Her shoulders slumped as reality set in. "My first class is at nine twenty. Then I have student teaching this afternoon. I don't get home until after four, but I need to study." Her schedule was a killer—hence, the no-dating policy. And if she needed another reminder why, here it was.

"Okay then, get dressed. I'll pick you up. We'll have breakfast. You've got ten minutes."

And the line went dead.

The phone was heavy in her hand. What just happened? A call. Ben. She replaced the handset. Did she want to do this? Meet the hot guy for eggs? Maybe she could get him out of her head. She raced for the closet.

"Oh, hell, why not?"

Somehow, impromptu eggs managed to turn into . . . exactly what she wasn't looking for. With books and notes strewn from one end of the couch to the other, Allie groaned beneath the weight a half-finished research paper. She lifted a glass of wine to her lips and let her eyelids drift shut as she sipped. She missed sleep. She missed her girlfriends. She missed . . . Ben.

"They're in Oregon? It's probably snowing in Oregon, for crying out loud." And she should kick herself for caring. The remainder of his chocolate birthday cake from yesterday sat on the kitchen counter, mocking her. "Do you know I dreamed about him last night? Disgusting!"

"You say something?" Reese had a mess of her own scattered across the living room floor.

She pried one reluctant eyelid open. Reese could just wipe away that smirk lurking across her lips. "Just muttering." With a decisive thump she deposited her empty glass on the coffee table. "No, damn it. I'm mad! This wasn't supposed to happen."

"What wasn't?"

"This is all your fault."

Reese continued to shuffle papers, sorting them into piles. "Seriously, if you're going to blame me for something, it's only polite to tell me what it is."

How could Reese stay so calm when gymnasts were practicing their floor exercises in her stomach? "Him." She jerked her chin toward the cake plate. "It's only been two weeks. Well, sixteen days actually, but we'll call it two weeks to simplify things."

"Ah, Ben. Now I understand."

"Of course, Ben." She picked up her empty glass and frowned into it. "We hardly spend any time together—and I should be okay with that—but I feel as if something's clutching at me—" She grabbed a fistful of the shirt covering her chest, "Right here, just because he's two states away." With a sigh she frowned into her glass again, shoved the pile off her lap and pressed to her feet.

Reese finally looked up. "They'll be home tomorrow. Bring me back some of that."

"Snippets! That's all the time we have together. Damn it, we barely even have time to grab a coffee." She reached the kitchen and snatched a clean glass from the shelf, filled it along with her own. Tossed the empty bottle into the recycling. "Oh, excuse me. We also had lunch together, precisely twice." It was tricky holding up two fingers along with the wine glasses, but she was determined. On tiptoe she navigated her way back through the minefield in the living room. "Sandwiches on the grass."

"Better known as a picnic. It's considered romantic." That smirk was back on Reese's face again, damn her.

Allie shoved the glass into her hand, then picked her way back to the couch and sank into it. She and Ben had spent an afternoon sitting in the sun and talking about nothing—books, movies, professors they both liked—and hated. And they shared a few knee-weakening kisses. Her shoulders drooped. "Yeah, it kind of was."

"Again, tomorrow."

Her heart skittered, so she scowled. "I don't even want a boyfriend."

"That doesn't seem to matter, now, does it?"

No, damn it, it didn't seem to matter. "But I don't want a boyfriend."

"I say it's too late, girlfriend. But maybe if you say it three times and click your sparkly red heels, your wish will come true."

Chapter Four

With a few good swings, Ben tested the weight of the bat. He'd been hitting well since he got back in the lineup.

Jake sidled up to the nearby chain link. "You're up first."

"Yeah, I saw." Members of the team milled around, cutting up before the game. With Jake bent over to tighten his cleats Ben lifted his gaze to scan the stands.

Jake straightened, bent a knee back and propped his foot against the fence. "They're here. Sixth row."

Ben scowled and spun back around to face the diamond. The opposing team was leaving the field. "Don't you have somewhere to be?"

Jake merely laughed and slapped him on the back. "Keep your head in the game, B."

"Fuck you." He waited until Jake got caught in conversation with the catcher, then turned back and found her. With a textbook open on her lap. His scowl settled into a frown. Why bother coming at all if she wasn't planning to watch the game?

With the sun glaring in his eyes, he scanned the rest of the stands, found Vivian sitting beside some stranger. She was hot, always had been. She'd stirred his blood for a while, too. But today there was no leap, no rush—and it pissed him off. He swung his eyes back to Allie, chatting with Reese on the bleacher. His breath quickened. His fingers remembered the feel of her and prickled. He wanted to glide them across her skin again. Find that little mole on the back of her shoulder and run his fingers over it. Run them through her curls and mess them up.

"Twenty-two now, huh?"

"Jesus, Jake. Don't you ever say hello?"

"Did. You were a million miles away."

No, only as far as the sixth row. "Go away."

But Jake merely picked up a bat, spun it like a top on his middle finger. "Heard you had a birthday party last night."

"No big deal. She baked me a cake." Chocolate. And he licked frosting from her fingers. Made a wish after she lit the candles, too. Silent, bawdy, and—sigh—unfulfilled.

She stood over the cake, waving a knife. "Hey Ben, what size piece do you want?"

He ambled up behind her and drew to a stop. His hands meandered down her sides and didn't stop until they reached her backside, where they gripped soft curves. "This big is perfect."

"She's waving at you."

He turned his back, faced the field before Jake could give him shit for his smug smile. "They're waving at *you*, moron." The opposing team was taking the field again, ready for battle. It was time to get serious.

Preparing for his first at-bat, he shoved a helmet onto his head, over hair that curled along his nape and defied the edge of the hard shell. His biceps bunched as he shifted the bat over his shoulder. He stepped up to the batter's box and performed the same warm-up ritual he'd had since high school, stomping his left foot twice, pawing the dirt with his right, a bull preparing to charge. A couple of strong swings and he stepped to the plate, took his stance.

The pitcher wound up and released the ball. Low in the outside corner, coming fast. His pants snugged against his butt and thighs as he stepped into his swing. There was a loud crack as lumber connected with leather and he skied it, sending the ball flying over the left field fence, mere inches inside the foul pole. Fist pumping, he rounded the bases until he landed firmly on home plate, surrounded by teammates.

The rest of the game was a blur, but he noticed Allie cheering from the stands as he left the field. Not that he was watching. Hair damp from a shower, he stepped from the locker room. Allie waited for him, that riot of curls caught up in a stubby ponytail, her tank top neatly tucked into cut-offs. Not his type, but damn, she looked good. Was it because he hadn't fucked her yet he was all tied up in knots?

"Reese and I came to watch you play."

It felt right to settle his arm across her shoulder. Natural. He led her toward her car. "Pretty good game."

"Pretty good? You were sensational, Ben."

Her enthusiastic smile was good for his ego. Loosened the ropes so he could breathe again. The scent in the air was pure Allie, fresh and sweet. He wanted to kiss her. Needed to taste those heart-shaped lips of hers. Glide his tongue across them until she opened up and he could slide it in and taste the honey inside. Long and slow and deep.

Jake cat-called from across the parking lot.

Somewhere private.

It was better he stick to the present, leave his fantasies for . . . later. He snagged her neck in the crook of his elbow and tugged until she bumped up against him. "Yeah, I did okay. Good thing we won. We needed that one."

"You won? Oh, sure. Right. Of course you won."

Allie, nervous? Imagine that! And damned if she didn't turn an interesting shade of pink. Just how far into her blouse did it go?

"You guys were awesome." She ducked out from under his arm as they approached her car. Her bright hazel eyes skittered between him and the ugly cracked blacktop.

What would she do if he kissed her—really kissed her—right here?

She beeped her car unlocked.

Would she kiss him back, run her arms around his waist and then up and over his shoulders? Lock them around his neck? Sink into him? Jesus, he was hard.

With a twist of her lush, rosy lips she turned away, reached out to open her car door.

Fuck it! He yanked her to him, spun her around until her back flattened against the door. And plastered his lips to hers. With her jaw trapped in his shaking palms, he devoured her with his heart pounding in his chest and his ears buzzing with the rush of blood that surged through his system.

Or maybe that was the cheers going up around them. *Stupid jerks.*

He closed his eyes against the brilliant afternoon sunshine, ran his tongue across the seam of her lips to urge her mouth open, and invaded her even as her arms wrapped around his waist. He found his hands loosened from her face and drawn down, down to the curve of her waist and felt his pulse ratchet higher. When her arms slid up his chest and over his shoulders there was a groan—his—right before they entwined behind his neck. He shut out the jeering of his teammates and with bold persuasion wrestled her tongue with short jabs, made long sweeps across the smoothness of her teeth.

She wrenched her lips away, left him bereft as she swept them across his face, his neck, while her hands raced over him. Down his shoulders, teasing the muscles of his back. She fused her lips to his once again. Her hands tunneled through his hair. Gripped his shoulders. Circled his waist and held on.

He burned where she touched him.

His hands swept her sides, his lips brushed her cheek, her throat, nibbled at the pulse so visible there. Palms cruised over rough denim covering her hips, then up again over the ribbed cotton of her top. His thumbs brushed the sides of her breasts and there was a moan—hers. He would have offered anything to cover the bareness of them with his hands or—oh, God, his *mouth*—which was so close now.

He let his hands glide down again, back to her waist, to the place where ribbed knit tucked into denim and ripped it out until his fingertips found smooth skin.

His knees grew weak.

Vehicles passed by. Honked. He pressed himself to her and sucked in air. Swept his hands down the length of her arms and back up again, caught her by the back of her head and nibbled greedily. Fulfilling his fantasy, he dug his fingers into her hair and popped the rubber band that held her curls hostage.

And finally, at long last, cradled her jaw is his palms as he gentled the kiss.

He reclaimed his tongue and brushed his lips over hers. Gently. Oh, so gently. Let them trail across her jaw to the smooth skin just beneath her ear. Propped his forehead against hers. And fought for breath.

Her chest heaved against his. Puffs of air gusted against his neck as she gasped. Her arms tightened around him, branded him.

He lifted his head. Her eyes were glassy, and as dark as storm clouds.

Whoa.

This—*he*—was out of control. He stumbled back a step. For years there'd been a parade of girls. Perky, sulky, witty, arrogant. Each beautiful, each different, each no more important than the last. Allie was just the next in line.

Wasn't she?

A lifeline was what he needed. He planted a smirk on his lips, which still tingled from her kisses. "Yeah, I suppose I was good today."

She was no longer breathless, and her eyes had lightened to pewter. "And you hit a home run." Her grin lit up her face and his heart did a slow roll.

Shit.

He was sunk. Defenseless. Wave the white flag, beg for mercy. Allie was not the next in line.

She was the end of the line.

His eyelids drifted shut against a flash of green amusement and he prepared to surrender.

Hell, no! He snapped his eyes open again and studied her features. The features that belonged to the woman he . . . loved. If he did this, he was doing it right.

He pulled her back into his arms. Let his face soften, his gaze warm her until she melted into him. "A home run, babe. Yeah, I guess I did."

Standing in the meager light of a single fluorescent bulb, Allie shifted the brown paper bag in her arms and knocked. After six hours in the library her mind was mush. All she wanted was a glass of wine and a hot bath. Okay, two glasses of wine. But instead here she was, juggling the makings for spaghetti. And what did that say about her willpower?

She was pathetic, following Ben around like a little lost puppy. But somehow she couldn't manage to stop. It was a battle she'd waged with herself for two weeks now, since that kiss in the parking lot. And every time he put his lips on hers her defenses grew weaker.

Oh, for Pete's sake. Get a grip. She pounded harder, then tried the knob.

The chest she stumbled against as the door flew inward was muscular, golden—and bare. Her breath escaped in a whoosh. Her shoulders sizzled where his palms latched on to keep her upright.

"Hi, babe."

His smile, just short of a leer, was positively sinful.

And that had the edge of her temper sharpening.

The lips that grazed hers widened into a grin as she marched across the threshold.

Oh, wasn't he smug? She swept past him, dropped the sack on the kitchen counter. "I hope you're hungry." With her wrist tugged, she found her palms pressed against sun-kissed skin.

"I could eat."

His lips were warm and soft as they touched hers again, but they didn't linger. "Put a shirt on."

His chin lowered as he followed her gaze. "I'm not cold."

No, but she couldn't concentrate. "Put a shirt on." Because she'd said it more harshly than she intended she took a sideways step and let out a long breath. Slid a short stack of mail aside and emptied the sack of groceries onto the counter.

With a box of pasta in one hand, a can of tomatoes in the other, she had to admit Reese was right. She'd been acting a shrew. She'd love to figure out why that was, but with her stomach quivering as if it had an infestation of butterflies, she simply couldn't think straight.

The bag was empty so she folded it, hid it in a cupboard. Reese had drawn her own conclusion, of course, and taken great joy in sharing it with her. It was a silly notion she had—outrageous really. After all, she barely knew the guy.

He still said nothing, was way too quiet as he stood with his head cocked and his eyes steady. Cans were now towered in a pyramid beside an onion and fresh mushrooms. Was he angry? Curious? She wished she knew.

Did she dare test Reese's theory? Did she even want to? What if love *had* actually crept into her heart? She moved toward him, allowed his arms to encircle her. She probably could have denied it. Would have sworn love was a tame, orderly emotion rather than this jumbled confusion. But the blue embers now gleaming in his eyes spoke to her soul. And the peck he'd doled out earlier with a bland smile only left her craving more of him.

The sweep of his hand over her hair and across her back had the butterflies settling down for a nap. Well, what did she make of that?

A brush of her fingertips eased the furrow in his forehead. "I'm sorry." Because she ached for him she tilted her chin, pressed her lips against his, let them rub until he pressed back. And immediately needed more.

With a shuffle of feet his back hit the counter, near a stale crust of sandwich and a half-empty milk glass, which he nearly upended. He tasted faintly of toothpaste, minty. His hands skimmed over her back and down to her waist, and her legs trembled.

Her heart stuttered. Her breath grew choppy when her fingers tunneled through the crisp hair sprinkling the chiseled plane of his chest. His heart thumped against her palms.

Her arms trembled too, grew weak when his lips traveled down her jaw, beginning at her ear and ending at the pulse pounding at the base of her throat. With his palms covering her hips he widened his stance and pulled her into the hardness of him. Her knees threatened to collapse.

Wait! This was crazy. Stupid. She wrenched away. Jerked back until his arms were forced to loosen around her. When her breathing slowed, when the tremors calmed—that's when it would be safe to lift her forehead from his. Eyelids she knew held stubby blond lashes breezed across her brow. Full lips which were parted even now blew out uneven breaths against her neck. The muscles of his forearms were firm against her palms. He was beautiful. So beautiful.

But was he hers?

She dragged her face from his, hoped to distract herself by peeking around the apartment, where beer bottles littered the coffee table and a layer of dust covered every surface. "How do you live in this pigsty?"

She would have thought he'd turn, take a look. Perhaps offer an excuse. Instead he merely grinned. "It's the cleaning lady's day off."

She could only roll her eyes. But when she spotted a jock strap poking out from beneath the couch she had to point it out. "Ben, that's disgusting!"

His toothy grin settled into a carefree smile before it slid away and he deadpanned, "I have no idea how that got there."

The pressure in her chest was achingly familiar as he tugged her close again.

"The hamper's in the bedroom, Ben. Right by the bed."

His smile bloomed again, even as the heat of a long gaze scorched her. "Is that right?"

Her heart surprised her with a jolt. Tripped and skittered and tumbled into a puddle of chaotic emotion.

It was those denim blue eyes, damn him, that she couldn't resist. It was that smile, sometimes shy, sometimes playful. And even now, it was the way he made her laugh when she wanted to stay angry. He was every young woman's fantasy—and she was nothing if not a typical young woman.

But was he *hers*?

His jaws bristled her palms with a day's growth of whiskers. It was interesting that his eyes darkened to midnight with her touch. Did it matter that his exes were plentiful enough to line Sun Devil Stadium? That far too soon she'd join that sisterhood and be left with only memories of his hard-muscled strength and summer bright eyes? She sucked in a breath. Did it matter that he'd take her heart with him when he left?

Her breath escaped in a rush. No, it was too late for those things to matter. She shifted, pressed her lips to his ear in a whisper, and let him know she was his.

"Yeah, that's right. Let me show you where it is."

With Allie curved to his chest Ben rode out the wave of tremors, let a soothing lethargy flood him as his racing heart settled. His palm swept the front of his shirt and was halted by two buttons fastened across her breasts.

He tugged her closer with ease, and slowly, slowly her pulse slowed. This was nice, easy. Nothing to be frightened of.

Her dimple intrigued him so he traced the corner of her mouth with the tip of his finger. "Have you always had this?"

"Always. My dad used to say it made me look mischievous." When she twisted to lay on her back her familiar scent hung on his pillow and teased his senses. "What about you? Were you a trouble maker? Ever break any bones?"

He brushed her hair from her cheek, considered untangling the sheet from her waist. "Nose once, thanks to Nick and a wild pitch. My pride many times." He missed the heat of her. Followed her onto the warmth she'd left on the sheet between them. "You have a brother. No sisters?

"Nope, just Ryan. How about you? Just brothers?" With a shuffle, she kicked her legs free of the covering.

He could have whimpered in thanks. "You kidding? With our pack she would have ended up pitching for the Yankees." When his hand had wandered an exposed length of thigh, he skimmed it back upward.

She chuckled. "So, your deal was baseball. Mine was always school. I made Ryan play it with me at home.

He traced a slow finger along her collarbone. Shifted onto his back, pulled her into his shoulder and was rewarded with a soft sigh as she wriggled closer still. "So you dreamed of becoming a teacher even back then."

"I guess I did. And T-Squared is under construction."

When she chuckled at her own pun he could only shake his head and grin. "I'll give you that one. Cheeky. Clever. You'll fit right in with my family."

And because the idea of it rocked him to the core he plowed ahead as if he hadn't just glimpsed his future.

"Plans for the company are coming right along. We're already bidding jobs, and my dad keeps us from drowning in paperwork. He tells us where to sign, we sign."

"So your dream is lumber and hardware?"

It was the timing as much as the question that made his heart suddenly stop. Perhaps if he hadn't mentioned family, if he hadn't just pictured her in a room surrounded by children, the query would have slid right through their conversation and fallen into a black hole.

Perhaps his silence wouldn't have been noted.

He closed his eyes so he could ignore the way her smile disappeared and the green flecks deserted her eyes.

He should have expected this. They were talking about their futures after all. So why, for God's sake why, did the idea of dreams suddenly conjure up a home with a yard, and—oh, sweet Jesus—the pitter patter of little feet?

But that was all in the future. He lifted his eyelids, brushed his lips across hers softly, with hope. And then more eagerly until her eyes sparkled again and soft purrs vibrated in her throat. With Allie in his bed all he would think about was tonight. In one smooth movement he landed on his side, trailed a finger down her arm, light as a feather and designed to raise another batch of goosebumps. "C'mere." He drew her to him, beneath him with the whisper. And as her eyes did a slow roll back to stormy he prepared to ride the tempest.

Chapter Five

The ordeal was nearly over. They'd studied for years. Ordered caps and gowns, and announcements, met with advisors for credit checks—a myriad of details. Suddenly final exams were behind them and graduation was here. The only thing keeping Ben from shouting for joy were the thousands of people packing the arena.

Allie's ceremony had occurred in the late morning. A smaller, dignified ceremony that he'd attended with her parents. He didn't mind sitting beside her dad; he seemed like a nice guy. They met at Easter and Ben received a warm welcome from the history professor wearing a worn corduroy blazer. The same man who earlier today sat in an elegant tailored suit as he clutched his wife's hand, beaming with pride at the young woman who was his daughter.

This evening he swam in a sea of maroon and gold, and people swarmed around him. He craned his neck, located Allie in the throng.

His heart skipped a beat and he waved. For months he'd run scared. She'd become too important, too fast. He didn't expect to fall in love. If anyone had told him he was ready he'd have sworn they were nuts. But once he admitted his feelings to himself he wasted no time moving forward. He smiled to himself. Graduation was not all he'd been arranging. A trip to see his father put the finishing touches on his plans for tonight.

The noise level was loud and lighthearted, and drew his attention back to the arena. Handmade banners waved, congratulating loved ones on their accomplishments. Over the din, the racket, the commotion, the orchestra tuned their instruments.

At last it was time to begin. In alphabetical order as they had since they were children, he jostled Jake good-naturedly and then stood stock still for the pledge and the invocation. He swallowed hard to hide the lump in his throat as the orchestra played the alma mater, and then, finally, with all the pomp and circumstance he'd worked so diligently toward for the past four years, he was a college graduate. And thank God for that.

He endured a final round of hugs and congratulations from parents and friends, then draped his arm across Allie's shoulders and led her to his car.

"Are you sure Jake and Reese have plans together?"

"Yeah." He opened the car door for her and helped her in. He was surprised, too, especially since Jake had abruptly pulled the plug on their relationship weeks ago. "He said they were meeting friends. Probably hitting the bars on Mill. They're big kids now, babe."

He started the engine and adjusted the stereo to her favorite station before pulling out of the parking space. Although the evening was warm he left his sport coat on during the ride. As they entered her apartment, however, he shrugged it off and draped it over the corner of the sofa.

Pacing the living room, sweat beaded and trickled down his back even as the air conditioning cooled the room. He picked things up from her tables, her shelves, turned them over in his hands, set them right back down again. He turned on a lamp and flipped the wall switch to turn off the overhead light. Chose a CD and slipped it into the stereo. Alabama. The music played softly and soothed him.

He took a deep breath and settled on the left side of the sofa. "Hey, come in here Al." He had hoped for a playful tone, but it was amazing he could speak at all over the thrumming in his chest. "Come sit with me." Stretching his arm along the seat, he patted the cushion.

"I'll be there in a sec, I just want to put these things away," she yelled out from the kitchen, then poked her head around the corner. "Hey, do you want something to drink? We've got wine, or there's beer."

"Beer, thanks. Then bring your cute little ass in here and sit with me. I'm lonely."

She grinned at him over her shoulder as she ducked back into the kitchen. The refrigerator opened, then slammed shut the way it did when she kicked it with her hip.

The bottles clinked as she set them on the coffee table. "Don't whine." She climbed onto the sofa and snuggled into him with her knees drawn to her chest. "You're a college graduate now, that means you're officially a grown up. Be charming." She leaned into him and nibbled the corner of his mouth, flirty little kisses that any other day would rev him up fast.

She leaned closer to deepen the kiss, but he backed away with a small smile. He let the smile bloom on his face as he smoothed her curls with the back of his hand. She was so damn beautiful. The song changed in the background, something soft and sensual. His hand lingered on the back of her neck, rubbing slowly. "I love you, Allie."

He released her nape, took both of her hands in his and smiled into eyes which were sparkling. I've been a jerk. I should have told you a long time ago, but I was scared. I thought I wasn't ready." And now he wanted to shout it out loud until the neighbors called the cops.

She shifted to face him fully, kneeling beside him on the cushion. Her lips curved slowly until she was grinning with her hands cradling his jaw. "I'm glad you're ready now, because I love you, too."

She loved him. He let his eyes slide shut as he hauled her into his arms and squeezed. His heart expanded in his chest. He was torn between laughing in relief and crying in thanks. Eyelashes winged across his brow as butterfly kisses tickled his eyelids.

"Are you still scared?"

His eyelids flicked open and a smile tugged at the corners of his mouth. Show time. "No, babe. I'm not scared anymore. Not of loving you." He paused a beat, tightened his arms around her, before he released her and hauled in a breath. "Of losing you, of not having you in my life—that scares the shit out of me."

Allie blinked sharply, and he allowed his smile to grow as his eyes searched her face. He rifled through his jacket, pulled a blue cardboard package from a pocket and proceeded to remove the lid. "Marry me, Allie."

At her gasp his smile faltered and his heart slammed against his ribs. He held out the small velvet box, sitting expectantly in one hand.

"I can't imagine a day without you, babe—your joy, your sweetness. His free hand reclaimed her face, his thumb sweeping the dusting of freckles over her cheek. Your curls, your dimple." His smile widened, the tension gone as her smile bloomed, his fingers threading through her hair, watching her eyes brighten and her dimple emerge.

"My life began when I met you, and I want to continue it with you." He popped opened the hinge, revealed the contents. "To make a family with you. To make plans for the future. To grow old with you.

"I promise I'll always be here for you. I'll make you happy. Please Allie, say you'll marry me."

Tears welled in the corners of her eyes, then overflowed as Ben plucked the ring from the box. Wearing a soggy grin she nodded, then cupped one hand on either side of his face, raining kisses on him.

"It was my mom's." He took her left hand in his and brought it to his lips. Kissed each of her knuckles and then slipped the ring on.

The nerves he'd fought only minutes ago were back and they brought friends. The fierce hammer of his heartbeat, the passionate song of blood roaring through his system had his head swimming.

She lifted her left hand, placed it back on his cheek and his breathing steadied. He let her pull him close and rejoiced as she murmured into his ear. "That was absolutely . . . charming."

Chapter Six

Jake peeled himself away from the blonde clinging to him like ivy—Bambi, she said her name was—and stepped away from the littered hi-top to answer the jangling ring of his new cellular phone.

"Hey, Jake, it's me."

Bambi openly scanned the room, hunting new prey with hopeful eyes. *Nope, definitely not a keeper.* "You ready to join the party or what?"

"Not tonight, man. Me and Allie, we've got our own party going on."

Through the line he could hear it. Ben was in a good mood about something.

"Yeah, what you guys up to?"

"Making plans for the future. Her parents are on board. My dad knows all about it and he's thrilled. That just leaves you."

In the background Allie was talking, too. Something about inviting Jake to dinner. He would show, sure. But why did they have to ask now? "What's the big deal, B?"

Jake waited a beat and then heard the grin in Ben's voice. "It's just . . . hey, buddy, I need to call in a favor."

Jake smiled in satisfaction as Bambi left his table, lurched to the dance floor and latched onto some sucker as drunk as she was. "Oh yeah, what now? You can't borrow my truck." Although if he continued to guzzle beer and the rate he had been, he'd need a cab ride home. He cast an eye over the crowded bar, landed on long copper curls and his heart stopped just long enough that he almost missed Ben's next comment.

"No, I don't need your truck. I just need *your* sorry ass. I want you to be my best man."

With a hand that suddenly felt weak, Jake held the phone against his ear, and his heart plummeted.

"Jake, you there? I'm getting married. Are you surprised?"

Surprised? No, not surprised. Shocked. That almost covered it. And envious. What kind of dick did that make him? What could he possibly say?

But Ben was waiting for something—anything. And he'd better somehow manage to sound happy. "Of course I will, Ben. Congratulations, to both of you."

"Good, because you promised me anything."

Ben laughed, but Jake could only manage a strangled chuckle.

"Besides, you got me into this."

Right. He finished his conversation, said good-bye and clicked off. Shoved his cell phone into a pocket as he stood in the middle of the teeming club, the graduation weekend crowd crushing him.

"Shit."

Ben sat behind a second-hand card table, their living room transformed into a makeshift office. So far the summer had been a whirlwind of activity. He tilted the folding chair back on two legs and idly followed a crack in the ceiling, his mind stuck on replay. The things a sleep-tousled Allie had done to him in her bed just hours ago—hell, the things he did to her—wreaked havoc on his concentration. Good thing they decided to establish the temporary office at their apartment instead of hers. Fewer distractions. He smiled in private amusement. They were already making good business decisions.

"Your dad is making good progress on all the paperwork—corporate papers and tax licenses, shit like that."

He dragged his perpetually horny ass back into the conversation—Jake was probably talking about something important.

"But digs are a little cramped here. We need a place to set up shop."

"I've been looking at locations with the realtor for two weeks now." His reminder was accompanied by a slow nod. "We've found a couple that would probably work. I have another appointment day after tomorrow. We'll find something soon."

Two days later he slammed into the apartment late in the afternoon, a legal-sized folder in his hand, a grin overtaking his face. "I think I found it."

Jake turned to him with a raised eyebrow. "It?"

"An office, dumbass. You want to see?" He waved the manila folder like a victory flag. "I have the lease right here."

Jake took the folder from him. "More good news—he held up his empty hand for a high five—the Peterson job came through."

Ben slapped his hand and grinned again. "'Bout time you did something around here." He paced the room while Jake studied the paperwork—reviewing each and every damn clause of the three-year lease like the girl he was.

Ben piled out of Jake's old truck at the proposed office site and examined the area—the building that would house their fledgling company, the yard surrounded by chain link to store building materials and equipment. They walked off dimensions, jotted down notes.

"Yeah, this will do." A satisfied smile lit Jake's eyes and Ben suffered a solid whack to the middle of his shoulder blades.

The whack he returned gave him his own satisfaction. "Then let's go celebrate."

He held open the sturdy wooden door for Jake and followed him into the franchise steak house, gave his name to the teenage girl behind the podium. Several minutes later he and Jake followed her to a table in the middle of the room.

"How's Allie?"

He winked. "Oh, she's good. Really good."

Jake's eyes skimmed the room, then fell back on him with a semblance of a grin. "Not only are you a prick, but you're a smug prick. You're whipped and you know it."

He opened his mouth to argue, then widened his eyes and chuckled instead. "I called her to meet us here."

Jake's grin died as his eyes bored into Ben. "Take good care of that girl. She's special."

"What? You my big brother now?"

"Nope. But you hurt her, I'm gonna kick the shit out of you."

"Message received. Now fuck off." He glanced around the room, spied Allie heading their way. Perfect timing. He stood, kissed her cheek as she arrived, held out her chair.

"Whipped." Jake mouthed the word from across the table.

"Thanks for inviting me." A waitress lowered her tray and set two tall glasses of iced tea on the table. She ordered one for herself, then picked up Ben's and drank thirstily.

"So, Allie. Wedding plans, huh?"

Ben snorted. "Please. Don't get her started."

"Like I give a skinny rat's ass what you want." Jake sneered playfully and turned back to the girl seated across the table.

Allie laughed, her hand engulfed in Ben's wide palm on the table. "I haven't really done anything yet. Kindergarten is over next week, then I can concentrate on wedding plans. We did decide to have the ceremony at my parents' church in Scottsdale, though. In the early evening."

Ben turned his gaze on Jake. "We done yet, Martha Stewart? We're borrowing Will's boat this Saturday, do some skiing. Want to come along?"

"Burgers, beer and Allie in a skimpy little two-piece? Hell yeah, I'm in."

Jake just laughed at his hard look. Maybe they should talk about weddings after all.

She had less than three months until their wedding date and a suitable location for a reception was proving hard to come by. Allie picked up the remote and turned off the news. "Ben, what do you think about this place?" She waved a fist full of brochures, collected from the venue she'd toured. "Reese and I checked it out today and it might do. They have a pretty patio in back."

Ben ignored the pamphlet. "Allie, it'll still be over a hundred degrees, even at six o'clock. Do you really think outdoors is an option?"

They were planning their wedding for the middle of August because neither of them could wait longer than that. And she wanted to write *Mrs. Tate* on the blackboard on the first day of school.

She held up another brochure. "I know it's late, I know you're tired. But pay attention. What about this place?"

Ben glanced up briefly and she started in on her sales pitch. "It's a little over the budget, but it has this big sweeping staircase that would be great for photos."

"You decide, Al. Whatever you want is fine."

She hit him with a throw pillow. "Don't be that guy, Ben."

His eyelids crept open. "What guy?"

"The guy that doesn't help with any of the decisions. This is *our* wedding. I need your input."

"All right then, we'll have it at my dad's house."

Allie plopped down beside him and grabbed his arm, pamphlets scattering on the sofa. "When did that become an option?"

"He only mentioned it today. I haven't had a chance to tell you."

"Ben, it's perfect! It's a big house with a great staircase, beautiful landscaping for photographs. It's a little far to drive, but so what. You sure it's okay?"

"Perfectly okay." His eyes drifted shut.

The next Saturday Allie, with the help of Reese and her mom, went searching for the perfect gown. After only three shops they met with success.

It was all shimmery satin and delicate lace. Sleeveless with a high, sculpted neckline. Seed pearls and sparkling crystals adorned the fitted

45

bodice. Standing on the dais, admiring her reflection in the triple mirror, tears of joy clouded her vision.

Katie Harper walked over with a veil in her hand. Stepped up beside her daughter and slipped the combs into her hair, smoothing the lace-edged netting over her shoulders and down her back. "You're an angel, the most beautiful bride ever." With a soft look on her delicately lined face she spoke tenderly. "Is this the one?"

With a smile whispering in her eyes, Allie answered. "Oh yes, we found *the dress*."

On Tuesday she shopped again with her mom and Reese, this time for flowers.

"Here, sweetie, this is like the picture you showed me last week." Reese held up a sample bouquet the floral designer had assembled ahead of time. Pink tea roses and white gardenias. "Do you still like this?"

She really did.

On a roll, Allie shopped for a cake. A bell chimed as she entered the shop alone and meandered through the bakery. A middle aged woman entered from the back, several years' worth of crullers and fresh sourdough plastered to her hips.

Martha Connor, the shop owner, was clearly knowledgeable, but after thirty minutes of looking through sample books, Allie was overwhelmed.

So many decisions to make over cake? What flavor to choose? Buttercream or whipped frosting? Filling or no filling? Flowers or no flowers?

"So, what do you think, Ben?" She stacked the last dinner plate in the dishwasher. "Chocolate, vanilla or red velvet?"

"What the hell's red velvet?" Ben was distracted—Red Sox on the tube and blueprints spread across the table. "Sounds like drapes. In a whorehouse."

She slammed the dishwasher closed. "Like it sounds, Ben. Red. Tastes like cake. Pay attention. Which would you rather have?"

"I really don't care, Allie. Pick one."

Tossing the kitchen towel on the counter, she steamed out of the room. "Fine!"

They were planning a simple wedding—fewer than a hundred people— but she was only doing this once; everything should be lovely. Reese and her mom were making it very easy, and the invitations were already in the mail.

"Ben, we need to go to the courthouse for a marriage license." She mentioned this as she dropped pasta into a pot of boiling water. Reese was at dinner with a new boyfriend and they had the apartment to themselves. "Can you take off work and meet me?"

Ben set the newspaper aside. "Sure, babe. Let me know when and I'll be there."

That was easy.

"How about your tux? Have you and Jake gotten fitted?"

Eyes wide, his look was sharp and cautious, a deer caught in the headlights. "Tux?"

She'd mentioned the black tuxedo to him several times in the past two weeks. She didn't bother to rein in her temper as she glared. "Yes, Ben. Tuxedo. The suit you're wearing to your wedding. I've asked you several times to get measured so you get the right size." Her frustration boiled over like the fettuccini on the red-hot burner. "Can you do that please? That one thing?"

"C'mon, Al. I've done more than one thing. It's all we talk about anymore. All you do. Everything's this for the wedding, that for the wedding. I can't wait till it's over."

Oh, really? On a huff, she let the bite of each word sting. "I'm sorry if this is *tiresome* for you, Ben, but there are more details than you can imagine in putting a wedding together."

Ben closed his eyes and dropped his chin to his chest, then scraped back his chair, sauntered toward her, took her in his arms. His eyes were hooded and a smile lifted one corner of his mouth. "Allie, honey? Will *you* be there?"

Had he lost his ever-loving mind? "Of course I'll be there."

"Good. That's all I need. I love you. I don't care about the writing on the invitations as long as they say Allie is going to marry Ben. I don't care about flowers, or cake. I don't really care about the dress you're wearing."

Then he paused for a beat with a long, thoughtful gaze and his smile turned wicked. "Although . . ." He drew the word out in that way he had. "I do care about what's under the dress. Make it sexy, okay?" Toning the smile down again, he went on, "You could wear silk or a gunny sack. I. Don't. Care. I don't care if there are only three people there."

He paused again, long enough to tighten his arms around her, each word emphasized with a kiss. "What I care about is you, and me, and the preacher.

Saying you will be mine forever. *That I get to love you every day for the rest of my life. Now do you understand?"*

Ah, hell, how sweet could one guy be?

She could only nod.

Finally—at last—their wedding day was here. Standing at the foot of the aisle, dressed in white satin and lace from the skin out, her eyes wandered the sanctuary. She gazed at her groom and his best man, both tugging bow ties and shuffling their feet. But they were stationed beside the minister in perfectly fitted black tuxedos. She tugged her father's hand. "Look, Daddy, he's almost as handsome as you."

Will turned a watery smile her way, squeezed her hand. "You'll always be my little girl, Alexandra Jane. But nothing makes me happier than the love I see when he looks at you."

Waiting for the music to change, her eyes misted over. Her heart was full, as full as the small church bursting with family, with friends. On cue she took her first step, glided down the aisle to the man she'd chosen to love for always.

Through a cloud of gossamer the preacher spoke his words, *"Dearly beloved, we are gathered here today . . ."* Reese held her bouquet while Jake handed Ben his mother's wedding band. He lifted her veil, sealed their vows with a lusty kiss. And grinning foolishly at one another, she scampered beside her husband back down the aisle, a brand new bride.

Standing in the receiving line, their future was full of promise; their lives were full of hope. They'd settle into a home of their own—a cramped two-bedroom apartment near her school that they'd put a deposit on last month.

As she accepted congratulations and blessings, standing shoulder to shoulder with the man of her dreams in the evening light, surrounded by loved ones, it was only right she should dream about the future with Ben. Ben, who loved her, who laughed with her. Who teased her about her dimple. She laughed, brushed bird seed from his shoulder, then leaned into his kiss.

She would run with him in the mornings, cook dinner with him at night, and draw him a map to the laundry hamper. And one day, in the same way she prepared for the school year to begin, for a room full of eager young children to grace her life, she would dream about a family of their own.

Chapter Seven

"Reminds me of the old days." Ben paused to stretch his back. Loading tools at the end of the day was heavy work. He pulled a bandanna from his back pocket and lifted his ragged baseball cap, wiping sweat from his tanned forehead. "Working like slaves for Old Man Billings."

Jake tossed a couple of two-by-fours into the bed of the truck. "Business is good. You complaining?"

"Hell no." He coiled an extension cord, looping it around his forearm and securing the end before he tossed it into the truck. "We need to get this company in the black as quickly as possible."

"We're getting there." Jake motioned for him to help lift the table saw and together they muscled it onto the tailgate. Jake gave it a healthy shove until it was seated in the bed. "Permits will be ready for that bigass house in Scottsdale next week, the one in Chandler the first of the month. I've got a handful of remodels on the line, too."

He nodded. He'd seen the proposals, the contracts. They'd be busy for a while. They unloaded their tools back at the yard and said goodnight. The next day would come early.

The apartment door opened to the sounds of Allie puttering in the kitchen. He kicked his boots off, left them by the door and padded that way. "Mmm, hello." After a slow, welcoming kiss he lifted lids, investigating. "Smells good. How was your day today?"

"I worked in the classroom all day, but it's all ready for the first day of school. I have lesson plans to finalize tonight." He found forks and napkins shoved into his hands to set the table.

She put the finishing touches on dinner, then passed him a loaded plate and took a seat across from him at the table. "Looks good, Allie. One day you'll make some lucky guy a fine wife."

"You think so? Do you think I'll make a good mom, too?"

His eyes shot up quickly. Surely his alarm flashed neon bright across his face.

"Gotcha!"

He grinned broadly and shook his head, then turned thoughtful. "You know I want to make babies with you, Al. Lots and lots of babies. But let's take this slow, okay? We both have careers to get off the ground."

"Mmm." She swallowed her mouthful. "There are lots of things I'd like us to do first." She glanced around. "And we'll need a house. This place is kind of small."

"It will happen when the time is right." He took her hand and rubbed her knuckles with the pad of his thumb. "I love you, but I want you to myself for a while."

She leaned across the table and kissed him. "I love you back."

"Good. Now be a good wife and don't *ever* scare me like that again."

She wouldn't have imagined it, but she was in love all over again. With twenty-five 5-year-olds. They kept her busy; some days they ran her ragged. But as she'd hoped, she loved every minute.

Allie locked her classroom and exited the outer doors of the school building, her arms full of paperwork she intended to go over that night. The sun, which had been bright earlier in the day, now hid behind thick gray clouds. Gusty breezes teased the stack of papers as she fumbled through her purse for keys. A tall, thin woman she recognized as a teacher in one of the other grades yelled from two cars down.

"Hey, do you need help? You look like you're about the lose everything!" She tossed her purse in her own car and hurried toward Allie, snatching a pile of papers before the wind scattered them like confetti.

"Thanks so much; you're a lifesaver!" Allie dropped her load onto the passenger seat and then reached around to relieve her rescuer of her burden. "I'm Allie Tate, by the way." With everything safely stashed, she turned to shake her new friend's hand.

Swirling leaves and trash danced their way across the parking lot, caught up in breezy flurries. "I'm Madison Andrews; I teach third. Call me Maddie." With a welcoming smile, Maddie grasped her hand, her long midnight black hair twirling as puffs of wind blew around them. "This is my first year; I just graduated. How long have you been here?"

Allie tossed her purse on top of the papers and slammed the car door. Her keys hung from one hand. "This is my first year too. Kindergarten."

"So, how do you like it so far?" The ends of Maddie's hair whipped into her face. She caught it in her fist and held it back while she lounged against the fender, settling in for a chat. "I have to admit, I get intimidated, mostly by the parents. Some days I feel like they're sharks and I'm chum in the water."

Allie smiled as she leaned against the car door, amused and jealous of Maddie's energy at the end of the day.

"I hate to admit it out loud, but my parents have all been very supportive." She smiled sheepishly, anchoring her skirt with her arm when the wind threatened to lift it. "I have quite a few who volunteer to help out during class." With the hand holding her keys she motioned toward the worksheets the children completed that day. "Unfortunately, the mom who was scheduled for today cancelled."

Allie desperately needed to get home, put her feet up. She pushed off the car and edged around Maddie, making sure warmth settled in her voice. "I'm glad I met you today. Maybe tomorrow we can have lunch together." Allie reached the door and propped it open.

Maddie's smile was in her eyes as she pushed herself off the car. "That will be great. School's been pretty lonely so far."

"Tomorrow, then. We can make plans for Saturday. We're having people over for poker. But you're warned, we generally last until the wee hours."

Maddie grinned and lifted her arm in farewell. "Sounds like fun. I'll tell my husband."

Allie slid in behind the wheel as the first fat raindrops fell. Smiled again and waved as she drove away.

Hopefully Jake would bring a date this time, but he usually showed up stag to poker. She'd brought up the subject with Ben the night before, but as usual, he told her to back off. Maybe they should just set him up on a blind date. A smile bloomed. Wouldn't that be fun? And a little like payback.

The next week Ben burst through the door in the evening, just as she sat to mark worksheets. It was nearing the end of the week, the end of September. "Hey Al, I've got a surprise for you. Throw some warm clothes together. We're leaving after work tomorrow."

After nearly an hour on the road she was finally relaxed. Questioning—interrogating—had done her no good. Ben was keeping their destination a secret. "This was a great idea, Ben." She lay with her head against the seat, eyes closed, tired from a long week herding youngsters. "Like a mini-honeymoon."

He reached across the car and smoothed her cheek with his fingers. "The softness of your skin is like velvet against my hand." The corner of his mouth twitched. "And if you tell Jake I said that I'll deny it."

Allie only smiled, turned to stare out her window, enjoying the ride and the desert scenery as it flew by in the waning afternoon light.

Wheels hummed as they cruised along the ribbon of patched asphalt, as if singing backup to the country music drifting from the radio. Ben took his eyes off the road long enough to glance her way. "You sure you didn't mind postponing our wedding trip?"

She let the peaceful surroundings seep into her. Towering saguaros stood resolute, their barrels pocked, arms reaching in surrender toward the swirling patches of high clouds. "No, it's fine. We both have so much to do."

"Maybe you need to dial it down. You'll make yourself sick if you keep up this pace.

"You're right. But there's so much. Lesson plans, meetings, the house. Where are we going, by the way?" They'd passed several road signs along the way. It had to be somewhere nearby.

Ben stretched his arm toward her and flicked a curl. "I was trying to be mysterious." He returned his hand to the steering wheel, flexed his fingers and rolled his neck. "I found a bed and breakfast in Sedona that's supposed to be pretty. Hopefully you'll feel better by the time the weekend's over."

She let a smile tug at her lips as she faced Ben and swept her gaze over his familiar features. Inside she glowed knowing that he was concerned about her, that he'd made the effort to plan this trip. She reached for his hand, laced their fingers together. "You're a great guy, you know that? I just might keep you."

Her attention was diverted as they left the interstate and travelled the highway into the quaint town nestled charmingly in a red rock valley. Through the dusky twilight, brightly hued blossoms lined the bumpy gravel drive that led to the inn's guest lot.

A Victorian two-story stood before them, its pale yellow clapboards highlighted with mustard and colonial blue trim and pristine white gingerbread, the steep rooflines covered in mottled gray slate. The front lantern was as welcoming as a lighthouse beacon. She mounted the wide painted steps to stand beside Ben on the wooden porch, and waited for Mr. and Mrs. Lange, the owners of the property, to answer their knock

"Come on in." The friendly couple who answered the door was probably in their mid-sixties. Ben trailed her as they were ushered through the front door and into the foyer. "We're so glad you made it. Make yourselves right at home.

Allie followed Mrs. Lange while the men carried their bags upstairs. She poked her head into room after room as the innkeeper chattered about the history of the house, the furnishings, the sights in the area, and ended in the dining room, which was painstakingly reproduced, comfortable and inviting.

"Breakfast is here on the sideboard starting at eight. High tea at four." She beckoned from the foot of the staircase. "Come, I'll show you up."

The rooms at this inn were named instead of numbered. Allie walked through the doorway to the Grand Canyon room and was immediately enchanted. The ice-blue beadboards and off-white crown moldings would wash the room with soothing cheer in the light of day. A tall, lace-covered window overlooked an expanse of lawn and into the pines, and there was a small stone-covered fireplace on the opposite wall. A fire was laid, ready for the strike of a match to ward off the chill of the autumn evening.

Buzzing with anticipation, she looked forward to snuggling with Ben on the chintz setee stationed before the hearth. But after removing the delicate antique quilt and tossing the mounds of fluffy pillows to the floor, it was the decadence of the king sized poster bed she longed to fall into with her husband.

"Town or Oak Creek Canyon?" He asked her the next morning as she lazed in bed. She could barely understand him through the blueberry muffin he'd confiscated from the buffet on his way upstairs. "Which do you want to explore first?"

He'd been for a run. Sweat trickled down his neck and into his T-shirt. She yawned and stretched beneath the covers. "Canyon."

"Up and at 'em, then." He grabbed her toes through the sheet and gave them a wiggle. "I'll be ready in fifteen minutes."

She held his hand as they strolled aimlessly through the rustling trees. "Luxury accommodations." Her sigh was pure pleasure. "Majestic red rock country. The maroon and gold of autumn leaves—" She drew to a stop, drew in her eyebrows as Ben simply slanted back and chuckled.

"I'm sorry." He snickered with no remorse at all. "But you sound like a travel brochure."

Yanking away, she jammed her fists into the pockets of her warm wool jacket. Kicked those leaves and continued alongside the fast-moving creek. "Well, don't call Fodor's just yet."

With a quick step he caught up to her, stole a kiss and she melted. He filled her—her mind, her heart, her soul. He restored her when she needed that. And right now she needed to spend the balance of their weekend quietly, together in their peaceful corner of the house.

They said good-bye to the proprietors on Sunday afternoon. Allie turned to Ben in the lee of the open car door, hesitating. He put his arms around her waist in a gentle embrace and dipped his head when she turned up for a kiss.

"We'll come back soon. You look like you're feeling better."

She was. Until the next morning when she awoke and made an abrupt dash to the bathroom. Ben had kissed her good-bye only an hour ago; she was glad he wasn't there to witness her misery. Nothing took the blush off a new marriage like the wife yakking over the toilet.

Six weeks had sped by since their getaway and she was still run down, but she attributed it to her hectic schedule. She lugged the laundry basket through the apartment, parked it beside the front door. Both she and Ben were busy with work, busy at home—running early in the mornings several days a week, watching the children squeal as they strolled through the neighborhood park after dinner. Ben charmed her, holding her hand and kissing her in public. She was always anxious to make love with him. But then, they were still newlyweds, still learning what pleased each other most. She grabbed a handful of quarters, scowled at the pile of dirty clothes. What would please her right now was a washer of her own.

Ben listened in on Allie's telephone conversation from the living room. Her voice was a murmur mingling with the splash of water as Allie dealt with dinner dishes. "No, Mom. We decided we'd spend Thanksgiving Day and Christmas Eve with you guys, then Christmas Day with Ben's dad and brothers."

This married thing was easier than he'd envisioned. There were adjustments to be made, of course, but he was a team player. Over the speculative comments of the football announcer, the refrigerator opened, glass clinked.

"Ryan's flying in tomorrow." Allie rounded the corner and entered the room carrying two longnecks. "And I promised my mom we'd be at her house by eleven on Thursday morning. She'll serve around four so there's time for football before dark.

She set the beers on a nearby table and settled beside him. He pulled her onto his lap as he stroked all his favorite places, extolling her virtues.

"You make it pretty easy to love you, you know." He grinned, picked up a bottle and raised it to her in a silent toast. "You bring me beer and I don't even ask." He took a long swallow from the bottle and set it back on the table, then nibbled kisses along her jaw. "You don't make me wash dishes. And really, *thank you*." She flashed him her dimple and wiggled until he hardened beneath her. Allie ran her hands up the sides of his arms, to the back of his neck and laced her fingers in his hair. She leaned forward, her lips beginning a teasing assault. Ben's arms tugged her closer, murmured as his lips brushed hers. "No PMS."

She froze. Like the human statues he and Jake saw in Vegas on spring break, she was immobile. He looked straight into her eyes. Something was very wrong.

"Allie? Honey, what's the matter?"

Even as she moaned, softly under her breath, he crooked a grin, rubbed her arms to get her attention. "Hey, what's up? I was only teasing, you know. You can be cranky if you want."

She sucked in a ragged breath, blurted what he assumed was a clue. "Ben, you know how I've been tired for forever?"

What did that have to do with anything? He tipped up her chin with a finger to see her face. "Sure, the semester's been a bitch. You'll feel better soon."

But she continued as if he hadn't spoken. "Anyway, I've never been regular, my cycle sort of keeps its own schedule. And one day I was sick—you were already gone to work." Her eyes were wild, darting.

What was he missing? Oh, God, was she ill? His eyes widened, his breathing became rough in his chest. He grabbed her hands for support—hers and his both. "Allie, for God's sake, what is it?"

She blew out a slow breath, locked her eyes on his and murmured. "I think I might be pregnant."

His jaw dropped. His breathing, which had been choppy, now stopped altogether. Of all the things he may have expected her to say, this was not one. "But we take precautions." How lame did that sound? But he bought a box of condoms—a damn *big* box—when they began sleeping together. They snickered about it at the time.

He wanted children, her children. But did he want them *yet*? His eyes skidded around the room. At the apartment, that was barely big enough for them to turn around in. At the ceiling, for what—divine intervention? At Allie, who wasn't ill, but instead was pregnant.

And miserable.

He was an ass.

He wrapped her in his arms, held her tight and rocked her as they would rock their child. Jesus. The idea took root, warmed him. Through the renewed pounding of his heart echoing in his ears he welcomed the slow grin that made its way across his face. "Al, you mean we're going to be parents?"

Without letting go he loosened her in his arms, tilted his head back, caught her bemused expression, the nervous grin hovering around her mouth. "Are you worried? Anxious? Allie, this will be great! We'll be great." He paused a beat with his eyes narrowed. "Wait . . . you said you think. We need to know for sure. Right now!"

He lurched from the sofa, but Allie pinned him. She squawked as he tumbled her into the cushions. Suddenly remembering her posited condition, he helped her find her feet.

It took them only minutes to hit the nearest drugstore, buy a test kit and return home. "Pee." Allie would probably call it an order. Maybe it was, but he didn't care. He followed it up by propelling her into the bathroom.

She stumbled across the threshold, her purchase clutched in her fist. "Impatient son of a gun, aren't you?"

"On the stick." He didn't care if he was grinning like a mad man. "Right now." Like a sentry he guarded the open doorway.

"Come on Ben, I need a little privacy." She grabbed the knob, swung the door closed in his face which was probably stupid with surprise, and spoke through the wooden panel. "Give me a little consideration, will you? I'll get this done and then show you."

He pushed the door back open, shut her up with a kiss. "I want to know if I get to be a daddy. I don't have time for consideration." He heaved a sighed, relented against her impatient glare, shut the door again. And begged from the hallway. "Now pee. Please?"

She peed.

He waited with his arms around her. Back to front so they could both watch the magic stick.

And there it was. Two pink lines.

Her hand shook only slightly as she held the plastic stick for him to see. "Okay, Daddy. What now?"

He had no idea. This was supposed to be years away. But he certainly couldn't tell her that. It was time to man up. She would need holding so he turned her into his chest, brushed his lips against her temple. "Hell if I know. What I do know is it's you and me, and we'll make it a good thing." His forehead against hers, he murmured the words against her skin. "I love you so much." His gaze lowered, followed his hand as it rubbed low on her belly. "And I already love our baby."

Even pale and skittish she was beautiful. And she was having his baby. How the hell did a guy get so lucky?

Chapter Eight

"In the kitchen!" Her shout came from that direction as he walked through the door after work. She planted her lips on his when he edged up beside her. "Boots."

With a look down he frowned, toed them off one after the other.

"I called my folks today. They're so excited, said the baby was better than the trip to Paris they had planned for the spring." She lifted a lid, gave her pot of stew a stir. "And Reese is already shopping for onesies."

"Happy, huh?"

"You could say. How about your dad?

"He cried."

Her brow furrowed even as the wooden spoon halted. "He's not happy?"

"Good tears. We're supposed to refer to him as Papa starting immediately."

Ben took a stack of bowls from the cupboard, passed them around the table. "I asked Jake to dinner. He'll be here any minute."

She ladled stew into Jake's bowl, passed it to him. Did the same for Ben. Let just the right amount of casual ride in her voice. "I stopped by the doctor's office today."

Jake lifted his eyes, ping-ponged a questioning gaze between her and Ben. "Everything okay?"

"Oh, everything's fine." She passed him the rolls, waited until he snagged one, bit into it. The taunt was devilish but much too hard to resist. "Just had to pee into a little cup."

To his credit, his food stayed in his mouth long enough for him to swallow. "A baby?" He pinned a glare on Ben. "You're married what, three months? Jesus, you know what causes that, right?"

Ben only grinned. "You jealous? Find your own wife, knock her up."

Jake's eyes dulled, quickly brightened and were accompanied by a loopy grin. "Yeah, easy for you to say. You got the good one." He got up from the table, kissed Allie on both cheeks and slapped Ben on the back. Hard.

A few weeks later Allie once again shifted against the headboard, propped up at the end of a busy Monday. She was once again herself—maybe a slightly larger self—but chasing the kids around all day wore her out.

"Are you glad it's a boy, Ben?" She was pretty sure he was, but he'd been kind of quiet since they returned from her sonogram earlier in the day. "I mean, most guys want to have a son, don't they?"

Ben stretched, lifted her pillow so she could get comfortable. "Sure, it's great. But you know I would have been good with a little girl, too." His absentminded pat on her arm did nothing to reassure her.

"Thanks." She wiggled into her nest. "What's the matter? You look pale. Do you not feel well?"

"I'm fine." Using a finger, he marked his place in the book on his lap and stared off into middle space.

"Maybe you shouldn't have gone with me today. Some guys get kind of freaked out about the whole *growing the baby* thing. Is that it? Did it bother you to see him on that monitor? I thought it was pretty cool, myself. And then to hear his heartbeat: *woosh, woosh, woosh*." She imitated the sound the best she could. "It was really fast. I didn't realize babies' hearts beat that fast." She was babbling, but Ben was really pale.

"What about his nickname? Are you sure you're okay with it? Because I really like that name, Trey. It means three, and well, he is. The third, I mean. Your dad is Bentley, you're Ben. I don't want anyone calling him Benjie. That sounds like a dog."

"Trey's good, sweetheart. That's a good name."

Oh, God. He wasn't having second thoughts about the baby, was he? Because really, it was too late for that now. She took a hard look at him, stiff against his own pillow with his eyes glued to the cover of that baby book on his lap.

"What are you reading, Ben?"

"What the hell's an incompetent cervix?"

"Good *God*, Ben." She grabbed the book from him and twisted to rearrange her pillows, scolding him with her best teacher voice as she tried to get comfortable. Again. Still. "If you worry about every single thing you read in those books I'm taking them all away from you."

But Ben was not intimidated. He speared her with a determined scowl. "We need to know what we're up against."

And there was the bossy voice. Is this what was bothering him? He could be such a trial. She softened her tone and scooted closer to him. "No, sweetheart. You need to know that we have an excellent doctor—you met her, remember? She's taking very good care of us. Everything will be fine." She handed the book back to him. "Now read the part about helping me with my breathing during labor. I signed us up for Lamaze classes in a few months."

Her twenty-third birthday fell on a Sunday. She was stuffed, the melody of classical strings lulling her from across the dining room. Their plates were cleared with a muted clatter and the waiter served their desserts—raspberry topped cheesecake for her and a decadent chocolate layer cake for him. She took a bite, then let out a low, appreciative sigh. "Delicious."

Ben's grin was expected. It was a joke between them how much she ate lately. "I had a call today."

She lifted her gaze and paused with her spoon raised to her lips, prepared to shovel in the next bite.

"Yep. From the zoo. Seems they're missing an elephant."

He was teasing. Of course he was. How many times a day could he possibly tell her how beautiful she was? But oh, he'd pay for that. With a retaliatory grin she set her spoon back in her dish. She stretched her arm out until her hand rested on his lap, adjacent to her. She let her fingers wiggle their way to his inner thigh. Hidden by the heavy linen tablecloth, she traced his hard length with her fingertips. Beamed up at him, all innocent. "Seems they're missing a snake, too."

With a muffled bark of laughter, he tugged her close and brushed his lips against hers, then pulled a gift from his jacket. Two fingers pushed it past the flickering candle and across the table to her, his warm blue eyes smiling. "Happy birthday, babe."

She picked up the flat, narrow box in one hand. It rustled when she gave it a little shake. "Is it a car seat? Because we really need a car seat."

"No silly, can't you tell by the shape? It's a stroller." She hadn't picked that out yet either. "Better open it to be sure."

She leisurely unfastened the tape, hiding her eyes with her lashes, taunting Ben with her deliberate motions. When all the tape was unstuck, she gradually peeled back the paper and exposed a jeweler's box. Her chin jerked up in surprise.

"Oh, Ben."

"You don't even know what it is yet. Open it!"

Oh lord, bossy voice again. But she knew him well now. He only used it when he was anxious.

She removed the smooth leather case from the box. Snapped open the lid to reveal a beautiful watch with a slim gold band and diamonds encircling its face. It was engraved on the back. *For all time. Love, Ben.*

"Oh, Ben. I love it." She plucked her new bauble from its cocoon and buckled it on. Her heart must surely show in her eyes, as it was so full of love, so swelled in her chest, she just might explode. She lifted her lemon water to his whisky sour in a toast, the lips of the elegant crystal touching with a discreet ring. "For all time."

She made it through winter, and warmer weather was again upon them. It had been more than a year since she first met Ben—such a busy year. With a waddle she swore she'd never resort to, she headed toward the kitchen for a glass of iced tea. A key scraped the lock and she halted. Ben stepped through the door and kicked off his boots.

"Like your dress." He leaned in for a welcoming kiss.

She scowled down at the acres of fabric. "Tent. You look tired."

"Hard week, just glad it's Friday." He dropped an arm across her shoulders. "I need to change. Tell me about your day."

Restless. Achy. I cried in the classroom after the kids left. "I'm just glad I made it to the last day of school before the rug rat made his appearance."

"Your due date was a whole week ago."

Her feet were evidence of that. "Everyone said first babies are late. I guess I'm glad they were right this time."

They passed the baby's room—a closet advertised as a second bedroom— which they'd painted soft yellow and hung with prints of nursery rhyme characters. A zoo animal mobile bobbed above the wooden crib Ben had assembled weeks ago. Everything was ready for Trey's arrival. There were stacks of diapers, tiny T-shirts and pajamas. Hand-knit blankets. Sweet smelling powder and lotion. And Jake brought a huge stuffed teddy bear with a big blue bow the day after the sonogram. They were missing nothing . . . except Trey.

Ben let his hand drift down to rest on his son. "Think Junior will let us sleep tonight?"

"It would be the first time this week."

"You look exhausted, babe. Go get off your feet. I'll have a quick shower and be out in a few minutes."

She nodded. "I just want something to drink first."

Padding across the cool tile of the kitchen floor, she removed the iced tea pitcher from the refrigerator. And stopped in her tracks as a gush of warm fluid ran down her bare thighs and soaked her hem. *Seriously?* She didn't even have to pee. She stared at the wetness surrounding her feet.

The puddle spreading across the floor suddenly took on a whole new meaning. Oh boy! *Ohboyohboyohboy!* She was having a baby!

"Um, Ben!" Stay calm. *Stay calm.* Had he heard her? She raised her voice. "Honey, can you come here, please?"

Her first contraction ripped through her, much stronger than she'd imagined. "Ben!" Damn. She wasn't planning to be one of those hysterical women. She *wasn't.* But calmness was overrated. She was done with calm. Right now she needed a chauffeur. One who was about to be a daddy. "*Ben!*"

Ben came running, tearing through the apartment with his shirt off, belt flapping. With her chest heaving, a vague hand waved toward the mess on the floor. "I . . ." Her breath came out in a whisper. "I made a mess." Oh, Ben. All he wanted was to relax in a hot shower and she was dragging him off to labor and delivery.

Ben took one look at the wet mess on the floor and immediately became a man of action. "Don't move. I'll get the mop." His worried gaze darted around the small room. "Did you drop the pitcher? I don't see any glass. Are you sure you're not hurt?" He led her by the shoulders to the nearest chair. "Here, sit while I clean this up for you." He was really so sweet.

"I didn't spill the tea." Women—lots and lots of women—did this every day. Maybe she could stay calm after all. Another contraction snuck up on her and she clenched the seat of the chair in a death grip. She took a deep breath against the pain. Blew it out.

Ben's gaze swung between the pitcher—still intact—sitting on the table and the splattered mess on the floor. "That's not tea." His eyes flew to her, and landed. "Baby?" At her nod he sailed to her side, dropped to his knees beside her. Patted her knee.

Another contraction came, riding the wake of the last one. Already? Was that *normal?*

"What do you need, Allie?"

She could barely breathe and he was asking idiot questions. She unclamped her hands, grabbed fistfuls of his shirt and dragged him so they were nose to nose. "Think . . . I need . . . hospital."

Ben's grin exploded across his face. He bent down and swept her into his arms. "Well, okay then, let's go get Trey."

Like they were running out for milk.

With a lead weight centered in his chest, Jake parked his truck, squared his shoulders and crossed the threshold of the hospital through wide glass doors. Was it bad, was it *wrong* to dread this day? He found the information desk. "Tate?"

The older woman—a volunteer, according to her name badge—pecked at the keyboard, beamed her response. "Ah, maternity. Room 334." And then pointed toward the elevator.

His stomach bottomed out at *maternity*. Jesus. Allie had a baby.

Ben's baby.

He'd had months to prepare, sure. Six of them. Fat lot of good that did him. He climbed into the empty car, stabbed the button for three.

His steps slowed as he neared her room. She'd never be his, but until today he could still hope. Still pretend he had a shot. The weight in his chest did a slow slide, landed in his stomach, which was already in knots. Suck it up, Taylor. The voices in his head were ruthless. You want her? Well, this is all you get. Don't fuck it up.

Echoes of his footfalls followed him as he searched for the correct room. Halting just outside her room he planted a grin on his face, popped his head around the doorframe. "I hear somebody had a busy night." He stepped into the room, was glad he'd chosen the roses, which he slid onto a counter beside two smaller bouquets. "Hi, babe." He leaned over the hospital bed, kissed Allie's cheek, checked his breath at the blond-haired angel alert in her arms.

Even as he smoothed a gentle finger over the curling tufts on the baby's head and nudged him under the chin, he turned to Ben, perched on the edge of the mattress beside Allie. "He's all red and wrinkly, what's the matter with him?"

"He's perfect. He has my eyes."

Jake snorted. "All babies have blue eyes, dumbshit."

Allie lifted the bundle toward him. "Do you want to hold him?"

Even in the ugly hospital gown she glowed. And her Mona Lisa smile shook him. If he wasn't convinced of it before, there was no way around the truth now. Allie was happy with her life—with Ben. And if he wanted to be part of that life he would find a way to be happy for her. "Of course I do." And he let her settle her son into the crook of his elbow.

His heart, which had at last settled into a smooth and steady rhythm, filled. "Well, hello, kid." He cradled the wriggling baby, rocked him with ease, kissed him gently on his soft little cheek and then rounded a grin on his two best friends. "You did good. I'm impressed."

"Hey Jake, I need to call in a favor." Ben's glance slid to Allie, and then they both turned to him.

With the soft flannel blanket peeled back, Jake paused as he played with tiny fingers, lifted his eyes to Ben, met his amused gleam. "Oh, yeah? What now? I suppose you want time off so you can get in Allie's way with the baby."

"Nah, I've got something better. We want you to be Trey's godfather." He waited a beat, the suggestion of a smirk riding on his smile. "Besides, you got me into this."

Jake stilled. Was he capable of this? Something—his heart?—lodged in his throat. Could he promise to help raise this child?

The baby was not his, but he was Allie's. He nestled him closer, humbled by the prospect. When he lowered his eyelids he found he couldn't shut out the weight of reality. How could he *not* promise? He started to speak, was surprised at the gravel he found in his voice. With a quick cough, he answered. "Yeah. I'd like that a lot."

Chapter Nine

Allie melted into the sofa with a sigh of relief and shuffled so the heating pad lay against her lower back. She picked up the photo album she'd set aside earlier and opened it on her lap. The cover was green leather, engraved with Trey's initials.

There was Trey as a newborn, in his parents' arms, still at the hospital. Trey at the lake, encased in a life vest so bulky he could barely toddle. She smiled at the memories as she flipped page after page. She came to last summer's vacation—including three days at Disneyland. She studied the pages until at last she came to the end. Trey's school photo, taken shortly after he entered kindergarten earlier in the fall. His vibrant personality shone through the brilliant blue eyes, so much like his father's.

The years had passed in a blur. For so long now there had been little to their days but car seats and play dates, lesson plans and blueprints. She set the hefty book on the table beside the sofa and adjusted the heat of the pad. Glanced at the clock. Her men should be home from their soccer game any minute.

Her stomach cramped and her smile dimmed. For five years she'd suffered a brutal monthly reminder that while their life may be full, it wasn't complete.

The slam of the front door and cleated feet clattering over the tiled entry had her swinging her legs over the edge of the sofa and straightening.

"Mama, Mama! Where are you?"

Ah, she recognized that voice. Loud, enthusiastic, and all boy. *Whoa, champ* echoed mere seconds before she was used as a roadblock.

"Hello, munchkin. How did your game go?" Her smile bloomed without pause. With her arms wrapped around her child she was content.

"Good. Real good. And guess what?"

Her smile broadened. She was quite familiar with the question-and-answer type conversations of a five-year-old. "What?"

Trey's face exploded in a grin. "We won! And our whole team got a trophy and a juice box." He shoved the award in her face. "Even Daddy, and even Uncle Jake, 'cause they're the coach. *And* Jax. *And* Jimmy. 'Cause they're on my team, too!"

"Wow!" She earnestly inspected the trophy. "Aren't you the lucky one?"

"Yep, I'm the lucky one." Trey grinned, spared her a quick hug, reclaimed his prize and shot through the house in a burst of little boy energy.

Ben folded himself onto the edge of the sofa, gentled a hand over his wife's back. "I'd say all is well in his world."

Allie pulled her eyes from the hallway. The heat and his hands united to ease her discomfort. At his snort she grinned into his shoulder. "At least through first grade, Coach Dad."

Later that night, Allie sat up in the dark. A slash of light from the hallway fell across the mattress, their covers thrown back.

"We've discussed this a million times, Allie." The hissed words were angry, and tired from overuse. "Now is not a good time. We're not ready."

"You mean *you're* not ready." But the ticking in her heart thundered. "Damn it, Ben, Trey's *five*. If we're going to have another baby, I'd like it to be soon." She was overcome by a swift and sudden resentment, an emotion that had been rearing its ugly head quite often lately. "Quit worrying about everything."

Ben stood at the foot of the bed and matched her glare. "Look, I take care of Trey as much as you do, and we're both dog-assed tired at the end of the day. How are we supposed to find enough time to take care of another kid, too?"

There was a new sense of urgency tonight. An unmistakable desperation in their words that frightened her. She climbed off the bed, brushed past him as she marched to the open doorway, shot out an arm toward the closed door across the hall. "We both love that kid asleep in there, and we *make* time for him. Just like we would make time for any other children. Just like we make time for anything important."

Ben paced the room, his strides eating up the carpet. "Think about the expense of a new baby. Remember how much everything cost when Trey was born? Diapers and formula and all the other shit we'd need. What are you willing to give up so we can afford all that again?"

The repetition was exhausting, and her shoulders slumped. "Look around, Ben." She spread her arms in helpless frustration. "What don't we have?" Their life wasn't extravagant, but they each had new vehicles; they took a family vacation each July; Trey was enrolled in a private school. She'd give it all up for one more mouth to feed.

Ben seemed to hesitate, then took a different tack. "You say you love him. What if we had another baby? How do you know you have enough love for two kids?"

Enough for him, *is that what he wanted to know?* She sank back onto the edge of the bed. Leveled her voice, refused to let the panic slither in. "Come on, Ben. Love doesn't divide itself when it's shared. Love multiplies."

Ben halted and leveled a long stare in her direction. He retrieved today's jeans from the floor, shoved into them as he muttered, "I'm tired of this bullshit. You don't understand." A quick step to the closet and he threw a shirt across his shoulders. "I can't take that chance." With a sweeping glance he marched from the room. Moments later the front door slammed.

The next afternoon, still dressed in her clothes from school, Allie chopped and diced, had marinara simmering on the stove. With the tension of last night's argument gnawing and nipping, the workday had seemed endless. She heard him stumble in some time during the night, but she didn't even bother to check the clock. Didn't give him the satisfaction of knowing she was still awake, either.

A door closed. Boots thudded. Should she brace for round two or was he as full of remorse as she? Allie held her breath, tracked muted footsteps as he traipsed through the house, turned the corner into the kitchen. She waited for him to approach her before she laid her hand on his chest, reached for a kiss. "You still mad?"

With lids lowered he drew her to him, his arms tight. One hand cupped the back of her head, as if she couldn't be close enough. "No, we'll work that out."

His chest pressed against her as he inhaled deeply, then let it out with a long, uneasy breath. Curiosity had her leaning back to look into his eyes. "What?"

His eyes were cloudy, not the sparking blue they usually wore. Tension radiated from him in waves. "I'm so damn sorry, Al. I love you, so damn much, and I'm so damn sorry."

She narrowed her eyes, her brow furrowed. She opened her mouth to question but a sense of foreboding had her closing it again.

Ben released her, turned and ambled toward the doorway.

"Wait."

He stopped in his tracks, then rotated back, his eyes lowered.

"Jake called. Said something about an argument and you should call when you got in. You two get in a fight?"

He lifted his gaze and met hers. "Sort of."

"But you guys never fight. It's kind of creepy."

His lips curved in a pitiful imitation of a smile. "Yeah, it's nothing, don't worry about it." And with no other explanation he turned again, headed for the hallway.

Time was elastic. Days stretched into weeks, and then months, and then years—each passing faster than the last. Allie gave the vacuum cleaner a determined shove over nubby beige carpet.

This mindless work was necessary and relaxing. She let her thoughts wander as she vacuumed her way out of her bedroom and down the hallway past Ben's office. She sucked up dust bunnies from beneath the ancient plaid sofa in the living room—why after three years in the house had it still not been replaced? As the machine glided into the furthest corner of the living room, she mentally ticked this chore off her Saturday to-do list. She'd mop the kitchen floor next. She had much to accomplish before the beginning of the week. And Ben had an overnight to Nebraska on Wednesday.

"Hey babe, I'm home!"

It was the jolt of alarm that had her hand flying up to cover her suddenly hammering heart, sucking in a surprised breath and whirling at the voice the behind her. She could only shake her head at her husband and used a nervous laugh to mask her fright. She bent, flicked the power switch. With the roar of the machine she hadn't heard the door, the thunk of his boots or his footsteps as he padded through the house wearing nothing but boxers. She could only hope his dusty work clothes were somewhere near the hamper in the laundry room.

His gaze heated her as it raked over her bare limbs poking through a form-fitting tank and cutoff jeans before he lowered his lips and sealed them on hers.

"Everything taken care of?"

"Yeah, the plumber needed in to fix his *modification*—the word was centered in air quotes—then I helped the foreman move a stack of lumber. Where's Trey?"

"With Jax. Maddie took the kids to the movies. There's a new Disney film out."

"Disney? Isn't he a little old for that?"

Allie grinned and rolled her eyes as she unplugged the machine. "There are probably girls involved."

His laugh of surprise erupted in a burst, then faded just as quickly. "Girls? Isn't he a little young for *that*?"

She paused in winding up the cord. Ben would always be a little boy's daddy, longing for the simpler days of skinned knees and loose teeth. "They grow up and move on before you're done being the parent, don't they?"

He only nodded.

The idea pricked her too, but she dealt with children growing up and moving on every year at school. The children from her first year teaching were already graduating from high school.

"I'd like to think he's too young to be interested in girls, but he is thirteen. They're probably at the top of a very short list." She picked up her basket of cleaning supplies, poked him in the chest with a finger. "You guys have that talk yet?"

"It's now at the top of *my* list."

She nodded, changed the subject. "So, what's on for today?"

"Jake's having people over to swim this afternoon, maybe get pizza later on. You feel like it?"

"Sure, sounds fun. Trey can work on his backstroke."

"There will be quite a few kids there. He can practice his backstroke another day."

With a fingertip she brushed the furrow in his forehead, smoothing it with a sassy grin. She tugged the elastic snugged around his waist. "Then how about you?"

His shorts were already halfway to the floor.

"You want to practice *your* backstroke?"

Time continued to trudge along. Ben finished dressing, his heart pounding, his limbs heavy. Even more time had passed now, and he'd let this farce continue for too many years. Allie threaded an arm through the sleeve of her blouse. "You don't look like a man ready for a road trip."

Ben gave his wife a falsely bright smile through the vanity mirror. Maybe she wouldn't notice if it didn't quite reach his eyes. "Sure I am. LA. Plumbing supplies. All gassed up and ready to go." He dug through the clutter on the bathroom counter. "Have you seen my keys?"

She patted his pants pocket. Sharp metal edges jabbed her hand through chino. "I hope you pay better attention while you're driving."

"Yeah, sure thing. What are you doing today?"

She reached up to poke an earring though the hole in her lobe. He admired the youthfulness the slight curve of her lips gave to her face and the way her breast lifted with her arm. Again he was knifed by the sharp stab of guilt that had haunted him for years. Allie deserved . . . better.

"Michael's watching all the kids so Maddie and I can do a little shopping, have lunch. Can you believe we've taught school for fifteen years already?" Her smiled brightened. "God, I love the first day of summer vacation."

His palms found her face, framed it, and his lips explored freely before he pulled away. "Always remember how much I love you."

Her arms wound around him. "Love you back, sweetheart."

The response, the soft silver of her eyes and the arms wrapped around his waist all warmed him. And made what he was about to do so much more difficult.

He slung the strap of his overnight bag onto his shoulder, stepped through the front door and closed it carefully behind him. He wasn't heading to LA. Like he hadn't gone to San Diego, or Houston, or any number of places over the years. He heaved himself into his truck, drove the few miles through late morning sunshine, and parked on the cracked concrete driveway. At the front door he stood a moment, his bag again strung over a shoulder, contemplating the tragic irony he was trapped in.

His glance swung from the neatly trimmed yard to the darkly stained wood of the front door. How many years had he come here, anyway? Many, certainly, but that didn't keep him from hating—no, *resenting*—it. Was it possible to stop *and* keep his honor? With a shift he transferred his duffle to his other shoulder. The idea had taunted him from time to time, but he couldn't figure how to manage it. The situation was beyond unfortunate. They were all victims.

Heaving a breath he dropped his duffle at his feet. He was tired clear to his bones. Tired of lying. Tired of feeling trapped. He needed to talk to Allie, make her understand. So many times he'd tried to tell her, to explain, then lost his nerve.

Oh God, he loved her. But what if he couldn't make her understand? The most frightening notion reared its head, turned him cold. What if he lost her?

And what about Trey? He was fifteen now, but that was still so young.

He would do anything to keep his son from hurting. Or worse, from hating him. The agony of that was like a sucker punch, swift, strong and painful.

But he was beyond tired of hurting.

He had to come clean, and soon. He was a good father. All things considered, he was a good husband. His love for his family was absolute. Maybe they would understand.

And he could stop hurting.

Ben stood to his full height, let out one final, weary sigh, then sucked in a deep, steadying breath and straightened his shoulders. He pressed the buzzer, pasted on a smile, and waited for her to open the door.

Chapter Ten

The lingering heat grabbed Trey by the chest and squeezed, and even though they'd already been there for hours, he wasn't quite ready to leave. The lights around the ball field flickered on slowly, one by one. Ugly grey moths dove into the yellow bulbs, swooped out, flew back in.

"Okay, champ, now go wide."

Dad tossed a short pass, aimed about six feet to his left. He cut sharply, caught the ball in his chest, tucked it close against his side.

Dad shot him a thumbs-up and lifted his voice to be heard from forty yards away. "Good job, champ. Almost perfect."

He fired back a wobble ball.

Dad got in formation, swung into the imaginary pocket and threw a perfect long spiral. "You all set for the weekend?"

It was his parents' anniversary this weekend—fifteen years—and they were leaving for Sedona the next day after work. His dad liked to joke that they were married for like five minutes before he was conceived, but he happened to know for a fact they were doing it before they got married. They didn't know he knew, but he heard them talking one night a few years ago, when they thought he was asleep.

He hauled ass to get to the ball and snagged it out of the air. "Sure thing. Aunt Maddie'll pick me up with Jax after practice." Ha! Hardly winded, even after that sprint. Coach had already started two-a-days, and they were a bitch, but they sure got you back in shape fast.

Again his throw back to his dad was weak, which was why Jax was the quarterback and he was a running back. Jax couldn't run for shit, but they both made varsity for next year, so they were cool.

"Nice catch."

"Thanks. We still going by Uncle Jake's to swim before we head home? I'm sweating like a pig." Uncle Jake wasn't really his uncle. But judging by the way they talked, he and his dad had been friends since God was in diapers. They also let him hang out with them on school breaks. Uncle Jake didn't treat him like a kid when he was around, which counted for a lot in his book.

"Yeah, sure. Here comes the last ball. It's a long one." Dropping a leg back, Dad raised his arm and let her fly.

Trey fell back, easily caught the pass, then ran in. Even though the sun was gone it was too friggin' hot. He was ready to jump in the pool.

The grass on the field was dry and crunchy, like it got every summer. A black asphalt track circled the field—the track his mom ran on almost every morning. After a few long strides they hit the parking lot. "You sure I can't stay home by myself this weekend? It's only a couple of days, and I'm not a little kid anymore." He was pretty sure he could talk his dad into it, but his mom kept a pretty short leash.

"Nope, not crossing the warden, champ." His dad clamped an elbow around his neck and knuckled-rubbed the top of his head. "I want to enjoy my weekend."

He ducked out of the fake hug. He liked it a lot, but he didn't want his dad to think he was a girl. "Yeah, I figured, but it was worth a shot. Can we go to the batting cages next week?" It was good to stay sharp, and his dad was a pretty good coach.

"Sure thing, champ."

His chest had that same puffed up feeling every time his dad called him *champ*, his special nickname ever since he could remember. His mom always called him something lame, like sweetheart, or honey. "Hey Dad, can I drive? It's only five miles."

"Ah, the question every father of a fifteen-year-old fields regularly. Dream on, champ." Dad chuckled and swung behind the wheel, gunned the engine and waited for him to buckle in.

"Are you sure they'll hold our reservation?" A couple of schedule snafus—a last minute consult with the lead electrician, final tweaks to the plans for a new office complex—and Ben had them running late.

"Relax, I called the B&B. They said everything's fine. We should be there by ten." His phone dinged. Stopped at a red light on the way out of town, his lips thinned as he read his text. He crammed the phone into his shirt pocket.

Her shoes pried off, she kicked her feet onto the dash. "I'm glad we didn't put off going north this year." If she sucked in her stomach and bent forward she could reach the air vent to adjust it. They wouldn't need air conditioning in Sedona. "I love the fall colors, but I am so ready to cool off for a few days."

She slid a glance to the face of her husband. That face was dearer today than when they first met over pizza fifteen years ago. The crow's feet when he smiled and the grizzle in his beard were something she still wasn't used to, even if they did radiate character and authority. And sex appeal—she smiled to herself—in a George Clooney sort of way.

Ben opened his mouth to speak. Snapped it shut in a move that reminded her of Trey's guppy and then faced her. "Trey could have stayed home alone. He's old enough not to need a babysitter."

"Maddie's not a babysitter. We're only making sure Trey doesn't get into trouble, Ben. I didn't want to worry about him over the weekend." She unclenched the fists resting on her lap—a reaction to the guilt trip Trey had been leading her on all week. "Besides, it makes it easier for Maddie to get him to football practice."

She didn't want to argue about this. Trey probably could have stayed by himself. But by the time today rolled around, the idea of not giving in to her son's pleading was simply a matter of principle. Thankfully, Ben remained silent, merely nodded and turned his attention back to the road.

Sunday afternoon, Allie stood alone on the porch of the ancient Victorian and scanned the yard; let the peace of the quiet afternoon seep into her. The gardens lining the stone walkways valiantly struggled against the warmth of the August sun, but the trees dotting the property still retained their full complement of green. It was still too early in the year for autumn color.

Their interminable weekend was finally over. This escape with Ben was supposed to be special, a relaxing break from work, away from the punishing heat of the city. Even—and yes, the guilt of it still niggled at her—away from Trey.

Even now she wasn't sure what happened. Saturday morning they did a little hiking, a little shopping—everything was fine. But some time during lunch his good mood vanished.

She'd sat across from Ben at a cloth-covered table, feet whimpering from the miles they'd trekked. "Maddie will love that pottery bowl we found for her." The server set her Cobb salad before her. She smiled her thanks. "I hope Trey didn't give her any trouble."

Ben sliced through his chicken breast, then raised his eyes. "Trey? Does he ever?"

"Not that I know of." A young girl sat perched in a wooden high chair nearby, blonde curls caught up in pink ribbons. Tiny white sneakers banged against the legs of her chair. Playing patty cake with her mother. Allie darted her eyes away; she hadn't meant to stare.

He hadn't said a civil word to her since.

She breathed deeply of the clean mountain air, wished there was more time before she had to climb in the car.

Ben finished loading their bags into the trunk and slammed the lid. "Hurry up. We need to get back." Impatience radiated from him in waves. "We'll be back for our anniversary next year."

Right now she wasn't taking odds. "Sure." She approached the car, climbed in. With a parting glance she scanned the oaks and the pines surrounding the house. Ben shot her an inquiring look and she nodded silently.

Next year could only be better. For now, it was time to get home.

Just before dark, Ben parked in the driveway and followed her into the house, rolling their suitcases, then went back outside. After starting the wash, Allie stepped back out and strode down the walk to the driveway, shoving her cell phone into the back pocket of her jeans. "Trey knows we're back. I told him you'd be by to pick him up."

Ben was just tucking his phone away. Preoccupied, he glanced up and merely nodded. He ducked under the hood of the car, digging deep into the mysteries of the engine as the lavender of twilight settled around them.

"This car's almost out of warranty. I want to find a new one for you, something safe." He jiggled and tugged, scowling into the dark recess. "The old girl needs a tune-up for now, though. I'll trade vehicles with you one day this week, have Steve in the shop take a look at it."

Now he wanted to talk. And about the car, no less. Go figure. She paused on her way back into the house. "Are you hungry?"

Ben slammed the hood back in place. "Not yet. Keep dinner easy. I've got a stop to make first, then I'll get Trey."

Jake scowled into the darkened interior of his car. He needed a life. No, not just a life, a *different* life. Of the upgraded, new-and-improved variety.

For fifteen years now he'd been hanging out, waiting. Surviving obscurely in the periphery of his own existence.

Well, fuck that.

Okay, so maybe he had women when he wanted them. Hell, he never claimed to be a saint. But they were merely diversions. An easy way to kill a few days, a few weeks at best. No relationships, no commitments, those were words to live by.

But his life needed purpose. Next week was his birthday, and nothing made a person question their presence in this world like a birthday. Starting now he was making changes. Moving on. He may be satisfied with his professional life—most days even proud—but his personal life was in the shitter.

The company he ran with Ben—a company they'd built with hope and sweat—thrived. And at the end of the day Ben went home to Allie and Trey. But at the end of his day who did he have at home? Nobody, not even a dog.

He was no longer a young man. The man in the mirror nowadays wore gray peppered in his temples and reading glasses tucked in his shirt pocket. He was now a middle-aged male—and lonely. It was past time to find someone to share his life with. What the hell was he waiting for anyway?

He sighed loudly. Didn't want to think too deeply about that.

"Sure hope that frown's not for me, sugar."

Jake jerked back to the present. Slipped his fingers around her hand and pressed it against her bare thigh. "Of course not. Guess I zoned out."

A sheaf of wheat blonde fell forward as Michelle stretched to turn down Brad Paisley, and the country superstar's tune lowered to a hum. "I surely have been looking forward to slipping away with you." Turned to face him, melted chocolate-colored eyes danced with excitement. "The bright lights, the action; I haven't been to Vegas in years." An Atlanta transplant, Michelle's voice dripped honeysuckle and magnolia blossoms. Her smile was seductive and inviting, even if he suspected it was practiced, yet Jake was glad they'd made a plan for the weekend. Michelle was intelligent and witty. And her long, long legs were incredibly sexy. He wished he cared.

He was first introduced to Michelle Lauder nearly two months ago. A senior engineer with Lauder and Martin, her firm provided consulting work on Rancho Encantado, T-Squared's latest housing development. This weekend was his chance to get away from Phoenix. Away from the reminder that every year for fifteen years *they* had a special anniversary trip and he had nothing.

It was a five hour drive from Phoenix to Las Vegas. As the glow of city lights appeared in the distance, bouncing off the low-lying clouds in the night sky, Jake settled into the seat of his luxury sedan. The CD changed in the player. George Strait.

"More country, Jake? Let's try something different." Michelle removed the CD, replaced it with something classical. "How about a little Bach?"

Bach? Where the hell did that come from?

Thankfully, his torture was short-lived as he pulled up to the hotel—a glamorous marble and white light property that was charging him enough to feed a third world country for an entire year. He handed his keys to the valet and rounded the hood even as an energetic bellman loaded their suitcases onto a wheeled cart. The polished floor of the luxurious lobby reflected the glistening light from the glow of an opulent crystal chandelier as he steered an unimpressed Michelle to the reception desk and gave the attendant his name.

Trailing the bellman through the open door of their room, Jake's eyes followed Michelle in the muted light of a crystal lamp as she investigated the opulent room, trailing one manicured finger over the silk duvet covering the king-sized bed, then stepping closer to the closed door of the balcony. He let the bellman out with a tip and nearly tripped over their luggage, lined up like soldiers in the suite.

He had one small bag. He raised his eyebrows at Michelle's two large suitcases. "What could you possibly need in so many bags, Michelle? It's Friday night. We're only staying until Sunday."

She turned away from the view of the strip, lifted a negligent shoulder. "Just the essentials, sugar. A little of this, a little of that."

He started to argue, but the words backed up in his throat. This was not a battle he'd win. Might as well check out the view instead.

With a dismissive toss Michelle's designer handbag landed on a nearby chair. Following him onto the terrace, she wordlessly slipped her arms around his waist. She had his shirt untucked, his belt unbuckled before he stopped her, took her hand and led her back inside. This was the start of his new life— he was damned if we wasn't going to enjoy it.

Allie waved good-bye as Ben backed down the driveway. She spent a good amount of time collecting more laundry and preparing chef salads. She slid them into the refrigerator to chill. With a second load of wet clothes tumbling in the dryer, she glanced at the clock on the way through the kitchen. What kept Ben? He was probably hashing out the upcoming Rotary project with Maddie's husband, Michael. As good friends, they'd worked on committees together for years.

With hair still wet from her shower, Allie switched on lamps as she wandered the house. It was fully dark outside so she flipped on the front porch light before heading back to her room. Her cell phone rang in the kitchen. She ran barefoot to grab it from her purse.

"Hello?"

"Hey, Mom. I thought you guys were coming to get me."

Her eyebrows drew together. "Dad left right after I talked to you; he should be there any minute." *Why wasn't he there yet?* "I'll see where he is and call you back."

Inexplicably, her heart raced. Her palms became moist and an uncomfortable foreboding settled in her midsection. She paced the kitchen floor as Ben's cell phone repeatedly went to voicemail.

She tried Jake. She could count on him to reassure her.

"Jake Taylor."

"Hi, it's Allie."

"Hey there, back already?"

"Um, yes." She paused a moment to take a breath, leveled out her voice. "Have you spoken to Ben?"

"Nah, I told him not to bug me this weekend. I was out of town, too. Just pulling into my garage. Is everything all right?"

She blew out another quiet, steadying breath. "Probably. But he left to pick up Trey hours ago and hasn't shown up yet. He's not answering his phone."

"I'm sure everything's fine." Jake's voice was calm, comforting. She focused on that. "Keep trying, he'll answer."

"Sure, you're right." This was silly. Ben and Trey would come crashing in the door any minute. But the knot in her stomach was growing. "Sorry to bother you."

She tried Ben's cell again.

Ben slowed, rounded the corner behind a cherry red compact, joined the scattering of vehicles already cruising down Grand. Tension radiated through his shoulders and down his spine, but the deed was done. He'd met his demon head on. Guilt snaked through his veins, so familiar anything else would be abnormal.

He was liberated, free. And the loss gutted him. A hot flash of shame flared and he beat back the flame until it was no more than embers, stuffed into a corner of his mind. He wouldn't allow them to die, though. They would glow and flicker again from time to time. And he would drag them out, allow them to rekindle.

After so many years he was granted a reprieve—which was more than he deserved. His lips thinned as he pressed them together. The admission was ruthless, yet true. Activating his turn signal, he veered into the left lane. His sigh rose from the depths of his soul. A fresh slap of remorse carried with it tears that burned the back of his throat and stung his eyes.

He slowed his pickup as he neared a red light, scrubbed his hands over his face. He'd been gone longer than he expected. Would Trey wonder where he was? Would Allie worry? Starting today he was theirs and theirs alone— no more *business trips*.

He needed his wife, to hear her voice, to say her name. He dug in his shirt pocket for his phone. She would hear the change in his voice, the contentment so different than his frustrated words of the day before. He allowed a fleeting tilt of his lips. Allie deserved to be happy.

"Oh, Allie." He breathed her name aloud. She didn't deserve his deceit. Yet deceive her he had. For years he'd lived in dread of the shadowy secret that dwelled between them. He'd tried to share it with her—so many times he tried—but in the end he shrank from tainting her with his ... predicament.

He let his eyes sweep the seat beside him. The bouquet of sunflowers and bottle of wine were for her. He had apologies to make. The naked yearning on her face as she watched the baby in the restaurant yesterday had been tortuous to him. He'd discounted her feelings for too many years, because he was a selfish, self-centered, ass. Completely in love with his wife, certainly. But still an ass.

Did she even realize she did that—ogle the babies like they were the last chocolate in the box? Probably not. She had been right all along, though. There was no reason they couldn't—shouldn't—have another child. He could only shake his head. Shit, she was always right.

A baby after all this time? His heart landed in his lap. Nerves? Excitement? Fear? Yeah, he was full of all that. This was scary stuff. He'd put her off for so long. But starting tonight, if she was still game—if she still wanted a baby—he was in.

He flipped his phone open with a thumb and spared a quick glance at the street around him. The only traffic was an older guy in a safe-looking foreign sedan slowing in the lane beside him. Allie needed a new car. She might like something like that, cruising around town with an infant buckled in the back.

The light changed from red to green as he approached. He pressed his foot to the gas, glanced down to dial.

At the unrelenting blare of a horn, his eyes winged up. *Oh, shit!* He yanked the wheel, launched forward against his restraint and held on as his truck spun across the intersection in a dizzying loop. There was no time for thought as he pitched back and forth, assaulted by the squeal of tires, the smell of rubber burning against asphalt, the deafening crunch of metal and a garish shower of broken glass.

Allie! No time to think of her, yet she was with him. In the noise, which surrounded him. In the blood, which covered him. In the pain, which sliced through him. And then finally—when all was silent—in the darkness, which enveloped him.

Chapter Eleven

Driving for five hours left his legs cramped and his head fuzzy, but these laps in the pool were both clearing the cobwebs and stretching him out. Jake flip-turned at the wall and glided toward the steps with long strokes. Enough was enough. He had an ice cold longneck and a lounge chair calling his name.

The ringing of his cell phone cut into the night. From habit, he checked the display. "Hey girl, did you give him hell?"

No response. But he could hear her. Her breathing was choppy in his hear. "Allie, are you there? Everything okay?"

"No. No, I don't think so." Her words were choked out. "I just had a call from the police. Ben was in an accident."

"An accident?" Surprise had him jutting forward in his chaise.

"Someone hit him. On . . . on his way to get Trey." They said it's bad, Jake." Her voice broke and ended in a whisper. "I have to go to the hospital."

Hospital?! He sprang to his feet. "Wait for me! Do you hear me, Allie?" He yelled over the thundering of his heart. *"Don't drive!* I'm on my way to pick you up."

He raced through his house, into his bedroom, stripping his shorts along the way. Oh shit, what happened? Did she say Trey was in the car, too? His heart hammered. No. No, on the way to *get* Trey." His breath left is body in a rush.

The Wranglers on the floor were dirty. They'd do. He ripped a clean shirt from the closet, shoved his foot into an ancient Red Wing. Where the hell was his other boot? And why did they never land in the same place? He found it, grabbed his keys and was out the door.

The drive from his house to theirs normally took twelve minutes. Tonight he blew through traffic and made it in eight. He set his jaw. He wouldn't be any help if he was panicked.

She waited on her front porch, pacing with her hands in knots as he tore up the driveway and squealed to a stop. The yellow glow of the porch light reflected off the wetness streaking down her face. She raced to his crew cab and clambered in.

"Which hospital?" He spared her a quick glance as he roared back down the drive.

"Desert Memorial." When she coughed the rasp in her throat cleared. "Do you know where it is?"

"That's where you took Trey when he broke his arm, remember?" He reached for her hand, squeezed it. How could his voice possibly sound so calm over the violent drumming of his heart?

He roared into a coveted parking spot near the building, shoved the truck into park. Grabbing her hand, he bolted toward the emergency room entrance. An ambulance was backing into a bay on the left side of the wing, its red lights cartwheeling, its siren no longer screaming. A squad car waited in a reserved space nearby. The wide glass doors screeched open automatically as they approached.

Please let Ben be all right. It had been so long since he prayed. Was anybody listening?

He drew Allie to the reception desk, staffed by a woman in a blue smock. This is Allie Tate. She was told her husband was in an automobile accident."

Anxiety emanated, resonated in his voice. Smiling was not an option.

With a tired nod she turned to her computer and typed. He paced alongside Allie and waited for information to spit out.

"Here it is." The woman jabbed a finger at the monitor. "He was brought in a few minutes ago. Treatment Room 15. She pointed to her right. "He'll be down that hall and on the left." She handed them each a pass which they clipped to their clothes, then sprinted down the corridor. On their way to Ben.

The antiseptic smell, the sterile white walls, the jangle of a gurney as it was muscled down the hallway were all a blur as they raced toward Treatment Room 15. Their feet clattered on the sparkling linoleum tiles, making an obscene amount of noise. Allie came up short as they approached the cubicle. Jake skidded to a halt beside her.

The doorway was blocked. Medical staff surrounded the bed. She slipped through the crowd and abruptly forgot to breathe. With a sheet to his waist he lay bare-chested, beaten and broken, torn and bloody. Her knees went to jelly. "Oh, Ben."

There was a hypnotic *drip-drip* of fluids being fed into his IV, an eerie slow *whoosh* of air being forced into his lungs. Doctors and nurses dashed around the room. Jake backed her away from the curtained entry and led her to an orange plastic chair in the hallway. They would wait to speak to a doctor. They would wait for Ben.

Jake sat beside her in the hallway, his voice low as he murmured into his phone. The glare of harsh fluorescent lighting filtered down from panels hidden in the ceiling.

"Trey's all right. Maddie said it was fine if he stayed another night. I only told her that Ben was in an accident and we were with him."

She reached for his hand and threaded their fingers together. "Thank you. I'll call them again later, after we know more."

Equipment beeped all around them and visitors shuffled past. A young boy cried in his father's arms, his arm wrapped in a bloody dish towel. Doctors and nurses darted efficiently from one room to the next. Medicinal smells collided with antibacterial cleaners.

Allie sprang from her chair and peeked in Ben's room yet again. Still asleep. Marilyn—the nurse's name badge wore a smiley-face sticker—fussed around the bed.

Jake would return any minute with coffee "I promise not to bother." She offered Marilyn a smile and hovered in the opening to the room. The nurse simply smiled and went about her business.

"How's he doing?" Jake came up behind her, offering two small plastic cups of creamer and a paper cup with a plastic lid. "Here you go. It's not too bad." Eyebrows drawn and eyes clouded, he stood beside her in Ben's doorway, sipping from his cup.

Poor Jake, he was so worried about Ben. But she didn't know how to make it better. She sipped, leaned against him and let the tension drain from her shoulders.

He held his paper cup in one hand. His other hand was cool when she reached for it to check his watch. Midnight—three hours since they arrived. People zipped in and out of Ben's cubicle regularly, doctors and nurses and lab personnel. And once orderlies in matching scrubs wheeled Ben out, not returning for forty five minutes. He was getting plenty of attention. But they were ignored.

Jake jerked awake when Marilyn left Ben's cubicle and drew to a stop beside him. She glanced at her watch, her quiet smile tempering his pounding heart.

"It's late, almost two a.m., but he's finally conscious."

At his nudge Allie's eyes flew open, but he was already standing. "Humpty Dumpty's awake."

The assessment Ben's physician had given them when he finally stopped by was brief yet overwhelming. He tossed out terms like contusions, abrasions and lacerations, so the white gauze dressings covered Ben's head, arms and chest were expected. But apparently there were indications of internal bleeding and swelling in his brain to be dealt with as well, probably requiring surgery. He was given a head CT hours ago.

Jake's throat burned. "We're here, buddy." From the far side of the bed, he placed his hand on Ben's shoulder. His eyes were glassy with pain. He grimaced when he tried to turn his head. "The doctor will come in and talk to you and Allie in a minute, explain what's going on."

Ben's eyes blinked, then skittered to search out his wife. "I love you, Allie." His rasp was slow, deliberate, but they could understand him. "I'm sorry. Tell Trey I'm sorry." His fingers stirred against the mattress.

Her hand quickly found his on the sheet, and she hovered over him, stroking it with her thumb. "I know sweetheart. I'll tell him. He knows."

His chest was tight. He stood to leave; they needed privacy. He was nearly run down in the doorway.

"Good evening, I'm Doctor Carter. I'll be the neurosurgeon handling Mr. Tate's case." The knot of anxiety that swept in with the doctor was just as quickly swept away by his confidence and energy. Jake let out a slow breath.

The doctor dropped into one of the chairs lining the wall and lowered his readers from their perch on his forehead. He glanced at the notes in his hand and replaced the glasses with the push of a finger. "As Doctor Fielding forewarned, we'll be taking Mr. Tate into surgery soon. There will be additional surgeons in the room to assist with abdominal bleeding and anything else that may arise." The doctor spoke with authority for several minutes, for a lifetime, even as he nodded to the nurse who followed him in and proceeded to check Ben's IV.

"According to test results, I have a clear indication of the extent of the damage. I'd like to outline the procedures I plan to follow." He stood and opened his tablet. Jake and Allie crowded around. "Let me show you what I have in mind."

With each of Doctor Carter's diagrams and detailed explanations, Jake's pulse took a slow and steady climb. All color drained from Allie's face. He shoved her into a chair beside Ben's bed. When he was finished, the doctor strolled to the edge of the curtain and turned back before stepping out. "The risks involved with this surgery are great. I expect it to last several hours." He glanced toward the nurse. "In the meantime I'm ordering more medication."

And for the first time fear sunk its gnarly fist into Jake's midsection and twisted.

Jake stood near the curtain. Doctor Carter was already halfway down the hall. He moved to stand beside Ben's bed and gave him a smile. He meant it to be reassuring.

Ben's eyelids drooped. Probably the new medication. "Hey Jake, I need to call in a favor."

His heart ached at the strain in Ben's voice. He inched closer and took his hand. "What now? No way will I loan you my truck." The jest fell flat, landed with a thud in his gut as Allie watched them from across the room. He studied Ben with what he was afraid was desperation looming in his eyes.

Ben gestured for him to lean closer still, lifted a hand to hook it behind his neck, locking their eyes together.

"I screwed things up bad." Ben's words were weak and grated against his throat. "I have to take care of this now, before I . . . go."

Ben's eyes bore into him, piercing and insistent. He would do anything to take away his pain.

"You've always been my best friend. If something happens—if I don't come back—I need you to look after them. Allie and Trey."

Jake jerked with a start, but Ben's grip held.

"You're the best person I know, Jake. Much better than I am." His glance found Allie, then skittered back. Jake followed his gaze. "You've loved her as long as I have." The quiet seriousness on his mangled face was heartbreaking. Every word was an obvious effort. "It's your turn now, Jake. Take good care of her. Promise me."

Guilt swamped him. The least he could do was look his friend in the eye. He cleared his throat, took hold of Ben's hand again. And let fear fuel his anger. It was the only defense he had. "Bullshit, Ben. You don't need any promises from me. You'll be good as new in no time. Take care of her yourself."

Shooting his hands up he spun, took a step back. He had to turn away. It was unthinkable that Ben would ask that of him. Absurd that he would consider it. He swiped at his eyes, which were flooded. But he would make that promise to Ben.

Because there was nothing he would rather do.

Jake stepped away from the bed and Ben sagged into the pillow. Allie edged closer. The soft beeps of the machines blended into the sounds coming from the adjacent treatment rooms. A tray clattered. Someone rushed down the corridor, their soft-soled shoes slapping the tiles. Her lips brushed over his, which were swollen and cracked, his fingers were cold in her hands. She was probably hurting him, but she couldn't let go.

He would be fine. He had to be fine. Hot tears drenched her eyes. The pressure on her chest made it hard to breathe. "I love you, sweetheart. Go to sleep. We'll be here when you wake up."

Ben's hand stretched out to caress her cheek. He would want to touch her dimple. He held her, loved her with his eyes, and spoke without turning away from her. "Can you give us a minute, Jake?"

Jake dropped a hand on Ben's blanketed foot and then left, pulling the curtain closed behind him.

She hovered over Ben, her hand resting on the metal side rail of the bed, tears dripping onto the covers, leaving splotches on the white sheet. He pulled her hand from the rail, lowered it to his chest. "If everything's not . . ."

"You'll be—"

He cut her off with his eyes. His voice was weak, soft and breathy. If only she could will her strength into him.

"You're so beautiful." He grimaced a crooked smile. In there was Ben's smile. "And I'm so proud of Trey. I wish—." His voice faded. He closed his eyes and wobbled his head. "But mostly, I'm so damned sorry."

Her tears started fresh. His eyes opened, his gaze unfocused. "Jake will be alone now, Allie. Take good care of him."

There was no controlling her tears, and the splotches on the sheet grew. The tissue she used to mop her eyes, to blow into, was useless against the stream running down her face. She nodded. "I promise." She would swear anything if it brought him back to her.

When his eyes drifted shut, she wiped the tears from her cheeks, and his. There were so many things they would do when he was well. So many things she would tell him.

His injuries weren't the only tragedy of his accident. It was time she realized that the resentment she'd carried all these years was petty and selfish. Acid wearing away the tender lining of their marriage.

Jake peeked through the curtain.

"Come on in, he's asleep." She held out a hand for him, then closed her eyes against the comfort of his arm draped across her shoulders.

They left Ben's cubicle and made their way to a waiting lounge to pass the time until his surgery was over. "I called Bentley a few minutes ago. Nick too." Her murmured words came from her place beside him on a cold vinyl sofa. "Let them know about the accident and the surgery. Bentley said he'd leave a message with his secretary and come down right away. My parents and brother are on their way, too."

"Have you spoken with Trey? Or Maddie?"

Trey. Her hands twisted in her lap. "I gave Michael an update. You remember Maddie's husband? He and Ben have been friends for years."

"Of course."

"He offered to bring Trey over. Oh, they're here." She stood.

They entered as a crowd, their voices raising and lowering as they greeted each other and then settled into seats to wait. Her eyes swept the room. Small groups of mismatched chairs sat in clusters. Low tables held scattered magazines. A nearby counter held a florist's vase of deep red roses. Periodically she caught their scent. Other families sat nearby, talking quietly, waiting for word of their loved ones.

A flat screen was mounted to the far wall, broadcasting the latest happenings in the Middle East in closed captions. Jake leaned forward in his chair, his elbows braced on his knees, studying a young child playing with blocks across the room. He glanced over his shoulder at her, then nodded at the child. "Almost hard to remember when Trey was that small."

It certainly was right now with his gangly arms draped over the back of the adjacent chair and his lanky legs kicked out under the coffee table. The elevator chimed in the hallway. She lifted her eyes to check the clock on the wall. Ben had been in surgery three hours already.

Doctor Carter, the surgeon they met during the wee hours of the morning rounded the corner, flanked by another man. Shoulder to shoulder they paused in the doorway and searched the room.

With deliberate movements she uncrossed her legs and stood. Jake unfolded beside her. She pressed her shaking hands together as he neared. He wore blue scrubs and throwaway booties, and his mask hung from ties caught behind his neck. In his hands he mangled a matching cotton skullcap.

His somber expression had her eyes welling. She reached for Trey, tugged him close. Ben was fine. Ben was fine. Ben was *fine*.

It was important to concentrate. The timbre of the doctor's voice as it rose and fell was like an echo bobbing in a deep well. Her throat thickened and stung and her ears clogged and the sound became an animated *wah, wah, wah*. She closed her eyes. Now she could focus on his words as they stuttered through her silly tears.

"I'm sorry ..."

Her eyes flew open.

"... everything in our power ..."

Her sobs unleashed when Jake hauled her into his arms and crushed Trey between them.

"No, No, No!" Someone cried out.

"Despite our best efforts ..."

It was her. Her knees were weak.

"No! Stop!"

"... didn't make it."

Jake guided her as she crumpled to the sofa.

"... dead."

The doctor quieted. And stood before them.

Trey's bleak eyes were huge in his face, their indigo irises flooded. Jake's hold firmed around them both. Tears flowed down his anguished face.

There was no escaping the truth.

Her heart, her soul, her Ben, would never return.

He was gone.

Chapter Twelve

The aroma of fresh coffee assailed Allie as she followed Trey into their home on the arm of her father-in-law. Mourners milled throughout, talking quietly in small groups. Some juggled paper plates laden with food, others held disposable cups of punch or coffee. She let her arm fall away from Bentley, and with a nudge from her, Trey followed his grandfather toward the kitchen, loosening his tie as they ran the gauntlet. Her mother immediately replaced Bentley, warm and comforting, guiding her to a comfortable armchair. Allie adjusted the skirt of her simple black dress and sat stoically, her hands quiet in her lap. Someone she didn't recognize brought her a cup of punch. She ghosted a smile, then set it on the table near her, untouched. One after another stepped up. She appreciated the condolences they offered, the anecdotes. They all had memories of the man they cared about. She made an effort to seem interested. These people were all feeling loss as well, but she didn't have the strength to focus on their needs. Her heart was broken. Nothing else mattered.

Ben's secretary—no, Jake's now—perched on the arm of her chair with moisture clinging to her lashes. "It was a beautiful service." Allie found her hand clasped along with Kim's offer of sympathy and a wispy smile. "Ben was one of the best bosses ever, and a good man."

She could only nod. "Thank you." Her chest was embedded with a weight that wouldn't ease as her eyes wandered the room, lighted on Jake. "This will be difficult on him, running the company alone."

Kim's eyes followed hers, found her new boss. "Don't you worry about him; I'll keep an eye out." Kim's smooth drawl was familiar and kind. "But you need to take care of yourself and Trey now."

She thanked Kim again with a lifelessness that was becoming familiar and let her eyes float around the room. So many people gathered in her home—hovering nearby, waiting to speak to her. Hysterically, a scene came to her from one of the movies Ben loved. *The mafia don was dead and the son sat, as if on a throne, a line of people at his feet, waiting to kiss his ring.* The head of her family was gone and here she sat. Her tears flowed freely again, great wracking sobs that refused to be controlled, ever since that brutal morning.

Jake, standing nearby, watching over her, witnessed her collapse. He caught Reese's eye and motioned her over.

"I'll take her into her room now." Her frailty was unsettling. But she would find her inner strength again. They all would.

Reese nodded and led the way down the hall. "I'll turn down the bed, help her out of her clothes."

He hovered as Reese got her tucked in and went to the bathroom for water and a sleeping pill. Allie had argued against the pills, but after two sleepless nights she relented and let him call her doctor. He and Reese stayed with her, talking softly, crooning nonsense until Allie fell asleep. In the kitchen he found Maddie packing leftover food away, stacking containers neatly in the refrigerator. It had been an arduous day for everyone.

Reese sidled up beside him. "Jax invited Trey home with them, and Maddie agreed. I think they're hoping to distract him with video games and late night refrigerator raids." He offered Reese a smile of gratitude as his eyes located Trey, sitting quietly by himself. "I'll spend the night tonight, in case

Allie wakes and needs someone."

The kitchen was clean, the refrigerator stocked; there was nothing left to do. Everyone gradually made their way out the door until the house was finally, mercifully, quiet. Only he and Reese remained.

Reese distributed floral arrangements around the living room and stacked sympathy cards on the kitchen table while he moved through the house with a trash bag, collecting discarded plates and cups. He stalled, hated the idea of leaving Allie, but Reese would be there. There was no reason to delay his departure. He peeked in on Allie, then left, headed to his empty house. He deliberated stopping by Michelle's on the way, remembered she was out of town.

Their trip home from Las Vegas had been a pleasant one. He'd ditched the scorned Bach when they stopped for gas, and they were happy and rested as they chatted about the weekend. They had seen a show—a popular comedian—and played a little blackjack, and again he was glad he suggested the getaway. It was a long drive, but he enjoyed having the time alone with Michelle, without the interruptions of their busy schedules.

"Hey, what do you have going on over there?" He was pulling into the outskirts of Phoenix, the lights of the skyline in the near distance. Michelle systematically jabbed buttons on her Blackberry.

"Getting a jump on tomorrow." As usual, her attention was on the backlit screen. "It looks like there's a problem with a project in Tucson. I'll need to head over there in a couple of days."

Jake's forehead furrowed and his lips thinned to a narrow line, but he said nothing. As he turned into her complex he commented again about the weekend. "I had a great time, Michelle. We'll do this again, one day soon."

Michelle frowned and looked up from the email she was composing. "Sure, sugar, but next time we should fly. Whoever wants to be stuck in the car for such a long time?"

Hiding the clutch of disappointment, Jake pulled up to Michelle's condo. He wheeled her suitcases to her door, kissed her good-bye and promised to call. He drove through intermittent weekend traffic to his own home with a vague sense of unease. As he pulled into his own garage, he parked the car and answered a phone call that changed his life forever.

Allie awoke groggy the next morning, a mind-numbing combination of grief, exhaustion and medication. She was curled up on Ben's side of the bed and shoved her whole face into his pillow, straining to catch his scent, but there was nothing left of him there. With a sad sigh of resignation she stumbled from the bed and ambled through the house to the kitchen, the smell of coffee and cinnamon a powerful lure.

There was Reese, pulling muffins out of the oven. The enticing aroma was a blatant reminder that she'd deprived her body of food for days. It rumbled in protest.

Reese turned at the sound of Allie entering the room. "Morning, sleepyhead. Ready for coffee?"

Allie offered a scrawny smile, her palm massaging the back of her neck. "Mmm, definitely."

Reese poured two mugs of the fragrant brew and Allie took a chair at the table. She idly thumbed through the stack of condolence cards, then set them aside. Allie doctored her coffee and took her first sip. Reese turned back to the counter and returned a moment later with her own mug and a basket of hot blueberry muffins.

Allie selected one, paused before taking a bite, her eyebrows furrowed. "Where's Trey?"

"Maddie took him home last night."

Her forehead smoothed; she nodded, then fixed a vague stare on her muffin. She pulled off small pieces, placed them one by one into her mouth and chewed sluggishly. When she was finished she took another sip, peering over her mug and gaining her friend's attention. She had no tears this morning. Her eyes were dry, but her heart was empty. "What am I going to do, Reese?" To keep her fingers busy, she shredded a paper napkin. "How do I get through this? I need to pull myself together, but I don't know how."

Reese's expression softened. She reached across the table and took Allie's hand. "Oh, honey. For now you get up each morning and you get through that day. Take it one step at a time, one day at a time. And don't make it any harder than that."

Pretty much what her mom had said for days now. Allie nodded and lowered her eyes, her palms both clutching her mug like a lifeline. "I'm worried about Jake, too."

"I know you are, sweetie. He called while you were asleep."

Allie nodded again, squeezed her hand around Reese's then pulled it away, lifted the coffee to her lips without tasting it. Tears snuck steadily through an invisible barrier, trickled down her cheeks. "I keep waiting for Ben to walk into the room, kicking off his boots." Her flooded eyes bounced off the entry and landed at the door to the laundry room, visible from her seat. "I hear his voice, but when I look of course he's not there. This all seems so unreal." She lowered her mug to the table, framed her face with her hands, whispered brokenly. "This happens to other people."

But this time it happened to her.

Allie thumbed her cheeks dry. "Trey's having such a hard time. They were so close."

Reese still spoke softly, her warm familiar voice comforting her friend. "He's been staying pretty close to home—to you. He's already figured out he's the man of the house now."

For the first time anger swept over her, through her, lightning fast and hot. She bolted upright in her chair. "Trey should not need to be the man of the house." She delivered her rant full steam and without reason. "That was his father's job. Ben had a teenage son who needed him. To go to his ball games, to teach him to drive. Now it's all up to me." Her voice abruptly lowered, turned sad. "Now I'll sit alone at his high school graduation, and at his wedding. Ben will miss holding our grandchildren."

"You'll get through this, Allie. You're strong. You and Trey will be fine."

Allie shook her head slowly. "I don't feel strong, Reese. Ben was always there to lean on, to back me up." She leaned back in her chair and lowered her gaze to her lap. "I don't want to do this by myself." But she couldn't change what was done.

"You have family and friends who will help you, you know."

Allie lifted her eyes to Reese, brackets cut between her eyebrows. "You're right, I'm sorry. Thank you so much for all you've done."

"Don't thank me. I love you."

Allie nodded and sat with Reese for long quiet minutes until Reese stood.

It was time for her to get home. The midday sun shone brightly through the windows. Allie straightened the kitchen, wiping counters and popping dirty mugs into the dishwasher as Reese collected her things to leave. Pulling Reese to her in a quick, tight hug, Allie murmured into her ear. "Don't worry about me. I'll call every day."

Reese dug her keys from her handbag, stood in the open doorway waving a fierce finger. "Every day."

Allie closed the door behind her friend. Dragged herself back into the kitchen, alone for the first time, and picked up the telephone to call the Andrews' house. She wasn't ready to be by herself in the house.

The telephone was answered by a deep male voice. "'lo."

She felt better simply at the sound of Jax's voice, and put a smile in her voice as she said hello.

High pitched whines and muted crashes clashed in the background. Her guess was a video game. "Oh, hey, Mrs. T. You want my mom?"

In her mind's eye he feinted left and then right with a controller in his hand. "No, mostly I wanted to thank you for inviting Trey to stay over."

"Mmm. Sure." Whatever had his attention, it wasn't her.

"Is Trey with you?"

"Nah, shower."

The whooping of a female voice added to the odd symphony. "Oh, will you please tell him I'll pick him up in about an hour?"

"No problem. Wait! Crap!"

She didn't want to know. She cradled the phone, jumped when it rang immediately. Couldn't possibly be Jax again so soon. Maddie perhaps? She picked it back up and answered.

"Hello?"

"Good afternoon, this is the office of Stephens and Sloan calling. Is Mrs. Tate available please?"

"This is Allie Tate." Allie's breakfast sat heavy in her stomach as the stilted, businesslike voice on the other end of the line set up an appointment for Monday. She needed to talk to somebody about Ben's will, and his life insurance. But was she up to this yet?

One baby step at a time. Take a shower. Pick up Trey. She could do those two things. And when she was done she would move on to the next step. Eventually she would come to Monday.

Allie collected Trey at the Andrews' door and walked back down the driveway to the car. She toted his backpack for him; he had his stinky practice uniform slung over a shoulder. She would wash that over the weekend. "How was practice?"

"Coach Murphy wants you to call." He dropped his gear by the car and dug through his pack. "This was my first day at practice all week so he needs to talk to you."

"What does he want, a written excuse?" The sarcasm was unusual for her, but so was the chaos in their lives.

Dear Coach, my son was absent because his father is dead. I promise it will never happen again.

"I don't know." The misery in his words was matched with the thin line of his lips. "Maybe. I suppose. Here's a paper you have to fill out."

"I'm sorry, honey. I'll take care of it." With a squeeze of his shoulder she dismissed the thought of the bulging refrigerator at home. "Are you hungry? We can stop somewhere for lunch."

Trey brightened instantly. "Can we get burgers and take them home?"

She smiled at her son. "That sounds perfect." They drove through the golden arches and ordered burgers, along with fries and chocolate shakes. Within minutes they were seated at the kitchen table, their meal spread out around them.

Conversation was halting. So much to say, but she wasn't in the mood for idle chatter. Evidently Trey wasn't either. The furrows in his forehead grew prominent as he picked up his burger, took a bite. As his jaw worked the glob in his mouth, his eyes strayed through the uncovered patio door, toward the back yard, eyeing a hummingbird as it buzzed the shrubbery.

Allie lowered her burger onto the paper wrapper, raised an eyebrow. "What's up, Trey?"

He paused, a ketchup covered French fry halfway to his mouth. He studied it a moment, then set it down. "Mom, are we poor now? Will we have to move?"

The belligerence in his voice surprised her. But it was natural for him to be frightened by the imagined ways his life may alter.

They were both grieving, but she sensed he needed to be assured they were in this together. "No sweetheart, we aren't poor." She kept her tone even. "I still have my job, remember? And there's insurance." She took his hand, reassuring him with great effort. "We're going to stay right here in our own house and everything will be fine. I don't want you to worry about it, okay?"

But his hostile inquiries made her contemplate their future, the questions spinning through her mind like a mouse on an exercise wheel. Ben held a life insurance policy, but the particulars of it were a mystery. It was her understanding they owed little debt other than the mortgage on their home, but Ben always handled their bills. And then there was the business, T-Squared Construction. A play on their names—Tate and Taylor. Only now there was no Tate.

She needed to get her affairs in order. After lunch she called Tom Gainey, their financial advisor. He owned a small firm and promised to meet with her on Tuesday afternoon.

Reese's advice was sound; she soldiered resolutely from one day into the next, not worrying about the future until it was upon her. When Saturday came she found comfort in menial tasks that lay forgotten all week. The laundry had grown to a mountain; she dug through it, shoved into the washer. She and Trey had eaten from the refrigerator the night before; today she took pork chops from the freezer, planning a little culinary therapy.

The washing machine finished its spin cycle and she yanked opened the dryer, wet clothes in hand, ready to be tossed in. She stopped short when she realized there was already a load there, forgotten for days, waiting to be folded and put away. She dropped the wet pile back in the washer and reached into the dryer. Ben's shirt—the shirt he wore on their last hike through Oak Creek Canyon was on top. She pressed the soft cotton to her cheek before hanging it up, caressing the wrinkled fabric.

Chapter Thirteen

Jake wiped his brow, knee-walked to the neighboring bush, vented his frustration by plying oversized clippers to the shrubbery lining his fence.

Arm muscles bunching with effort, he muttered in huffs of breath while abusing branches that wanted attention weeks ago. "Bitch just takes off like everything's fine. Sure, why not? " Standing, he glugged from a large bottle of water. "Blows me a kiss and a *sorry for your loss* on her way out the door." The memory still caused him to fume, out loud.

Times like this he really wished he had a dog. Robby Duncan had a dog he needed to find a home for—his kid was allergic. Damned ugliest dog he ever saw, but sweet tempered and obedient. As protective as a whole squad of US Army Rangers. The dog wouldn't abandon him in the middle of a crisis. And she damned sure wouldn't turn her back when he wanted to scratch her belly.

Jake stripped off his sweat-soaked T-shirt, adjusted his battered work jeans and moved on to the two citrus trees, stripping suckers from the trunks and gleaning old fruit. "I'll try to make it home early, we can do something." The acerbic mimic dripped off his tongue in disgust. "What the hell? Did she think I'd feel like *socializing*?" No, what he *needed* was somebody to keep him company while he figured out how he would manage without his best friend.

Grappling with hurt and disappointment that were swelling into anger; knees and back strained with overwork, he moved on to the neglected planting beds, weeds and sun-withered plants plucked and relegated to the ever-growing pile of yard debris.

His best friend died on Monday, and Tuesday she left for a business trip. In whose world was that more important than losing a friend of thirty-some-odd years? He studied a fistful of dry stems for the answer. And she hadn't come home early. Hell, she wasn't home *yet*. "Too much work to do. More problems than they realized." Wasn't she just full of excuses? He tried talking to her on the phone, but of course she was preoccupied. A talk—someone to help him survive the crap that was his life—had to wait.

Hedge shears dangling, Jake stood back, surveyed his work. To cool his thoughts, and his body, he dropped his jeans and shorts, dove from the ledge into the deep end of the pool where the clear water was refreshing. After several vigorous laps he pulled his sodden body from the water and traipsed through the house without a towel, dripping as he made his way to the bathroom and the soothing spray of a hot shower.

Barefoot, he padded to the kitchen for a soda, dressed only in navy boxer briefs and an ancient college tee. With longing he glanced out the glass door, wished the weather was milder and he could crash in a lounger. But most of the day had already been spent in the blistering heat so he opted for air conditioning. He fell into the sofa and flipped channels until he found baseball. But his mind was stuck in the past, on Ben. He muted the game and reached for the phone. There was one person he could count on to understand.

He always could count on Allie.

Allie clutched Ben's jeans in her hand as she dashed into the kitchen, caught the phone on the third ring.

"Allie, it's Jake. Just calling to check on you."

She paused. Forced a smile into her voice. He didn't need her drama. "We're fine here. Laying low."

But something must have bled through, because he pounced. "What's up? Something upset you?"

She paused before answering. "No. Well, nothing really. It's silly." She paused another beat. "I was doing laundry and I found clothes in the dryer from . . . that night. Sunday."

"Oh babe, I'm sorry." His gentle caring nearly undid her.

"My heart just aches." One fist lifted, pressed against her breastbone as if to relieve the pain as the other dragged the crumpled Wranglers. "It hurts for Ben, and for me. But mostly for Trey." Leaning a hip against the counter, her hand lifted, shoved through her tangle of curls. Her words heated. "He's only *fifteen*, Jake; he needs his dad."

But Jake needed Ben around as well. Her voice grew softer, apologetic. "My guess is work hasn't been much fun, either."

"Yeah, well. Nick's been doing a great job keeping the jobs on track, but Ben was his brother."

Silence hung on the line. Was Jake remembering that summer Nick graduated from college and hired on with the company? Over the past ten years it was a decision none of them regretted.

"Yeah, he's really stepped up, but Ben will be missed for a long time."

The knowledge that someone felt the same loss was somehow comforting. "I don't know much about this stuff, but one day we should talk about the company and how Ben's death affects it. I need to know you'll be okay." Ben's words haunted her.

He'll be alone. Take care of him, Allie.

"The company will be fine, Allie. Ben can't be replaced, but there are life insurance policies on each of us specifically to protect the company. It's a common practice."

Allie nodded as she edged around the counter and dropped onto a chair at the table, her chin propped in a palm. "Good, then. I'm glad you did that."

"There will be a few changes to the corporate paperwork. Minor. I'll need you to sign."

Her brow lowered. "Why would you need my name on company papers?"

"With Ben gone, half the company belongs to you now."

Allie popped to her feet. "I can't do that, Jake. I've never been involved with the company." Her heart dropped. What was Jake thinking? Ben was the business whiz; not her.

"It's already done. Besides, it would make Ben feel better." His voice was nonchalant as the refrigerator slammed shut on Jake's end of the line. "The attorney is drafting the paperwork; it should be ready next week."

"We'll talk about it." Allie perched back on the edge of her seat. Reached for the salt shaker and twirled it on the table. "That reminds me, though, I have an appointment with him Monday at ten to go over Ben's estate. Do you have time to go along?"

"Of course, sweetheart; whatever you need." A pull tab hissed and clicked in the background. "Everything else okay? Trey? There are a lot of changes in his life right now."

She closed her eyes, massaged tension from the back of her neck. "He's scared, angry, worried about the future, that we'll be broke and have to move. I told him about Ben's life insurance, but I don't even know what it will cover. I'm worried I made him promises I won't be able to keep."

"Allie, you'll never move unless you want to. I'll make sure of that." That fierce, protective tone was so Jake. "I'm sure Ben provided well for you; I can't imagine otherwise."

"Well, I guess we'll know on Monday, won't we?" She leaned back in her chair, staring through the slider into the backyard. "George has copies of all our insurance policies."

"Is there anything I can do for you? Anything you need?"

The yard was two weeks' high. A few dandelions poked their fuzzy heads through tall blades of grass. Ben didn't have time for yard work the previous weekend because they were gone. Had it only been a week?

"What I need is for Trey to mow the lawn. Either that or get goats." The amusement in her voice startled her, it had been so long. "I'll have to pull the mom card soon."

"Give the kid time to adjust, Allie. I'll come over in a few days and help him out." Amusement rode in Jake's voice; but then, he'd always had a soft spot for Trey.

A hummingbird fluttered against the door. She'd have to remember to refill the feeder. "Thank you for that. How's Michelle?"

"Gone." The word was uttered with uncharacteristic bluntness. She didn't push.

"You okay? Need anything?"

"Nah, I'm good. Monday, then?"

"Yeah. I'll see you then."

The line clicked, Jake was gone. She pressed Ben's jeans against her chest, went back to confront the rest of his laundry.

Monday morning, Allie arrived for her appointment early. She'd been up with the dawn, paced the house for as long as she could stand it, and when she deemed it late enough to leave without beating the receptionist to the office, got in her car for the trip downtown. As she rode the elevator to the fourth floor she stifled a yawn bought on by the mostly sleepless night. Her palms were damp, which was just silly. As was the wild, erratic beating of her heart. Ben's will was no secret, after all. They were together when George wrote it up. There was an identical one with her name on the cover.

But the life insurance. Why didn't she know more about that? *Dear God, please let them be able to keep the house.*

Allie's heels clacked against the marble tiles of the lobby. As she crossed the room she met the open gaze of Gladys Williams, the silver-haired guardian of the mahogany desk parked in the corner. "I'm Allie Tate. I have an appointment."

"Of course, Mrs. Tate. Mr. Stephens isn't quite ready for you yet." She waved a hand boasting nothing but a plain gold band toward a seating area. "Please, make yourself comfortable."

Allie perched on the ivory brocade sofa and stopped herself before brushing her palms over the fabric of her green sheath. She picked up a glamour mag, then lifted her gaze at the ding of the elevator. Relief flooded her as Jake stepped from the car.

Mrs. Williams looked up with a professional smile. "Good Morning, Jake.

His smile was a quick flash of hello for the silver-haired receptionist before he met Allie's gaze and crossed the room. He dropped a peck on Allie's cheek before relaxing into the seat beside her. She abandoned the unread magazine to a nearby table and sank back into the cushion. Her eyes scanned the original oils decorating the silk-papered walls as they sat together. Ben hadn't mentioned they'd redecorated the office. She slid her eyes shut, blindsided again. She was here because Ben was dead. Would it ever stop sneaking up on her?

Jake tipped his head to look her in the eyes. "Everything okay?"

"Excuse me, but if you'd follow me?"

Allie glanced up at Gladys, pushed to her feet. It was better to ignore Jake's question than lie to him. Gladys led the way in her smart, tailored suit, stopping at a small conference room where the attorney was already seated. A legal sized folder lay open, stacks of papers spread on the table before him. Jake, of course, had done business with George for years already; she had met him several times in the past.

George Stephens stood as they entered. His dark brown hair cut conservatively short and black utilitarian eyeglasses easily pegged him as ex-military.

"Allie, I'm glad you could make it. Again, I'm very sorry for your loss." George gave her hand an easy press. The ridges of scarring covering the back of his hand was soft, smooth, which surprised her.

"Jake." George shook his hand. "Please, take a seat." George pulled his hand back, used it to motion them in.

The scarring on George's face and neck caused Allie to recall that George had returned to private practice following an explosion his last tour in Iraq. She looked up, thanked Gladys, who'd slipped in with a tray of coffee while everyone got settled, then left, closing the door behind her. Jake poured himself a cup then took the seat beside her, exuding strength and support.

George shot her a *straight to business* smile. "First of all Allie, after going over your late husband's estate, I find there are several items to be discussed, several decisions to be made." George skated a gaze to Jake, then back again. "This is rather sensitive material; would you prefer privacy?"

"Actually, I would rather Jake stayed." She smiled to convey a confidence she didn't feel. No way was she tackling this solo.

"No problem." The smile, the nod, were probably meant to reassure, but were gone before they took. George tapped the papers on the right side of the open folder. He picked up the first document, weighed it, leafed through it. "I have here your late husband's current will, along with copies of insurance policies. Your late husband, um … Ben, was very thorough. He made certain I had easy access to all his important papers, in case of a situation such as this."

Allie seethed. Who was George to repeatedly refer to Ben as late? Ben wasn't *late* for anything. He was *dead*. Never going to show up again. Permanently.

George cleared his throat. "I'll go through the will first."

Her anxiety eased even as he listed the details of each of her major assets—some held in trust and some not. He persisted relentlessly about community property, and probate, which should not be an issue because of the careful way Ben constructed his affairs.

"Do you have any questions?"

Confusion was probably etched on her face. "I don't even know where to begin."

He laid the will face down and selected the next document, paused to pour himself a cup of coffee, add exactly one tablespoon of cream, and suck in a sip. "Moving on to your late husband's insurance policies." George flicked the sheaf of papers in his hand. "There are several."

He soldiered on, detailing coverage, expounded the benefit as well as the terms, and then the accidental death rider, which would double the benefit of the policy. She, Alexandra Harper Tate, was named his sole beneficiary.

George laid the paperwork face down on top of the will and lifted the next document. Allie raised her eyes to George, her hand securely ensconced in Jake's much larger palm.

George lifted the next document—a secondary life insurance policy he clarified upon sight of her furrowed brow. He forged ahead, detailed the policy and explained that, again there was a rider doubling the benefit in the event of accidental death. Before the question could form he continued, marching forward in true military fashion. "The beneficiary of this policy is a son, Bentley Logan Tate the third."

Her heart quickened. "Trey."

Jake gave her hand a squeeze.

George added those papers to the discard pile and reached for the next set. He was not yet finished. This was a major medical policy, with limits adequate to cover any of Ben's medical expenses not covered by their health insurance, effectively leaving her with no out-of-pocket expenses. George set this last policy with the others he already read.

Jake squeezed her hand again and cast her a small smile when she turned to him. The information overwhelmed her, but her greatest fears were erased. Her son's life would not be disrupted by hardship, and they would not be leaving their home any time soon. Ben provided well for his family, but the price they all paid was high.

George seemed to have finished with Allie. Jake spoke up. "About the paperwork I asked to have completed?"

"Yes, I believe it should be ready. Let me check, save you both a trip back to the office." He reached for his cane, hobbled from the room.

Allie let them settle, the words, the reassurances. Stood and wandered the room, her eyes skimming the burgundy leather bindings of reference books lining two walls, caught the light of relief on Jake's face. The corners of her mouth pulled outward even as her eyebrows lowered. "I had no idea."

"Your life can be as easy as you want now." He reached for the coffee, topped off his cup. Replaced the pot when she declined a refill with a shake of her head. "What do you want to do first? Vacation in Europe, purchase a new car. Perhaps a small island?"

He laughed when her eyes widened, then crinkled with a grin that faded as the doorknob rattled. George entered the room, a short stack of papers folded into the crook of an elbow. As he settled himself in his seat he pushed Ben's folder aside and addressed Jake. "Before we start with the corporate amendments, let me go over this final life policy." He pulled a small binder from the middle of the pile, resumed his elucidation. "Are you familiar with it? It's term policy, naming the corporation as beneficiary."

"Sure. Seems like it's somewhere around two hundred grand. We each had one."

"Well, no. No." Now it was Jake's turn to narrow his eyes. His gaze flew to Allie at the window, then back again when George spoke. "Five years ago, Ben brought new policies in to my office. Said your company was larger, financially sound. He wanted to protect it, so he added coverage. You would have signed paperwork."

Jake dug into his memory, recalled papers shoved across his desk, a vague explanation about insurance. He signed by the red X and shoved them back with barely a glance. They were just starting site work for Canto del Agua at the time; the details of the seven mammoth waterfalls scattered among the commercial pads were a bitch. "The specifics are sketchy, and honestly, I didn't pay attention to what I signed."

George frowned. "The benefit is a million dollars, Jake. With an accidental death rider that doubles it."

Jake's jaw dropped. Damn if Ben hadn't covered their asses again. Now it was definite—Ben's share went to Allie. There wasn't much he could do for her right now, but he could do this.

His mind reeled as George pulled out the corporate docs, explained, answered questions, assured him it would take less than a month to have Ben's name removed and Allie's in its place.

The air conditioning clicked as it cycled on, then hummed quietly as the system blew cool air into the room. George shuffled his papers again, wrapped a thick elastic band around them, dragged Ben's folder closer.

"What is that?" There still lay a lone unopened packet on the table. Allie was emotionally drained; the last thing she needed was to return for a forgotten file.

George seemed nonplussed, looking from one to the other of them, clearly unprepared for her question. "I'm sorry, Jake, I'm not at liberty to discuss that."

"It's another insurance policy." There was with no tangible reason for the knotting in his gut; he snatched up the papers, slid out of his seat, crossed the room to Allie before George was out of his chair

Allie skimmed the document. The policy was similar to Trey's, the beneficiary to receive a tidy sum upon reaching majority. She mentally clicked through the short list of Ben's female relatives. "Who is this, Meredith Jane Wilson?"

With his cane shifted to his left hand, George relieved her of the papers.

She returned to her seat, her eyes centered on George, who seemed to be waging an inner battle. Jake dropped into the chair beside her.

"She is your late husband's child."

Two heads snapped up in unison.

"What!?"

Rage rolled off Jake as he spit out the single word—a split second before George's next words had her surging to her feet.

"Meredith Wilson is Ben's daughter." George met her eyes. "She'd be about ten or eleven by now."

Allie drew herself up, her hands fisted at her sides. She stared straight ahead, a coldness settling over the stone in her chest. Her words were deliberate, dragged from her throat. "Could you tell me, please, when this policy was taken out?"

George limped back to the table, consulted the file. "This second policy is dated six months ago."

Six months. She choked down bile; it rose again. All the times she begged him, fought him for another baby, he refused. Because the selfish, lying, cheating bastard already had another child. Wasn't it odd she didn't cry? She'd cried—did nothing *but* cry—for days after his death. But now—no, now there were no tears. Her heart was hollow. The man she lived with—and loved, damn it—had slept with another woman.

Then gave that woman the one thing that meant the most to *her*.

Chapter Fourteen

The heat in Jake's gaze seared her but she refused to look at him as he stood beside her. Perhaps her world wasn't the only one shifted on its axis. But then again, he and Ben were close. She was betrayed by his best friend—there was no way he didn't know about it.

In the elevator to the ground floor, through the double glass doors of the building and onto the sidewalk she remained stoic. Jake halted before they reached the parking garage, grabbed her forearm. "Allie, stop. Let's go someplace. Talk about this."

She could only offer him a terse nod. "Third Base." The sports bar was just up the street.

She ordered iced tea and—at Jake's insistence—a grilled chicken sandwich. She sat across from him in their quiet booth, reeling from mental whiplash as her mind relived the past few hours.

A bell tinkled softly. A shaft of sunlight entered through the opening door, dust motes hanging loose, trapped in the glare. A small family appeared through the murky brightness, glancing around for an empty table. A young girl skipped over the bright linoleum. The man caught a pudgy hand in his own, slowing her progress.

"Stay with Daddy, Karen." Evidently, the girl was his daughter.

She, Allie, didn't have a daughter.

But Ben had a daughter.

The odor of old grease tickled her nose, mixed with the sizzle of cold meat as it was slapped onto a hot grill. Allie squeezed lemon into her tall plastic tumbler. Complete thoughts were elusive. Stringing words together in a logical, comprehensible order was a struggle. In the end she gave up, simply lifted her eyes to Jake. "Talk."

Staring at his hands, Jake white-knuckled the edge of the table, his mouth set in a grim line. He glanced away, out the window as a woman passed by, then back to her. "I knew he was with someone." His admission was wrung from somewhere deep. Was it from hurt or anger? Or possibly guilt? "Way back then." He paused and she was silent, waiting for him to continue. He met her eyes. "I don't know who she was. Only that she was divorced, her son was on a team with Trey." He opened his mouth. Closed it again. Picked up his tea and gulped.

She looked away, focused on the pennants, the framed jerseys lining the wall to let some of the anger slide away, then pinned him with a still unrelenting glare. "Everything, Jake."

He lowered his glass to the scarred Formica in mottled blue and shook his head. "That's all I know." He scrubbed his hands over his face. "It's the only time we've ever fought in our whole lives." He lifted his glass again and took a long drink, watched her from over the rim. "He said he didn't love her, barely knew her; it just . . . happened. It was only one time."

It hit Allie that she knew the woman, had probably spoken with her. Maybe she was a friend. She remained mute in her seat, absorbing the details, each word burning white-hot inside her until finally she spoke, each word spit out with deliberate harshness. "I just learned that the man I lived with for fifteen years, who refused to have any more children with me, did exactly that with another woman. Do you think I want to hear excuses?"

Jake dropped his forearms to the table, leaned forward, spit out, "Christ, Allie. I'm not making excuses for the prick; I'm telling you what I know. Like I said, we fought. I asked him what the hell he was doing, did he realize everything he was throwing away. Anything I could say to a guy about to screw up his whole life." Jake slammed back against the booth, his voice a low growl. "He swore it was over."

Her eyes were hot; her words dripped ice. "Apparently not."

As their lunch arrived it occurred to her that this was a whole new Allie. Allie the Bitch. Not a person she liked at all.

Flashbacks played over, over again, screaming to be heard. *I need you to know how much I love you . . . how much you mean to me. You both have made me so happy . . . the happiest man in the world.* And then, *But mostly, I'm so damned sorry.*

She forked a tomato slice onto the bun and stabbed Jake with her eyes. "Tell me about the girl."

Jake shook his head. His eyes sought her gaze, held it. "I heard about her the same time you did. He never mentioned her."

She searched Jake's troubled eyes. The truth was undeniable. The selfish, lying, cheating bastard was someone he didn't know either.

"I don't want Trey to know about this."

Jake nodded. "Understood."

She stared out the window, saw nothing. Her rage, once so bright, had forged itself into a glowing white ember, branding her heart.

"You don't really plan to die." It startled her that the word came easier already. It was heavy, though, and echoed as if hauled from a deep cavern. "I wonder how all this would have played out if he had more time."

"He had ten years, Allie." Her eyes flew to his at the sharp reminder. "I keep thinking that I should have been more aware of what Ben did." He scrubbed a hand across his face, over the short hair on his head. "Maybe I got too involved with the projects. He never said anything, though."

"This has brought a few things into perspective for both of us." And didn't that understate the matter considerably? "I went to school; I took care of Trey, Ben, the house. The rest I took for granted." The anger flared again, this time accompanied by guilt, all directed inward. "The more I think of what he did, I'm ashamed." She'd remained composed at the attorney's office, and up until a moment ago, but she gave in to tears now, let embarrassment and humiliation intensify her grief.

The server came to refill their tea. Allie turned away, wiped her eyes with her napkin. When she was gone Jake reached across the table and took Allie's hand, curled his fingers around hers on the cool table top.

"No need for shame, Allie. You didn't know. I think he didn't tell you because he did love you—you and Trey." Jake's glanced skipped around the room—the diner was busier now, the noise of the lunch buzzing around them. His eyes drifted back to Allie. "It was what he did to take care of his family. He would have done anything in the world for you two."

That night she thought back over her conversation with Jake. The steel trap was still locked around her icy heart, but her brain was ready to process the alarming revelations.

For his own reasons her selfish, lying, cheating bastard husband turned to another woman rather than ride out a black time in their marriage. Had he loved the woman? Did he really end their affair? The facts did not throw a favorable light on her husband. Looking back with a suspiciousness borne of betrayal, chunks of time were now haunted by great big question marks emblazoned on them in red.

She made it easy for him to cover his tracks. Took the easy way out when he offered to manage their finances. Or did he insist? Who could remember after so many years? Either way, she didn't want to do it back then, and she still didn't.

He'd played cards with the same group of guys for longer than she could remember, but somehow it was never Ben's turn to host poker night. Allie blithely accepted his reasoning that Joe and Steve, both men she couldn't pick out of a lineup, owned large homes with green baize tables already in place. Allie would need to rearrange furniture to squeeze a pair of card tables into their living room. Sick, she recalled several times she shoved a hot appetizer or a twelve pack into his hands as he left the house.

Conjecture was pointless. Even so, how *would* this have played out? Would she have found out at some point? Would there at last, at some point in the future, have been a tell-tale clue that would have broken through her naïveté? A hotel receipt? The wrong name uttered in the heat of passion? It was all so cliché.

An affair that lasted nearly as long as his marriage. It was bizarre, to say the least, nearly beyond comprehension. And though it galled her, she was at least thankful he took care of his daughter.

Memories floated to the surface. Business trips—trade shows, conventions. Did Jake go as well? Her thoughts shifted, chasing an obscure conclusion. The Christmas he ran out for whipped cream—Trey was eight that year, he played Rudolph in the school program the week before. Ben was gone for hours and seemed especially quiet the rest of the day. Was he really gone so long because nothing was open? And finally, the Tuesday nights. Poker with the guys. Why wasn't Jake part of that? How many of those nights did her husband come home late and hold her in the dark, smelling as fresh as when he left, proclaiming his undying love? Allie dragged in a breath, blew it out.

Damn his selfish, lying, cheating bastard heart.

Still riding the emotional roller coaster that was her day, hope and relief lifting her temporarily from her grief only to plunge her to new depths of pain and betrayal, she was more than chagrined that she did not know more about the business end of running a household. No matter how disagreeable the chore, it now fell squarely on her shoulders.

She now had a new life, this life that was dumped on her, and she needed to learn how to live it. She would start the next afternoon.

She sat in Tom Gainey's office and pored over investment statements like her students tackled phonics flash cards. There were money market funds, and retirement accounts. And for Trey, a big fat college fund, drawing interest and exempt from federal income tax. She gave Tom the information about Ben's insurance policies and together they came up with a strategy for preserving her newfound wealth.

And as she left his office, walking a little more confidently through his tiny lobby, the first building blocks of a new life slipped firmly into place.

Chapter Fifteen

Allie was mad. No, not mad. Livid, that about covered it. She flung her purse onto the kitchen table. Tossed her keys to land with a clatter beside it. Nothing had gone right for the past two years and it was all Ben's fault. Not her problem he wasn't here to defend himself, the selfish, lying, cheating bastard. She had a laundry list of problems and they could all be laid right at his doorstep. Or . . . wherever.

It all started way back then with the automatic sprinkler system—and a timer she knew nothing about. One afternoon as she strode across the lawn, her eye on the daily paper, it suddenly began spewing. Geysers gushed that would put Yosemite to shame; every last one of the heads completely sheared off.

She ran to the controls on the wall just inside the garage door, blindly flipped switches and twisted dials until the water shut off. Oh, that Trey, she'd seethed, plowing the mower straight ahead rather than veering around those pesky pop-ups—all in order to finish the chore fast, damn kid. And Ben—they lived together in this house for five years—don't you think he could have mentioned, just once, how to operate the system? So, besides needing to learn about the damn timer, every sprinkler head in the entire yard needed to be replaced.

They were idiots.

Both of them.

Today's bout of retail therapy had done nothing to improve her mood. With a firm grasp on her shopping bag she strode into the living room toting her new paperback and trio of scented candles, her mind still spinning.

"Jake, I have a problem with my sprinkler system." She'd called him as soon as she'd had a chance to change her clothes, to dry her hair. "Trey ran over the sprinkler heads with the mower." Her frustration buzzed through the atmosphere, circled the satellite and crash landed in his cell phone.

"How many?" Bless his heart, of course he'd drop everything to come over, pry her out of a jam.

"All of them."

"All of them!"

Poor Jake.

With her new candles scattered on a shelf of the wall unit, wicks lit and jasmine floating on the air, she stormed into her room. It was shortly after the sprinkler incident that her car began to chug and choke. Out of warranty, it was in the shop so often that she'd named the sardine can the dealership offered as a loaner.

She'd scarcely sprung her car from the mechanic—if God was kind, for the last time—and was trying to make it home before rush hour when her tire popped. *Damn it!* Ben was supposed to handle these things. She steered the limping vehicle to the shoulder and parked while a dust storm rolled in from the west. There was nothing to do but call for help and wait, random acts of mayhem gleefully flitting through her head, aimed directly at her dearly departed.

Tossing her new romance into the seat of her reading chair—at least *someone* got to have a happy ever after—she continued into the bathroom and walk-in closet beyond. But *that day* she'd picked up the handset and called Jake.

"*Can you believe it? It took them three hours to get there! Three! I was a damn goldfish in a glass bowl, everybody staring at me as they zoomed past.*"

"*Hold on. The game's too loud.*" *The phone clunked like it was dropped on a hard surface, then he was back.* "*Now, what are you talking about?*"

"*Triple A. I got a flat and it took them forever to get there because of the storm. I was stuck on the side of the freeway, getting sandblasted in the dark.*"

"*Really, Allie? You thought they'd rush right out to change your tire in that wind and sand? You were lucky they got there in three hours.*"

Allie changed into drawstring cotton pants and a thin tee, finally comfortable and well on her way to calmer. That was, until the squeal of electric guitar and the battle fire of twenty-third century weaponry poured from Trey's open doorway and followed him like a cloud down the hallway and toward her room. Which brought her temper flying full circle, and back to his son. That's right, *his*. *Her* son was conscientious, helped around the house without nagging. Was polite and pleasant. Dubbed the Stepford student at a very young age.

Now he acted out, rushed through chores irresponsibly. Sassed her relentlessly. Was moody, inconsiderate, argumentative. And the frosting on the cake? His grades had dipped dangerously into the red zone. Not only that, but he'd figured out how to push her guilt button, too. He was getting on her nerves. The worst part was, she was pretty sure she brought this on herself, giving in to him too much—the poor kid, doesn't have a dad . . .

The long, long stare she leveled his way was hot, the arm she thrust out as he crossed her threshold wordlessly pointed the way back out. He gusted out a laugh and turned around. "Come on, Mom, you gotta let me out of the house some day. Today works for me."

"Dear God, give me the strength to not kill him." She could not allow this to continue. She was holding up her end of the deal, damn it, but he was clearly not holding up his.

Just shy of his sixteenth birthday, Allie taught him to drive, like a good mom. Took him to the mall in the evenings so he'd have a great big piece of asphalt all to himself. Demonstrated the knobs, the buttons, and then braced herself against the dash and the door while he mastered the intricacies of an automatic transmission. And at eight o'clock in the morning the very day he turned sixteen there they were, waiting in line to take his driving test. And of course he passed the first time, the little creep.

Allie dropped into her scarlet chenille chair, reached out to switch on the reading lamp. Nestled in the corner of her bedroom, she opened her paperback and then ignored it as she contemplated problem number four with a sigh of frustration. Once the kid in question could drive, he thought he *could drive*. Whenever he wanted. Her car. Without asking. That was the kicker. *Little creep* was tame compared to some of the things she called him under her breath these days. She'd tolerated this for a full year already, but now the little creep was grounded. Restricted to the house. And turning into a monster.

And, oh yes, there was more. Kicking off her shoes, she twisted in the chair, dragged her feet up and tucked them beneath her. Her son, the monster, was not playing fair. He was out of school for the summer now so he was *there*. In her face. Unfortunately, Allie hadn't remembered that part of *restriction* when the word hurled from her in a moment of wholesome wrath. Trey had never been grounded before. But oh hell, he was making her pay for using that awful word now, wasn't he? Television on all day, space aliens warring and machine guns blasting from the damn video games at a brain-numbing volume. Snacking at an Olympic pace and trashing the kitchen in the process. Wheedling and cajoling, begging to be exiled to the mean streets of The Greater Phoenix Metropolitan Area. He was supposed to work for Jake this summer but she fixed that with her little plan, didn't she?

As if conjured, the door cracked open and his head appeared. Thankfully, the cacophony didn't chase him this time. "C'mon, Mom." He rolled his eyes. "You have to let me go. It's summer break. I can't be stuck in the house all day." When she didn't kick him out again he eased the door open fully and entered the room, his hands splayed. "Look, I'm sorry. I won't take your car again without asking, I promise."

"Give it a rest, Trey." Her words rode on an exhausted sigh. Giving up on the idea of reading, she laid her new book on the lamp table, tilted her head back and closed her eyes. "Quit bugging me and I'll think about it." *How many mothers around the world were saying those exact words today?*

"Well, think hard and fast, will you?" Trey hovered at her elbow, his words braver, animated. "All my friends are hanging out. Jax has a new girlfriend and she has this really hot friend. We're all supposed to go to the movies tomorrow." He finally paused to take a breath. "And Jake's planning to take the boat out this weekend. Do I have to miss that too?" He laid it on thick, and was barely shy of rude.

And then, as if the knife of uncertainty, of frustration, of anger wasn't already lodged firmly in her gut, he gave it a little twist.

"You know, if you bought me my own truck you wouldn't have to share." Her eyes snapped open in disbelief. "I could work for Uncle Jake this summer and make my own money, pay for my own gas." He had what he probably thought was the perfect solution to his problem, and a downright smug expression. "I could ask a girl out without asking you for money and—"

Oh, hell no. "No way." She surged to her feet, her face lifted so she stood nose to chin with him, her fists planted on her hips. "No way are you spending the summer hanging out with a . . . a . . . girl." The idea of her only child ending life as he knew it on the whims of a short skirt and rampant hormones scared her witless.

"And where on earth would you get the idea I'd run right out and buy you a truck simply because you wanted one, huh?" She was into it now. A finger speared his chest, punctuating each of her objections. "You've been a brat around here. You haven't been respecting the house rules and you haven't been respecting *me*."

He quick-stepped backwards. "I told you I was sorry." Summer blue eyes earnest, he raked a chunk of hair from his forehead. "If I had my own truck I could even help you run errands. Go to the store for you, stuff like that. I'm growing up, Mom; you can't keep treating me like I'm twelve."

"I liked you better when you were twelve."

Trey merely rolled his eyes, went on as if she hadn't spoken. "Think about it. I could drive myself to school in the fall. I don't know a single senior whose mom drives them to school. It's downright embarrassing."

That's it, go for the emotional hook. Someone was giving this kid lessons.

"Plus, it would be easier if I have to stay after to study. My grades—"

He was too far away to poke so she jabbed the air with one stern finger. "We haven't even gotten started on your grades, young man! You're lucky you don't have summer school. Your GPA took a plunge this year; you realize that, don't you?" *Argh, preaching now.* She took a deep, calming breath, a step back. And lowered her voice to a reasonable tenor. "Look Trey, before there are any changes to your punishment there must be changes to your behavior."

Oh, she liked that. Sensible. If only she had more practice with this punishment stuff. You'd think for a teacher she'd be better at it, but she was flying blind. Maybe she needed to buy a book.

"I promise to change my behavior, Mom. Really, but you don't understand."

Would he ever give up? She pinned him with a hard stare. "I understand you're old enough to be responsible for your actions, Trey. The punishment stands. But I'll think about what to do." When he opened his mouth again, when his whole body said bluster, she added steel to her voice. "I'll *think* about it. That means 'don't bug me.'"

She welcomed the interruption of the telephone, returned to her chair as Trey dove to grab the receiver at its first shrill ring.

"Hello? Oh, hi." Trey paused a beat, dropped onto the side of her bed, causing it to bounce, hooked his heels on the rail. "No, I was trying to talk her into letting me out of the cell block." He waited again, glaring at her across the room. "Yeah, I told her all that."

Who was he talking to? Could be anybody.

"No, I told her that, too. She's still mad."

Trey stopped, listened to the mystery caller before continuing his rant. "Well, you said that, but she doesn't think it's a good idea. Maybe you could talk to her?" Another brief silence. "Yeah? Thanks Uncle Jake, she's right here."

Allie surged to her feet, grabbed the phone from his hand. "You've got to be kidding!" She didn't even say hello. "He's harassing you, too?" Long strides took Allie all the way to the kitchen where she splashed white zin into a nice, tall tumbler and headed onto the patio.

"Relax, Allie, he'll be fine. He's simply testing boundaries." Jake sounded so relaxed and certain. When was the last time she was relaxed? "He's never been cooped up like this. It's hard on you but it's hard on him, too."

She sank into a wicker chair. Took a sip but she wasn't ready to give the boy a pass yet. "It's *supposed* to be hard on him. But he's not supposed to make it *harder* on me."

"Still torturing you, huh?" He had the nerve to chuckle, damn him.

"Wondering if I'll survive. I swear I'll never put him on restriction again. I'll find some other way to punish him. Or sell him to gypsies." She huffed out a laugh. Stood to pull an errant thistle from the geraniums. "So what were all those mysterious things you told him to say?" Weed disposed of, she wandered the yard.

"Nothing so mysterious. He was sorry, wouldn't do it again. He'll bring his grades up." He paused a moment, glugged in her ear right before glass clinked on glass. Was he stretched on a pool chaise with a beer? She envied his calm, bent at the waist to tug at a dandelion as the sun inched over the horizon. "He asked me if I thought you'd buy him a truck."

Like a jackknife she unfolded, fisting the plant, releasing fuzzy white seeds to parachute on the breeze. "That's unlikely. He's got quite a bit of ground to make up."

"Understood, but he *is* supposed to work for me again this summer. You don't plan to chauffeur him to and from job sites all summer, do you? That's not much fun."

She unrolled the garden hose, dragged it to water her potted plants. "No, I'm not planning to drive him anywhere. I'm planning to keep him locked in the house." But like a hissing teakettle with the heat turned off, she was losing steam.

"Sure you are. What about when you're done with your mad?"

"Damn it, Jake."

"What if we go out, look at used trucks this weekend? Leave the kid at home."

Whose side was he on, anyway? "I suppose we could." *Really?* "Wait a minute—"

He cut her off. "Saturday work for you? Say eleven? I've got stuff I should do early."

Her shoulders stiffened before she blew out a breath, let the tension flow from her as water flowed from the hose and into colorful petunias that thrived in the warmth of late spring. "Why not?"

"Settled. Now, Sunday. We're taking the boat out—first time this season. You up for it? A little sun, skiing, food, beer. The usual cast of characters."

Allie found she could smile for the first time today as he bullied her out of her mood. "Sure, sounds like fun; I haven't seen Michelle in a while." She didn't see the attraction, but was willing to make the effort for Jake's sake.

"She's out of town this week; should be back home Friday."

They'd skied together for years, since college. With Ben. With Trey. She always looked forward to it. Flowers soaked, she turned off the water, rolled the hose.

"Have Trey bring Jax along. Otherwise it's all adults, too boring for him."

She ambled back to her chair, folded herself onto the cushion. "Nah, Jake. Trey loves hanging out with you. Don't you know? You're *cool.* Evidently I only think I am."

"Hey, Allie, Can you see outside? The sun's going down in a blaze tonight."

"Darn. I'm right on the patio and didn't even notice." She stood, tugged her chair until it faced west and the ball of fire kissing the horizon. In two minutes it would be gone. "Now I know why some animals eat their young. Boy, that kid can rile me." They were linked by the sound of their breathing, the sun continued its descent into the abyss, leaving behind a glorious array of color. Rosy streaks of fuchsia and melon churned together, trapped beneath low swirling clouds in a graying lavender sky. They were only moments away from the inky darkness of night.

"Beautiful." She breathed the word on a sigh. "If I ever moved from Arizona, I would miss that most. That and the stars."

"I love that about the lake. When we stay until dark and build a bonfire. There are always so many stars out." Neither mentioned Ben, who would break out his guitar once evening fell and everything settled down. Ben, who broke their hearts.

She looked forward to Sunday, but Trey's attitude still upset her. "I almost don't want to bring him along. He's given me such a hard time."

"He's a teenager, Allie. It's a lethal combination of hormones and unanswered questions. With a little patience, you'll both survive." Jake was such a rock. He could calm her out of her worst mood.

"He told me about a girl he wants to ask out."

"Has he ever been on a date?" Jake sounded surprised. "He's never mentioned one to me."

"To a dance at school, with a group, sure. But a *date* date? No." Allie released a heavy breath. "I'm afraid I'm blowing it with him, Jake. I'm too bossy, but he scares me." A blanket of stars appeared, flickering on one at a time. Crickets chirped in the lawn. She tilted her head against the back of her chair and pushed off with her toes, rocking.

"You're the mom, Allie. That's your job. And Trey's a smart kid; he'll use his head."

Her lips twisted in a dubious frown. "He's seventeen, Jake. And like you said, he's ruled by hormones. Which head will win?"

Jake choked on a laugh. "Come on Allie, give the kid a little credit. Ben talked to him about sex years ago."

"Sex, sure. The common sense talk, that's what he needs now." The moon was a bright orange smile, hanging low in the sky. "But I'm just the mom. I may as well speak a foreign language for all he listens to me."

"I could talk to him if you want." He paused, and a smile entered his voice. "Girls are evil, you know."

She chuckled in return. "How is it you're so good with Trey? You don't even have kids."

"I'm winging it as we go along, I guess. He's a good kid, Allie. And I was a teenage boy once."

She caught the wistfulness in his tone and would have bitten her tongue to bring the words back. Who else could she talk into the night with? Not Maddie, busy with her own family. Not Reese, tangled in the social whirlwind of her husband's career. A yawn escaped.

"I heard that. You should go."

"It's been a long day." She waited for him to say something more, hesitant to break their connection. "You're right." She stretched out of her chair. "I'll see you this weekend, then."

"G'night, babe."

Jake arrived Saturday as promised. Shirtless, Trey bent over the mower in the front yard, removing debris from the blade. Glaring orange wires snaked from his back pocket and into his ears. He sauntered over to Trey, tapped his shoulder.

Trey jolted upright.

"Jake! You scared the sh— . . . heck out of me!" He grinned, removed one of the earbuds, let it dangle, leaving the other inserted. "I didn't know you were coming over today." He crouched to finish cleaning the blade, righted the mower.

He eyed the boy playfully. "Yeah, well, if you plan to cut the grass maybe I ought to babysit the sprinklers."

Trey cringed, then barked a quick laugh that trailed him to the house. "Jeez, will you and my mom ever let it go?"

After his dad died Trey was devastated, same as his mom. He'd lost his best buddy, the one who hung out with him, made him feel special. Taught him guy stuff—like working in the yard. When he was younger Dad would cut and trim and he would sweep the clippings, and as he got older he got to use the trimmer. But Dad always mowed. The yard was his baby, and nobody touched his baby.

After his dad was gone, Jake took over their yard work. Trey didn't think much of it at first, but several months had passed now. Maybe being the man in the family included taking on the yard work. He was fifteen after all. Uncle Jake didn't mind helping out, but he was there all the time. It was time to step up, to man up. So he would start with something simple . . . like mowing the lawn. Problem was, he didn't know how. How hard could it be? He'd worked beside Dad a hundred times, probably more. So he got out the mower, filled the gas, and off he went. Once he was done with the front yard, he stood back, inspected his work.

Shit. The swaths Dad made were always straight and true, perfectly even. Looking out at the yard that day, there was nothing resembling straight *or* even. And the pop-up sprinklers kept getting in the way. But he could fix that. Every time the mower cut one off, he twisted it back into the dirt by the black plastic pipe thing. There. Then one day Mom came storming into the house looking like a wet T-shirt contestant, yelling about the sprinkler system. Yeah, he probably screwed that up too. So he ended up bugging Jake after all.

"I think I messed up a few of the sprinkler heads. Mom's pissed."

"A few?" Jake didn't have to laugh at him, He was only trying to help. "I heard it was more like all of them."

"Yeah, it's more like all of them." He shuffled his feet where he stood, rushed on. "I don't want to bother you. Just get me started, I'll take it from there."

"Trey, you're never a pest. Besides, I haven't seen you in a couple of weeks. I can come after work. We'll get everything all fixed up, good as new. Maybe we'll throw something on the grill when we're done."

That evening they made a pilgrimage to what Jake called the big boy toy store and returned with supplies—replacement heads, a sack full of skinny black risers, a roll of white plastic tape. They raided the garage, dug out Dad's tools and Jake taught him the basics of sprinkler repair. Then Jake got out the lawn mower and showed him a few tricks; before he knew it, his lawn looked as good as Dad's.

The slamming door had him looking up, waving good-bye as his mom climbed into Jake's pickup.

Allie skipped out of the house wearing jeans that rode a little low on her hips and a ruffled white blouse. Silver earrings played peekaboo through her long curls, and brightly painted toes peeped through her open-toed flats. Jake opened the truck door for her. His fingers strained to trace the path of freckles that danced across her chest. Damn Ben and his promises. He agreed to take care of Allie, not maul her in front of her son.

At last Allie saw reason. It was only logical that in order to keep their collective sanity—all *three* of them—she couldn't continue to share a vehicle with her son. With money not an issue, all he had to do was rationally demonstrate the advantages of purchasing Trey his own truck. The difference, quite obviously, was that she was not being browbeaten by an emotional teenager. No, he was more subtle than that. *All right, devious.* But still, once they actually checked out the selection, Allie decided a used truck wasn't at all what Trey needed. He would be leaving home in one more year, after all. She didn't want to worry about him breaking down.

So she wandered the new-truck lot. Inspected stickers, peeked in doors. He rode shotgun while she test-drove a white sun-roofed model, smiled when she said it was *it*. Then she saw the black one. How could she have missed it?

"Oh, this is what he needs." She circled the lifted chassis, four fingers trailing high-gloss ebony. "Four wheel drive. Extra cab. Big tires."

"Huge tires, Allie. Hell on gas mileage." So much for being mad at Trey.

She merely glanced over her shoulder at him, grinned. "You started this.

Oh, a bed liner, even better." She yanked open the driver's door, stood on tiptoe to peer inside. "Six-CD changer, premium speakers. I can't tell, does it have that remote start thingy?"

He'd created a monster. He could only shake his head and hold on for the ride. "I'm sure it can be arranged."

"And we'll need the extended warranty." There she was—practical Allie.

He and Ben had dealt with Dave Michaelson, the salesman, many times over the years and he always gave them a fair shake. Jake sat to one side, his chest puffed out, while Allie made a deal for the truck of Trey's dreams. As with so many things she'd done in the past two years—on her own—making this purchase was a rite of passage, almost a ceremony. She was doing fine, and Trey was about to be shocked.

She turned to him from time to time, but he merely smiled and nodded as Allie, in a very un-Allie moment, wrote a whopping big check and bought her son a truck.

He followed her outside. She was still riding a wave of excitement, of confidence. "It will be a couple of hours before they have it ready to go. How about lunch?"

Oh Christ, Allie wanted to celebrate. She felt empowered and probably needed that feeling to linger a while longer before divebombing back into real life. He really shouldn't. He left Michelle at home working.

But Allie was impossible to resist. "Sounds great!" With a light hand on the small of her back, he guided her to the parking lot.

"He'll flip!" The echo of her gleeful crowing still echoed as she bit into her sloppy stroganoff burger. He mentally groaned as she used the tip of her tongue to lick sour cream sauce from the corner of her mouth.

"I'm sure you're right. It's definitely a great truck." He grinned back at her, hoped it didn't much resemble a grimace. He loved the truck, was happy for Trey. But mostly he tried not to squirm in his seat, captivated by the way the overhead fluorescents caught the bright highlights in her hair and how her dimple flashed when she smiled. Or talked. Or sat. *Shit.*

It was mid-afternoon by the time he pulled up to Allie's, where Trey was framed in the front window. Following him, Allie pulled into her driveway in the brand spanking new black truck, remote start thingy included.

The front door slammed open and Trey hurtled out, skidded to a stop mere feet from his mom, hands clasped to his head, bug-eyed, slack-jawed. Grinning, Speechless. Allie stuck out a hand and let the key fob hang.

Trey's eyes volleyed between Allie, him and the truck as he found his voice. "Holy shit! Mom! Really? What do I—? Can I—?"

Jake stood beside Allie, just grinned like a proud papa with a wad of emotion trapped in his chest while Trey whooped, hugged, bounced, opened doors to climb inside before hopping right out again, hugging yet again.

He caught Trey in his arms, pounded him on the back and handed him to Allie, who laughed, the sound a reminder that while he could happily watch them both, this mother and child that meant so much to him, they were merely his to watch over, not his.

Chapter Sixteen

Jake turned the key in the lock and swung open the door. He could still envision the look of unadulterated joy on Trey's face, hear the sheer glee in his voice. The kid was on cloud nine. And had a right to be. Fifteen was a hard age for a boy to lose his dad, especially when they were as tight as he and Ben were. He tried to fill in for Ben, but he fell way short. As much as he wished it was different, he wasn't Trey's dad.

He met Michelle as he walked down the hallway and gave her a quick kiss. "Hello, get your work done?" He snaked his hand out, reached for her.

She coolly evaded him and he held in a sigh. The iciness in his house had nothing to do with the air blowing through the vents, but served in sharp contrast to the home he'd just left. "I got done what I needed to. I was beginning to wonder if you forgot the way home."

"It took longer than I realized to buy a truck." He kept the words casual, then kicked himself. He had no reason to feel defensive. She was snippy more and more lately for no reason he could name. "Allie did great." A forced grin across his face. "You should have seen the look on Trey's face—boy, was he surprised."

Michelle hummed a bored sigh and turned away, heading toward the kitchen. "We're having chicken for dinner. It's roasting in the oven."

Jake followed her and leaned against the counter. "You should have waited, Michelle. I thought we'd go out."

Her shrug dipped the collar of her blouse, exposing the milky skin she pampered. "I go out all the time. I thought it would be nice to eat in."

She went out all the time. Meetings and out of town trips were the very heart of her existence. While he stayed home and waited. "It sounds fine. Chicken will be fine." He reached around her to grab a beer from the refrigerator. "Don't forget we've got the lake tomorrow."

Tomorrow?"

"We talked about it, remember? We'll meet the regular crowd there. Allie and Trey will ride with us."

She flashed him an impatient look. "I have a report I need to finish. I leave for Colorado on Monday to meet a prospective client."

His free hand hung limp by his side. He wanted beyond reason to reach out to her, but sensed the gesture would be useless. "Can't you finish it another time? Everyone's expecting you to be there." With a heavy heart he shot her a coaxing smile and took a stab at convincing her. "C'mon Michelle, it's the first time this summer. You might even enjoy yourself."

"I don't think so."

Yeah, probably not.

The next morning Jake stepped into the kitchen to say good-bye. Michelle was already at the table, her long blonde hair caught up in a tail, a cup of coffee beside her laptop as she keyed in figures. It was early, the dawn not yet a memory. Her eyes briefly met his as he strode in, then she went back to her spreadsheet. He laid his hand gently over hers, forcing her to stop.

"I wish you'd change your mind, come with us. Everyone will wonder why you're not there."

She pulled her hand from beneath his and stood, facing him. "They're your friends, Jake. Not mine."

"No, they're *ours*."

Michelle rolled her eyes dramatically. "Whatever."

Moving away, he poured himself a cup of coffee, blew across it before taking a slow sip. "Allie said she's looking forward to seeing you again."

"Allie!" Michelle spit the word like a piece of used gum.

His eyes went hot. He edged his words with warning, forced then through a clenched jaw. "What is that supposed to mean?"

Michelle drew her shoulders tight, let them drop. "Nothing."

His eyebrows drew together. Her brown eyes that used to warm him, soothe him, held something new this morning. Something frightening. Something a lot like indifference. How long had that been there?

With a tentative smile he took a step toward her, wrapped a hand around her nape, leaned in for a kiss. "I'll miss you. When I get back we'll go out, get dinner. All right?"

She turned her face away and retreated, her hands hanging loose. "Fine."

He left the kitchen, a knot of tension eating at his insides. The muted rat-tat of the keyboard followed him as he opened the front door.

Pulling his truck away from the curb he towed his ski boat down the slow lane of the interstate. Streaks of pink and yellow lightened the lavender sky and he kept an eye on the other early risers as they zoomed past.

Something was different with Michelle; wrong somehow. He couldn't pinpoint exactly what it was, or when it started, but things weren't as they should be. Too much work, probably, not enough time together. He and Michelle weren't happy.

The revelation settled over him like a cooling mist. But he could fix this. When she returned from Colorado he'd take her away again, rekindle the romance, the heat. And once the romance was back, she wouldn't be obsessed by her work.

Jake bobbed his head along with the music streaming from the radio. He was anticipating a clear, warm, sunny day and he had a plan. He resettled himself in his seat the way he planned to resettle his life. Pulled up to Allie's curb as Trey and Jax lumbered down the walkway, lugging an ice chest between them.

"Hey, Jake! We're ready to go. Mom will be right out." They dropped the heavy cooler near the boat.

"Great! I'll go see if she needs help." Jake trotted across the lawn to the door.

He rapped quickly and let himself in. Rumpled sleeping bags and empty soda cans littered the floor. Smiling at the remains of a teenage sleepover, he picked up the remote, clicked off the television on his way to the kitchen, looking for Allie. She wasn't there, but a plastic container of potato salad, a few bags of chips, towels and a beach bag were all stacked on the table. He reversed his steps, heading back into the living room. Allie turned the corner from the hall, smoothing a short sundress over her bikini. He caught a quick glimpse of smooth thighs before they were hidden beneath bright cotton fabric.

"Oh, Jake. I didn't hear you." One palm splayed against her chest. "I just need to get my stuff." Allie gathered up her things from the table, glanced around the room. "Where's Michelle?"

Her load shifted precariously. "Let me get that." He pulled the towels and beach bag from her arms before they slipped to the floor. "She had work to finish. It will only be us."

"That's too bad." She shrugged the balance of her load back into place. "It will be too nice a day to be stuck inside." She grinned saucily. "I intend to take full advantage of your hospitality."

He winked at her over his shoulder as he led the way to the door. "At your service, ma'am."

Everything was hauled outside. At Jake's whistle Trey and Jax ceased lobbing a football back and forth, ran over to help. Between them they got loaded and were on their way.

The sun shone clear and bright over the crystal blue lake. The early season crowds were sparse. Allie moved to the bow of the boat, slipped out of her dress and sandals. Stretched out on the white vinyl seat she soaked up rays, bouncing whenever the boat hit a wake. Jake's eyes swept over her from behind shaded lenses. Her bound hair blew loose with the wind; her golden skin shimmered with the lotion she'd smoothed on. She was faced toward him, eyes closed, lips smiling, singing softly with the music pouring from the speakers.

He steered to an unoccupied area of the lake and the boys took turns jumping in, bobbing in their life vests as they donned skis. Rope taut and gripped firmly they gave the thumbs up and off they went, sailing across the cool, smooth water.

Peering over his shoulder, Jake checked the progress of the skier. Jax, stationed at the stern, held the orange signal flag in hand. Trey, balanced ably on a wakeboard, knees bent, guided himself from left to right and back again, jumping their wake, laughing as he did so. He was a good looking kid. Tall and lean with blond hair whipping in his face. Jake was transported back in time, watching Ben ski while he stood in the boat, flag at the ready, his own dad at the wheel. He shook himself back to the present as Trey let go of the rope and gently glided across the water.

Trey swam to the ladder and hauled himself in, shivering and shaking water like a mutt. "Oh, man, that felt good." He laughed as he removed his ski vest. "The water's still a little cold, though." He wrapped himself in a large towel. "Uncle Jake, you want a turn? I'll drive."

A dunk in the lake was exactly what he needed to get the picture of Allie in a swimsuit out of his head. He snagged the vest from the seat where Trey dropped it and put it on, sucking in a quick breath as the cold, wet nylon hit his sun-warmed skin.

Trey grabbed his shades, got comfortable in the driver's seat and sat back, waiting for him to hop in the water. Roused from her catnap, Allie staggered toward the back of the boat, body parts jiggling with the rocking motion of the vessel. Yup, a shot of cold water was a definitely good idea.

Trey slowed the boat, steered around to pick him up. Jake's teeth chattered and goose bumps covered his skin as he pulled himself up the ladder and into the boat. He removed the ski vest and grabbed a towel. "That first run gets harder and harder every year."

"Well, I'm impressed. You were as good as the boys." Allie was back in her sundress. *Thank you, Jesus.*

"You are so good for my ego." He grinned and kissed her forehead, then reclaimed his place in the driver's seat. "Okay guys, Mom's turn."

Allie laughed, raised her hands in mock surrender. "Waiting until the water is warmer, thank you. How about lunch? Hours on the water always work up an appetite."

It was a day like so many they'd enjoyed before—warm sun, burgers on the grill, tunes blaring from someone's portable stereo. It was nice to visit with people she hadn't seen in months, some since before Ben's death. Trey was already busy, tossing horseshoes in the sand with Jake and Jax, along with another man she met earlier. Bob something, an electrician. The old guys against the young guns, and the teenagers were merciless.

Picking her way down the gravelly beach with a plate in her hand, she staked out a smooth area to sit. Setting her lunch on a nearby rock, she spread her towel. She'd scarcely started in on her burger when Jake made his way to her, a couple of cold drinks in his hands.

She scooted, made room for him on her oversized beach towel. He plopped down beside her, handed her a bottle of water, took a long pull off his beer, and shot a glance toward the horseshoe pit behind him. He pointed his bottle to where Trey and Jax were now matched up against a couple of guys in their mid-twenties. "Those boys kicked our butts."

She laughed, followed his gaze. "They're ruthless. You should've heard them playing video games last night." She took a sip, then a bite of her hamburger.

Jake picked up her fork, sampled the potato salad. "They're good kids. They crack me up." He shot another quick glance their way. "I envy you."

She raised her eyebrows. "I'll send Trey home with you for a week. That will cure you, I promise." She took one last bite of her hamburger and set the uneaten half on her empty plate.

Jake laughed, snagged the uneaten burger, and finished it off.

"What about you and Michelle? Any babies in your future?" She studied him hard. Did he realize the desperation she sensed in him lately? "You would be a great daddy, Jake."

He studied her empty plate. "Could be. Someday." His gaze drifted back to the horseshoe pit before yanking it back to her with a heavy sigh and a frustrated frown. He pulled his knees up, let his forearms rest on them and stared across the water. "No, I doubt it. Things aren't great right now, to say the least. She's always gone."

"Every relationship has bumps."

"Even when she's home all she does is work. I don't remember it that way last summer, or maybe I wasn't paying attention. But now?" He stopped and turned his head, staring at Trey, "I really don't see her as a mom."

Allie couldn't help but touch his arm. "I'm sorry, Jake."

The smile he aimed her way was humorless. "Yeah, me too." He took another long drink of his beer, which must be warm by now. "Last year, when she moved in, it all seemed so simple. The next logical step. I almost wish she hadn't now. It would be easier. The end, it would be . . . less messy."

When he looked directly at her with his eyes so haunted, she had an uncomfortable urge to wrap him in her arms. Instead she inched closer, sat beside him hip to hip, offering unspoken comfort as he vented.

"I was tired of being alone. I'll try to make it work. But the idea of children? That's a tough one to let go."

Her heart just skittered. It was hard to watch a man in that much pain. And Jake deserved so much more. She turned to face the crowd. The music was still loud, the teenagers were still pitching horseshoes, someone was toasting marshmallows for s'mores at the barbeque. She glanced back at Trey. She couldn't imagine her life without him.

"Dreams are hard to give up." The acceptance of this was relatively new to her. "It took a long time before I stopped thinking of having another child." She tilted her head to the side and shrugged in one fluid motion. "I always hoped Ben would come around. But once he was gone I had to face the reality of it never happening." She let her breath out in a deep sigh, stared out at the water lapping between the boats lining the shore. "That was the part that bothered me the most about Ben's . . . situation. He refused to have another baby with me, yet he had one with whatshername." She took another deep breath, blew it out in a long whoosh.

She turned back to Jake, a lopsided grin on her face, "I should go on one of those tabloid shows. Or maybe I should just shut up."

He reached over and traced a finger down her cheek, kissed the crest and caused her stomach to drop. Her eyes, which probably showed her confusion, flew to his, which were smiling.

"It was my pleasure. I think we both unloaded a little today."

Jake left work Wednesday night anxious to start Operation Rekindle.

Dinner Sunday evening had been disappointing, nothing more than silently sharing a restaurant table with Michelle, and Monday she left pre-dawn, and without a good-bye. But today she was due back from Denver and he wanted to beat her home. He had a great idea for a vacation and already talked to Nick about taking time off. He pulled into the driveway beside her sedan.

"Damn." He had the whole seduction scene planned. Along with a bottle of her favorite wine and a stack of travel brochures. And in the bag, rose petals and bath bubbles. Smoothly shifting to Plan B, he hurried through the house.

He found her in the bedroom, still in her business suit and heels, her suitcase open on the bed. "Hey, there." He smiled when she turned to him, wrapped his arms around her, settling his lips on hers. She pulled back, then melted into him with a sigh, kissing him back as he rested his palms across her back.

"Welcome home. Why don't you leave all this for later?" He waved the pamphlets at her and gave her a hopeful grin. "I've got a great idea I want to talk to you about. Then I'll show you how much I missed you."

Her hand fluttered as her eyes darted around the room. "I'm not unpacking."

He paused, and his eyes bounced around the room. A large gap loomed in the open closet. Articles of clothing lay scattered on the bed. A matching suitcase stood near the door.

His gaze flew back to her, blazing. "What the fuck's going on, Michelle? His eyes swept her from head to toe. "Tell me this isn't what it looks like." His eyes raked over her again before he threw the cruise brochures to the floor. "Or were you even planning to tell me at all?" Sparing a last searing glare at her, and then at the wreckage strewn around the room, he pivoted and stalked out.

His stomach growled. The irony didn't escape him that now, under these bizarre circumstances, he finally had Michelle's undivided attention.

Weary, he braced his palms against the patio slider. The moon cast a silvery reflection across the surface of the swimming pool. The night was still, the water placid. A calm word.

Nothing calm going on here.

She'd taken a seat at the kitchen table, her knees neatly crossed beneath her navy pinstripe skirt. Right now he'd like a little of the coffee he left near his chair, but it was long since cold. They'd been beating this horse for hours. He pushed off the door and stalked to the center of the room. The front door was within view, Michelle's cases were lined precisely beside each other.

"We've been together two years." He tamped down the frustration that oozed from his words. "How can you simply blow this off?"

"We've been through this, Jake. I'm not blowing anything off. I've given you everything I had."

The slow trickle of honey was gone from her tone. The magnolia blossoms he'd originally been attracted to. He'd admired her warmth, her serenity. But now she was just cold. Calm.

Placid.

"I deserve someone who will give me that much back."

His ears pricked. Funny, but it seemed those should be his words. In awe, he let her continue to play the victim. Her sniff was dainty. He could only admire the melodrama.

And wanted to applaud the wobbly, sad smile, the tears pooled in her eyes.

"I need that much, Jake. It's time for me to say good-bye."

A performance like that surely deserved an Oscar. He had no defense against the humorless smile that tilted his lips.

His pulse kicked even as his heart plummeted. There must be something left to salvage. Some reason he fought for this relationship. There must be words to keep him from returning to his lonely bachelor life. "But we're . . . compatible." And the lame justification sent him stalking back to the glass door.

Again her eyes met his openly. "You don't love me, Jake."

Love? The word pierced him, knifed him in the heart. "I . . . can't . . . .feel that." He moved, marched the length of the room, back to the table.

"Yes. You can."

He glowered as his weeping heart dropped to his feet. "What the hell are you talking about?"

"Sit down, Jake."

With a scowl he landed in a chair.

Thoughtful, she rose and wandered across the room. Stood leaning against the slider, mimicking his prior stance, staring into the darkness. "Now do me a favor. Close your eyes."

He opened his mouth to object, then closed it and did as she asked.

Her clothes rustled across the room. "Now, think of yourself thirty years in the future."

The request was outrageous, yet the vision filtered into his mind even as he simmered.

"You're married, you have grown children. Maybe grandchildren who come to visit. Your hair is gray, your sex life isn't what it used to be, but you're happy.

"Now, without picturing a face, think of your wife standing beside you, the woman you love." Her voice lulled him. "She has gray hair, too, her boobs sag, maybe she snores when she sleeps. But this is the woman who still makes you laugh, who keeps you on your toes. Now . . . in your mind . . . look up. Whose face do you see?"

Oh, God! His eyes snapped open.

Michelle clicked through the kitchen on her high heels. Passed him— still sitting at the table—and the bag holding rose petals and bath bubbles, and warm chardonnay.

At the front door she paused, her head lowered. "Do you know you've never called me anything but Michelle? It's never honey. Not baby or babe. Certainly not sweetheart. Not one single time. It's always Michelle."

Still seated in his chair, with his back turned, the door ticked opened . . . and then closed.

Their relationship had never had a chance of surviving. Michelle had merely hammered the final nails into the coffin. He dropped his chin to his chest. Took a series of deep breaths to steady his heart, which was no longer in his gut, but back where it belonged. This day was destined to occur. He fully accepted the blame. There was nothing he could do to change it, though. He'd given his heart a lifetime ago. It wasn't up for grabs.

He would be alone now. He'd resisted this, feared the desolation. His stomach growled again.

He got up to make a sandwich.

Chapter Seventeen

"Those are truly excellent shoes!"

Allie grinned, brushed crumbs from her lips. How typical of Reese to gush over designer footwear. Allie lifted her cardboard cup to sip fragrant chai, replaced it on the varnished table. Music drifted from overhead—something New Age that at this very moment got points for soothing away the last of the morning's stresses. Her final counseling session with Doctor Baker—a stint that left her surprisingly introspective—was behind her. As was an emotionally wrenching visit with Ben. Reese's call for a spur-of-the-moment round of shoe therapy just as she left the cemetery seemed like a sign.

"Perfect for a night on the town."

Allie pushed away the remains of her snack, dug the shoe box from her shopping bag. "They are fantastic, aren't they?" She grinned, caressed the heel of silver metallic peep toes with a pretty little bow at the back. "Not Manolos, but hey." She nodded pointedly at her friend's stilettos.

Reese stuck out her foot, twisted her ankle and gave her footwear critical regard. "Mmm. Last year's."

Flipping the shoe back and forth, Allie studied her new pump before tucking it away. "I have no idea when I'll wear them. But I haven't bought a great pair of shoes since before Ben died."

"Any self-respecting girl cannot go three years without splurging. Pretty sure there's a law."

Allie bent to stow the box. They *were* pretty great, even if they'd just gather dust in her closet. "Now you're the shoe police."

Reese chuffed out a laugh, tilted her head back, finished off her decaf skinny latte. "Isn't it about time you joined the world again, Allie? Midgets and teenagers are all well and good, but it's time to do something grown-up. Wear the shoes."

As much as her chest tightened, trapping her breath, she'd had similar thoughts lately. Could she go through with it? She lifted her gaze. "Reese—"

"Okay, don't panic." Reese threw out a hand, covered hers. "What about ladies' night? Pretty dresses. Girly cocktails." A finger sporting a blood-red nail waggled at her shopping bag. "Killer shoes."

Allie's spirits lifted. She'd survived a crap morning. Trey was gone and she hadn't fallen apart. Everything else was cake. Dinner, a couple of cosmos—yeah, appealing. Her teasing smile came naturally. "I guess you make a pretty good date."

Reese's thoughtful frown was not the reaction she expected. "Or you could save them for a real date."

She blinked, her smile flattened out. "What? What date?"

"I thought you and Jake might be—" With a flick of her wrist, Reese left the end of her sentence to dangle.

Her heart stopped. Then restarted in double-time. Hopefully Reese would take her silence for anything—*anything*—other than this mysterious panic roiling through her.

"Close your mouth." Reese reached across the table, tipped up her jaw with two fingers. "You can certainly understand why I'd ask. He spends half his time at your house."

"He was Ben's best friend, Reese. His business partner. I love him like a brother."

"Has he ever even had a serious relationship?"

"Sure. Michelle, remember? They were together until about a year ago."

"Oh, her. Snobby bitch." Reese dismissed her with a shrug. "You two belong together. You suit." In Reese-world all was settled, but Allie's heart skittered again. "I would have sworn you had a thing for him. Back in college."

Allie jittered out a shaky laugh. "Your imagination knows no bounds." No way would she admit that to Reese. She'd gnaw on it like a hound with a soup bone. "Jake and I have been friends for almost twenty years. Just friends."

"Hel-lo. Are you two the only ones who *don't* see it?"

A dark-haired woman walked past their table to the front counter. Beside her was a young girl, perhaps eleven or twelve, quite clearly arguing with the woman—with her hands. Compassion came over her in a rush. Such a brave young girl.

She turned back to Reese and blinked. "See what?"

"Sparks? Fireworks? Rockets' red glare? Any of this sound familiar?"

Allie laughed at her friend. "I love you, Reese, but you're crazy."

"Huh. I would have sworn . . ." Her voice trailed away before she brightened. "Then how about the principal from my school? His wife divorced him a couple of years ago. He's a nice guy. Not too hard to look at either." Reese raised her eyebrows and added a wink, a steamroller with a boring, drab life directly in its path.

The woman and girl stepped to the pick-up counter, their backs to the room. The barista handed them their drinks—Frappuccinos for each of them. The girl politely signed what she assumed was thanks. Turning toward the exit, they again passed her table, the girl smiling shyly as she scampered by with a plastic cup in her hand.

The girl seemed familiar somehow. Allie eyed the woman. Did she know her? She seemed vaguely familiar also, perhaps someone she knew long ago. What name had the barista called? Maggie, that was it. Didn't ring any bells.

Oh, jeez. Reese was still wound up.

"It's time to dive back into that proverbial dating pool. At least dip a toe."

Butterflies took up residence with the raspberry scone. Was she ready for this? Whatever happened to ladies night out? But maybe if she agreed Reese would get off her back about Jake. She carefully framed her response. "It might be nice to meet someone new."

"Like I said, nice guy. His name is Gary Benson. It will be fun!"

Allie pasted on a smile, not quite as natural or eager as before. "You're probably right." She checked her watch, got to her feet. She still wanted to prep her classroom for a new batch of munchkins.

"I'll see Gary at school tomorrow, give him your number."

Allie pumped enthusiasm into her voice. Leaned in for a hug. "Okay, fine. I'll wait for his call."

Allie's phone rang as she entered the house Wednesday afternoon, her arms full of groceries. About time Trey called to check in. He'd been gone for days already. The market bags landed on the counter with a *thwump* as she grabbed the handset.

"Hey there, I was getting worried." She fished out the eggs, opened the refrigerator to shelve them.

A hesitant voice answered. "Sorry, I only spoke with Reese today; I didn't realize you were waiting for me to call."

At the abrupt lurch in her pulse the cardboard carton bobbled, slipped. She lunged to catch it before it hit the tile.

"Who *is* this?" She squeezed her eyes shut. *No! No! No!*

"Gary Benson. Is this Allie?"

"Afraid so." She cleared her throat and thus, the squeak. "I'm sorry. I was rude. I thought you were my son. Rather, that my son was calling. He's away at school and I expect him to call. He hasn't called yet." Her voice was now her enemy. She stammered, babbled on, sounded like a complete idiot.

"So you weren't waiting for me to call?"

The amusement in his voice made her laugh. "Reese said she would talk to you, but I haven't heard back from her. And right now this entire conversation is feeling slightly surreal."

"Let me make the whole thing a bit more real. Reese told you I'm divorced, right?"

"Well, yes."

"I'm tied up this week, but would you like to do something next weekend? Lunch, a movie, a museum. A baseball game. Your pick."

"Baseball?" It was probably the doubt in her voice that caused him to chuckle, but it was a friendly sound.

"Just thought I'd throw that out there. You know, on the chance."

Okay, she could do this. The smile in her voice was almost natural. "Tell you what, Gary, I haven't been to a ball game in years. Let's see what kind of sports fan you are."

"A challenge?"

"I've seen grown men cry at baseball."

"You're on. The game's Saturday at three."

"Sounds good. Do you know where I live?"

"Chandler, isn't it? Quite a bit out of the way. I'll meet you at the stadium, by the main entrance at two o'clock. Reese showed me a snapshot of you."

Wow! Not even willing to make the effort on a first date? Strike one on Gary. "All right, I'll meet you there at two." She hung up without any of the anticipation she had three minutes ago. Was she was doing the right thing?

At two o'clock the next Saturday she paced the rotunda scanning the crowd for a stranger. She looked as good as she could with a new green peasant blouse topping freshly pressed jeans. She checked the time. Two twenty five and he still wasn't there. She plopped down on an empty bench. Was anything worse than getting stood up on a blind date? He had ten more minutes and she was gone.

"Allie!"

She spun her head toward the booming voice. Found it attached to a long-legged man in jeans and a red team T-shirt jogging her way.

"Oh my God, Allie. Sorry I'm so late." He halted beside her, waves of thick dark hair falling over his forehead. He shoved it back and uncovered brilliant blue eyes. High cheekbones, strong chin, and grooves framing his mouth that said he smiled often . . . *Good job, Reese!* "My ex was supposed to pick up our son by noon and didn't arrive until one thirty. Then Corey couldn't find his homework. To top it off I was in a rush to leave and forgot to bring your number. I couldn't even call to let you know what was going on."

Okay, so everyone's day falls apart from time to time. "Don't worry about it. Let's just enjoy the afternoon."

She followed Gary up the escalator, located their seats on the upper deck. The stadium room was open today, the warm afternoon sun angling in and blinding her, but from this height she couldn't see more than the vague shapes of the players on the field anyway. The stadium was far from full. *An ex-wife must take a good portion of a principal's salary if these are the best seats he could come up with.*

She settled into her seat beside him. He seemed like a nice guy. She should be kind and enjoy what she could see of the game. But added to his request to meet at the stadium, and then his tardiness, prickles of apprehension ran down the back of her neck and had Gary teetering on the edge of strike two.

"Yo!" Gary yelled to a beer vendor, stuck up three fingers. The paper cup sloshed suds as he passed it to her. He fisted the other two, drained them, roared out a belch. Nice guy, her ass! By the fourth inning he'd downed two more beers and his comments to the surrounding fans were obnoxious. So much for fun. Her face seared, and not from the blistering sun.

Six cups were stacked beneath his seat by the end of the sixth inning, each as empty as his threats to the opposing team, and she was done. Strike three, she was out of there. She popped to her feet, the folding seat clattering shut without her weight.

"Hey, Gary, thanks for a great time, but I'm heading home."

Her sarcasm sailed right over his head.

"Why you leavin' toots? Game's not over."

His game was lost long ago. She forced a smile. "It's getting late. I want to get a head start on traffic." She bent to pick up her purse, but by the time she stood Gary was already distracted by the action on the field. And here she was, worried about making a scene in the bleachers. She made her way downstairs, outside, into her car. Which she wouldn't have if Gary wasn't an ass.

What a waste of a perfectly good Saturday afternoon. Which was really too bad, because she'd done a lot of thinking in the past week. It might be nice to have someone to spend time with, after all. She didn't want a long-term relationship, no. But as she hit the drive-thru for a lonely dinner, she decided a little company would have been far more pleasant.

Allie tossed her sacked dinner and purse onto the kitchen counter. At the blinking telephone message light she pushed play, listened while she pulled a glass tumbler from the cupboard, filled it with juice.

"Allie, I'm dying here. Call the minute you get home. With details!"

That made her laugh. Reese was a lot of things—subtle was not one. She waited for the next message to boot.

"Hey, there. Haven't talked to you since the kid left, wanted to make sure you're okay." There was a short pause, then, "Bye, babe." Her lips spread in a smile. *Jake.*

The unwrapped burrito sat in her hand while she punched in Reese's number, waited until the fifth ring for her to answer.

She took a bite of her burrito. "I was about to hang up." The glob of machaca and tortilla in her mouth was hard to talk around.

"I was watering the garden and had to run to catch the phone."

Allie swallowed what she was chewing. "So, how are the tomatoes?"

"Screw the tomatoes, Allie. Spill the goods!"

"Anybody ever tell you you're nosy?"

"Sure. All the time. Now tell me."

She could just picture Reese's smartass grin. "I think I know why Mrs. Principal chose to get un-married." Allie lifted her glass, sipped apple juice. and detailed the events of the day.

"Oh, the dirty rotten creep. I thought he . . . Jeez, he's just a creep."

Reese's seething buzz snapped through the phone line. Allie shook her head and smiled. "Down, Fido. We'll simply list this in the 'worst date ever' column and move on. Everyone needs a funny story to tell."

"Maybe, but this kind of funny just stinks."

"Agreed." Reese may not have children of her own, but her maternal wrath was firmly in place. Warmed, Allie stretched to her feet, sacked up her wrappers and walked it to the trash. "So tell me something funny from school. With all that prepubescent angst swimming the hallways of Jefferson Middle School, something's bound to blow."

"Yes, but will it be their hormones or my temper?" Reese laughed out loud. "You have a classroom full of five-year-olds. I'll bet they keep you in stitches."

Allie leaned against the counter, stretched out her legs. God, she needed to unload. "Usually. Not this year. This year I have a boy whose parents are in the middle of a nasty divorce. They're using their kid for the rope in this epic battle of tug of war and it's turning him into a real . . ." She hesitated. There had to be a more politically correct word, right?

"I believe the word you're looking for is *brat*."

Allie blew out a relieved chuckle. Bless Reese again for letting her whine, but not letting her wallow. "Did I sound like I was playing the pity card?"

"You were, and you win. Let me tell you about this seventh-grader who locked himself in the john."

Later that evening, Allie grabbed a dust rag, and room by room dragged the cloth over the low wood tables, the bookshelves against the wall. Her mood was lightened. She had Reese to thank for that. Even the housework with its tangy aroma of lemon oil was enjoyable.

When she came to the living room, she paused as she ran the rag over photographs of Trey when he was a baby, and then a young boy, and then a young man. She and Ben were in many of the photos. Why hadn't she removed those yet? Now was as good a time as any.

She wandered the room, moving from surface to surface, collecting several frames, a lifetime of firsts. Ben with his fists punching the air as a very young Trey tumbled across the goal line holding a football. High-fiving Trey as the youngster hopped on home plate, celebrating his first home run. The ceremonial first shovel of dirt on their first project, Ben standing alongside Jake, both grinning, both still so young. Trey's high school graduation, standing beside Jax. She and Ben holding Trey, grinning proudly on the day of his birth. The last two photos she returned. They would stay. The others she gathered in her arms and carried into Trey's empty room, where she shoved them between trophies and souvenirs, on wall shelves and the wooden dresser. Now these mementos were Trey's.

She folded the last towel from the dryer and placed it atop the pile, gathering the stack in her arms. She was almost to her bathroom when the telephone rang. Setting the load on her bed she checked the caller ID, prepared to ignore the call if it was Gary.

Jake. Her face lit up.

She punched the answer button.

"Hi, Jake." She sank into her armchair and drew up her knees, wrapping her arms around her shins. "What's up?"

"Sitting in the pool, cold beer close by. Thinking about you and the kid. It's been a couple of weeks since you dropped him off at school. Is he all settled in?"

"I got him into his dorm room, and Jax was already there. Classes started on Tuesday, but I haven't heard from him yet. Maybe I'll call soon. I don't want to be that helicopter mom."

"Helicopter?"

"You know. Hovering."

He laughed softly. "Clever. You sound like you're doing okay. No mommy meltdowns?"

They'd had these conversations for years. She was comfortable telling him what was on her mind. "Actually, I'm fine. It's pretty quiet around here though. Times like this make me wish more than ever we had more children."

"I always wondered about that, but I figured it was the choice you and Ben made. I remember, though, you always talked about having *kids*. Plural."

Water sloshed around Jake's words. Wouldn't it be nice to be there, too, relaxing in the pool? "No, it was Ben." She could finally say this without a sad sigh attached. "After Trey came there was always some reason why we should wait, why it wasn't a good time." She paused. "He was afraid we didn't have enough."

"Enough?"

She wiggled deeper into the chair. "Hmm. Time. Money. She hesitated. "Love. It frightened him. I used to beg him. Actually, we fought about it. But in the end, it's just Trey." She hesitated again. "There's something . . . oh, never mind."

"Regret is hard to live with."

His voice was mellow in her ear, as if he'd given this thought. Her chest grew tight with the regret she tried to forget. Regret for herself. For Jake, who'd never held his own newborn child. Even for Ben, who probably didn't deserve it.

"And I think we're a little past *never mind*."

Yeah, they probably were. She stumbled ahead. "Do you ever feel that there's something missing in your life? That something is calling out from your soul? Like something important is unfinished, incomplete?"

"Who doesn't? It probably sounds foolish after all these years, or corny at the very least, but I wish I'd found someone to . . . to have that big romance with. I would have liked to share my life. Maybe have children. It's too late now."

Allie marveled that he could sound merely retrospective. She was pretty sure her plea sounded desperate. "It's not too late. You're a great guy. You'll find someone and have everything you ever wanted." She sat in the dark shadows of her bedroom, curled into her chair, with only the fixture from the hallway to dimly light the room. He did deserve it all. "What ever happened with Michelle? I thought you two would end up married."

"It was good for a while, but she worked so much. Then it sort of . . . fell apart."

"She travelled a lot. Was there someone else?"

Jake paused a beat before he answered. "I guess you could say that."

Oh, no. "I'm sorry. You know, you're always there when I need someone. You can talk to me, too. If you need somebody."

"I know, babe. I appreciate that." Jake's slider scraped open and after a moment the refrigerator slammed shut, a can hissed open. "But, she's in the past and the mood is way too serious." His voice brightened. "So until Ms. Perfectly Wonderful shows up, we'll just talk about funner stuff."

She laughed. "Let me tell you about today's experience with funner stuff."

"Yeah, what did you do, ride the elephant at the zoo?"

Hey Allie, the zoo called. No, not going there tonight. "No, actually, I had a date."

Jake's voice sputtered like something he drank went down wrong. "A date?"

"Yeah, if you can call it that. We went to a baseball game. Sounds like it should be fun, right?" She steamed ahead, her earlier irritation poking through. "First of all, I had to meet him there. Then we had nosebleed seats. And to top it all off, the entire game he was a wasted, obnoxious ass."

"Charming."

"Yeah, a real prince. Thankfully, I was over it by the time I got home. Poor Reese got an earful, though. She's the one who set us up."

"Poor Reese is right." Jake's laughter rumbled in her ear. "So now we're both on the prowl?"

So not funny. "I don't want to think of myself that way. I won't. I just want *something*. Someone who's interested, who's interesting, who makes me laugh."

"The perfect man."

". . . ish, Jake. Nobody's perfect." Her tone was light and cheerful, despite her words. "I'm tired of being lonely. "This is weird for me, like my life is on do-overs."

"What if we do something next weekend? Then we won't be lonely together. Do you already have plans?"

"With Maddie for Saturday, and I usually bring work home. Why don't you come for dinner Sunday? Bring a movie." And the loneliness was already sliding away

Chapter Eighteen

Jake arrived the next Sunday at four o'clock with a bottle of wine and a DVD. Allie took a peek at the cover as he walked through the door and burst out laughing. "Oh, Jake, that is such a *guy* movie!" She continued to chuckle as she stepped over to the stereo to turn the music off. "You are such a guy."

"You say that like it's a bad thing." He couldn't control the huff in his voice so he strolled to the entertainment center and inserted the movie disc in the player. Allie set the wine on the kitchen counter and got out the opener. His gaze shuttled between Allie and the empty box in his hand. "I'll have you know this is a great action movie. A big heist, a hot girl, cool cars. What more can you ask for?"

His only response was a laugh from the kitchen.

The smell of clam sauce wafted into the living room, mixed with the clink of glass as Allie lifted a lid. He wandered in, lifted his wine, then stood beside her, peering into the pot. "*Mmm.* Something smells delicious." And standing so close to her, dinner wasn't the only thing, but he didn't dare say that.

"It's spaghetti night." With a final rap of the spoon on the lip of the pan, Allie led the way back to the living room.

By force of will he kept one eye on the movie as his mind wandered. What would it be like to sit like this with Allie every night? For her to cuddle close to him? To smell her cooking and know she made the meal for him. For them. To talk about their day. To turn out the lights and walk down the hallway together when the day was done.

Oh hell, what brought on these thoughts tonight? Then it hit him, and blades twisted in his gut. Allie was dating. She was ready to share her life with somebody new. How could he stand it? Could he do nothing while she went out with other men? But what could he do? She was Ben's wife. He was supposed to take care of her. He promised.

The final credits rolled. "All right, I liked the movie." She rolled her head against the back of the sofa. "And the boy gets the girl, always a satisfying ending." When he didn't return her grin, she let hers fall, inched closer. "Are you all right?" Her hand landed on his forearm. He was pale, and he looked ill.

His smiled seemed bright enough though.

"Fine, didn't get much sleep last night. So the movie wasn't a bust? Do you trust me now?"

"Oh, I trust you. It's the devil inside you I don't trust." She stood, tossed a saucy grin over her shoulder. And laughed.

"Ha! My favorite line. Next time you pick the movie. Let's see what you come up with."

"I accept your challenge." With Jake trailing her, his hands occupied with empty stemware, she hit the kitchen still wearing a smile—dropped pasta into a boiling pot of water, pulled out romaine for a salad.

"So, hear from Trey yet?"

While he uncorked the wine with a *pop*, refilled glasses, his eyes soft with caring, she mixed croutons and dressing into lettuce, gave it a toss. Her voice softened with a smile. "Yes, he finally called. Everything's good." Parmesan shavings fell from her grater and fluttered like snow over dressed greens. "Said he'll come home in a couple of weeks." She gave the sauce a stir, lifted the spoon so he could taste.

"God, that's good. And now you're not worried."

She lifted her eyes, met his gaze. "I'm always worried." And blew it off with a shrug. "It's a mom thing. He said to tell you hi." She pushed the salad bowl into his empty hands, nudged her chin toward the table.

"I have a job starting soon up in Cottonwood." He walked the bowl across the room as directed. "Maybe I'll make a quick detour

"He'd like that." And suddenly she laughed again. "He's come a long way in the past few years. Remember when he learned to drive? I was ready to put him up for adoption."

He shouldered her away from the stove, hefted the heavy pasta pot, drained it into a colander in the sink. "Aw, he's a good kid. You did a helluva job with him."

She dished a serving of noodles, blanketed it with clam sauce, handed it to him. Shooed him to the table. Her voice turned thoughtful as the face of a light-haired girl came to her. "Just lucky, I think."

Salad tongs hovered in midair as his eyes searched hers out across the room. "Lucky? Why's that?"

She took the seat across from him, scooped noodles and sauce onto her plate. And couldn't get rid of the ache in her heart. "Reese and I were in Starbucks the other day, and in comes this mom with a girl who was deaf. She was young, the girl, like one of Reese's students." She twirled pasta, took a bite. Jake was nearly done already. "For some reason it really hit me, made me stop and be grateful for everything we have—our health."

Jake leaned an elbow on the table; his forearm spanned the table, his palm so near. "Surely you see special needs children at school. Why would this one bother you so much?"

It was natural to reach a few inches, rest her palm on his, so she did. "She looked so familiar. So did the mom."

"Did you know them?"

With their fingers entwined, familiar and comforting, she shook her head. "I don't think so. I forget the mom's name, but it was like maybe I knew her once upon a time. But the girl—I thought maybe I should recognize her."

The squeeze of her hand gave her comfort. She shook off the mood, pushed her empty plate away, changed the subject. "I want ice cream. How about it?"

He stood to help her clear the table. "I'm full, but I'll share a banana split with you."

"You're on."

Ten minutes later they were huddled over an oblong dish of tasty soft serve. Jake grinned at her, licked a dribble from his bottom lip. "Same time next Sunday? I'm curious to see what movie you pick."

Allie scooped up ice cream, held it aloft. "Sure. I'll make sure it's a good one!"

"I have no doubt."

Eyes closed and with a slow moan of orgasmic delight, Allie sucked in the spoonful of ice cream covered with pineapple sauce.

Jesus. His pulse leapt. He couldn't watch. He popped a bite of chocolate covered banana into his mouth and turned away, scanning the crowd.

Seated two tables over a boy about Trey's age faced him. A dark haired woman and a young blonde girl shared his table, their backs to him. His mom and sister? Most likely. The young man glanced over and caught him watching. Then did the oddest thing.

Smiling and waving, the boy yelled to him, "Hi, Coach!"

"Who the heck?" He shrugged when Allie lifted an eyebrow, excused himself, strolled to their table, and did exactly what he usually did when he found himself in this predicament.

He faked it.

"Hey man, haven't seen you in a while." He bumped the boy's fist with his own.

"Here visiting for the weekend." The boy motioned to the two across from him, his hands a wave of gestures. "It's my mom's birthday." The young girl smiled up at Jake, mutely waved hello. He introduced her with a smile. "This is my sister, Merrie, wearing her chocolate sundae." Jake stepped closer, his hand stretching out to the woman, prepared to shake.

"Happy . . . ." The greeting hung in the air unfinished. His heart kicked even as he went rigid. His hand drifted to his side. Maggie Jensen. Holy shit, it was Maggie Jensen. His eyes darted back to her son. Jimmy. He remembered him now, soccer. His gaze sought the girl, whose features suddenly answered so many questions. Dark hair, dark eyes—like her mom. But the nose, and the smile, those he recognized. *Fuck.*

His head spun to look over his shoulder. Was Allie watching? No, talking on her cell. Good. He turned back; his voice went taut. "Maggie."

She gave nothing away. "Jake. Good to see you again."

He let his eyes slide from mother to daughter and back again, sitting beside each other on a concrete bench. "I'll bet."

For years he'd wondered, and here it was. The proof sat right before him—with fudge sauce smeared across her face. And there the mother sat. Pretending there was nothing *significant* about their meeting while he fumed.

He drug his eyes away, lifted his hand again to shake with the boy. "Jimmy, it was good to see you again. Have a safe trip home." He turned back to Maggie, his words edged in ice. "We need to talk." Let her worry how to explain that to her son.

"Yes, I imagine we do." But the cold-hearted, husband-stealing bitch was unmoved.

Jake reached into his billfold, pulled out a business card. Held it out to her. "Call me tomorrow. We'll meet."

She took the card and nodded.

Pivoting on his heel, he marched back to Allie, grabbed her arm. "Let's go." And hustled her toward his truck.

She dug her feet in when he opened her door. "Jake, what—?"

He swiveled to look behind them, to a table where half-eaten ice cream was left to melt. And a familiar woman fled across the parking lot with two kids in tow, gesturing rapidly.

He let his eyes slide closed. Didn't open them again until he'd taken a deep breath. But still had to grit his teeth to speak. "Get in. Please."

Dear God, how did he tell her?

Allie studied Jake as he sped through town—the slash of his mouth, eyes black as coal, glittering with temper. What could that woman have said to set him off? Her own stomach knotted. By the time he pulled into her driveway she could ladle the tension with a spoon.

"Enough, Jake. Who were those people back there?"

He sat staring straight ahead, eyes glued to a spot on her garage door, both hands clutching the steering wheel.

"The boy was Jimmy Jensen; he played soccer with Trey for a few years when they were little."

Her eyebrows pulled together. "I remember Jimmy; nice kid. He pissed you off?"

"The woman, Allie? Did you recognize her?"

The woman? "No. Wait. Was she the woman from Starbucks? She was Jimmy's mom?" Her stomach unwound; a jittery laugh escaped. Jake was still attached to the wheel. "No wonder I recognized her. She probably thinks I'm terribly rude for not saying hello." She twisted to look back the way they came. Stupid, Allie. She can't see you here. "And now she has a little girl. She must have remarried. I remember she was divorced, but that was a long time ago."

"I don't know if she's remarried or not. But Allie, the little girl—"

She studied Jake, her eyes wide in the darkened truck. And finally prompted him, "Yes, the little girl *what?*"

Finally, his features softened and he turned to her. He took a deep breath and met her steady gaze. "The girl is Ben's daughter."

Her eyes shot wide, then lowered, along with her brow. But where was the blinding rage? The twisted knife of guilt and humiliation? All she had was ... nothing. Wait, maybe a vague interest.

Long ago she'd resigned herself—her relationship with her husband wasn't what she believed it was. She spent years heeding the advice of a professional. Meeting after meeting emptying her soul to a group of strangers, sharing her humiliation. Reliving her life, one still frame at a time strobing through the dark corners of her mind whenever she closed her eyes, and often when they were open.

She worked tirelessly, for Trey's sake as well as her own, to put her anger behind her until all she allowed herself to feel was regret. Regret for what could have been, what should have been. For herself and for their son. Regret that what she offered was not enough for her husband, and that he was not willing to communicate this to her. So she put her memories aside and lived in the present, moving forward.

That her memories emerged from time to time to haunt her was natural. After all, she lived with his mirror image. And she'd loved her husband for fifteen years. But through the passage of time she finally understood that she could not change Ben. She could not change the past. But she could—and did—change her life. She put the past behind her and found peace. She put behind her the feelings of anguish at his duplicity, and her stinging anger. She no longer needed them.

But she wouldn't mind a few answers.

The play of emotions over her face was arresting. *Jesus.* The one person he hated to hurt more than anyone. She stared straight ahead, her face a mask while he waited for the betrayal, the pain, the anger. But her face remained impassive. And then her features softened, loosened even as his whole body tensed and his pulse roared. He could handle it, whatever she threw his way.

Her lips tilted in a slight smile. "I'd like a chance to talk to her."

His stomach dropped, bounced. Jesus. Here he was, expecting hysterics and she was only curious? Never in his lifetime would he understand the workings of the female mind. "I told her I want to talk. She's supposed to call tomorrow."

"Good. Are you okay?"

She was worried about *him*? Remarkable. "I'm fine. But I'd like a few answers."

Allie bent a knee onto the leather seat, turned to him, a wry smile on her face. "Yes. I have questions of my own."

"Are you okay?"

She nodded. "I am." She turned forward again, stared through the windshield. "I didn't realize how okay I am until now. I guess it simply took time."

He understood. She would need that. Time to think, time to feel, time to get over feelings.

"But I'm okay." She turned another smile his way, this one embarrassed. "I want to know what I did wrong."

"Christ, Allie. You didn't do anything wrong."

She scowled, quirked her lips. Lifted a shoulder. "Call it pride. Or vanity. It won't change anything, but maybe I'm curious."

He reached out, rested his palm on her nape and pulled her forward. Let his lips brush across her forehead. It would be so easy to tilt her chin, shift his attentions lower, but it was a really bad idea. Instead, he took a deep breath of her flowery scent, and released her neck even as he released his breath, and moved back to safety. "You amaze me."

"I'm not amazing. I loved him. For a long time I loved him. And I have to believe he loved us too, the best way he could." She reached across the interior of the truck and laid her palm on his forearm, let it feather down to his thigh. "He's my son's father. Somewhere there has to be a way to live with what he left us.

His leg warmed where her hand lay, before she pulled it back, heaved open her door. Hot air flooded the interior, overriding the coolness of the air conditioning. She clambered down, out, and turned back, peering at him seated across the cab. "Well, it's been quite an evening."

"Yes it has."

"Call me. When she calls and you set something up, call me. I'd like to meet the girl. Meredith."

"Of course."

She stood, studying him. Raised one hand with a smile. "Well, 'night, Jake."

He lifted a hand in return. "G'night, babe."

He took his time driving home, he had a lot to think about. Allie wasn't the only person betrayed. He was deceived by the friend he knew longer than his earliest memories. The friend who was not inclined to share a facet of his life that was so crucial, so vital. But over the years he'd dealt with Ben's betrayal in his own fashion. Because he loved Ben. And Ben loved him. The best way he could.

He woke with a waiting-for-the-next-shoe-to-drop sort of feeling in his gut. He went through the motions at work, his cell phone never more than a few inches from his hand, important calls hurried through, all others ignored. But by five o'clock he hadn't yet spoken with her and his nerves were frayed.

Usually hours behind the rest of the office staff, he set the alarm and locked the office door one step behind Kim. Maneuvering his way through rush hour traffic he held his cell phone in one hand, calculating the easiest way to reach Maggie. Was she listed in the book? Maybe he could Google her. Or he could hire a private detective. They would be listed in the book; maybe he should start there. Did he know any investigators? The phone rang in his hand. He caught the Blackberry an instant before it sailed to the floorboards. "It's about time you called."

"I'm calling now. You said you wanted to talk."

"We do. And we want to meet the girl." He sounded like a heavy-handed thug and he really didn't care.

Maggie's reply was soft and tentative. "I don't want her hurt. She doesn't know the whole story."

For the little girl's sake, he let up. A bit. "We have no intention of hurting anyone. But we'd like to meet her. And ask a few questions."

His breath hung in his chest, until she finally answered.

"All right. Can you come by the house around seven?"

"Just give me the address. We'll be there."

Mondays alone were bad enough, but Monday with a cloud hanging over her head took serious fortitude. It wasn't a gray cloud exactly, but that was little consolation. She had a stomach full of what was undoubtedly unresolved anxiety, and therefore it was deemed a cloud nonetheless. She'd dragged herself through the day, escaped to the relative safety of rush hour traffic the moment the classroom was clear. Now that she was home, she needed something to do to keep from losing her mind until Jake called.

Plugging her iPod into the portable speaker and turning the volume up loud, she gave the oven a thorough scrubbing, then moved on to the refrigerator. While she reloaded the cold food, her smartphone danced its way across the counter. Reaching for it, she turned down the music as she pressed the device to her ear.

"She called."

The tightness in his voice made her laugh. "Hi Jake."

His breath whooshed in her ear. "Sorry. I've been on edge all day."

"Tell me about it." She replaced the milk carton and loaf of bread onto the top shelf of her sparkling refrigerator and closed the door. "But she'll meet us?"

"Tonight at seven. Can you make it?"

"Even if I have to reschedule the apocalypse."

It was his turn to chuckle. "Your house is between mine and hers; can I pick you up on the way?"

"That would be nice, thanks."

"Good. I'll see you in an hour."

"See you then. And Jake?"

"Yeah?"

"Relax."

He let out another whoosh and chuckled again. "Seeya, Allie."

"Seeya, Jake."

She fit the sliding racks back into the oven and turned for her bathroom. It was amazing how a quick shower, a little make-up could make her feel better. She stood in her walk-in closet, inspecting her wardrobe. What to wear to meet the lover? She chuffed out a laugh. What a bizarre question.

She fingered her options. Her navy linen suit? It was generally reserved for funerals and such, but hey, this almost qualified. A dress? She snorted. Who was she trying to impress? Jeans? Well, she wanted to impress a little. Muttering an impatient oath, she yanked the slacks and pullover she wore to school that day from their hangers and put them back on. With her feet wedged into three inch heels she was ready to meet Maggie Jensen head on.

The bell rang. Allie retrieved her purse and ran to answer it. She threw open the door and there stood Jake, in brand new black Wranglers, tugging on the collar of a starched button-down. His timeworn Red Wings even had a good cleaning.

She slipped through the open doorway, couldn't resist a tease. "Poor Jake. You couldn't look more uncomfortable if you were wearing a three-piece suit."

More than uncomfortable, now he also looked embarrassed. "Don't laugh. I had it on for about a minute." He held her door, and then her hand as she climbed into the cab of his truck.

"I won't laugh at you if you promise not to laugh at me."

His eyes touched on her as he hoisted into his seat. "But you look great."

"Maybe, but I considered wearing my blue suit."

He did snicker. "Your funeral suit?"

"Yeah, that one."

"Oh shit, we are a pair." He grinned in her direction.

She grinned back. God, she was glad he was with her. "Aren't we though."

Weaving his way through traffic that was finally lighter, Jake followed Maggie's directions, pulling into the driveway of a nondescript stucco ranch within fifteen minutes.

She lifted her eyes, studied the windowless front entry—the six-paneled door, the roller skates propped against the wall beside it. A shallow breath escaped through parted lips. "I'm nervous."

He took her hand, laced their fingers. "Me too. Shall we get this over with?"

Chapter Nineteen

Maggie opened the door to them. Barefoot, dressed in worn jeans and a sleeveless blouse, she stepped back and waved them in. Allie refused to feel overdressed.

Jake cleared his throat. "Thank you, Maggie, for seeing us."

She gestured them into the living room. "It needs to be done."

He crossed the oatmeal berber and took a seat on the patterned sofa.

Allie lowered herself beside him. "Yes, well . . ." Her idle glance around Maggie's home found it comfortable with a pair of russet wingbacks facing them and shelves full of books lining the far wall. The kitchen could just be seen from where she sat. Her hands wanted to flutter; she locked them together on her lap. "Where's your daughter?"

"Next door, playing with a friend. She'll be home soon."

Allie nodded, rubbed her thumbs together, met Maggie's gaze. "We don't want to cause trouble for you. We simply want to understand."

Maggie perched on a chair across the coffee table. Her voice was quiet, calm, which was almost admirable.

"There's not much to understand, really. I ran into Ben late one night. He was coming out of the supermarket with a twelve pack. He said he was on his way home, but my battery was dead in the parking lot. He gave me a ride home." Maggie stood and moved behind her chair, her fingers kneading the upholstery.

"I guess you two were fighting. He seemed very upset. I asked him if he wanted to come in and talk." She let her fingers loosen. Lifted her chin a notch. "Jimmy was living with my ex by then. We polished off the beer and moved on to a bottle of scotch I had in the cupboard. One of many I had in the cupboard back then." Maggie's voice changed, became less confrontational, almost apologetic. "Anyway, one thing led to another and . . . you can imagine the rest."

Woodenly, Allie dropped down beside Jake. "You make the whole . . . situation . . . seem so straightforward."

"Yes. Back then my entire life was one whole . . . situation."

Maggie resumed her seat, let a sardonic smile twist her lips. "It was a mistake from the beginning. We both knew that." She barked a scoffing laugh. "Jesus. You should have seen the expression on his face when we were done. If ever there was a man who regretted his actions, it was Ben that night. He couldn't get out of here fast enough."

Allie lowered her eyes. Hated that she just sat through that monologue and still needed to know. "And yet he continued to see you."

"No. I didn't see him again. I hadn't even planned to tell him about the baby. I mean, I had no illusions about breaking up your marriage; you guys were happy." She waved her hand for emphasis. "He was just screwed up one night and I was drunk enough to not care. We ran into him a couple of years later, though. He guessed she was his."

Allie had only seen the child's face once, but it was apparent why she seemed familiar. "She looks a lot like him."

"Yes, she does."

"And you never saw him again?" This seemed unlikely.

"He came to see Merrie. I'm an accountant. I have clients out of town and eventually he offered to stay with her. I don't have family in town. He'd stay for a couple of days, if I needed to be gone for work." Maggie's eyes bored into hers as she spoke insistently. "You have to understand, he didn't come to see me. He came to see Merrie. He hated coming here, hated lying to you." And then, sadly. "I think he almost hated Merrie. But he felt . . . obligated. She was his daughter."

Maggie's story had a ring of truth, but for years she held one scenario firmly set in her mind. It was hard to dispel. "How does that explain poker nights?"

"Poker nights?"

"Ben was gone. Every month, first Tuesday."

Maggie tilted her head to the side. "Poker night."

Allie hesitated, held her breath. "He said that's where he was. You can see how I may have my doubts now."

"He wasn't here. My guess is he was playing poker."

"Oh shit." Jake leapt from his seat, prowled the room.

"Yeah." The quaking in her knees was unnerving. She let her eyes follow him as he stalked between the sofa and the bookcase, then back again. Was he thinking the same thing she was? Years ago she confronted him about these nights. Why was he not a part of this ritual? He simply explained that he spent every day with Ben, and while he may be his best friend, they needed time apart. Jake didn't know if he played cards every month or not. Without a clear answer, Allie let it drop.

Troubled as he was, Jake faced Maggie, arms folded across his chest, his square jaw set. "Did he come here the night he got in his accident?"

Maggie's long breath sounded across the room. She lowered her eyes before responding. "Yes." Her nod was slow, diffident. "He hadn't been here for a few months, and then he showed up out of the blue. He never did that before. I always called him to let him know when I needed to be gone."

"Why did he come here that night?"

Maggie turned to look at Allie. "You just returned from your trip north. He came to tell me he was done, he couldn't do it anymore. He couldn't stand lying to you. He planned to come clean, tell you about Merrie. And he planned to stop seeing her."

Jake dropped back onto the sofa, reached for her hand. His palm was sweaty.

"Honestly, he was more upset than I was. You see, Merrie doesn't know he was her father. To her, he was just Ben."

Oh, Lord. Was anything she knew real? "Did he give you money for her?"

Maggie shook her head. "The night he came to say good-bye—the night of his accident—he offered again but I told him no. I'm a partner in my firm, I have good benefits. There was a life insurance policy, which was a surprise to me. It's in the bank. Hopefully, she'll use it for college."

Yes, hopefully she would. "If you don't mind my asking, how does she handle her condition?"

Maggie lifted one shoulder. "She's bright, well adjusted. We deal with the rest day by day."

The door flew open and Merrie, dressed in hot pink from the ribbon in her hair to the laces in her grimy white tennies, barreled in, hands flying.

Maggie turned in her seat at the sound of the door crashing against the wall, smiling and holding her arm out to her daughter. She signed as she spoke. "Come in here, honey; there are people I'd like you to meet."

Breathless, the girl spun into the room, a bright smile on her face. She stared at Jake for a moment before lifting her hands to gesture.

"I remember you. You were at DQ." Maggie's hands were smoothly confident as she translated.

He smiled and nodded to her. "Yes I was. I used to know your brother. And I wanted to say hello to your mom."

Merrie stood with her mother, who used her hand motions to pass on Jake's words then introduce the visitors. "Honey, this is Jake and his friend Allie. They were friends of Ben's.

Merrie nodded to her mom with a happy grin. "I remember Ben. He moved away." Maggie put Merrie's signs into words. "He used to play with me when I was little. He was a nice man."

Merrie then turned back to Jake, a study in seriousness. "My brother told me you used to be his soccer coach when he was younger than I am. I want to play soccer, too."

Allie melted. Just grinned at the girl with so much energy, so much enthusiasm. She found Jake's eyes. He was grinning, too.

"You need to talk to your mom about that."

Maggie's hands lifted, moved. "Yes, I did already." Merrie screwed up her face. "She thinks I need piano lessons instead."

The girl was adorable. Jake's laugh rumbled against her side. "Well, they say mommies know best."

Merrie pouted, then grinned. "If I have to play music, I want to play the drums. I can feel the drums better, anyway. I could play The Little Drummer Boy on my birthday."

"Your birthday?"

The girl bubbled with energy as her hands flew. Again, Maggie's voice told the story. "Uh huh. My birthday's on Christmas. That's why they call me Merrie. Get it? It's really short for Meredith, but I like Merrie—it sounds happy."

Maggie smiled indulgently and reached for the girl, wrapping her in her arms. "Honey, time for your bath. Say good-bye please."

Merrie skipped across the room to the pair on the couch, gifted Jake with a two-armed squeeze around his neck, then Allie. Standing back, using her best company manners, with a grin that crooked up a little more on one side than the other, she signed, "It was very nice to meet you. 'Bye."

And she was gone.

Jake stood. Allie followed him up, her eyes following the path the girl took. "Maggie, if you don't mind, at some point, I'd like to spend more time with her."

Maggie, still seated, was more curious than suspicious. "Why?"

The woman was as much a casualty as any of them. Why did Allie feel the need to apologize? Maggie was a person she knew long ago, whose life was dramatically affected by a twisted series of events. But it was her nature to focus on the positive. She chose to glean any good that may be wrung from this odd situation. And to her, that meant Trey had a sister.

"She has a brother she's never met."

Maggie's head bowed. Tears silently drenched her eyes before she dashed them away.

Allie reached out a hand, let it touch Maggie's shoulder before returning it to her side. "My son has a sister. I'd like him to know her."

Maggie nodded, rubbed her eyes again, led Jake and Allie to the door. "Please don't feel that you must have a relationship with Merrie. But if you want to see her, let me know. We can set something up." Maggie passed her a business card, her contact information neatly listed.

Allie took the card, glanced at it. Had she ever received one before, years ago? "I'll be in touch. Hopefully soon, but I need to discuss this with Trey before Merrie simply appears in his life. Needless to say, this will come as somewhat of a surprise."

Maggie's expression was impassive. "I agree, that will be best for both of them."

Allie leaned in to hug this woman she had a bizarre link to. There was no bitterness, no resentment. They were merely two mothers, each protecting their child.

Jake sat beside Allie in the dark confines of his truck. "I feel like the earth just tilted."

Allie nodded, then shook her head. "I can't even . . . oh God, Jake. Poor Ben."

"Yeah, all these years I've been mad at him. Thinking he was such an ass, stepping out on you. I mean, what was he thinking? I never even considered that maybe he suffered too."

He started the ignition and backed out of Maggie's driveway. Cars passed them, their headlights shining as he merged into freeway traffic. He needed this quiet time for contemplation. Pairing old beliefs with new knowledge, reconciling the two.

"I've spent a lot of time and energy learning to live with what I thought Ben did to me. It's incredible, but even after all the pain he caused, I can still hurt for him. I wish he told me. We could have worked it out."

No, Ben never would have done that. Jake checked the rear-view, moved out from behind a semi. "He would have protected you from anything, Allie. And he did try to tell me. It was the next day, after his . . . time . . . with Maggie. I stormed at him, called him everything hateful I could think of." How many times over the years had he given that day a different ending? Full of guilt, he slammed a fist into the steering wheel. "Damn it, Allie, we were friends. I worked with him every day. Why couldn't he talk to *me* about the child?"

With her palm soft and quiet on his arm the acid churning in his gut eased. His eyes flew to hers; the anguish there was not betrayed by her soothing voice.

"He should have let us help him. You knew Ben. You knew him with Trey. Can you imagine him having a child and having to sneak to spend time with her, hating that he had to? We planned elaborate parties for Trey, clowns and magicians and trips to the zoo, but he couldn't even see Merrie on her birthday."

"But he planned to give her up for you. For you and Trey."

She pulled her arm away; he immediately felt the loss. "I don't know if that makes me feel better or worse."

He drove, lost in his memories. Exited and turned onto her street, and then into her driveway. He turned the key in the ignition and twisted to face Allie, shoveled his hair off his forehead. "He loved you a lot."

She smiled, fingered a lock that tumbled back. "He loved us both."

He captured her hand, laced their fingers across the console. "I'm glad we know what really happened."

"So am I." She shared a rueful smile. "I could live with what we imagined. But this is easier."

"You okay?"

"I am." It was true, she truly was. Not back to the place she started, but forward to a better place. The truth tore down the last of her barriers. She was already at peace in her new life. And now she was at peace with Ben. "I really am. How about you?"

"He was my best friend, even if his moral compass did point directly south, to his dick." His grin quirked up one side of his mouth. "He was an ass."

A laugh bubbled in her throat and escaped. "Yeah, he kind of was."

Jake leaned forward to kiss her cheek. He climbed out of the truck and ran around to pull her door open, then helped her down until she stood on the driveway beside him. "How will Trey handle this?"

Her heart lurched. "I have no idea. It may be difficult."

"I'm here."

She lifted her eyes to Jake, who was there for her so many times, in so many different ways.

"I'm counting on it."

Allie walked toward the door, then stopped and turned back, grinning.

"I still owe you a movie. Do you still want to come over on Sunday?"

"You up for it?"

"Sure. I've got one all picked out—it's perfect."

Chapter Twenty

She met him at the door in a skimpy little tee and yoga pants. No way would he notice what they did to her ass.

"Streisand and Redford, it's perfect. What could be more romantic than star-crossed lovers as political opposites in a controversial time in American history?"

The damn girl was nearly licking her chops in anticipation. "I'd rather have a kidney removed."

"It's tragic. I cry every time."

She had that dreamy look in her eyes. The look usually associated with kittens and brand new babies. The look that played with his good intentions. "By the time it's over I may cry with you. Please tell me you're making something good for dinner." The back of her hand slammed into his gut. *"Umph!"*

"Pot roast."

Halfway through the epic tale of Katie and Hubbell, he loved the movie. Well, not the movie as much as its effect on Allie. Tucked up against his side; she snuggled in with her head nestled against him, wadded tissues heaped beside her. Her hair smelled like spring flowers and her skin was as smooth as silk.

God bless a good old fashioned love story.

"Thanks again for dinner, the roast is delicious. I get tired of my own cooking." Sitting across from Allie at her kitchen table seemed almost intimate tonight. He had flicked the CD player on. Adele. Carried candles in from the living room and turned off the overhead fixture. Did she notice it, too? His heartbeat knocked against his breastbone.

"I like your new glasses. They make you look very distinguished."

He laughed with a scoop of potatoes hanging on his fork. "I finally chucked the readers. Life is so much easier when you can see what you're doing." With a two-fingered nudge he adjusted them on his nose. "Now tell me about your week."

"I had another date last night." She smiled, lifted her wine glass. "With Tom Gainey; you remember him."

Yeah, he knew him. He used to like him, too, the rat bastard. He hunted for words that sounded supportive, but the best he could come up with was, "Really, how do you like that?" He didn't, not one bit.

"I had an appointment on Thursday to go over Trey's college fund and a few other investments and we got talking. I didn't know his wife died. A year or so ago, I guess. Anyway, he asked me to dinner."

"Did you have a good time?" Did he have you home early, drop you off at the curb?

"Well, dinner was good." The devil was in her smile, along with the dimple that snagged his attention. "The company, not so much. All he talked about for over an hour was this type of bond, that type of mutual fund. I was afraid I'd fall asleep before dessert."

"Maybe we should hook him up with Maggie."

Allie laughed and stabbed a roasted carrot.

"I'm sorry you didn't enjoy yourself." And now he didn't have to kick Tom

Gainey's ass. "Better luck next time."

"Yeah, thanks. Until then I have my kids at school." She forked a bit of meat. "Oh, and Maddie. We're still training for that race in January."

He rambled on as they finished dinner, asked about the kids in her class, told her about the new office project in Cottonwood. Even though she had no interest in running the company, she'd always seemed interested in it.

Plates clanked and silverware jangled as he loaded the dishwasher. "I'll be back a week from Sunday. Flying to Oregon next weekend."

Allie finished wiping the table, rinsed out the dishcloth in the sink. "Oh? Business?"

He looped an arm across her shoulders, herded her back into the living room. "A family wedding. Should be fun." He stayed until he caught Allie stifling a yawn in her own corner of the sofa, then left her there with a kiss to her forehead.

Allie set aside the worksheets she was marking and stretched to pick up the jangling telephone.

"Hello?"

"It's Maddie. You busy?"

Allie stretched her legs out, propped her bare feet on the edge of the coffee table. "Hi, just finishing up worksheets, then I thought I'd bake cookies to send to the boys, maybe snickerdoodles this time. They can pass them around the dorm, make a few new friends. How are you doing with Jax gone, by the way?"

"You kidding?" The words erupted on a chuckle. "I'm better than good. No more hollow leg at the dinner table, and the girls' schedules are a breeze compared to his. I feel like I have nothing but free time on my hands."

It was easier for Maddie to laugh it off; her house wasn't a silent tomb. "Well, enjoy it while you can.

Maddie let out a melodramatic sigh. "Yes, Em starts high school next year; my work begins again. I'll call you for backup, Auntie Allie."

"Nothing I'd love more." Even Maddie didn't know how much she enjoyed her daughters. Jake was the only person she ever told her deepest secret to. "So, what's up?"

"I forgot to tell you the girls have orthodontist appointments before school tomorrow. Doctor Campbell is away fishing so his new partner will be seeing them. Anyway, I won't be able to run."

"We run every day, Maddie, I'll see you tomorrow. If you're worried about my safety, don't." She let the warmth in her voice bleed through the telephone connection. "I'm more concerned about you, dragging those girls kicking and screaming to their ortho appointment."

Her cell phone rang on her way home the next day. She dug around in her purse until she located the source, dragged the device to her ear. "Hello?"

"Oh my goodness, he's gorgeous!"

"Maddie? Who's gorgeous?"

"Blake. The new orthodontist. He recently moved here from back east. Oh my goodness, as sweet as can be. I think Emily's in love." Maddie was as giggly as one of her daughters.

"Well, oh my goodness." Maggie's laughter was infectious so she giggled along. "Maybe they'll actually enjoy wearing braces now."

"I sure hope so. Emily and Tory have both fought the metal every step of the way."

Trey fought his, too, back when he was thirteen. Ben was still alive.

" ...so he said he would. That sounds nice, don't you think?"

Oh no, what did she miss? "Sorry, you lost me. Said he would *what*, Maddie?"

"Blake mentioned he hadn't made many friends yet." She repeated it like she was speaking to a dimwitted child. "So I asked him over. Friday night at our house. We'll invite people. Barbeque. Of course you'll come." Maddie seemed to have it all worked out. "Like I said, he's hot. He's single. Who knows, maybe something will come of it." Ah, now Allie understood.

"Don't get your hopes up. The last couple of men I met were perfectly nice guys until we went out."

But Friday night, much to her amazement, she found herself having fun. Lots of fun that was leading absolutely nowhere. Blake Dobson *was* gorgeous. And witty, and charming, and intelligent. And *young*.

Allie grabbed her friend and dragged her around the corner, out of earshot. "Jeez, Maddie, when did he graduate from college, last week?"

"Now don't get upset, he's not as young as he looks. Besides, what're a few years? You two could end up having a great time together." Maddie gave Blake an exaggerated once over and waggled her eyebrows at Allie. "He's in his *prime*. Can you imagine." Maddie was practically drooling as she drew out the word.

She peered around the corner for another quick look. "A boy toy's really not my style, Mad. Why don't you set him up with one of the new girls at school? Like Ginny Tolover from fourth grade—she's a lot closer to his age."

Saturday morning Allie went for her usual run around the track. She did the laundry, vacuumed, dusted every item on every shelf—all in an effort to keep her mind occupied.

Why did Maddie think she would be interested in Blake? Did she seem desperate? It had only been a few weeks. She wasn't ready to throw in the towel yet.

Maddie honked and Allie ran out, hopped into the car, blowing kisses at the girls in the back seat. She caught a flash of color as the girls grinned, and twisted her head around.

She cocked an eyebrow, shook her head, and grinned. "Orange, very festive." The girls were a constant source of amusement. "You two ready for Halloween by any chance?"

"What do you think?" Tory slipped her long dark braid back over her shoulder and leaned forward, running her tongue over new stubbly rubber bands in the rear view mirror. "I think we look like we have Cheetos in our teeth, but Em likes it. Next month it's my turn to pick the color. What's a good color for Thanksgiving?" A new conversation erupted between the teenagers, fall colors and the excitement of the approaching holidays. Allie listened with half an ear, loving the sound of their giggles as they chattered.

"Blake says hi, by the way."

Allie could imagine Maddie's little matchmaking brain scheming away beneath her fall of dark layers. "You can tell him I said hello, but get that look off your face right now."

Maddie shot her a different look, this one all innocence. "What look?"

"The one that says '*boy, have I got the guy for you*.' This is so not happening, Maddie. I told you, he's too young."

"And I told you . . . he's just for fun." Maddie lowered her voice. "The sweaty, sheet-twisting kind of fun you haven't had in a good long while." A giggle erupted at that, then stopped as her eyes darted with Maddie's to the back seat.

"I wonder what Jake would say about him."

"Really? Why?" Maddie stopped at a red light and twisted in her seat to face her.

Instead of answering, Allie pointed out the license plate cover on the vintage Mustang idling before them, broadcasting to all that the driver's other car was a broom. They both chuckled.

"Well?"

Allie growled low in her throat. Why was she suddenly defensive? "He's a friend. We talk." She shrugged. "Actually, I've told him about all my dating disasters."

"Allie, honey, I love you like the sister I never had, but you can be so naive. You've got to know how he feels about you."

Naive. Yeah, history already proved she was that.

"Jake?" What was with everybody? "We've been friends forever. He came over a couple of times to watch movies. We have fun together. He likes my cooking." She paused. "He is not my next first date."

"Okay, if you say so." But Maddie was clearly a non-believer.

Maddie pulled into the salon parking lot. Allie shot out a hand to hold Maddie back as the girls climbed out. "It's relaxing to simply hang out; not feel like I'm sixteen again, hoping the new boy likes me." The girls shot to the door, then drew to a halt and waited, bouncing with impatience. "Now drop the whole inquisition. Please, Maddie. I want to enjoy our girl time."

Maddie nodded like maybe she understood.

Allie relaxed into the vacant chair between Emily and Maddie, with Victoria on the other side of her mom. The massager worked the stress out of her back. Her feet sighed as they soaked in the warm swirling water of the jetted tub. Something upbeat and twangy played softly through hidden speakers, barely audible over the hum of motors and the melodic voices of the Asian girls sitting before them.

She did enjoy spending time with Jake, probably too much. Was that why he didn't call? A memory—her cuddled into him on the sofa, sporting soggy tissues, no less—misted through her mind and she cringed. Of course he was uncomfortable. She kneaded her temples with two fingers.

She needed a stern mental sit-down and trapped in this chair was as good a time as any. Starting now she would step back, wait for Jake to feel comfortable enough to call her again. To trust that she wouldn't violate their friendship. She would miss him, sure, but she missed him now. The music changed to a slow ballad. She began to hum along.

Maddie opened one eye and gave her a peek. "Tory and Em have tickets to see this group next month." Allie shot a smile to Emily, who joined the conversation.

"It will be our first live concert." Emily's smile lit up her face even as she rolled her eyes. "Mom said she'd rather let us go by ourselves than have to sit through two hours of rednecks in cowboy boots wailing about pickup trucks and two-timing women."

"Ha! She doesn't know what she's missing. My first concert was my junior year of high school—Aerosmith." She faced the girl with a grin. "You'll have to tell me all about the hot guys in those cowboy boots."

Her house was spotless; her windows washed. She reorganized the kitchen pantry. And the linen closet. She purchased two flats of petunias which even now marched a path along the driveway to the front door. A pot of stew simmered on the stove, its aroma beginning to flavor the house. Allie paced her house, wearing a path on the shiny clean tile, but all the tasks, all the distractions, could not keep her mind from replaying last night's dream. She who never remembered her nighttime imaginings could not get this one to stop. The Technicolor reel played on a continuous loop, over and over again.

She was dressed, brushing on mascara, nearly ready for her date to arrive. New shoes adorned her feet—silver metallic peep toes. There was a feeling of anticipation. Of excitement. She checked her purse, made sure it held her house key and lipstick. Anxiously listened for the doorbell. And then it rang. She gathered her purse and wrap from the bed where she tossed them and, heart thundering, ran. Standing before the front door, she took a deep breath. Eagerly she turned the knob, opened the portal and said hello . . . to broad shoulders, jet-black hair with a touch of silver, and bright sable eyes behind steel-rimmed glasses.

What did this mean?

The question screamed in her head all day. Jake was her friend, her pal, her second brother. He treated her like a sister. With respect and humor and care.

Oh, God, what could this mean?

She made a promise to Ben. She had an obligation to Jake. She couldn't let him suspect that she cared for him more than she should. She would never hurt him that way. He was due any minute. She had to get a hold of herself.

The bell rang and she rushed to the door, sandals tapping across the tile. She sucked in a deep breath and turned the knob. Jake—with thick, broad shoulders snugged into a baby blue polo shirt, short dark hair with a hint of gray at the temples and deep set eyes gleaming through metal-framed glasses—leaned against the doorjamb, waving a DVD, grinning like a Cheshire cat.

"Guy movie night!" he crowed, pushing the case into her hand and entering her house. "Have you ever seen this one?"

She examined the cover, raised her eyebrows so high that wrinkles creased her forehead. "I can't believe it! You've picked the perfect movie. Cool weapons, battles, blood, all wrapped up in a romantic adventure."

Had she lost her mind?

Jake grabbed the case, thinking maybe he picked up the wrong movie. Yep, this was the one he wanted. Revolutionary War battles, Indian attacks, seriously wicked weapons. Not a speck of romance.

"Are you crazy?" He waved the box right in her face. "This here is a serious guy movie. And after last week, you owe me."

"Whatever, Jake, but think about it. They're trapped in a cave and the Huron are almost there. Hawkeye knows he has to escape, but he's torn; he wants to be with Cora, to protect her. He's yelling to be heard over the thundering sound of rushing water. And right before he jumps off the ledge into the waterfall he shouts to her to be strong, to survive, no matter what. No matter how long it takes, he will find her. Oh Jake, it's one of the most romantic scenes *ever*."

He was speechless. Leave it to Allie to take a perfectly good war movie and turn it into a love story. *Shit.* He put the disc into the player, fully prepared to hate the flick he liked so much the last three times he saw it.

But again he found himself enjoying the love story. More importantly, he enjoyed Allie enjoying the love story. She started out sitting stiffly on the other side of the sofa, but here she was, tucked into the niche of his shoulder, using his hand to cover her eyes during the bloody battles. Oh good Lord, he could get used to this. The smell of her hair, her soft sighs during tender moments on the screen. He tugged her closer. Before he could stop himself he kissed her softly on the top of her head, then rested his chin there. She was a perfect fit. He closed his eyes, sighed deeply, and let the rightness of it wash over him.

The movie ended, the powerful soundtrack playing through the sweeping panoramic landscape of the final scene. Jake reached out and trapped the tear that travelled down Allie's cheek, smoothing it away.

"Maybe we should pick a comedy next time; I don't like to see you cry."

She wiped her eyes with a tissue and lifted a negligent shoulder, a rueful smile lifting her lips. "It's a character flaw."

"You don't have any flaws that *I* know of. Oh, maybe one." He flashed her a lopsided smile and answered the question shimmering in her eyes. "You haven't fed me yet."

She gave a soggy laugh and led the way into the kitchen. "The evenings are finally cooler, why don't we eat outside tonight?" She ladled stew into chunky stoneware bowls, handed him one along with a lined wicker basket heavy with warm crusty rolls and motioned him to lead the way.

Jake dipped into his bowl; spoke with his spoon hovering before his mouth. "Have you heard from the kid?"

"No, not this week." She let a smile tilt her lips, it amused her when he referred to Trey this way. "Tell me about your trip to Oregon."

He dug into the basket, came out with a warm roll and tore off a bite. "You would have liked the wedding. It was held in my cousin's backyard and the weather was perfect. They have a huge garden on a hill—colorful flowers, big shady trees all around—you would have loved it." The bread dipped into broth, he popped it in his mouth, spoke around it. "It's been too long since I've seen them last. Probably since my mom died, four years ago."

He may not even realize it, but the wistfulness in his voice was telling. He was a warm, loving man. Would he ever have a family of his own? "You should see your family more often. It's important, you know. One day you'll look back and regret not knowing them better."

"I thought the same thing on the flight home. Then he smiled at her. "You know what else I thought?" At her raised eyebrows he kept talking. "I thought about Trey. My cousin's son and his fiancé graduated from college last May. In only a few years that could be the kid. Kind of scary, huh?"

"Hard to imagine. I don't think he's ever had a serious girlfriend. But it is amazing how fast he's grown up."

As the shadows lengthened in her back yard she told him about school and about the child whose parents were divorcing.

"It's heartbreaking to watch the turmoil this little boy goes through. We both have friends who are divorced with children, but it's different, stuck in the drama day after day." The familiar ache in her chest returned as compassion swelled. "As a teacher it's certainly not the first time this has occurred, but as a mom . . . my heart hurts for the kids caught in the middle."

His hands captured hers, halting them as they wrung together atop the glass patio table, his gaze far steadier than the sudden surge of his pulse. He was caught in the moment, caught in the web of emotion in her eyes. In self-preservation he turned away before he drew her to him, maybe rubbed his hand across her back and soothed them both.

Because that was a *really* bad idea.

Instead he dredged up a convincing grin to lighten the mood. "So have you been hanging out with any new guys lately?"

Her wry smile told him he succeeded. "I had dinner at Maddie's last Friday, she wanted to fix me up with her daughters' orthodontist." With a burst she chuckled, dropped his hands with a quick squeeze. "You should see the surprise on your face. It probably matches mine when I first saw Blake. This guy's drop dead gorgeous, charming, funny, obviously intelligent, and has a killer body."

Jake scowled and shoved down the lick of jealousy.

"And he has big hands."

Okay, now that was just mean. Her eyes twinkled in the glow from the fixtures flanking the slider, telling him she was teasing. But still. He pushed away from the table to collect their empty bowls. "Are you going out with him soon?"

Allie scrunched up her face in distaste. "Absolutely not. He's about fourteen years old. I don't know what Maddie was thinking. Really, do I seem desperate?"

She may not be, but he was beginning to feel that way. He answered Allie's question with the same answer she gave him.

"Absolutely not. The right person will come along, probably when you least expect it." One day he'd tell her that right person was sitting across the table, but it wasn't tonight.

The frustration was killing him.

He carried their bowls into the kitchen and wiped counters while she loaded the dishwasher. When they were done, she gave a last look around. "Everything's all right here, I'll walk you out."

"I'll call you in a few days." He kissed her cheek at the door. "I've got a busy week, problems on a job, but we should do this again."

"We should, it was fun." Smiling, she gave him a quick hug of farewell. "You're a good guy to have around."

Chapter Twenty One

The shower brewing on his way to her house had him soaked by the time he dashed past the freshly planted border and scrambled into his Corvette. Damn the rain! He slammed the car door, dragged in a lungful of intoxicating new-car chemicals and settled into what Nick laughingly referred to as his mid-life crisis. Said all he needed now was a sexy young babe in the passenger seat and he could be the poster child.

He scowled into the privacy of the darkened interior. Screw Nick. He could drive any car he wanted, even if his head did damn near hit the roof. And it wasn't a sexy young babe he wanted to drive it with. With a shudder he dragged his palms down the thighs of wet jeans and allowed his gaze scan Allie's house. Overhead lights went out in the living room, momentarily a rosy glow filtered through the drapes of her bedroom. He gripped the steering wheel, studied his knuckles as his palms soaked the leather wrapping before starting the engine. Big hands.

Yeah he knew what that meant.

He unwrapped his hands, turned them over to examine their palms and his eyes glazed over. His breathing became shallow, labored. His imagination took over—his fantasies—as he envisioned running his fingers through Allie's soft curls, then along her jaw to the sensitive spot at the base of her throat. Over the curve of her shoulders and on to the valley of her waist, exploring the curve of her . . .

Stop already! He dragged in a deep, ragged breath, pressed the back of his dripping head against the leather headrest and allowed the agonized groan to seep out. He couldn't think. Could only feel in great sweeping pulses that addled his brain. With effort he sucked in steady streams of air, blew them out between gritted teeth. Okay, it was a start. His breath, his breathing, that was easier now. He stretched out his left leg, shook out his knee and adjusted his jeans. Jesus. When was the last time he sat outside a girl's house with a fucking hard-on?

This had to stop. Sitting here, hesitant to leave, hoping for a glimpse, he was no better than a stalker. He had to back off. Back away. Put her needs before his. This, this—what exactly was it? Infatuation? Attraction?—had gone too far. He needed to keep Allie safe, and he couldn't do that if it was him she needed protection from. With a grunt of frustration, he turned the key until the engine roared to life.

Allie's plan to plant flowers in the back yard was discarded with the wet Sunday paper. It was still raining. She spent her morning indoors—ironing clothes for the new week and checking school papers. Late in the afternoon, after the pregnant steel clouds dried out and thinned to silver ribbons, she headed to the grocery store for her weekly supplies. Her eyes wandered through the meat case, searching for inspiration. She missed the days of cooking for a family. She missed cooking for Trey. And for Jake. The packages were all too large for a family of one. Maybe Trey would come home soon. He hadn't been home since he left for school. Hardly ever called. Was this normal? She'd have to ask someone. Morosely, she headed for the freezer section.

Allie was curled into one side of the sofa, her painted toes tucked beneath a blanket. Her microwave dinner on her lap, she picked up the remote and flipped through channels until she found a classic movie—the opening credits were still rolling. Two people, each already in a relationship, meet on an ocean liner and fall in love. At the end of their voyage they agree to separate and meet again at the top of the Empire State Building in six months. The original version, not the remake—one of her favorites.

She was on her second tissue when the phone rang. Irrationally her pulse leapt. What if it was Jake? If she promised to stay on her side of the sofa perhaps he'd come over and watch the rest of the movie with her? Tease her as he handed her a tissue?

Distracted, she answered the call.

"Allie, hi! So is it serious?"

Allie let her shoulders slump in disappointment, then shook her head and straightened in her seat. "Reese, just what I need tonight." Reese's casual breeziness always cheered her.

"Ha! The last time we talked you said would call me after your doctor's appointment. Then nothing. You going to live or what?"

Allie was late. Three months late. Since she hadn't had sex in over three years she probably wasn't pregnant. That left one daunting possibility—one she wasn't ready for.

"Her office called to reschedule, but I looked up my symptoms on the internet. I'm sure it's menopause."

"Don't sound so miserable; it's a wonder what they can do with replacement hormones these days. Think about it, pregnancy won't be an issue anymore."

That idea had already trekked boldly through her mind and left its sticky footprints." Before the seething misery had a chance to root she changed the subject, eager to chat about anything else—school, Halloween, the bestseller she recently finished. By the time they made plans to meet for a matinee she'd missed the end of her movie. As she said good-bye Reese was still nagging her to call the doctor.

"I promise I'll call first thing, Mom." She softened her chiding voice with a chuckle. "And I promise to let you know if it's fatal."

But the starter was acting up in the morning and it took forever to get her car going. Late for school and cranky, she dodged mud puddles on her way in the building. Her kids didn't deserve her foul mood, though, so she shook it off and got started with a counting game. However, by the end of the day she was still unsettled. She ran her vehicle by the garage and luckily got right in.

Somewhat mollified, she wrote a check and drove her newly repaired vehicle home, windshield wipers swiping at full speed. Pride swelled inside her, coursed through her system. She'd solved her problem without running to someone else for help. She liked this feeling of independence. It was warm, energizing, encouraging.

Now if she could only get her son home for a visit.

The week was a busy one, and flew. She ran with Maddie each morning, volunteered at the library Wednesday after work. And twenty five kindergarten children tugged at her like Stretch Armstrong all day long. Her evenings were busy, also with lesson plans to review and Halloween art projects to prepare for. Trey called on Thursday, everything was going well, he'd be home the next weekend.

Allie met Reese for lunch on Saturday before the movie. Over spinach salads and raspberry tea they laughed about antics at school and their plans for the upcoming week. Allie worked at the library Tuesdays after work, and there was a committee meeting about Christmas at the women's shelter scheduled for Wednesday evening. It promised to be another busy week. Allie dug into it with gusto.

Leaving the library Tuesday night, her cell phone rang. She checked the caller ID. "Maddie, how are you?" She probably had to back out of running again.

"I'm good thanks." Cheerful Maddie sounded harried. "But Emily, not so much. She came home from school sick today, and you know how the girls are. Once one of them gets something she's good about sharing with the other. I expect them both to be ill tomorrow."

"That's too bad. Is there something I can do to help?"

"Well, no and yes."

Allie's eyebrows dropped at the cryptic answer. "What do you need?"

"They've got those tickets for Friday night. The concert, remember?"

"Oh right. I'd love to buy them from you. I'm sure I can find someone to go with me." It was well known Maddie would rather listen to fingernails scratching the chalkboard; she was not a fan of country music.

"Oh, thanks! You're a lifesaver. I'll bring them with me to school tomorrow.

"Sounds great. I'll get them from you during lunch. She hung up, drove along for a few minutes, then picked her phone back up and called Reese, wondering if she was interested in a girls' night out.

"This Friday, Allie? Rats! One of the guys in John's firm is retiring and there's a dinner." Reese seemed dismayed. "I'd much rather spend the evening with you than a bunch of stuffy tax attorneys."

Allie laughed at her. "Right. If I didn't know how much you loved one of those stuffy attorneys I might believe you." Reese and John were married fourteen years now and opted out of parenthood. Reese announced—a little smugly—to anyone crass enough to question their decision that they were still on their honeymoon.

Reese sighed, a deep mocking sigh. "Truly pathetic, but true. His job may be boring, but nothing else about the man is."

"Lalalalala, hanging up now." Allie laughed again. She'd always liked John—he was brilliant, and a fine example of male hunkiness—but Reese never did master the fine art of censoring. "Have fun at your dinner."

She pulled into her driveway, hit the garage door opener as she said good-bye. Who else could she call? Thumbing through a mental rolodex of possible companions as she parked in the garage and walked into the house, one name immediately popped into her head.

She quashed it just as quickly. She couldn't call him. She made a promise to herself that she wouldn't. It was getting late—too late to call anyone tonight—but tomorrow she would talk to Ginny at school. Ginny was quite a bit younger than she, but she might enjoy the concert. If Ginny couldn't make it she could ask Marie from the library. Or maybe she should ask Blake. The thought made her chuckle.

Yeah, right!

She wasn't chuckling Thursday afternoon as she placed a call to his office. She punched the number into her cell as she pulled her car from the school parking lot. The good doctor was with a patient so she left her number and asked to have him call. Her phone rang as she pulled up to a red light, three blocks away.

Allie laughed as she said hello. "I only called a minute ago. You're done with your patient already?"

He laughed with her and confided, "I'll tell you a secret . . . I wasn't really with a patient. Jill, the receptionist, she's supposed to say that to everybody who calls for me. That way I don't get stuck with something unwanted—like a sales rep."

"Ah, very sneaky, doctor."

"What can I say? You now know my one vice. Other than that I'm as honest as they come."

"I'm relieved to hear it. I have an offer for you, and I'd hate to have to worry about your moral character." She was foolish for even calling him, but she was running out of options.

"An offer, huh? This is intriguing." Amusement lingered in his voice. "Whatcha got, Allie?"

"I've got two tickets to a concert and I'm looking for company." She named the group that would be playing. "I wondered if you might be interested."

Instead of interested, Blake seemed embarrassed. "Wow, Allie. I'm flattered that you'd call, I am. But actually, I'm seeing someone right now; we already have plans to attend."

Now it was Allie's turn to be embarrassed. She pulled up to the last stoplight before her house. There was a vehicle stopped alongside her. Could the woman driving the midnight blue convertible see her discomfort? She propped her left elbow on the window ledge, hid her face with her palm. With a quick blurted apology she hurried off the phone.

She pitched her handbag onto the kitchen counter and carried her tote bag into the living room. She had papers to mark, but they could wait until later. In a while she would check the DVR, see if anything sounded good. How many nights were spent in front of the television with nothing but schoolwork to keep her company?

The walk down the hallway to her room was endless tonight. With curious trepidation she removed her school clothes, stepped into black sweatpants and a fleece sweatshirt like she was donning chain mail. After slipping her feet into fuzzy armor she headed for the kitchen. The flick of a light switch eradicated shadows in the kitchen, she poured a fortifying glass of merlot. With a steeling breath she picked up the telephone on her way outside.

She hung her booted toes over the edge of the flagstone deck, the receiver dangling from one hand, half-empty stemware clutched in the other. She closed her eyes against the blanket of stars draping the night sky. She could still change her mind, but . . . she missed him.

Calling may not be wise, but . . . she missed him. She dialed his number before she could talk herself out of it.

Jake sank onto the edge of a deck chair, nursing a cold beer. The heat was finally gone, his chest rose as he filled it with crisp fall air. He tilted his head, guzzled half the bottle, set it on the table. Work on the Cottonwood Commercial Center had been ceaseless for weeks now with one setback after another—materials, sub-contractors, weather—you name it. Nick could handle the job himself, but the investors insisted he get the job back on track personally. So emails flew continually, his phone had been glued to his ear, and his truck could practically drive the route to Cottonwood, a two hour journey, without his assistance. But the relentless babysitting paid off. After eighteen days the development was back on schedule and the investors were off his back. Mercifully, the project once again rode Nick's broad shoulders. He'd more than proved himself as an adept project manager in the years since he finished college, even more since his brother's death.

Easing back in the chaise, he studied the haphazard array of stars blanketing the inky sky. He could locate the most common constellations like the big and little dippers, and then the North Star. He could recite the names of others, but could never find them in the sky. Mostly he liked the stars because they reminded him of Allie's freckles—scattered over her silken skin the way stars sprinkled across the heavens. He let his eyes drift shut, imagined being able to trace the path of each of her constellations. Imagined running his lips over each one, and giving it a name.

His phone rang and he let it. Ignored the voicemail notification as well. There was nobody he wanted to talk to. Allie hadn't called in weeks. She slipped into his thoughts, though, uninvited—he was unable to keep her out. But face it, he didn't want her out, didn't turn her memory away once.

What was she doing tonight? Was she busy with her young orthodontist? Did she have someone new by now? An emptiness crushed his chest, heavy and familiar. Why did she stop calling? Could she tell how he felt? He hoped by staying away she would stop invading his every thought. He woke up thinking of her; left for work wondering if she was home, getting ready for school. At the end of the day he fell into bed exhausted, wishing she was there, to hold while he slept. It was a good thing work was so busy these past few weeks. But now he was tired.

His phone rang again. Out of habit he picked it up, checked the caller ID. His heart stuttered when her name came up. *Play it cool, Taylor.* "Hello?" A stab of anticipation ran straight to his gut.

"Jake?"

The one word nearly melted his resistance. "Yeah. Allie? How've you been?"

She answered after a short pause. "I'm good. Did . . . did I catch you in the middle of something?"

God, all he wanted was to be in the same room with her. "Not really. Why?"

"You sound funny. And you haven't called." She paused again, then blurted out, "I miss you." .

Jake slid his eyes shut and bit back a groan. "What's to miss? You must have plenty of guys around." And how petulant did *that* sound?

Her chuckle rumbled softly in his ear. "Nah, don't be silly.

Really? He wanted to dance at the thought—like Gene Kelly, posed dramatically with an umbrella in one outstretched hand, his fedora in the other while raindrops slicked over him. *Defenses firmly in place, big boy.* He relaxed against the cushion again, took up his beer. "That's too bad. So what *have* you been up to, besides not dating?"

"Same old, same old. The kids at school, the library. I had a committee meeting last night. And I got a pedicure with Maddie and the girls last Saturday."

He liked her toes painted a startling pink, shuffling on his dashboard. A reluctant smile tugged on his lips.

"Oh, and I cut my hair."

He bolted upright in his chair. "You did what!?"

"Well, *I* didn't do it. I went to a salon."

She sounded amused now, her mischievous grin came across loud and clear. His resistance tumbled, crumbled into a pile of useless rubble.

"It was an impulse. I thought I'd try something new. You'll like it, I promise."

Yeah, sure. "I can hardly wait." Some of his greatest fantasies involved his hands and her hair and she just shot them all to hell.

"Oh stop pouting. What is it with men and long hair anyway?"

Not in a million years could he tell her what was with *this man* and *her* long hair, so he said nothing—simply sulked wordlessly.

"Anyway, you sound tired."

He shivered, the chill breeze seeping through his thin T-shirt, causing goosebumps. "I am tired. The job in Cottonwood has been kicking our asses—mine *and* Nick's. Too many road trips, too much diner food, too little sleep. I'm sitting by the pool, dozing. I'm glad you called."

Her hesitation was imperceptible, nothing more than a faint hitch in the conversation. "What does your day look like tomorrow? Will you be in town?"

"Yeah, sure. I'm planning to sleep in, catch up around the house. I have a dentist's appointment late in the morning, so it will be after lunch before I get to the office. I thought I would hang out tomorrow night, probably order a pizza. You want to come eat pizza with me?" Where did this feeling come from—like he was jumping out of an airplane without a parachute?

Her chuckle warmed him instantly. "It sounds great, but I have something funner."

"Funner, huh? How could it possibly be better than pizza and the tube?" God, he missed teasing her.

"How about a concert at Airways? Maddie's girls are sick, so I bought their tickets." It's a country band, but they're pretty good seats. What do you think?"

That free-falling feeling swamped him again. He hadn't seen her in nearly three weeks, but that wasn't near enough time to get her out of his head.

"Sounds perfect. What time does it start?"

"The concert's at eight."

"I'll pick you up at six. We can grab dinner downtown, somewhere near the arena."

She agreed so quickly his pulse leapt.

He would see Allie again. His heart sang. He missed her fiercely. Tomorrow could not come fast enough.

Waking Friday was a painful venture, his chest full of lead as it was. He'd dreamed of her again, dreamed of kissing. Dreamed of a lover with short, curly hair and slim shoulders shrouded in fairy dust. Oh, shit, did he agree to a date?

Not a date; the little voice was reassuring. Just food and a little music. But dread hung heavy—like knowing he was on his way to the gallows where he would be hung by the neck until dead. Or perhaps he would face a firing squad. Okay, yeah. At least that was quicker.

He grappled with alarm that threatened to overwhelm him. How would he make it? A tangle of anticipation and terror twisted through his mind and knotted his midsection. He would never survive.

The house was already presentable—the cleaning lady came on Wednesdays. He threw a load of jeans into the washer and went to the garage to drag out the lawnmower. The palm trees towering over the front yard swayed, rustled in the breeze. The autumn day was sunny with a bracing nip, the type of day he usually relished. But today there was little enjoyment; he was a man on the way to his demise.

When he finished the grass he shoved the mower back into the garage and then his laundry into the dryer on his way through to the backyard. There he sprayed off the patio, then rolled up the hose, skimmed fallen leaves from the surface of the pool and trudged through the house to shower.

Heat and steam cascaded over his body, easing muscles achy from physical labor, almost relaxing him. He let his mind ease, as well, and listen to his saner self. Spending time with Allie was not torture. He enjoyed her, for chrissake. He *wanted* to be with her. He would just remember to play it cool.

A new voice spoke to him, made him pause as he lathered his hair. What if he didn't have to play it cool? What if he could make this work? Allie missed him too; he could hear it in her voice, in her words. Was it possible he was overlooking something? These thoughts all warred with his feeling of imminent doom as he dressed for the day.

He ran his tongue over the slickness of his teeth as he left the hygienist's chair and was led in the direction of the examination room. He reclined on the exam chair while the assistant covered him with a lead blanket, then shoved x-ray slides into his mouth while he concentrated on not gagging up his breakfast. That bit of pleasantness over, he relaxed, waited for the dentist to tell him he was cavity-free and free to get to work.

"A root canal? You've got to be kidding!" Bloody hell, wasn't that the way his world spun lately? Still muttering, something about the dentist and the silver Ferrari sitting in the parking lot, he made the needed follow-up appointments and left the building.

Whirling hope lobbied with sweeping despair all morning. He was up and down like the see-saw Allie's kids liked to play on at recess. He needed to rein in his thoughts, restore order to their chaotic flight. Anguish still hovered in the background, but optimism was straining to take control.

Jake pulled his truck out of the medical complex parking lot, swung toward his office. Driving down the boulevard, he came to the onramp and made a quick detour, something strong inside him urging him in this direction. Arriving at his destination, he pulled over, sat for a few moments, staring through the windshield as the idling engine vibrated through the cab of his truck. Shutting down the engine, he kicked through dull fallen leaves, stopping beneath the dubious shade of a venerable jacaranda.

This needed to be done.

Jake reached out, palmed the cool granite headstone. His eyes darted, following the murmur of a nearby voice. An older gentleman stood at a plot several rows across, fresh flowers lying on the ground before him.

His gaze swung back, the memory of a warm, soft hand attached to an IV machine replacing the cool, solid granite beneath his unsteady palm. He let his heart have its say. "Hey Tate, I made you a promise years ago, but I don't know how to do it anymore." No preamble; cut straight to the chase.

Once said, the words opened a floodgate of emotion. Did a promise made before his world turned upside down still hold weight? He had to be honest with himself—it did. Ben screwed things up, but Jake couldn't discount a life-long friendship. Then again, didn't he owe himself? He withdrew his hand, his footsteps hesitant as he paced across dormant Bermuda grass.

He allowed his rambled, nearly disjointed thoughts to spill at random. "What do I do? Do I tell her? Is there room for me in her life?"

Back and forth he trod beneath the thin-leafed, blooming canopy, blossoms drifting like lavender snowflakes, scattering at his feet. "I don't know how . . . how *did* you sense that I love her?" He'd guarded that secret for so long. He punted a fallen twig. "She still hasn't figured it out."

He paused with his breathing labored, keeping time with the beat of his heart. "I can't let her go." He stopped pacing, then resumed, shuffling through the floral carpet swirling in a sudden eddy. "No one else will love her better than I will. But can I love her *and* keep my promise to you?" He drew to a stop. This was the crux of his dilemma.

Nobody could care for her and Trey better than he could. The knowledge came from the depth of his soul. But he needed absolution to move forward. He had to swallow hard, twice, before he could turn, face his friend with his heart thudding and his fists clenched, dragging out words from earlier days, happier times.

"I hope you don't mind buddy, but I've got to call in a favor."

He collapsed on to the stone bench he sat on so many times before, his chin tucked against his chest. With his eyes open, he allowed his thoughts to turn to Ben, to the past. There was a lifetime spent playing together as children, on the swingset and then on the baseball diamond. On the gridiron in high school, pretending not to watch the cheerleaders on the sideline. As roommates in college, when fate, that fickle bitch, brought Allie to one of them instead of the other.

As he sat lost in thought his eyes scanned the blossoms that lined the lane and at the blooming oleanders dotting the lawn, searching for the source of the trilling that tickled his ears. From high on the left it flew in—a bluebird, singing merrily as it landed on Ben's gravestone. And the song was like a benediction.

Chapter Twenty Two

He pulled into her driveway right on time. Strode past her bed of vibrant petunias and rang the doorbell, heart drumming like a teenager on his first date. But this wasn't a date, was it? This was Allie, who happened to have an extra ticket. But *what if?*

The thought would not rest.

She pulled open the door and he stood, breathless, wanting to be nowhere more than exactly where he was.

"Jake!" She pitched forward and his arms were instantly full of her. Silver hoops flashed through a sleek bob as she canted back, grinned, then squeezed him tight again. "I'm so glad you're here."

He tightened his hold, had sorely underestimated how much he missed the feel of her tucked beneath his chin, his arms doubled around her.

She wiggled out of his embrace and broke into a full-throated laugh. "It's not good for friends to stay away so long."

Friends? *After that greeting?* God, he hoped not. She disappeared into the kitchen, returned with her navy pea coat and her purse slung over her arm.

"Ready."

His mind held a vivid image of him picking his tongue up off the porch and slapping it over his shoulder. Of their own volition his eyes dragged upwards, starting with brightly painted toes peeping through sparkly silver shoes, raked their way over lucious curves tucked into fuck-me jeans and white tuxedo pleats and landed on . . .

Hair. Not like his new fantasy, but better still. Smooth and silky and sexy as all hell—her auburn curls were gone, replaced with a highlighted fall that swung across her shoulders with the motion of her head. Her hair never did that before. His fingers tingled as he quickly conjured a whole new set of fantasies.

To defend himself—and her—he grabbed her hand, herded her to his car. "You were right—I do like your hair." The finger that waggled in that direction drew her laughter. He pulled her close, closed his eyes and pressed his lips to her forehead. His voice was husky when he spoke. "I missed you. I'm glad we're doing this." He released her, helped her into the low-slung seat, then darted around the hood of his cherry red sports car and settled into the driver's seat. He reached down to turn the key and the powerful engine roared to life.

Jake drove downtown, parked in a lot on Jefferson, near the arena. Hand-in-hand like lovers, they strolled. When the beguiling tang of tomato and garlic spilled through an open doorway and onto the sidewalk they turned in, found a table, and over lasagna and crusty bread caught up on each other's lives.

His was full of work, getting the Cottonwood job back on track, and his dentist's appointment. She told him about school, about how volunteering at the library wasn't as much fun as she hoped. She'd had several meetings with the group organizing fundraisers for the women's shelter. And Trey was due home around noon the next day. Monday was a holiday, he had three days.

He was happy, hopeful, for the first time in what seemed like a lifetime. He slipped his hand around Allie's as they melted into the stream of bodies leaving the arena, knots of traffic tangling their way through the downtown streets around them. Impulsively, he sang a few bars, pulling her loosely into his arms for an impromptu two-step right there on the sidewalk. Laughing together they continued, talking about the music, and Trey, and a movie they both wanted to see. Jake held the car door while she climbed in. Pushing her door closed, he rounded to the other side.

She slipped off her heels as he settled in his seat, lifted her bare feet onto the brand new dash. "Oops!" Abruptly she stopped, shot him a quick look of chagrin, and dropped her feet back to the floor.

His eyes found hers, lingered for an elongated moment as green flecks danced. "Please, feel free." He reached across the gearshift and with a wink lifted them one by one, cradled them with his thumb running across her instep until they rested on the leather.

Jake maneuvered the throaty sports car through heavy post-event traffic, negotiating the freeway exchanges around the airport with Indy precision until they were heading south through Tempe. Without commenting, she let her eyes follow his finger when he pointed out a granite and glass high-rise under construction off to the east. "One of Ryan's."

She nodded and let her eyes slide back, over bare feet featuring brightly-hued toes until she sat blindly, the road, the traffic, obscure images flashing past her window. After an evening of music, laughter, conversation, Jake was suddenly so quiet. What was he thinking? She rubbed a palm across her forehead, smoothing the tension there. Oh, man, she was confused.

She was happy when she was with Jake. Content. This was true. They enjoyed quiet evenings at home as well as rowdy moments lost in a crowd. She'd enjoyed herself tonight, but then, he made sure she did. He was always—always—considerate, attentive.

She pushed the fast forward button, landing in an uncertain future. What if? What if this was more than friendship? What if Reese and Maddie were right and Jake's feelings for her were . . . strong? How did she feel about that? About Jake? He was Ben's best friend, but Ben was gone. It took her years to make her own life, free from the anguish his dying left.

Jake was an important part of that life. If he left how would she feel? She kneaded her forehead again, bracketed her jaw in her hands, unable to even glance his way.

She couldn't imagine her life without Jake in it. What if he left and never came back? She always thought she loved him like a brother, and she had, for many years. But now—what she felt for him now went soul deep, far more consuming than anything she could have imagined.

She chanced a peek at him, found him studying the road as he twisted his way through her neighborhood, his mouth tight. What was he thinking? She couldn't imagine. But her thoughts were suddenly clear. There'd been so many questions, so many problems over the years. But Jake was always there. With him there was only one possible solution.

Pulling into her driveway, he killed the engine, lost in thought. His hand lay idle on the gear shift knob, not far from hers, lying motionless on her lap. Before she had time to catch her breath, to talk herself out of it, she lifted her palm, stretched her arm mere inches, and covered it.

Jake expertly steered through traffic. Tonight he was resolved. A mission, a plan, a purpose—whatever he wanted to call it—soon he would put it into action. The red glow of tail lights bled through the starlit darkness around them. The glaring headlights of the truck behind him blinded him in the rear view mirror. Soft strains of melody wove their way through the interior of his car. But Allie was quiet. Sober eyes stared out the window, still and solemn. He dug, rooting for the words he needed. The feelings he had for her ran deep, but how did he tell her, let her know what he wanted? He frantically searched, but his mind was blank, a dark, cavernous void. His heart plummeted, his breathing grew ragged. Once again he was a convict on death row, awaiting the executioner.

He pulled his car into Allie's driveway. Shoved it into park and turned the key, killing the hum of the engine. If he didn't do something with his hands he'd reach for her, embarrass them both. With his right he seized the gear shift lever like a drowning man desperately clutches a rope.

"Tonight was fun. Thanks for calling."

She didn't respond, but her hand lifted, hovered, sheltered his, resting on the leather-wrapped knob. His heart lifted, found its home, and raced even as his questioning eyes raced to meet hers. He turned his hand over, wrapped her fingers within his and added the slightest pressure.

Her mouth tipped in a delicate smile. "Do you want to come in? I bought an espresso machine, I could make lattes." Her voice was high and fast, but also beseeching and his worry eased, a bit.

Coffee was the last thing he wanted tonight, but he wanted to come in. "Coffee sounds great."

Wordlessly, Allie fumbled with the coffee maker, pressed freshly ground beans, steamed milk and added vanilla syrup. He carried the untouched drink into the living room and settled into a corner of the smooth leather sofa. She followed him into the room, pressed a remote and the voice of a powerful tenor filled the room. With another press the volume lowered. Grasping her mug, she eyed him as she crossed the room.

She drew closer—with a puzzled look in her eyes, lips slightly parted, and a sway in her hips that he'd practiced not noticing for years—and his brain clogged, his thoughts scattered like a herd of feral cats, unwilling to be tamed. The sofa shifted as she sat, crooked a knee and faced him. His heart beat erratically, trapped somewhere on its way to his throat.

He set his latte on the table, grateful his shaking hands could accomplish it without splashing. Allie still held her mug; he set it beside his and folded her hands in his, trapping them. He'd held her hands before, hundreds of times, but never with clammy palms. Hopefully she wouldn't notice.

"Do you remember the night of Ben's accident, Allie? We were talking to him before his surgery."

She lowered her eyebrows, glanced away before meeting his eyes again. "Sure. How could I ever forget that night?"

"What Ben said to me—" His eyes hit the ceiling, searching for guidance, then drifted back to her. A small smile quirked one corner of his mouth. "What Ben said to me was if something happened, if he didn't make it out of surgery, he wanted me to take care of you. He made me promise."

Her eyes widened, then narrowed, and her head shook from side to side. "Jake, you were the best friend a man could ask for. Ben loved you." With a tug she freed her hands, reversed their positions so his large palms were held within hers, so much smaller. "And you have been here for me, and for Trey, whenever we needed you. I couldn't ask for more than that."

But he needed her to ask for more.

He bent one knee and pulled his leg onto the sofa, twisted to level their gazes, hands held, his thumbs locking them together, his heart thrumming in his chest. Words of love floated on the air, drifting through the room on seductive notes.

"Yes, well, there was something else, too. Something he knew, even though I never told him."

Allie cocked her head. His eyes darted away and then back again, he sucked in a deep, unsteady breath and blew it out slowly through parted lips. Sitting on the sofa, facing her, he allowed his lips to curve in a hopeful smile. It was time to take the plunge.

"I'm in love with you, Allie. I've always loved you."

Allie gasped and jerked her hands from around his, slapping her fists to her chest like it would protect her. "No. Jake, no. You can't. I can't." Frantic now, her eyes were wide with alarm, her breaths coming in short gasps. "I promised I'd take care of you, too. I . . . can't."

The corners of his lips lowered until his smile was but a flimsy substitute. He'd come so far already. He'd taken the first halting step, he couldn't let her shut him down. To see this through he had to leap.

"I learned—long time ago—to be your friend, Allie. It was the only way I could be part of your life." A lifetime of yearning clotted his throat as the words, full of emotion, spilled from his mouth like floodwaters breaching a dam. "But now, now Ben's been gone a long time and we've both done a lot of healing." He reached for her hands again, lifted them from where they'd drifted to her lap.

"You're an amazing woman, resilient and strong. I want to be your friend, but I love you. I want more." Amazingly enough, the words he was unable to rehearse earlier came instinctively now. He brushed his lips across her knuckles.

"I need you, Allie. I need to be with you. I need to come home to you at the end of the day. To share my life with you, and to share yours. To sleep with you at night, and wake with you in the morning. And I think you need me too."

There it was. His heart, laid on the line for her to cherish or destroy. It cost him, but the past three years cost Allie as well. Cost more than the time spent taking back her independence, but the reward was ineffable—Allie as a strong, resilient woman. Could he ever make her understand how proud he was of her?

A large gray moth fluttered against the screen of the open glass door. The antique Regulator clock ticked against the far wall. He sat, facing her, searching her eyes, searching her heart, waiting for a sign, scared to death.

Allie lifted her chin, determined steel gray eyes connecting with his, her fingers tightened around his, her face impassive.

"No, Jake. I don't need you."

His eyelids squeezed shut. His breath hitched and faltered. His heart was breaking. Splintering into a million tiny shards, freefalling into the black hole of a life without her.

Then Allie, the woman he loved, the woman who was his life, released his hands to slide her fingers through the hair at his temples, then cupped his jaw in her graceful palms, drawing him nearer. His skin burned where her fingers lingered. The familiar scent of her shampoo and the subtle fragrance of blossoms floated over him a heartbeat before her words registered.

"Lord help me, I want you, but—."

His world exploded like a kaleidoscope, bursts of color shifting and reflecting before spinning back to a pinpoint of emotion centered on three words as his eyes snapped open and heated and two fingers covered her lips, preventing her from finishing her thought.

His heart leapt and he smiled, more from relief than happiness. "You want me." He withdrew his fingers, the memory of her still warm on them. Testing, his lips brushed hers with the force of butterfly wings. Just let them skim, soft and querying before drawing back, her soft scent surrounding him. He had dreamed of this, wanted this, but hadn't dared to hope. Could it be real?

Eyes locked on hers, his hands skimmed the thin cotton at her waist before drawing her against him. He'd held her narrow waist before, helping her into his truck or out of his boat, but tonight her heart fluttered against his chest where they met, making desire pool in his belly.

She scraped his bottom lip with bared teeth even as his palms skated over her shoulders and down her arms. "I want you in my life, too."

The quivers chasing down his spine had him groaning. His abdomen sucked in as her hands drifted across those muscles and locked behind him. "I want you every day." Her lips teased the column of his throat, pausing to murmur against the throbbing beat that pulsed throughout his body in time to the bold, passionate rhythm of the music.

He let his lips become bold as well—firm, strong, insistent—as he lifted her jaw and met her lips and his brain struggled to process this glorious chain of events. *She wanted him!* His blood quickened in his veins. At last, she was his! His hands trembled as they moved again, mapping her familiar figure in an unfamiliar way. His thumbs brushed against the sides of her breasts and she arched into him. Her low hum of pleasure against his mouth had his dick surging against his zipper. "Oh, God, please don't pull away."

With eyes dilated, as deeply black as his must be, she withdrew and he nearly wept as his arms loosened around her. But she merely searched his eyes, then his face, and lifted her lips in a smile. "I love you." Sweetly, quietly, so very Allie, she lowered her lips again, took his mouth, claimed it in a kiss full of promise.

A kiss that questioned, tenderly and cautious.

Boldly and without reserve, he allowed his lips to answer.

As if dazed, she rose.

As if connected, he followed, and without hesitation gathered her lean curves to him and pressed his mouth to hers in a kiss so deep the heat of it spread throughout his limbs.

She pulled back again, studying his features. "I want to wake up with you in the morning." Her deft fingers freed his shirt button; her gaze turned hot before it lowered to follow her hands, baring a fine sprinkling of chest hairs that tapered to trail down his abdomen.

His heart thundered at the novelty of her gentle hands on his bare skin. "Mmm. Tomorrow morning."

Spreading the separated halves of his shirt, sliding it off his shoulders and down his arms, scattered kisses followed her fingers. "Mmm hmm. Every day." Hooded hazel eyes finally lifted, glittering with hunger.

He stopped her hands as they reached for his zipper. "Sounds like a hell of an idea." And as he reached down to scoop her into his arms, shifted her with a bounce and carried her down the hallway, his heart soared in his chest.

Chapter Twenty Three

Waited. He'd waited a lifetime for tonight, he could do without the anxiety twisting a knot in his gut. What did he have to be afraid of? This was Allie in his arms, he knew her. Knew her humor, her laughter, had witnessed her tears of both compassion and grief. Recognized the floral scent she wore. And now he knew her taste. "I've waited for you." His words were murmured as she slid his glasses from his face and laid them on the nightstand.

A grin stretched across her face as she pushed to her toes and linked her wrists behind his neck. "Waited? I seem to remember several women over the years." She rubbed her breasts over his bare chest.

Oh, he wouldn't mind if she did that all night long, but he wanted his hands on her skin. He unbuttoned her pleated blouse, removed it to skim his lips across one freckled shoulder and breathe in her scent before meeting her eyes. "Yes, well, there was also the small matter of a husband."

Her head fell back when his lips lowered to her satiny collarbone. "Mmm, the husband. That feels good, don't stop."

His hands forged a path down her rib cage, her abdomen tightening with a quick intake of breath as his thumbs grazed the sides of lace-covered breasts. The mewl of satisfaction that escaped on her gasp had his erection throbbing. His breaths came in harsh gasps. He dropped to his knees. His work-roughened palms rasped against the satiny skin of her hips as he tugged open the snap of her jeans and lowered the zipper. "Jesus, Allie, did you *paint* these on? Help me out here." With a laugh she wriggled until he had the curve-hugging denim down and off.

Lust threatened to consume him as he uncovered her silky limbs and left her standing in nothing but mind-altering scraps of pink silk. She palmed his head, her fingers tickling through his hair and across his scalp as his hands explored the firmness of her toned runner's thighs, roamed her trim hips and kneaded the lush globes of her ass. Jesus, she was . . . perfect. Better than anything good and soft he could ever imagine. He dragged open– mouth kisses over the front of her panties and was rewarded when she drew in a ragged shudder. His heart raced in his chest.

More. He needed more and he needed it now. Needed to bury himself—. Ah, *fuck!* Abruptly he tightened his arms around her thighs and dropped his forehead to her belly. "Shit."

Her hands held him close. "Not the reaction I was looking for, Jake."

He raised his eyes, met hers, dark with passion yet suddenly amused. "Tell me you have condoms, Allie. He rose, floundering, desperate. "I'm not . . . prepared . . . for this." His imagination hadn't dare stretch this far.

Her amusement fled and her hands lifted to cup his jaw. "No I don't, but I've already started my change." She released his face and his pecs tightened as her hands raked across his shoulders then flicked his nipples.

Allie. Her babies. "I'm sorry, baby." he murmured while he still could and caught the quick flash of regret that clouded her eyes.

Then he couldn't think. Could only feel as those hands coasted lower and, "Ah, fuck, Allie. What are you—?" His knees buckled. He couldn't breathe. She was going to kill him. "Jesus. Baby. Do that again."

The soft morning light sneaked through the slats of the window blinds and warmed her face. She'd been warm since Jake first held her last night, hot since she uncovered his bare skin and caused his heart to sprint with just her hands. Her blood scorched her veins when he laid her on the bed and nibbled every inch of her body, inflaming her sensitive skin with his hot, lashing tongue. Describing in exacting detail what he wanted to do to her.

She melted when he crowded into her body, inch by unhurried inch and then burned when passion built and he powered into her in a series of hard, grinding thrusts. He drowned her in a sea of endless kisses that left her chest heaving for breath and her body slick with sweat. And when his fingers found her and set her blazing, his body was fused to hers as they came apart together.

Sated, energized, she stretched out her arms, and then her legs. Oh, a little achy. Her heart bumped, then smoothed, settled. "Jake." The word slipped out on a satisfied sigh.

He was awake. She lay cradled, wrapped in the warm cocoon of his arms, with the proof pressed urgently against her hip. She turned her head back and he dropped a lusty kiss on her lips.

"Good morning, babe. Sleep well?"

"Eventually." She rolled and landed facing him, letting her palm ride the firm ridges of his abdomen. "How about you? That smile looks satisfied."

He smoothed her hair back, a grin spread across his face. "I was. Several times, in fact."

She let her grin match his. "And points to you for that."

Lying on his side with an arm resting heavy across her waist, his lips lowered to tease hers again before continuing across her jaw and down the column of her throat. "We have hours before Trey's due home. Care to up the score?"

Her breath quickened in her chest. His hand roamed along her hip, dragging her closer until she was beneath him, kicking at the tangle of sheets. She wrestled him, rolled until she lay across his chest, propped on her elbows. "This game could be addicting, you know."

Quick as a cobra, he raised his head and stole another kiss. "Oh God, I hope so."

Rumpled and exhausted but hungry for food Allie climbed out of bed, then straightened the bedroom and changed the sheets. Jake belted out an upbeat tune from the shower, and she smiled. Gathering the linens, she headed down the hallway as the shower spray ceased. She was still smiling as she turned the corner.

And ran smack into Trey.

"You guys should consider putting a sock on the door." He had the nerve to chortle as she bounced off him.

Oh, God! She stumbled to a full stop, enveloped in the heat of a full body blush, and tugged at the sash of her robe.

Trey's laugh subsided gradually, landed in an amused smirk. "I think I may be traumatized."

"Trey!" The working corner of her brain recognized that her son was here. Home. *Early.* And he was speaking. "What, what are you talking about?" She glanced down at her armful of rumpled sheets, gave them a quick toss into the laundry room.

"You and Jake, of course." His eyes gleamed with mirth. "Isn't that his new car in the driveway? You two were making so much noise you didn't even hear me."

"Babe, is the coffee . . . ?"

Jake's words trailed off as he edged around the corner, buttoning his jeans as he entered. His hair was wet and tousled from his shower. He came up short when he saw Trey.

Jake's eyes pinned Trey and his voice sounded strangled. "You were *here* last night?"

Trey laughed again, mischief dancing in his eyes. "Well I drove all that way. I thought I may as well stay."

Jake's muttered *oh shit* got hung up in a groan as his eyes skipped over to Allie, who was fading to an adorable shade of pink. Gingerly wading into the waters of Trey's acceptance, he ignored the jackhammer pounding in his chest and listened in while he started a pot of coffee.

"My last class got cancelled." Trey was still grinning with unholy glee. "I thought it would be a nice surprise—I just didn't realize the surprise would be on me."

Jake was capable of guarding the coffee pot, but Allie was a kindergarten teacher for two decades now—she was a master at sticky situations. He could have dropped to kiss her feet when she grinned widely and spread her arms for an openhearted hug.

"Welcome home, Trey. What a nice surprise!"

Her grin grew, turning into a chuckle as Trey wrapped his arms around her and lifted her before setting her bare feet back on the kitchen floor. Stepping out of her son's embrace, she held out her open palm.

"Now give me your key."

Trey's grin faded to amusement mixed with incredulity. "Ah, c'mon, Mom. Really?" He rolled his eyes. "You're gonna take my key? How am I supposed to get in the house?"

Allie reached into the refrigerator for juice and milk, setting them on the counter. "You can use the code on the garage door. Come in through the laundry room." She dove back into the fridge. "I think that makes perfect sense."

Trey, clearly not. His smile faded further. "Seriously? Even late at night? It's loud."

She pulled out of the refrigerator, hands full of bacon and eggs. Her eyes met his. "Exactly!"

Jake had to laugh. A full snort that had fresh coffee shooting through his nose. Hell yeah, he could get used to this.

Jake poured coffee for Allie. She took it and stepped up against him. With her free arm wrapped around his waist, she lightly stretched up to brush his lips with hers.

"Mmm, good." She smiled sweetly. "I think your shirt's still by the sofa, somewhere. You want breakfast?"

He paused in the doorway. "I could go for seconds."

She tossed a kitchen towel at him, causing him to laugh, and began laying bacon strips on the sizzling griddle.

Pancake batter was mixed. Trey poured juice and refilled coffee mugs. "Hey Jake." Trey grinned at him as he reentered the room. "That's a nice ride you've got."

"Yeah, thanks. You should see it on the open road. She's a racehorse." He barely had time to wonder at Allie's glare before the gleam in Trey's eyes registered.

"Sweet! Think I can take it for a spin?"

Ah, shit. That's why Allie was pissed. "That would be a hell, no." He shot

Allie a helpless shrug before shaking his head and laughing as he took a seat at the breakfast table. This was what breakfast was all about.

Jake filled the stainless steel sink with hot, sudsy water while Trey attacked the countertops with a wet sponge. A feeling of contentment infused him in an easy breath. If everything went the way he wanted this would be his family. *Family.* Did he dare to believe?

"Hey Trey?" With the dishwasher loaded, up to his forearms in soapy dishwater he concentrated on scouring the griddle.

"Yeah?"

The heat of Trey's curious glance warmed his back. "I imagine it was something of a surprise, finding me here this morning."

Trey answered with a chuckle. "And commando, no less. Now t*hat* was a surprise."

That easy breath was probably only one wrong word away, but as long as the kid was joking around he wasn't pissed. He let his hands still in the suds long enough to catch a confirming glimpse from over his shoulder, then focused his scrubbing on an imaginary speck. "We can talk, you know."

The sponge squeaked against the granite countertop. "You mean like, *what are your intentions for my mom?*"

Gripping the sponge, scouring the griddle thankfully kept his hands from shaking. "I don't know. I guess so, if that's what you want to know."

The sponge flew over Jake's shoulder to land in the sink with a *plop*. "Okay, so yeah, I suppose so. What *are* your intentions? I didn't realize you guys were hooking up."

Jake gave up any pretense of cleaning the griddle, rinsed the soap and dropped it in the drainer. It gave him a moment to dispel that quick flash of irritation. He leaned a jean-clad hip against the counter and crossed his ankles. "Not hooking up, Trey. I love her. She loves me too."

A small smile hovered around his mouth, but his voice was earnest, his gaze direct. "This is kind of new for me, for us. I don't know what happens next." He allowed his expression to turn solemn. "I would never do anything to hurt her, you know that, right?"

Trey continued to face him, and finally he smiled again. "Yeah, I know that."

"If I asked her to marry me, would you be good with that?" A small hopeful smile tugged at his lips; it would mean disaster if he got the wrong answer.

But Trey lit up. "Uncle Jake, dude. That would be awesome. I would be totally good with that. Will you ask her soon?"

Jake's smile widened. "Yeah, very soon." This was the second part of his plan. He meant to ask her last night, and then again this morning, but they were . . . distracted.

"But dude, what if she says no?"

Trey's look of horror had Jake's pulse pounding in his temples. Oh crap, he didn't think of that. What if she did? The eggs he had for breakfast were now sloshing around in his stomach.

"Jake, you should see your face . . . priceless." He hooted, then became earnest. "But seriously, why would she say no?"

"Yeah, why would she say no?" Okay. Good. Got that figured out. Easy. His heart rate tumbled back to something resembling normal.

"One thing, though."

There went the hammer again, but his pulse relaxed when Trey merely smirked. "Yeah, what's that?"

"Do I still have to call you 'Uncle'?"

Jake swooped around the island and grabbed Trey in a bear hug, laughing with him as he lifted him off his feet.

"I love you, Trey. You know that? You are definitely one great kid." Content hell, he was overcome.

"Yeah, Jake. Love you, too. Welcome to the family."

Battle cries and boisterous laughter—along with the unmistakable sounds of splashing and sloshing—drew Allie to the kitchen, raising both suspicions and curiosity. Trey, manning a lethal weapon in the form of the sink sprayer, was on the verge of claiming victory. Jake crouched behind the island cabinet, a long-handled skillet serving as his shield. She could only shake her head in mock exasperation. Little boys came in all sizes. Water cascaded over the countertops, creating miniature waterfalls which fell freely to the tile. Scattered puddles and mounds of suds dotted the floor. She let it all go and withdrew to the safety of the living room. Trey was the only man in her life for years now, but, oh yeah, she was ready for a change. And Trey seemed ready, too.

Woeful cries of surrender came from the kitchen. Perhaps it was safe to reenter now. She stole around the corner, dodging pools of water as she made her way to the mop. Jake, no longer in mortal danger, dried the griddle and put it away. Trey poured them each one more cup of coffee before he rinsed out the pot.

Allie paused, a questioning eye on her son while leaning on the mop handle. "So tell us about school."

"And what keeps you too busy to come home." Jake shamelessly edged that in, then shrugged when Allie frowned at him. "Your mother worries."

Trey tracked the volley of expressions with a grin. "Oh, I manage to stay busy. I found a football team to join. It's a club league, but there's pretty good talent. Except the QB sucks. I sure miss Jax."

"What about your classes?" The rise of panic pouring from Allie's eyes had her asking more emphatically than necessary. Jake draped a comforting arm across her shoulders and led her to sit with her coffee.

"Yes, classes, too, Mom. Biology and math are pretty hard." Trey rolled his eyes, then laughed. "You'll be glad to know I'm on a first name basis with everyone who works in the library."

Trey joined them at the table. "I know kids who barely go to class." Disgust was written on his face. "C's get degrees, that's their motto. They spend the weekend partying and Monday nursing a hangover. It's kind of sad, really. One day they'll come around and wish they put in more effort."

Allie's mother's eye bored into the kid sitting beside her. Okay, where was her son and who was this imposter? Trey was only gone two months and already he seemed more mature.

Trey eased out of his chair. "I didn't have time to do my laundry this week, so I brought it down. It's still in my truck; I'll go get it."

The only time she'd ever seen Trey do his own laundry was one day back in August. Imagining him coming home with all his clothes the same dingy gray, she dragged him to the washing machine under squawking protest and showed him how to sort white socks from blue jeans and how much detergent to use. She hoped he was using that lesson at school, but she could also picture him wearing his clothes until they were stiff.

"Well, I guess I should go now." Jake stood to pull her into his arms, lowered his cheek to the top of her head. "Mmm, you feel good. And you always smell nice. Like flowers." He planted a soft kiss on her forehead. "I still have a hard time believing this isn't a dream." He lifted his head and smiled down at her. "I love you, have I told you lately?"

"No, stay. And feel free to tell me anytime the mood strikes." She paused, searching for the words. "Does this seem unreal to you, too? I feel almost like I'm too happy. Like I don't deserve this."

Jake nuzzled her neck, sending goosebumps down her arms. "You do deserve this . . . and more."

The calm contentment on his face after the possible fiasco with Trey should make her smile. Instead, dread had her shoulders slumping as if she wore a cement shawl. She pulled out of his arms. "There's something we need to talk about." But Trey would be back any minute. "Let's take a walk."

She was already pushing her arms into her jacket. She handed Jake's to him and passed Trey on the front porch. Jake paused to hold the door open for him as he entered the house with what was possibly his entire wardrobe shoved into a large plastic hamper. "Have at it, kid."

"Thanks, Jake," he drolled, and headed for the laundry room.

A brisk wind had kicked up and brown leaves hurtled across the dormant lawn, swirling in the curb. Allie huddled into her coat; Jake laced her fingers with his as they strolled down the sidewalk, leaves crunching beneath each step. He waited for what, he had no idea, but she wouldn't meet his eyes and his heart rate ratcheted.

In time she sent him a sideways glance, then spoke slowly, her words seemingly chosen carefully. "Thank you for last night, Jake."

He drew his eyebrows together in confusion, tightened his fingers around hers and drew her to a halt. "You waiting for me to say *you're welcome*, Allie? Because *thank you* doesn't begin to cover how I feel about last night."

"You're right. It was wonderful, but I've been thinking." She pulled their joined hands to her heart. "This is hard for me to say, and I need you to hear me out."

Hear what? Was she having second thoughts? *Oh, hell no.* He dropped her hand to grasp her by the shoulders. "Hard to say what? Where are you going with this?"

She lowered her eyes to study the sidewalk. "I hope you agree that what we have here—what we need to have, I should say—is an affair. Just sex."

What the hell? "You think I can agree to *that*?" He frowned down at her, flummoxed. After the night they'd just had? The words they'd spoken?

She tilted her head back and peered up at him, shoving her bare hands deep into her pockets. "Remember last night, when I told you I've started my change already . . . menopause, and I couldn't get pregnant?"

His frown deepened. "Yeah, what about it? That doesn't matter."

"Of course it matters." A combination of anger and misery rode the harsh statement and only her upraised palm stopped him from pulling her closer and locking his arms around her. "I can't have children anymore, Jake. When you find someone to settle down with you'll want that. And I can't . . . do that. Not anymore."

Her eyes turned haunted as she pulled out one hand and laid it on his chest. "It's so hard to explain, but I feel . . . incomplete." She patted her hand. "In here. And now the choice is not mine to make. I love Trey, but I always felt there were more children inside me, needing me. It was a concept Ben never understood." She paused and finally he pulled her against his jacket.

"I always felt I was still young enough to have another child, but I guess Mother Nature has a different plan for me." She widened her eyes and blinked back tears.

He leaned back and thumbed the moisture away. "First off, you love me, right?" The drawn out moment before she answered had his heart pounding.

"Of course."

Jesus. Was she trying to give him a heart attack? "Of course. And what we have here is not *just* sex, Allie. It's *great* sex." At her puny smile, he added more earnestly, "We are not having an affair. I love you." No way in hell was she cutting him out now. He'd make her see they needed to be together. He trapped her face, his calloused palms cupping her cheeks, and dropped a gentle kiss on her lips. "Marry me. Babies or no babies, I want every day and every single night with *you*."

He glanced up the street, at two teenage boys skateboarding on the sidewalk, and the next-door neighbor unloading groceries, then turned back to her. "This isn't exactly the way I wanted to ask you, though." He smiled at her, and released her to hold her hands. "I wanted candlelight and champagne, soft music in the background. And a ring. Can we go shopping this afternoon and find a great big rock to put here?" He lifted her left hand and kissed her bare ring finger. She'd worn Ben's rings on her right hand since that first day with the attorney. He stopped talking. She hadn't said anything yet and his heart pounded again. Christ, he may have that heart attack yet. "Allie? Babe, what do you say? Shall we go pick one out?"

Allie pulled her hands to her sides and turned away. "I love you, Jake. There's no doubt in my mind, I love you." He took a deep breath, sensing an important *but* coming next. "I'll stay with you as long as you want. But I can't marry you." She turned around now, her eyes beseeching him to understand. "My son is the best thing I ever did. I want you to know that happiness too."

Hell no. She was not pulling that on him. "Don't I get to decide, Allie? Don't I get a say? Babies were a dream, but dreams can change. I love you. And I love Trey. You're my family now."

"I'll be with you. For as long as you want. But I won't marry you." Sonofabitch. He couldn't be this close to the brass ring only to have her yank it away. "We only get one chance to live our life. One day you'll change your mind and then you'll be free."

He didn't want to be free, damn it. How could she be so cruel? Didn't she realize each word was a dagger, plunged unerringly into his heart? He had no intention of letting her get away with this shit. He wasn't going anywhere, and neither was she. But she was in no mood to be reasoned with. Taking her hand, he led her back to the house. "All right, babe. We'll do this your way, for now."

Chapter Twenty Four

Allie took a pork roast from the refrigerator, seasoned it and set it to brown it on the stovetop wearing a frown that had nothing to do with the slab of meat sizzling in the heavy Dutch oven. Jake needed to understand that this troubling need to protect him plagued her. Plagued, yes, that was a good word for how she felt. Wouldn't it be nice if she could not worry about what was right for everyone and just take what she wanted? Because she would have chosen a future with Jake.

Using tongs, she flipped the meat to sear the top. Whether this was due to Ben's request or on her, it didn't matter. Her conscience wouldn't allow her to be the anchor that kept him from a life he wanted.

Oh, she was thankful for what they shared now, but despair weighed heavy on her mood. She added liquid to the meat and hefted the cast iron pan into the screaming hot oven. How long would they survive if she was already pulling away?

Allie passed the plate of sliced meat to Trey. "Do you already have plans for tomorrow?

Trey passed mashed potatoes to Jake and took the platter from his mom. "Jax and I are planning something tomorrow night; his girlfriend Kiley is in town and she brought her roommate with her. But I don't have anything planned during the day."

"I wondered." She glanced up at Jake. "Maybe we can all do something. Go to a matinee, or bowling."

Jake swallowed his bite and spoke up. "How would you like to go to a football game? Not sure who we're playing, but we're home this week."

Trey didn't bother swallowing first, nearly bouncing in his seat. "Dude! I'm totally down with that. Do you think we can still get tickets?"

"Let me make a call, see if I can come up with something."

Allie sat, bemused. "Forty-five-yard line. That's good, right?"

"It's excellent, Mom. And only a few rows in from the field! Jake, you totally scored! But what will we do with the fourth ticket?"

Maybe your mom would like to invite a friend." Jake's deadpan expression had her smothering a grin."

"Sure, that's a pretty good idea."

But Trey was less than enthusiastic and she nearly laughed while she finished clearing the table. "Or," she drew out the word for drama, "Maybe Jax would like to come along."

Jake followed Trey with his eyes as he lit down the hallway. "I think he liked that idea a whole lot better."

"I'd say so. He had to make the call before we change our minds." She rinsed plates and began stacking them in the dishwasher. "How did you manage that, mister? I'm impressed."

Jake gave a quick jerk of his shoulder. "No big deal, really. We have a supplier with season tickets. He uses them mainly for customers." Simple as that.

"Wow! A man with connections. I may keep you around after all, if only for the perks." She gave him a mischievous smile.

"Oh, I can think of better perks than football tickets." Jake had a mischievous smile of his own. "Trey's going out tonight, what do you say we find a sock?"

Allie followed Jake into the living room, plopped on the sofa beside him. What a day, she was exhausted. As promised, he arrived this morning loaded down with a barbeque grill and a cooler filled with food and drinks, then trashed her kitchen cupboards hunting for the forgotten paper goods. She pushed up the sleeves of her bulky green turtleneck. "Tailgating. Now I remember why we had to leave four hours before game time.

Jake picked up the remote and flipped channels until he came to the news, then turned down the volume. He picked up her right hand, absently twisted her ring. "Sure. Like when Ben and I used to take Trey to games."

She looked at her hand, at his fingers toying with her jewelry and pulled her hand away. "Right." The stadium parking lot was a sea of pop-up canopies with red and black logo banners snapping in a breeze that carried enticing aromas of grilled meat. Swarms of noisy fans dressed in replica team jerseys were clustered around grills and portable firepits. She stood to light a scented candle and smiled from across the room. "Actually, I had fun. The boys did too. I should have remembered sunscreen, though. My nose is a little pink."

He leaned back, dropped an arm across the back of the sofa and nodded toward her feet. "What you should have remembered was to not wear those three-inch heels. You would have landed on your ass if you lost your footing on those steps down to our seats."

Um hmm, those seats in the third row. He really did spoil them. She returned to the couch, sat and dangled one jean clad leg over his knee. "Would you save me if I started to fall?" He lifted her leg, straightened it and ran a palm down the denim of her jeans, ending with her boot in his hand. It had been so long since a man touched her with an end game objective. She smiled to herself. It felt really good.

"You bet." He lowered his voice and the tingles she was beginning to associate with him snaked up and down her spine. "If your butt was broken you wouldn't be able to wrap these babies around my waist later tonight."

Her face heated. "Oh." The word escaped on a short breath, not nearly all she wanted to say, but all she got out before Trey wandered in, freshly showered. Darn his timing! Watching him cross the room, she took a deep breath and shook her head to clear it. The scents of soap and cologne followed him as he dropped into the easy chair, drumming his fingers on the arm.

His hand stilled. He looked at her, then down at his chest. "What? I have something on my shirt?"

She took another deep breath. There, calmer. She shook her head again. "Um, no. We were just talking about the game."

Trey lit up in a beaming grin. "Yeah, it was great! Thanks again, Jake. For the jersey, too."

"No problem. Can't have everyone representing except you and Jax." Jake leaned forward and fist-bumped Trey, then sat with his forearms braced on his knees. "So what are you guys up to tonight?"

"Pizza, then a movie." Trey rolled his eyes. "I hope it's not some chick flick." His smile turned uneasy, matching the uncertainty in his eyes. "I'm a little nervous, can you tell? It's my first blind date."

"Don't sweat it. Just have a good time."

His grin was a little shaky. "Good time. Got it." A car honked at the curb and Trey sprang to his feet with a feeble wave. "I'm out."

As the front door slammed, Jake sank into the cushion beside her. "Even though his timing stinks I've really missed him." He chuckled and dropped his arm across her shoulders, the thick nubby sweater rubbing against her skin under his fingers. "Has he mentioned coming home more often?"

"No, and I won't ask." This was his time. To grow up, to explore. She laid a tentative hand against Jake's chest, let it wander. "This is our time now."

"Our time, I like that." He stopped her hand, pulled it to his lips and brushed them across her knuckles. "But if it bothers you to not see him, we should talk to him about it."

She pulled her hand free, looped it across the hard width of his waist, then tilted her head to the side when he lowered his lips to her collarbone. "No. He knows he's welcome, he'll be home when he can."

He lifted his head and pulled her to his chest. "I doubt you could ever make him feel unwelcome."

She sat quietly for a moment, distracted by the beating of his heart under her ear. "I should put something together for dinner." She moved as if to stand, but Jake's words stopped her.

"Pizza sounds good. Why don't we order in instead?"

Jake woke to an infomercial touting the wonders of food dehydrators. The pizza box lay open on the table before him, two leftover slices lying shriveled inside. Was Trey home yet? *Hey Tate, you got plans Saturday.* He shook off the memory.

Allie slept soundly against his chest. When he stood and lifted her into his arms she snuffled through her parted lips and retreated into her dreams. Tucked into bed with a crocheted afghan covering her and her hair spilling over her pillow, he envied her sense of peace.

He released a sigh as he watched her sleep. He understood her need to shield him from a life he may regret. It was bullshit, but he got it. She loved him, though, and that was a good start.

Patience, bucko. She would come around. She had to.

Hopeful, he retraced his steps to the living room, then snatched up the pizza box to drop into the garbage container on his way to his truck.

Halloween was behind her, Thanksgiving hovered in the near future. Allie stretched, reaching high from her perch on the stepstool. She grabbed the cardboard cutouts from the wall and stepped down carefully, Jack-o'-lanterns and candy corn gripped firmly in her hand. She stacked them on the nearest desk as Maddie walked past her open door.

A moment later she reappeared, as always full of energy. "Don't you love it when Halloween is over? I swear that holiday was invented for the sole purpose of classroom disruption! It's all the kids can think about for weeks—costumes, parties, candy. Costumes. Their concentration flies right out the window."

Allie laughed softly at her friend. Maddie idly flipped through the discarded decorations as Allie collected a handful of fall leaves and moved back to the stepstool. "I freely admit that holiday is hell on lessons. And Christmas is even worse. But Thanksgiving, that's always my favorite. Other than a few leaves, and maybe a couple of pilgrim stories, Thanksgiving is a breeze." She had to look down to see Maddie from her vantage point on the stool. "I remember one year Trey's homeroom tried to do a Thanksgiving feast." She shook her head as she remembered. "It was a fiasco. That poor teacher. She was new and so full of ideals."

"And tell me you're not."

She dimpled down at her friend. "What can I say? Hel-lo, I love my job." Done hanging leaves in a random order, Allie climbed down again and reached for the pilgrims. She lifted the stool and carried it to the opposite side of the room. "So what do the Andrews' have planned for Thanksgiving?"

Maddie moved to the door and hung a cardboard turkey. "We're going to Prescott, to Michael's family. It should be fun, no snow yet, though. How about you, is dinner at your mom's?"

Allie glanced around the room in a quick double-check and nodded, climbed down and stowed the stool in the closet. "It always is, but I haven't talked to her about it yet. My brother Ryan and his family are usually there, but now that his wife is gone I don't know what his plans are. And I need to see if Jake already has plans. I'd love for him to go with us. My family's only met him a couple of times, and that was years ago." Allie picked up the Halloween decorations from the desk and put them away in the cabinet. She checked the time. The morning bell would ring in five short minutes.

"Of course he'll go. His parents are both gone and he has no siblings, what else would he do?" Maddie helped Allie distribute worksheets to each desk, readying the room for the invasion of youngsters.

Allie shrugged. "I don't know. In the past he's always gone to some friend's house. We never could get him to go to Scottsdale with us."

"Yes, but now he wants to marry you." Maddie laid a paper on the final desktop and met her gaze. "You're nuts, by the way. I can't believe you haven't changed your mind yet. He's a great guy, and he loves you more than the legal limit. If he's good with the way things are, why can't you be?"

"I must admit, it's hard to remember why I keep saying no." Allie shook her head in consternation. "He asks me every time I see him, but I don't want him tied down to something he'll want out of someday."

"Allie, I've been listening to your excuses for weeks and I've got to tell you, I think you're batshit crazy. He wants to be tied down; for chrissake give him what he wants and tie him down."

Allie headed toward the door to line her kids up for school. "Thanks, Maddie, we'll see how things go."

"I only want you to be truly happy." Maddie leaned in, hugged.

Allie smiled, squeezed back. "I'm happy."

Jason, the boy whose parents were divorcing, slipped up as she stepped onto the playground. "I learned a new joke, Mrs. Tate. Wanna hear?"

Allie squatted to his height and gave him a bright smile. The boy rarely spoke anymore. One knock-knock joke just might make his day. "Sure, why not?"

Tuesday after Thanksgiving Allie sat in Jake's kitchen, trying to enjoy a quiet dinner. With a few exceptions, things had been going smoothly for weeks now. Jake spent the holiday with her family, piling his plate high and joining in conversation. But ever since that night he'd seemed to be on edge. And he was terribly quiet tonight. Was he rethinking their relationship? She studied him as he spooned take-out kung pao over his rice, then traded her for the curry. He hadn't spoken in so long the sound of his voice made her jump.

"I heard from Trey today. He wanted to know if he could work for me while he's home for Christmas."

Allie took a bite of curry; hopefully the spicy dish wouldn't upset her stomach. She'd been off—achy and nauseated all day. It was a lousy time to come down with something. "Really? Is there enough work that you can keep him busy?"

Trey spent the past two summers working for T-Squared and had picked up a number of skills. "Sure, I can throw him on a crew while he's home. He told me he's interested in learning more about the business." He took another bite, then added, "They have a pretty good management program up there."

"It must run in the family."

When silence thickened the air she lifted her eyes to him. "What?"

"What about us, Allie? Our family, you and me? How much longer do I have to wait?" He choked out the words even as his voice escalated, a side of him she'd rarely ever seen. "When will you be done with this . . . this . . . *damn it!*" His voice exploded as his fist pounded the table, bouncing dinner plates and upsetting his water glass. "I'm tired of living apart. I want us to be a family."

He sprang from his seat, towering over her, then stalked to the kitchen for a towel. He spun at the sink, his neck corded with strain, ebony eyes piercing her. "I want more, damn it. I want you to marry me."

She lifted her hands, palms raised upward. "I'm here, Jake, but that's all I can give you. "I don't know what more I can say."

His voice bellowed as his palms slammed the table. "You can say you'll marry me!"

Enough! Her chair clattered to the floor as she surged to her feet. She slapped her palms to the table, face to face with him. "But I can't have babies!" She yelled in his face, "I refuse—*refuse*—to take that away from you!"

She found his finger shoved in her face. "You're full of it, you know that? Why Allie? Why is this enough for you?" His palm slashed between them, emphasizing his question. "Why do you think us having or not having babies is important to me?" His voice was suddenly quiet, defeated. "I've loved you, wanted you, for . . . ever. Do you think I'd throw all that away so there's another little Taylor running around?"

So it had come to this. Her voice caught in her throat. "I don't know. You just . . . don't understand."

Jake sank back into his seat, eyes on his unfinished dinner. "What will it take to convince you?" The pain in his voice had tears clogging her throat. "The idea of my own child is a thing of the past. My life is yours now; I can't imagine it without you. Not for ten minutes or ten days, certainly not forever. Can you really live without me?"

Oh God, could she? She needed him, probably more than he claimed to need her. But this was no time to make a life-changing, potentially disastrous decision, angry and about to lose what little dinner she ate. "I need to leave now, Jake; there's too much to think about." Eyes brimming, she strode into the living room, grabbing her purse along the way.

He ran after her and caught her arm at the couch. "I'll call you tomorrow."

"No. Please. Give me time. I'll call you." She tugged her arm free, swiped at the streaming tears and continued to the door.

"I love you, Allie."

The gruffness in his voice stopped her hand from turning the doorknob. She stilled, unable to move, but unable to stay. Didn't he know this was killing her too? "I know you do. I love you too. I'm just not sure if it's enough."

He reached for her again, turned her to him and ran the backs of his fingers down her cheek. If only she had the will to pull away. His lips whispered against hers before he opened the door for her, opening a wound in her soul that she alone was responsible for.

The pain in his eyes was nearly her undoing. The hurt in his voice echoed as she pulled out of his driveway and drove to the corner stop sign. Her teary glance in the rear view mirror provided nothing but a blurry kaleidoscope of light. Was Jake watching her drive away from him? If she turned around right now would he welcome her back? Wrap her in his arms and love her?

There was no doubt he would.

But for how long?

A car pulled up behind her. She needed to make a decision. Should she change her mind and turn back? Could she risk her heart, her future? Could she trust that Jake was willing to give up babies of his own? Was she strong enough to let him? The car behind her honked. She took her foot off the brake and continued straight.

Chapter Twenty Five

Trey was on his way. He called Allie to let her know he was almost home. They had two feet of new snow up north and even with new chains and four-wheel drive, he was uneasy driving on the recently plowed highway. Allie held her breath until he called, letting her know he was clear. He would be home in an hour.

Erratic hormones were still giving her fits. She was irritable and short-tempered and the waterworks had not yet let up. And now she was ill with the flu. It had been coming on for weeks. She was achy and nauseated and no matter how much sleep she got during the night she woke up tired. She forced herself to run with Maddie each morning, but by the time she returned home she was exhausted.

It was only six o'clock, but Allie was already in her sweats. The kids at school were keyed up about the upcoming break and her days had been spent in a frenzy of activity. She endured parent conferences, and the annual holiday program, but her evenings were full of nothing but time to think. It was what she asked for and, like he always did, Jake gave her what she wanted.

She thought of him as she woke in the morning, reaching for him and finding nothing but cold sheets. What was he doing today? In the classroom, between interruptions by busy five-year-olds, she thought about their time together. Eating dinner alone, she wished he was there to share her day. And at night . . . nights were the worst. At night her memories and imagination took over.

She relaxed into the corner of the sofa, a mug of herbal tea cradled in one hand. The aromas of simmering soup and Trey's favorite pumpkin cake flavored the air. Covered with a light throw, she munched saltines, a murder mystery she'd been dying to read open on her lap.

The front door opened, letting in a blast of wintery cold. "Hey, Mom, I'm here!"

She untucked her feet to stand as Trey yelled into the house, ducking her head to take a quick swipe at her eyes and plaster on a semblance of a smile. "Welcome home, sweetheart." She wrapped him in a welcoming hug as she neared him.

Stepping out of her arms, Trey dropped his duffle bag near the door. "Hey, are you okay? You look like you were crying."

"No, it's just, um . . . I'm happy to have you home." She could hardly tell him she was afraid she was screwing up her life.

"Just wait until you have to feed me every day. You'll change your mind in a hurry."

A genuine grin spread across her face. She pointed at his duffle. "Is this all you brought?"

"Are you kidding? I'll be here for a month. I brought so much stuff down you'll think I'm moving back." He turned and headed back out the door.

She followed him, forcing enthusiasm into her voice. "I heard you're planning to work for Jake while you're home." Thankfully, he didn't seem to notice the way she stumbled over Jake's name.

"I called him a couple of weeks ago. He said he could keep me busy while I'm here." He opened the truck door, began unloading his stuff. He slung his backpack over a shoulder, then grabbed another duffel bag. A box full of video games and DVDs came next. Finally, a garbage bag full of who knew what.

She surveyed the clutter scattered around her driveway and sighed. Welcome home, Trey. Farewell to her peace and quiet for the next four weeks. Maybe that was a good thing.

A bag in each hand, she traipsed inside. Trey followed her with the rest of his things, lifting a beaten-up Red Wing and kicking the door shut behind him. He dropped everything in the middle of the floor and pulled out his cell phone. "I need to give him a call. I'm supposed to work tomorrow, but I don't know where."

The hum of Trey's voice faded as she hauled his gear to his room. Yes, she should probably ask him to do it himself, but knowing Jake was on the phone made him almost . . . here. The sound of approaching footsteps had her dropping her armload and looking up.

"Hey, that soup is really good." Trey waved a spoon in the air. "Can we eat soon? I'm starving." He turned toward the kitchen again, and she followed. "By the way, Jake says hi."

"I'm planning to make biscuits to go with it." The tremor in her voice was easily disguised in a cough as she slipped into the pantry. Before she could control them, the tears were gushing, streaming along her nose and dripping from her chin. Leaning her forehead against the wall, all she could do was let them fall.

Two weeks. It was two weeks since she last saw him, talked to him, touched him—felt his touch. She could still smell him, taste him. Oh God, she missed him badly. Sometimes it was hard to remember why she was so resistant. Using her shoulder to scrub her face dry, she grabbed the flour.

With biscuits browning in the oven, Allie set the table. Trey ambled back in and poured a glass of milk. "You don't have a Christmas tree yet, mom. What are you waiting for?"

She leaned to pull the bread from the oven. "There's still a week so I waited for you. I thought you might like to get one together."

"Can we go tomorrow after work?" Trey took an empty bowl to the stove and dished his soup, grabbing a couple of biscuits on his way to the table.

She ladled soup into her own bowl and tore off half a biscuit. "We can go whenever you want. I don't have anything planned at all. I'll get out the decorations while you're gone." Allie took the seat across from Trey and dipped out a small spoonful of soup.

"Hey, Mama?"

"What, sweetheart?" She met his gaze across the table, wondering what was wrong. He never called her *Mama* anymore."

He looked uncomfortable. "When I talked to Jake today, he said to tell you hi, but he also said to tell you he missed you."

Allie's biscuit paused on its journey to her mouth. Her eyes darted away as they filled.

"He sounded sad, really quiet. What's going on?"

Allie swiped her eyes with her napkin then gave him a weak smile. "It's nothing for you to worry about, sweetheart. We just have a few things to work out."

Trey leaned forward, his forearms braced against the table. "You're still treating me like I'm twelve."

"No, I'm . . . yes, sorry, but—" She knit her brow. "It's complicated. Things may work themselves out."

Trey leaned back again, angling his head. "Or maybe they won't?"

"Or maybe they won't."

He stood and circled the table, then put his arm around her shoulder, kissing her cheek. "I'm sorry, Mom."

He was definitely no longer her little boy. His tenderness brought on a watery smile. "I know honey, but no need to worry."

Her bowl was still half full but her hunger was overridden by the chaos in her heart. She cleared the table, then settled on the sofa with a fresh mug of tea. Her stomach seemed to settle in the evenings; hopefully that would be the case tonight. She picked up her novel, hopefully the drama on the page would distract her for a while.

Trey walked through with his dirty laundry and she looked up at the thumping of the hamper against his thighs. "Leave that and I'll do it tomorrow."

"It's fine, Mom. I'll put in a load before I leave."

"You're going out?"

"Gonna hang out with Jax."

How could she have forgotten how he was never still? Within minutes he was gone, backing out of the driveway. She lived alone for months now . . . why did it seem so lonely tonight?

Trey was at work. And even though she moved about the house as quickly as she dared, tables would get dusted and rugs would get vacuumed quicker if she didn't get lightheaded every time she moved too fast. She dragged a few small pieces of furniture, rearranging them inch by inch to make room for the tree. From the high shelves in the garage she yanked down several large clear tubs of holiday decorations staggering under their weight as she hauled them into the living room.

Uncovering the first bin, she pulled out Trey's stocking; her mom quilted it for his first Christmas. She rooted around until she found its hanger, then hung it from a shelf of the built-in bookcase. Only one stocking. It always looked so lonely.

The house was a little more festive with the wreath—an artificial arrangement of greenery, pine cones and ribbon—adorning the front door. Maybe this year she should get a real one, one that actually smelled like Christmas. Shrugging, she knelt before the box of decorations, reacquainting herself with a lifetime of colorful treasures. Delicate glass ornaments were tucked away beside papier-mâché grade school projects, craft bazaar finds, and gifts from students. Each piece had a story behind it, a celebration of the history of their family.

Tossing the last bit of tissue wrapper back into the bin, she surveyed her work. The scented candles she loved were scattered about, table lines were stored in the kitchen and her favorite, a wooden nativity crèche, had a place of honor on the entry table. Her home held just the right mix of fussy and functional, but her eyes drooped with exhaustion. She left the empty containers where they lay and dropped onto the sofa for a short nap.

She swatted at the persistent fly. Swatted again as it landed on her cheek, but hit something solid. She cracked her eyelid and found Trey, grinning at her.

"Hey, sleepyhead, I'm home. Time to get us a tree."

Trey hauled the cumbersome Douglas Fir through the doorway and to the far corner of the living room—the same corner that held their tree each year. The strings of colorful lights were in the same tangle she unsnarled every year, but eventually he could coil them around the fragrant branches.

Trey pawed through the same box of ornaments she dug through earlier, held up a cheesy animated cartoon character. "Where did this one come from, Mom?" A little guy in overalls and a hardhat dangled from his finger.

It wasn't surprising he didn't remember it. She'd left it in the box the past couple of years. Today she took it from him with a nostalgic smile.

"Here, open this one," Ben said, but she already knew what it was. Every year he gave her a pretty ornament, something special. She unwrapped the package. "Oh, look Trey . . . it's Daddy!" She giggled at the character, then leaned forward to give her husband a thank-you kiss. He drew her onto his lap, tickling her as they rolled on the floor.

"I'll have you know, I only wear overalls on Thursdays." And with leering eyes he whispered in her ear. "But I'll show you my tools any time you like."

"Your dad. Several years ago." She handed the little guy back to Trey. "Hang it on the tree."

His eyes were clear as he did so, no hidden animosity, no lurking pain of betrayal. What did he think of when he remembered Ben? The day he removed his training wheels and gave him a push? His high fives after scoring another touchdown? Taking him along in his truck as he checked job sites? All great memories, true, but that was right. A boy should worship his dad.

She slid a sidelong glance to Trey, who had changed so much in the past three years. He wasn't a boy any longer, he was nearly a man now. Didn't he have the right to know what kind of man his father really was? There was a little girl involved now. A sister Trey deserved to know about. She held in a troubled sigh that Trey would surely pick up on if released.

Wherever would she find the courage to tell him?

The week ground by but Allie didn't need a calendar to remind her that tomorrow was finally Christmas Eve. She was prepared—her gifts were all wrapped and under the tree. Of course there was a package for Jake, and it glared at her each time she passed through the room. She still hadn't spoken with him. What would she say? She might miss him terribly, but she still couldn't give him what he wanted.

The front door slammed and muffled footsteps headed for the kitchen. "Mom, you here?" Trey's voice trailed off as he turned the corner.

"Oh, no! Look at you." The words punched through her laugh and left her chuckling even as she stopped him with a raised palm. "Let me guess. Sheetrock today?" Her hand waved to indicate the fine white powder smearing his hands and face and coating his clothing.

He looked down, brushing his hands against his thighs and sending up an impressive cloud of dust. "What gave it away?"

She could only shake her head. It was too late to stop the mess from drifting to her kitchen floor. "Just a lucky guess." She looked him over, head to toe. At least he left his boots outside. She turned to the oven, reached in to check the meatloaf. Her stomach lurched, a not-so-gentle reminder to stand slowly. "How was work today?" Trey eyed her closely even as she forced the grimace from her face.

"Everyone knocked off early and Jake had a barbeque in the yard." He snapped his fingers and disappeared around the corner. "I'll be right back. I forgot something."

He returned moments later, his cell phone at his ear, and handed Allie a small gift bag. He put his hand over the receiver. "This is from Jake. He said you can open it any time."

Jake. Her heart dropped, then pounded in her chest, as it did for weeks now. She took the bag from his hand. She peered inside, but its contents were well hidden in a crush of tissue paper. "Thanks. I'll . . . I'll open it later." But Trey was already gone, his voice fading as he disappeared into his room.

"Yeah, I wish you were here, too . . . But it's snowing there . . . No, I'll be back the day before classes start . . . I miss you, too."

Interesting.

There were plenty of places she'd rather be than lying on the bathroom floor. But with her knees drawn to her chest and her face pressed against the cool tile, sucking in slow and steady breaths helped relieve the worst of the nausea taunting her tonight.

Trey's voice drew closer, calling out for her. Darn it, she'd wanted to ask him—well, grill him, actually—about his mysterious phone conversation earlier, but all during dinner her stomach kept her preoccupied. And laid out on the floor was not an ideal setting for snooping into her son's personal life. Then again, what about her life was ideal lately? "In here, Trey."

There was nowhere to hide once he rounded the corner and spotted her shifting to sit against the wall. "Whoa. You sick, Mom?" His black padded vinyl guitar case slapped against this thigh as she skidded to a halt.

"Just a bug I picked up from school." She mustered a smile. "See, better already."

"You need anything? Pepto?"

"Nope. I'm good."

"I was going out, but—"

"Go."

He shifted the case to the other hand, shifted the weight from one foot to the other. "Tomorrow's Christmas Eve. Have you called—?"

Not having that conversation tonight. "Grandpa Bentley is coming for dinner at six. I think Uncle Nick's coming, too. Where are you going tonight?

"Just to Jax's. You sure you're okay?"

No, but she would be. "Go. Tell Maddie I'll call her tomorrow."

A few moments later the front door shut.

Perched on the edge of the bed with her teeth brushed and her stomach settled, Allie picked up Jake's gift bag from the nightstand. Midnight blue with a scattering of gold stars, overflowing with metallic gold tissue. She'd turned her back on him. Didn't trust him to know his own mind. But he loved her anyway.

A simple card depicting two white peace doves was inscribed in Jake's precise block lettering.

WHENEVER YOU'RE READY. I LOVE YOU.

No. He couldn't have. Oh God, what if he did? She rooted through gold tissue and uncovered a small square box tied with a gold ribbon. *Did he?* She palmed the crimson foil-wrapped package, then closed her eyes and clasped her other hand around it, pressing it to her heart. He was willing to set everything aside for her. Why wasn't she willing to let him?

The answer pealed through her heart, as clear and exalting as church bells on Christmas Eve. The strain and anxiety of the past weeks melted away. *She was.*

She had to be.

The same sad scenes had flashed through her mind for weeks. Her, alone and unhappy, with nothing but class papers to keep her occupied at night. Wishing for something she denied herself. Denied them. Would Jake be alone too? Possibly not. Nerves kicked in, flip-flopping in her stomach. The idea of it was unthinkable. They belonged together. She would be brave now; she would take the last step. Dragging in a breath that was more determined than fortifying she dropped the gift back into the bag.

Jake glared at the jumble of detailed spreadsheets and financial statements strewn across the table then tossed his glasses on the whole mess. *Damn Nick to the seventh level of paperwork hell!* He and Nick were supposed to review these printouts together. But Nick had been scarce for weeks now, and this week he was gone altogether. *Skiing in Big Bear with the guys,* my ass. He was probably holed up in the lodge with someone warm and curvy.

He replaced his glasses and turned back to the numbers swimming before him then stopped, rolled his neck and rubbed his eyelids under his glasses. It was no use to continue. No use pretending he wasn't sitting here waiting for the phone to ring. It was already ten. She wasn't calling tonight.

A light rap sounded on his door. Who could that be? He stood, stretching his back before making his way through the living room to the front door. It was probably just the neighbor boys, knocking then hiding in the bushes lining the house. Wouldn't be the first time. He threw open the door.

Allie! She leaned against the stucco wall with a small bag swinging from one finger, a lazy grin stretched across her face, the cool breeze swishing her silky auburn hair along the collar of her green wool pea coat. His heart kicked.

"I got this gift today, but there was no name on the card."

He flipped the switch for the porch fixture, bathing her in the yellow glow. Relaxed against the door frame, he returned her look, soaking in the sight of her. She looked thinner. But her gray eyes flashed green with amusement in the harsh light. "Must have been an oversight." He accepted the gift bag, peeked inside at the wink of red paper and lifted his eyes to her. "You haven't opened it."

"Mmm. I thought you might want to give it to me in person."

Teasing? He cocked his head, stepped out of the doorway. "Maybe so.

She paused as she entered the living room, tossing her coat over the back of the armchair. "Well, Scrooge, I see you've gone all out this year."

He glanced around at the missing Christmas tree, the lack of holiday cheer, and his mouth quirked. "That's Mister Scrooge to you, thank you very much."

He followed her onto the loveseat and dropped the bag on his lap. Her reaction to its contents had the entire Riverdance chorus line pounding out a number in his abdomen. Had she finally changed her mind? Would she accept it? Accept him? She seemed calm, and almost cheerful. His breath backed up in his chest. "What's on your mind, Allie?"

"I'm ready."

Ready? As in *ready*, ready? His pulse leapt, then raced. She sat so relaxed, hands folded loosely on her lap. Was the suddenly nervous smile flitting across her face a clue? Did she mean ... ? Sweet Christ, it would be too cruel if she didn't. He cleared his throat. "Explain that, please."

The hands in her lap twisted together. "I love you, Jake. I don't want to wait until it's too late."

His hands flew to hers until they were trapped between them. "Allie."

Her eyes winged to meet his gaze. They were clear, bright, and full of promise. "You've proven in so many ways, for so long, that I can trust you, that you're there for me. I need to trust that what I can give you is enough." Her palm traced his forearm, rubbing it lightly and causing his muscles to bunch. Her grin rocked his soul. "I want to spend the rest of my life with you. You and me, and Trey."

That was exactly what he wanted to hear. Heart thumping, he leaned forward and placed a hard, happy kiss on her mouth. Lifting the bag he glanced at her, optimistic for the first time in weeks.

He removed the small package from the gift bag and ripped off the paper, tossing it aside. Opening the velvet box he plucked the ring and slid in onto his much larger finger, wagging it at the woman sitting beside him, his own smile blooming. "I love you, Allie. I missed you more than I ever realized I would." He had to pause, had to kiss her.

His hands capturing her jaw, he lowered his head until their lips met in a warm, soft promise. With his eyes closed he savored the brief taste of her.

They would have time now. Time to taste more fully, time to take . . . it all.

"Maybe we won't have everything we dreamed of, but we will make these our best days. And whatever happens from now until the end, we'll be together." He lifted her left hand and slid the ring from his finger to hers.

She scooted closer to him, pressed her lips against his again and curled under his shoulder, to the place she fit so well. She stared at her ring, getting a good look at it for the first time. Nick assured him it was impressive—an emerald cut diamond set in a platinum band. She held her hand out. "Wow, I could take someone's eye out with this thing." She turned her face to him. "You forgive me for being a little bit stubborn? You still want to marry me?"

A little bit stubborn? He snorted. "Of course. And yes, as soon as possible."

"Tonight?"

"Really?"

"Very soon. There's something we need to do first." The promise in her tone had his blood running hot, and pooling in his gut.

She turned and straddled his lap. Leaning into him, she kissed him, her teeth gently grazing his bottom lip, quickly followed by the tip of her tongue, soothing, inflaming as her kiss deepened, demanded. The light scent of her, the velvet feel of her, the low, throaty sound of her as she ran her lips over his all crashed down on him, paralyzing him with love, with lust. His arms tightened around her as he mindlessly returned her kisses. He pulled back, found his voice, breathless and rough. "Can you stay?"

Her own answer was husky. "For a while. Trey will be home tonight."

He stood, scooping her up. Cradling her, he shouldered open the door to his room. She flipped the wall switch to turn on the lamp and stopped him, her eyes on his bed. She wore a worried look on her face and the corners of his lips tipped up. "Second thoughts?

"Um, no." She looked away. "Not exactly."

"What's the matter, Allie? Don't you like my new bed?"

"You just got it?"

She was so predictable. And she never failed to amuse him. "I thought we should have our own bed. Besides, this one's bigger." He finished walking toward the bed, dropping her onto the new comforter. He stood, still smiling, looming over her. "You spoiled me with your big bed. Which you slept in with your husband by the way."

Allie popped off the edge of the bed, wrung her hands. "Yeah, about that."

His amusement grew until it turned into a chuckle. He took a seat on the foot of their bed and nestled her between his knees, holding her hands. "I don't care who was there before me, babe. As long as I'm there now."

She sighed and sank onto his lap. "You spoil me every day, Mr. Taylor. And . . . you read me like a dimestore novel."

"A dimestore novel? Is there sex in it?"

A giggle sputtered up, and lit her face. "I don't know. I've never actually read one."

He cradled her face in his hands. "What do you say we write our own?" Jake lay back on their new bed, pulling her with him, joined his lips to hers, and began the magic he missed.

Jake shifted, pulled Allie against his hard length, threw a leg over her under the blanket.

"Wait, Jake. I can't stay. Trey."

Shit. Trey. He nuzzled the flowery scent of her throat but the frustration was hard to tamp down. "How soon is 'very soon' Allie?"

"Don't growl." She grinned as her palm drifted over the sparse furring on his chest, plucking and teasing. "Whenever you say, sweetheart. As soon as you want it to be."

Satiety still trickled through his limbs, but her wandering hands were about to land her on her back. "Do you want a big wedding?"

She pushed herself up so she lay across his chest, studying him. Her hair fell forward in a curtain, trapping their faces. "I did the whole wedding thing. It's not a big deal to me. I would be perfectly happy with the Justice of the Peace." She grinned impudently as she spoke. "But this is the only time you're getting married, mister. If you want the whole veil and black tux thing, I'm in."

His look mocked her, then turned soft. "You, me and whoever's doing the ceremony. That's all I need. And Trey." Jake lifted his head for a quick kiss. "Do you think he'd stand with me?"

"He'd be hurt if he didn't." She rolled to her back, lying beside him, staring up at the ceiling. "He kind of likes you, you know."

He turned his head so he faced her. Grabbed her hand and interlaced their fingers. "Yeah, I kind of like him back."

"So . . . When?"

"Friday?"

"I've got nothing better planned."

"Friday it is. Where would you rather live, here or your house?"

"Well, you do have a pool . . . and a fireplace. But my bathroom's bigger."

"Your house it is. We can build a pool."

"But bring our bed." She stretched out all four limbs. "This is really comfortable. What time is it?"

"Eleven forty five. Why?"

She answered by rolling to her side and running a bold palm over the ridges of his abdomen, her gaze going as deep and dark as thunderheads and locked on his. His lips lowered to hers with a groan of need, his tongue dipping inside to tangle itself around hers. She lifted against him, demanding . . . more. He had more. He added pressure to their kiss, licking and sucking, then rolling her until she was trapped beneath him, his heat pressed shamelessly against her core.

"Jesus, woman, I love you." The need in her eyes sparked a fuse in him, reigniting a passion that merely simmered, but never died. This was the woman who had occupied his dreams, and his nightmares, for nearly half his life. This was where he belonged. Above her. Beside her. Home.

Chapter Twenty Six

"Bentley's coming for dinner tomorrow. Nick too. I'm making a ham. Do you already have plans?" It would be much easier to wiggle into her panties if Jake's hands didn't keep getting in the way.

"Nope, I'm all yours." He palmed her bare behind, pulled her close.

With a laugh and a halfhearted slap at him she took a step back. "Jake! It's Christmas Eve and you don't have plans?"

"Well, I sort of made plans, but it worked itself out." He grabbed her blouse and held it out of reach.

She picked up her jeans and climbed in. His comment stopped her and she studied him, balancing like a flamingo with one leg pushed through, the other stuck midway. "What does that mean?"

He dropped the blouse on the bed and took hold of the dangling pant leg, used it to reel her in. "It means you had until tomorrow to come to your senses. Then I was coming over."

Grinning, she hopped toward him. "Oh."

He dropped a quick kiss on her lips, then let go of her pants. "Yeah. Oh. Now what time can I come over?"

"Is six too early?" Jeans up and snapped, she reached for her shirt, but Jake was too fast and held it over his head.

"You know, it will be damn nice watching you get dressed, *and undressed*, every day."

She scowled and grabbed for her shirt. "Damn you, I'll never get dressed at this rate."

He sighed and handed it over. "Spoilsport. What time are you eating?"

"Four." She shrugged into her blouse, poking tiny buttons through holes.

His hands snaked up under hers, fumbling and unfastening as he went. "Then why do you want me to come at six?"

"Six in the morning, sweetheart. I can't wait any longer than that."

He hauled her onto his lap. She bounced up quickly, his naked guy parts were much too tempting. "Jake!" Exasperation was written in her voice. "Trey will be home soon."

"I hope you're more fun next week."

She chose to ignore him. "I hope Ben's family doesn't have a problem with . . . you know." She held her hand out, her ring sparkling in the lamplight. "Us."

"It will be a little hard to hide." He motioned with his chin to the new bauble on her finger.

She rebuttoned her blouse and hunted for her shoes. She found them under the bed and slid her feet into them. "Well, luckily they all love you, too." And besides, now that she finally had it she wasn't taking it off.

With one last thorough kiss to get her through the night, she left him lying on the bed.

Jake chafed his palms together and pounded on the door. Again. No answer. Rang the doorbell. No answer. He sauntered around to the garage, intent on helping himself in the house via the code panel when he spotted Trey jogging toward the house. His sweatpants and hoodie sported his school logo, his sneakers plop-plopped as they hit the concrete sidewalk. He slowed as he approached the yard.

"Jake!" Trey waved a welcome. "You're here early." Smoke signals wafted from his lips as he spoke. Sweat trickled from his temple.

Jake stepped back the way he came. Crap, he didn't count on Trey being awake yet. Invited or not, what excuse could he use for his early arrival? Rooting around the closet of his mind, he dug out a lame one. "I thought I'd help you get the grass mowed." He settled deeper in his coat, rubbed his bare hands together again then shoved them into his pockets.

Trey drew to a halt when he got to Jake, folded at the waist and braced his palms on his knees, still panting out puffs. "Doesn't my mom have a service?"

"Their contract expired." He was pretty sure that wasn't true, but maybe Trey didn't know that.

Sucking in deep gulps of air, Trey's eyes narrowed. "So why are you really here?"

Jake removed his hands from his pockets, covered his ears with them. He really should have remembered a hat. And gloves. "I told you, I'm—"

His breathing evening out, Trey smiled. "No, seriously. Did you work it out with my mom?"

Jake let a satisfied smirk bloom on his face. "Yeah."

Trey stood, stretched. His smile grew wider. "Too cool. So is she going to marry you?"

It was tempting to puff out his chest caveman style, fist-pounding it with a series of pure satisfied male grunts. Mere hours ago it would have seemed perfectly natural, in fact—with a naked Allie draped across his chest as soft and warm as a cashmere blanket. But standing beside her teenage kid? Probably not such a great idea. He buried his fists in his armpits. "Yeah. Um, I wanted to talk to you about that."

Trey reached out to fist-bump him, his excited words clambering over Jake's nervous stumbling. "All right! When? What do you want to talk about?"

Jake sucked in a deep breath. Let his words spew out with his frosted breath. "This Friday. I want you to be my best man."

"Woo-hoo!" Trey fist-shot the sky then spun back with panic in his eyes. "I don't have to wear a tux, do I?"

He couldn't have held back his grin if he wanted to. Damn, he loved this kid. "Hell no. No tux. But you do have to dress a little nicer than that." A flick of his right hand indicated the sweat-stained fleece.

"I can do that." Trey turned thoughtful. "Wait a minute, why so soon? Is she pregnant?"

Jesus. That was probably a logical question for an eighteen-year-old male, but it caught him off guard so his laugh was shaky. "No, but I've waited . . . long enough."

Trey nodded. "Well, you don't need to make up an excuse to come over." Trey wrapped his arms around himself. "Dude, it's cold out here. Let's go wake up the bride." He took off, racing across the front porch.

Jake followed him through the front door. What the hell, let's go wake up the bride.

Trey sped through the house in search of his mom, but he paused just inside the doorway. As always, the Christmas tree took up an entire corner of the room, every branch adorned with ornaments, the whole thing strung with popcorn garlands. Brightly decorated gifts were scattered underneath. The whole house had Allie's stamp on it, her signature combination of sophisticated and homespun, decked for the season with color and scent.

He never bothered with holiday decorations. After all, there was usually nobody at his house to appreciate them. But this was a home. Soon it would be his home.

Still calling out for Allie, Trey flew back through the living room. Jake caught up with him as he barged through the door of her bedroom. She was sitting on the edge of her bed, deathly pale. Was she ill?

Trey rushed across the carpet and prepared to pounce. "Hey, Mom! You're getting married! Con . . ."

Jake threw out his arm to block him. "Trey, no, don't . . .

Trey sailed through the air and landed in the middle of the bed.

Unable to move fast enough to avoid the jarring bounce, Allie sprung from the bed and ran into the bathroom, knees hitting the tile with no time to spare.

" . . . gratulations! Mom?" Trey yelled after her. "Hey, are you okay?"

Jake was already in the bathroom, a moment behind Allie. He knelt beside her, holding her hair and rubbing her back. "Babe, you feel better now?"

She scooted back, leaning her cheek against his chest. "No. Leave me alone."

"What can I do for you?"

Just let me die. "Nothing."

Jake chuckled at her dramatics.

Trey crept around the corner. "Jake, is she okay?"

"She'll be fine, Trey. It's probably something she ate."

"She spewed earlier this week, too."

Jake looked down at her, frowning with new concern. "Why didn't you tell me you're ill?

"Just stomach flu. I'll feel better soon."

"Trey, wet a washcloth for me, please." He used it to wipe her face and neck. Her thready voice concerned him. "What did the doctor say?"

"Um . . . nothing much."

"Allie." His warning tone was well suited to a naughty three year old.

Mutiny glared in her scowl. "All right, I haven't been."

Jake stroked her shoulders as she lay against him. "Allie. Be sensible. I don't have a bunch of fancy initials after my name, but this isn't right." Using his finger he turned her to face him and tipped up her chin. "What if there's something seriously wrong? Please, promise you'll see the doctor soon?"

She nodded agreement as he helped her to her feet.

Allie leaned against the refrigerator, then tugged the door open and lifted out the ham she planned for dinner. Jake entered as she struggled to carry the heavy piece of meat, took it from her easily, and set it on the counter. "You still don't look well, Allie. Go sit at the table and let me do this for you."

"You know how to cook a ham?" Build a twenty story office building? Sure, no sweat. But the Christmas ham? This she had to see.

"You questioning me, woman?" He read the vacuum sealed package, then glanced at her with a smug grin. "Ha! It says right here, 'Fully cooked.' How hard can it be?" His gaze bounced from one cabinet to the next as if trying to divine what was hidden behind each closed door. Finally he halted with a heavy sigh and a roll of his eyes. "Okay, tell me where to find the roasting pan."

The aroma of ham baking warmed the house. Allie snapped green beans, throwing away the ends and dropping the wet beans onto a pot. Trey peeled potatoes at the sink.

He looked at his mom. "Are you sure you're not pregnant?"

Her head came up with a snap. "Not possible, Trey."

"I think she's pregnant."

"Wouldn't that be something?" The doorbell chimed and drowned out Jake's murmur. At least now he didn't have to explain his last statement.

"I'll get it!" Trey dropped a half-peeled potato into the sink with a splash, ran to the door and swung it open. Right behind him, Jake gripped the door panel as a cold gust threatened to snatch it from Trey's hand. "Gramps! Uncle Nick! Merry Christmas!"

Bentley's arms were full of wrapped gifts. Nick carried a bottle of wine in each hand. Trey hugged each man as they entered the room, then ran the wine into the kitchen and squatted to place the new presents under the tree.

"Merry Christmas, Bentley." Allie grinned as she entered the living room. "We're glad you came today. We've missed you."

"Allie, as beautiful as ever, Merry Christmas!" Bentley grabbed Allie in a bear hug and placed a fatherly kiss on her cheek.

It had been several years since he'd last seen Ben's father. It was amazing how regret and worry could age a person, but the Tate dimples still emerged when he grinned and his grip was still firm as Jake shook his hand. "Merry Christmas, Bentley."

"Jake, good to see you, son. You look well also. Merry Christmas. And will you look at Trey. I swear he's grown two inches since I saw him last."

"Aw, Gramps." Everyone laughed at Bentley's predictable exaggeration. "You say that every time I see you."

"Glad you could make it, Nick." Allie leaned into his warm hug and turned her cheek up for a chaste kiss. "Jake tells me you've been gone quite a bit lately. He wondered if you had some lady friend stashed away."

Jake laughed. The wheels were obviously turning and a scary gleam shone in her eye as Allie kidded him.

Nick's gaze shot to him with a scowling sigh. "Thanks a bunch, boss. Now she'll never leave me alone."

Crap, he could already see he'd have to cover for Nick if he wanted any peace at either home *or* work. But Nick was what? Thirty-six or thirty-seven already and hadn't had a serious relationship since that dancer chick in high school. Yeah, the story sounded kind of familiar.

Nick stuck his hand out for him to shake. "Merry Christmas, anyway. Glad to see you here."

He glanced around the room and grinned as he took a seat beside Allie. "Yes, well, I expect you'll be seeing a lot more of me here from now on."

Nick looked confused, but his dad wasn't a lawyer for nothing. Bentley's gaze panned the smiling faces lined up on the couch—his, Trey's, Allie's—before landing on Allie's hand. His face lit up brighter than the decorated tree standing steadfast in the corner. "I'm glad you two finally came to your senses."

Nick popped up from his chair, beaming. He stepped forward and again embraced his sister-in-law. "I'm thrilled for you Allie. You deserve to be happy again." He then shook Jake's hand. "And you too, Jake; congratulations!"

Allie passed the beans while conversation rose and fell around the table. "The wedding will be Friday. You'll come, won't you Gramps, Uncle Nick? I get to be best man." She could only shake her head. Trey hadn't even given her a chance to issue an invitation.

"Wouldn't miss it for anything." Bentley's acknowledgement was cheerful. "Friday you say?"

"Yes, Friday." Even Jake wasn't leaving her an opportunity. "And of course you're invited. It will be at the courthouse. Just family and very close friends."

"So." She patted her mouth with her napkin. "Have you heard from Gavin lately?"

But at the mention of his youngest son Bentley's mouth went tight and the laughter in his eyes died. Apparently that was a *no*. Her heart landed in her lap. "I'm sorry."

Nick patted her hand from his seat beside her. "Not your fault, doll. The prick hasn't been home in years, and evidently a damn phone call or card at Christmas was just too much to ask for this year."

If anyone knew what caused Gavin to give up a full ride and leave town, they weren't talking. But the day following his high school graduation he took off without a word. Three weeks later he called and announced he'd shipped out for Army basic training. They'd gotten a few short notes from him since, seen him sporadically over the years, the last time at Ben's funeral.

And she'd totally ruined Christmas dinner. With effort she brought up

249

the wedding again. Thankfully that brought a spark back to the conversation. And finally, as everyone finished up their meal, Trey just couldn't hold it in any longer.

"I think she's pregnant."

Allie jumped as her fork clattered against her plate.

"Why do you think that, Trey?" Bentley asked after swallowing his bite of potatoes.

"She's puked twice, and she's tired all the time. And she keeps falling asleep on the couch."

Nick looked across the table at her. "Allie, you're not feeling well?"

"It's nothing. Just had a little flu."

Jake zeroed in on Trey. "What do you know about being pregnant?"

Trey puffed out his chest. "I hear things. Besides, four girls in my school got pregnant last year." He turned to Allie. "You remember Angie Muldoon?"

"Sure. She was that cute little redhead you had a crush on in middle school."

Trey nodded sagely, eyebrows quirked upward, lips twisted to the side.

Whoa. What? "But those girls were only seventeen." And how naïve did that sound? Jake leaned forward in his seat. "I thought you guys got a safe sex lecture at school."

"Sure, Jake. Every year since seventh grade." Trey's dramatic eye roll spoke volumes about the efficacy of the program.

Bentley and Nick were silent, probably in shock. Allie's face fell. Jesus, Christmas or otherwise, this was so not dinner conversation. "It's time to clear the table, Trey." Jake stood, carrying a load of plates to the sink. "Allie, honey, you all go into the living room and sit. We'll be out soon." The murmur of voices rose and fell as they settled in the living room, the television turned on to a holiday variety show.

Jake placed the last glass in the dishwasher and stacked the pans to soak in the sink. Drying his hands on the dishtowel, he took a breath—a deep bolstering breath—and turned. "Trey, what do you know about menopause?"

Trey looked confused for a moment. "Isn't it that Jewish candle, the one with lots of lights on it?" He used his hands to demonstrate. "Are you Jewish?"

At sea, he thought a minute, then chuckled. "No, knucklehead, that's a menorah. Menopause is something women go through."

The light dawned on Trey's face. "Oh yeah, I saw an article about that in my mom's *Cosmo*. It's for old ladies. Why?"

The whole Trey reading *Cosmo* discussion could wait. And since his face was already heating, he needed to make this as simple as possible, for both their sakes. "When your mom says she's not pregnant, she means it, Trey. She says she's already started going through menopause, which means, among other things, that she can't have babies anymore." He jammed his hands into his pockets. How much of this should he—or *could* he—discuss with Allie's son? "She does seem a little young, but I guess they go through it at different times."

"Well isn't that good? It means you don't have to worry about condoms."

Ah, just found the limit. "Just do me a favor, kid. Drop the subject of babies around your mom, okay?"

Confusion was still written all over his face, but it was Christmas and there was a gift with his name on it so Jake was off the hook.

"Sure, whatever. We done here? Gramps has presents for us."

He gave a final glance around the kitchen. Everything was clean except the pans in the sink. "Yeah, we're done enough for now."

Together they walked into the living room, where Christmas music poured from the television. Trey stopped in the middle of the room, pointing. "See, what did I tell you?"

Jake followed his finger and spotted the sleeping Allie, slumped down in the corner of the sofa, wrapped around a throw pillow. His brow furrowed at the dark smudges under her eyes. He hadn't been doing a very good job of taking care of her lately, but that was over now. It was time to wrap this party up. He crouched beside her and shook her gently. "Wake up, Sleeping Beauty."

Allie peeked her eyes open, stretching and sitting up. She snuggled into him as he sat beside her, draping his arm around her and rubbing her shoulder.

"Mmm." She dimpled up at him. "Prince Charming, I presume."

Jake crowded into the doorway with Allie and Trey, waving farewell as Bentley and Nick braced against the icy wind on their way toward Nick's SUV. Shouts of *good-bye* and *Merry Christmas* rode a gust back toward the house.

With his arm across her sagging shoulders, he led a yawning Allie back into the littered house. Gift wrap and empty boxes were scattered across the living room floor, the kitchen table held the remnants of dessert—china plates scraped clean of apple pie and empty glasses filmed with egg nog.

The contentment he'd known briefly and then lost returned as blinding serenity. His throat worked as he pulled Allie to him and the comfort of her arms surrounded him. If he had a choice, he wouldn't be anywhere else. This was it for him. His home. His family. His reason to care.

Trey pushed the door closed and was gone, shot as if from a cannon down the hallway to the seclusion of his room. Allie followed him with her eyes, her smile bemused as his door slammed shut. "He really likes that laptop Bentley got him. Maybe you can—"

He tipped up her chin and cut her off. Regret sat like a stone in his chest but she was pale again. "Time for me to leave now, too. It's been a long day."

He caught the finger she ran down his shirt before it reached his belt. The kiss she breathed across his lips nearly stopped his heart. "Stay."

"But you're tired. And ill. And Trey . . ."

Again she quieted him. "You're home. Stay."

He pulled her back into his arms. Yeah, he was home.

She woke with Jake warm and hard and wrapped around her, dark morning scruff shrouding the firmness of his square jaw, creases that typically etched the corners of his eyes smoothed out in sleep. She rubbed a thumb against the barely visible grooves. When he smiled they'd be back. She hooked the sheet and lowered it, exposing an impressive amount of muscle for a guy his age—well, for any guy, actually—and grinned as he blinked awake.

He raised himself onto an elbow. "What you got in mind, babe?"

She continued to pull, a grin tugging at her lips. "I got myself a pretty great Christmas gift here. Just wanted to take a look."

His eyes flared, and weren't the only part of him that blazed awake. Goosebumps chased across her skin as he lowered her to the bed, looming over her. Warm hands caressed her as he nuzzled her throat, growling as he tugged the straps of her nightgown. "You're right, babe. This is the way to unwrap a present."

Allie pulled fresh undergarments from her dresser. Then laughed at the unconcealed interest in Jake's eyes as they followed her movements. "Now I know why you want to marry me." She laughed again as he snatched his hand to his chest before she closed the drawer on his fingers. "Here I thought the reason was my charming personality, but all along it was really just me in my panties."

He finished tugging his T-shirt down and over his abdomen. Barefoot, he backed toward the doorway, pausing to brace his palms against the jamb. "And you'd be wrong, babe. It's really you *out of* your panties."

Allie let Jake lead her to his truck, waving one last farewell to her family as she climbed in and buckled. Sinking into the chilly leather of the bucket seat, she tightened her coat around her and covered her mouth as it stretched open in a yawn. It had been a truly exceptional day—the excitement on Trey's face as he opened his gifts, the horror and then delight on Jake's as he unwrapped the box containing all her favorite soppy love stories, late morning church services and then dinner with her parents and brother. But the best part was definitely when Jake raised his glass and announced their engagement. Evidently, he'd already chatted privately with her dad because they both fairly beamed with happiness. She reached for his hand across the console.

"Merry Christmas, sweetheart. I love you."

"Not nearly as much as I love you. Five more days until you're my wife." She grinned. The countdown was a daily ritual. "Seems like a lifetime." So was the grumbling.

"Big baby. It will be here before you know it." She kissed him lightly to take any sting out of her words.

Yes, the day had been nearly perfect, marred only by the heartbreaking sadness on her brother's face.

"I don't like seeing Ryan so unhappy. It would be nice if he and Tess worked things out."

Ryan's wife of only five years had been gone for several months now, taking their twin sons to live in her former hometown. It was really too bad. They appeared to be so happy in the beginning.

Jake put the truck in gear, sparing her a glance as he pulled away from her parents' curb. "I talked to him tonight about coming to work with me and Nick."

She straightened in her seat. "Oh, yeah?"

He nodded. "Sure. We could use an in-house architect; it would speed up some of our projects."

And give Ryan the chance to be home more often. "Jake, that's great. Think he'll do it?"

He shrugged. "Can't say, but I hope so. It's hard to tell what's going on with him and Tess, though."

She shifted back and laid her head against the headrest. Rain poured down the windows in streaming rivulets. Heated air blew in from the air vents, warming the interior. Her son was on the back seat. The man she loved was beside her. She reached for Jake's hand again and closed her eyes. She'd forgotten what it was like, how comforting, to have someone to share her life with. How gratifying it was to have a complete family once again.

The truck door slammed, and she fluttered her eyes open. Trey was running across the yard and into the house, shaking moisture from his hair like a mutt as he crossed the threshold. Jake was still, intent on the wipers swishing against the windshield. Abruptly he killed the engine. His hand covered hers, stopping her before she opened her door.

"I'll say goodnight here. With this weather I'll to need to start work early and I don't have clothes here."

Aggravation and impatience collided in his voice. With her free hand she fingered the locket hanging around her neck—the one he'd given her just that morning already loaded with photos of Trey and himself—and fell into him when he tugged her arm.

"Are you sure you can't stay? I'm getting used to you in my bed." His lips pressed against hers. She captured his jaw in her hands and sank into the kiss. Her pulse kicked up when his arms pulled her closer. The warmth of his hard chest bled through the layers of his heavy coat. Her hands strayed, roamed across the width of his broad shoulders as she pulled away. She would much rather he stayed and finish what he'd started here. She'd have to talk to Trey, because really, she couldn't take five more days of this delicious agony. "Will you bring your stuff tomorrow? You may as well start moving in."

"What about Trey? Will that cause a problem?"

"I'll talk to him tonight, but I'm sure he'll wonder what took you so long."

"So long? It's only been two days."

She grinned and pulled on her mittens. "That's what I said; it's been two whole days."

Jake raced around the hood of the truck and led her to her front door. Grinding his impatient lips against hers, seeking entrance with a slash of his tongue, his eyes darkened to black, his arms tightened, his kiss spoke to her.

Good night, I'll miss you. I want to do this all night long.

With regret she pulled away, murmuring into his hooded eyes. "I know. Me too."

He kissed her once more, on her nose. "Tomorrow I'll bring clothes." Grinning, he dashed back through the rain to his truck. She entered her house and stood at the window like a lovesick teenager. She stayed until Jake was out of sight, and only then walked down the hallway to bed.

Chapter Twenty Seven

The next day, Monday, dawned overcast and dreary, but rain no longer pelted the roof. She hopped out of bed. She had too much to accomplish to laze around.

Glancing at the clock to make sure she wouldn't be late to meet Maddie, she laced up her runners. She didn't need to hurry to make their usual meeting time, but with the holiday they hadn't hit the track in days. She was anxious to get back. With only three weeks until their marathon, they both needed to stay on their training schedule.

She cringed as she trotted through the house. She hadn't even shared her news with Reese and Maddie yet. But they had four days, what were friends for? They could probably pull off this wedding without her. She paused as she locked the house behind her. Maddie. Reese. One of them would be her maid of honor, but which? How did she choose between two best friends?

Taking off at a slow jog, she let her tight muscles warm up gradually against the cool morning air. She took in a deep, refreshing breath as she ran along the route to the high school and let her mind work. Did Jake own a suit? The last time she saw him in one was at Ben's funeral.

They'd need flowers, too. And reservations for the wedding dinner. *Yikes!* That list just kept getting longer and longer.

She spotted Maddie as she approached the school. She waved and yelled a greeting. Maddie looked good today in green running shorts and her effervescent smile. "Good morning. How was your holiday?"

Maddie laughed. "Where to begin? Family . . . food . . . madness. I wouldn't trade it for the world, but I'm glad it's over."

Allie kept pace as Maddie took off around the track, her ponytail bobbing with each step. "Something exciting happened."

Maddie's eyes flew to her and widened. "Exciting? I like exciting!"

Ha! This would be fun. "Come to lunch with me and I'll tell you all about it. I'll call Reese, too. Let's eat early and we can do a little shopping afterwards."

"Sounds perfect. The girls want to see a movie today. I'll drop them off before lunch and they can hang out at the mall while we shop."

"That will work. Now, tell me about your Christmas. It's so much different when your kids are younger; I miss that a lot."

Allie hung up the phone after her call to Reese. Their lunch date was all set. Only a few more calls to make—to their favorite Mexican eatery and then her salon—and her to-do list would be blissfully shorter. She stepped into the shower.

With agility she maneuvered her car into a parking space narrowed by an oversized SUV crowding the dividing line. The *Check Engine* light glowed red on the dash as she shut off the engine. Great! One more thing added to tomorrow's list.

The lunchtime crowd hovered in the restaurant lobby waiting to be seated. Reese and Maddie sat in a booth under a window, waving her over. She removed her jacket as she veered to meet them. Sliding in beside Reese she grinned and set her left elbow on the table, propping her chin on her hand. Who would notice first? Either way, this wasn't going to take long.

"Squeee!" Reese. She would have guessed Maddie to notice first.

"Ow!" She slapped at Reese when she grabbed for her hand.

"Show me. I wanna see!"

"Oh my goodness." Maddie inspected the ring and used her favorite phrase, squeaking over Reese's babble. "You are such a rat. You didn't even tell us you were back together!" Then she paused, eyes wide. "It *is* Jake, right?"

A bubble of laughter burst out. "Of course it's Jake. And I didn't tell you *yet* because we weren't back together until two days ago."

The server appeared to take their orders and was quickly gone.

"Oh, Allie . . . I'm so happy for you." Uncharacteristic tears brimmed in Reese's eyes as she blubbered and clasped her manicured hands together. "You deserve to be happy. Jake's a real find, and lucky to have you."

She reached over, grabbed Reese's hands and squeezed. "Thanks, Reese." She'd been an amazing friend for so long, and she didn't make it weird that Jake was her boyfriend first, so long ago. She squeezed her hands again.

"Well, he is. He reminds me of a hunky guy from the cover of one of my romance novels."

And just like that, Maddie got them laughing again.

Reese picked up her hand to inspect her ring again. "It's about time you realized you were perfect for each other."

"Have you set a date? Will you be a June bride?" She chuckled. Maddie was such a romantic.

"No, actually it will be this Friday." Her friends were so good for her, and predictable. She sat back to enjoy the fireworks.

"*What!*"

"*This* Friday?"

She had to laugh at the horrified and incredulous looks on their faces. "Yes, this Friday. And I'll need help to get this done."

"Of course, anything you need." And then the light dawned. "That's why you want to shop today. You need a wedding dress!"

"That, and maid of honor dresses."

"Dresses? As in more than one?"

Oh, this *was* fun. "Well, only if you both agree."

"Agree? Of course we agree. Don't we agree, Maddie?"

"I agree!"

They spent an enjoyable hour making plans and giggling like schoolgirls. As they finished their lunch Maddie glanced at her watch. "The girls will be out of their movie soon. Do you mind if they join us?"

"Of course I don't mind. They're always fun to have along." Allie looked forward to spending a couple of hours with her friend's teenage daughters.

Allie let Reese drag her through the first of the department stores. "Nothing's right, Reese. The rose pink sheath was too plain. The dove gray was nice, but I can't sit in it." She glanced at her watch. "Maddie needs to get here soon. We need backup."

Reese dove into her enormous handbag and with laser accuracy came out with her smartphone, tapping buttons on the touchscreen. "I'll text her, we can send photos."

She held up a yellow full skirted suit. "I like this." Reese snapped a shot and sent it to Maddie.

Dress #3 . . . What do you think?

Says MOB, not bride ☹

"What about this one?" A hunter green A-line with a printed jacket.

Dress #4??

She looks like a tree

Reese giggled.

"What?" Allie looked over Reese's shoulder at the message, then pulled a face at her reflection. "It kind of does, doesn't it?"

"Jake will like this one." She tried on a sea green gown with a plunging neckline.

Dress #5 . . . Well?

Ewww on the dress, but when did Allie get boobs?

Reese held the phone so Allie could read. She stood at the mirror and tugged at the dress. "Don't ask me! I don't know where they came from."

They both eyed Allie's impressive cleavage and giggled again.

Allie eyed the rejects lining the changing room and sighed. "Time to try the next store."

Once there, Reese took a picture of a beige linen suit, on clearance from summer stock.

What about this one?

Hell no.

Allie let out a frustrated huff. "Enough technology; we needed her pronto."

Get your a** here now!

Maddie finally arrived, frantically dragging two red-and-green-toothed teenagers behind her. "No luck?"

Allie shook her head. "No luck."

Emily spoke up, pointing down one of the aisles of stores. "I've seen really pretty dresses in one of the boutique windows down that way. They're for older ladies." Her panicked eyes widened. "Not that I'm calling you old."

Allie laughed off Emily's embarrassment. "I'm willing to try anything at this point." Holiday music poured from invisible speakers as they dodged holiday bargain shoppers and kiosks selling everything from knitted beanies to cell phone service. A glass-fronted display showing a mannequin in winter white cashmere caught Allie's attention.

"Ooh. I see something I like here." As one they stepped through the open double door and onto gleaming hardwood. The melodious strains of something classical flowed softly from somewhere above crystal chandeliers. Cherrywood cabinetry with glass shelving lined the walls. Glass-topped circular racks were scattered sparingly throughout the space. An employee strode up to them.

Reese waited as she came out of the fitting room, her eyes lit. "It's perfect Allie. Look at the way it just flows over you. It's beautiful."

Allie stepped up to the three-way mirror and smoothed the front of the dress. The fine wool draped smartly, shaping her curves, stopping short of her knees. The deep cowl highlighted the elegant line of her throat. Five crystal buttons fastened by loops ran from her wrists halfway up the forearm of each long tapered sleeve. She twirled and suddenly she was six again, playing wedding with her cousin Sarah.

Maddie sauntered near from across the floor. "That dress looks wonderful on you, Allie. I especially like it with your zebra flats."

With a grin Allie turned back to the mirror. "It is amazing, isn't it?" On a pivot she studied all sides of the dress. "I love it."

She'd found her dress. And it looked like Maddie and Reese were making progress as well. They were each in front of the wide mirror as she exited her fitting room, glamming it up in classic fitted suits. The sapphire skirt and short jacket complemented Maddie's newly slim figure. She spun, the kick pleat flaring on the silk skirt. Reese laughed and threw out her arms, showing off her emerald green selection. "Hey Allie, you like?"

What could she say? They were both crazy. Crazy beautiful.

Standing at the checkout counter, Allie hefted her garment bag in one hand, her purse on the other arm. It was a trick to retrieve her credit card from the saleswoman. They'd had so much fun, but she was drained. What she wouldn't give to climb into her cozy pajamas, but there was work to do. Progress to be made. She took a deep breath and plunged ahead. "So what color shoes?"

"Silver!"

She grinned as the words exploded from four different mouths. Guess it was unanimous. Even better, she already had it covered. "I can wear those peep toes I bought last summer. I've only worn them once."

Maddie beamed. "I have strappy silver heels I haven't worn for ages."

Emily and Tory both groaned. Lost chance for a shoe adventure.

"Well, I want new."

"Of course you do, Reese."

Reese paraded across the carpet of the Nordstrom shoe department in four-inch heels, then perched on a padded bench. "First try! I love these." She lifted a foot, twirling it to model exquisite Prada ankle cuff sandals, perfect for spring, not so much for a blustery December. But she was happy. "Yes, I am the shoe champ," She smirked as she bent to remove her new treasures.

And so modest.

Thank God, their mission was complete, shopping was exhausting. With effort she followed the herd toward the parking lot. Maddie was parked near their exit, but she and Reese were each several rows over, nearer the restaurant. Waving as Maddie and her girls got in their vehicle, she and Reese walked along together until they arrived at her sedan. Allie opened the back door and hung her dress, then turned to say good-bye.

"Still want to scout for flowers in the morning?"

"Call me. I should be ready to leave by nine or so."

"Too bad Maddie can't come along. I guess the girls have registration for dance." She slid into her car, leaving the door open, then turned the key to start the engine.

Click.

Oh, no. She tried the ignition again. *Grind. Click.* Flopping back in the seat didn't change anything, but her growl released frustration. "This I do not need right now."

"Oh no! Can I give you a lift home?"

Allie frowned. "It's getting late and I'm too tired to wait for a tow, but Reese, I'm really not on your way."

"Whatever. It's on my way if I take the other freeway. Here, get your dress." She opened the rear door and pulled out the garment bag.

Within minutes they were settled in Reese's sporty two-seater, whizzing through rush hour traffic. Jake's truck was backing into the driveway as Reese pulled up to the curb.

He smiled and met them as they climbed out of Reese's little car. "Hey, Reese."

Reese nodded. "Hear you're gonna be a husband. Better take good care of my girl."

Jake laughed as he kissed her cheek. "The best, Reese." Then he turned to Allie for a welcoming peck. "What happened to your truck, babe?"

"That thing is falling apart around me, I swear," she grumbled as she stepped onto the sidewalk, her plastic encased dress hanging from her hand. "It wouldn't start so I left it at the mall. I need to call for a tow truck."

"I can take care of it."

Her gaze was worshiping and probably looked stupid, but he was a god. Like rescuing her from the wreck of the Titanic kind of heroic. "That would be so great." He deserved so much more than just another kiss. Soon. "Reese, can you stay for a few?"

"Thanks, but I better get home. John will be wondering about dinner." She waggled a two-fingered good-bye and called out as she slid into her car. "I'll see you in the morning!"

Jake grabbed a couple of duffle bags from his truck. Then he took her dress and carried it in for her. "What did you find today?" He nodded toward the garment bag.

She tilted her head and smiled. "Something special for Friday. Which reminds me . . . do you have something to wear?"

"All taken care of." He shifted the bag to open the front door. "Trey too." With his arm holding the door for her, she entered the house.

She grabbed a Coke from the fridge, then walked through the house and into her walk-in closet. Why had she not noticed that her clothes hung on the rods in such an unorganized jumble? Leaving her drink on the dresser top, she squeezed the garment bag between an old coat and her navy blue suit as Jake stepped into the closet and craned his neck left and right with a frown.

He lifted his duffle bags. "Where do you want these?"

She chuckled at his desperate expression. "Just leave them. I need to make room."

He dropped the bags. "We need to get our marriage license. Can you meet me at the courthouse?"

Her gaze slid from rod to shelf. Ben's clothes used to fit in that closet. She simply needed to organize. "Sure, let me know when you can get away from work."

She left the closet, taking a long swallow of her drink as she wandered her way down the hall. "I'll start dinner now."

He caught up to her before she reached the kitchen. Pulling her into the living room, he sank into the sofa, pulling her onto his lap. "Aren't you going to show me that dress?"

She leaned into him and wiggled her nose against his. "Yes I am. On Friday."

His fingers traced a pattern over her collarbone, making her shiver. "Very secretive."

She grabbed one of his hands and lifted it to kiss his fingertips. "There's not much you haven't seen already. The dress will be a surprise."

"Fair point." He looked out the window, into the darkening sky. "I should go look at your truck before it gets any later. Trey can come with me."

"Trey's here?"

"Yeah, in his room."

She got up and knocked on the closed bedroom door. Trey was leaned back against the pillows on his bed, talking on his cell phone. He put his hand over the receiver when she walked in.

"Hi, Mom. I'll be done in a minute."

"Jake needs you to go with him to look at my car. It wouldn't start."

"No problem. I'll be right there." She closed the door and went into the kitchen, getting out ingredients to put together pizza.

Jake wandered in while she chopped vegetables. Reached around her and snitched a slice of pepperoni. "If the car won't start, I'll call a tow truck and have them come get it. Then we'll go to my place and get the bed too, as long as Trey's with me."

She smiled and nodded. "Our bed." Then pressed a good-bye kiss on his lips. "See you later, then."

Chapter Twenty Eight

The two pizzas were in pans and set aside until it was time to pop them into the oven. She had time on her hands and the caffeine-laden soda had worked its magic so she wandered into her room. She stripped the sheets from her bed, shoving them into the hamper. Tonight her old bed would be gone, replaced with their new bed. The way her old life was about to be replaced with their new life together. A new life she would build with Jake. This would be the final step to putting the past behind her.

With renewed energy she moved to the closet. Ben's clothing was removed long ago, but it was ridiculous how she'd managed to take over that space. She moved her wardrobe back where it was when she shared the closet in the past, restoring order and removing items she no longer wore. Her glance skimmed over Jake's bags tucked against the wall. Sliding open one long zipper, she unpacked shirts and slacks, smoothing wrinkles from each item as it was hung. His jeans, showing the wear and tear of work, were removed and placed on hangers as well. She took the second bag to an antique dresser in the bedroom, its empty drawers gliding open smoothly as if happy to be of use again. Pulling out the wads of gym shorts, undershirts, boxer briefs and mismatched socks that were shoved unceremoniously into the bag, she neatly stacked them in their new homes. In the bottom of the bag were his shoes. She walked them back into the closet, placing them on the floor shelf, dress shoes and work boots lined up neatly beside running shoes and heels.

There was one last thing. Removing his shaving kit, she returned to the vanity. His toothbrush went in the holder with hers, personal items into the medicine cabinet. She stood back and soaked it in. Starting tonight they would each be part of *them*, never again alone. She turned off the light as she left the room, smiling.

The phone rang as she slid the pizzas in to cook. She closed the oven door and picked up the receiver. "Hi babe, how's my truck?"

"Down for the count, I'm afraid. I had to call for a tow."

Her heart sank. "Darn! I have a few things to take care of tomorrow."

"That'll still work. When we're done loading the mattress I'll have Trey bring my car over for you."

What? "You mean you'll let Trey drive your 'Vette? Your shiny *new* Corvette that I've ridden in exactly once?"

"Um. Yes?"

She could only laugh in astonishment. He was a very brave man. "That will certainly make you his idol for life." As if he wasn't already.

There was a smile in his voice when he spoke. "I've waited half a lifetime to finally say you're mine, Allie. I'm feeling generous."

A quiet sigh slipped out. He took such good care of them. She let her voice go sultry. "Then hurry home so I can thank you properly."

There was an endless pause before he broke the silence, his words caressing her heart in a voice that was exceptionally deep and more than a little strained. "Babe. It's you. It's always been you." He paused again to clear his throat. "You're all the thanks I need."

Her heart fluttered. Oh, my.

The air was spicy with the aroma of pepperoni as the front door slammed and Trey trailed Jake in, the mattress they wrestled between them more awkward and unwieldy than a full-grown crocodile. "Here. Set it down . . . now," he said, and let go. Jesus, it was a good thing Trey was there to help. No way could he have managed the cumbersome bed alone. He stretched the stiffness out of his fingers and headed toward the master bedroom. "The old bed comes out first, remember? Let's carry it into the garage."

Jake tugged the replacement mattress into place, Trey helping him push at it until it was installed on the black iron frame. Allie stood nearby, offering suggestions she called it. He grinned. He called it acting like a wife.

But as a reward, he got fresh hot pizza with his woman and her kid. What beat that? By the time Allie had the dishwasher loaded she was yawning. She disappeared while he flipped channels in the living room, but came back minutes later wearing pajamas, her breath minty fresh when she leaned into him.

"I can't keep my eyes open a moment longer. I really need to go to bed now."

He anchored his hand around her neck and let his lips skim along the softness of hers, parting them with gentle pressure. Trey was preparing to leave, meeting friends for a late movie and he was sprawled on the sofa with his eyelids drooping. The sexy soft scent of Allie's skin buzzed his senses. He stood and clicked the TV off. Might as well tag along.

Jake was relaxed from a warm, soothing shower. With a towel tied to his hips he entered the darkened bedroom. "*Ow!* Damn it!" He nursed the toe that stumbled into the oversized nightstand. A little light would be good here, he patted the tabletop blindly. Ah ha, the lamp. He flicked it on and checked the bed. She was still asleep, good. Now, where were his clothes?

The upper drawer held a mother lode of lace and satin; he remembered that drawer. He tried the next drawer down. Running shorts and stretchy tops. "Where the hell'd she hide my clothes?" He finally found them in the other dresser, all neatly folded. He glanced at Allie again, sleeping soundly on his side of the bed. "Thanks, babe." He stepped into underwear and joined her under the covers, tucking her up against his still-damp skin.

Jake was gone when she awoke the next morning. He left a note on the bathroom counter, along with keys.

Allie—Will get truck repaired today. Have fun with Reese. Courthouse at 4? Love you, Jake

Short and sweet. She missed him already. She tucked the note into her vanity drawer and stepped under the steaming hot shower.

She stood in the center of the living room, arms crossed. She'd already had a busy morning selecting flowers with Reese, but there was still so much to do. First off, what to do with the Christmas tree? She checked the clock. If she retrieved the storage boxes from the garage it would take an hour or so to have everything packed away. Forty minutes later she had a stack of bulging containers, her treasured memories safe and snug in their tissue wrappers, ready for the next year.

When Trey returned from work she'd enlist him to haul away the dry tree for recycling. She inspected the surrounding carpet. It wouldn't do any good to vacuum up pine needles until the tree was gone. She plopped on the sofa, turned the television on to a cable music channel and picked up her novel from the side table.

Jake counted the persistent rings of the telephone until Allie answered. She had so much on her plate this week he'd bet anything she lost track of time.

"Hello?"

Oh, sweet Christ! He jerked the steering wheel. Caught in heavy traffic with the phone pressed to his ear, he nearly swerved into a minivan. Apparently she'd been asleep. That deep, throaty voice was pure sex and cut straight to his gut. "Babe. Are you ready?"

He waited through the pause. "Sure. Just walking out the door."

The little liar. She'd definitely been sleeping. He let a smile creep into his voice. "Okay, then. I'll meet you inside the courthouse."

Walking through the smudged glass door minutes later, he scanned the room and sought Allie out while shrugging out of his flannel-lined jacket. There she was, perched on a chair in the waiting area with her coat neatly buttoned, a magazine propped open on her lap. When she looked up, found him, her smile was sweet and welcoming.

He had to pause, soak in the emotions flooding through every fiber of his being. Anticipation stood front and center, combined with the desperate desire she ignited with no more than a glance. And if he read it right, the jitters he'd had all morning indicated a little nervousness. But he was okay with that—*husband* was a new role for him.

There were so many other feelings poking around his brain and his heart—peace, contentment. Relief. But above all else he was blissfully happy.

If he were a poet he'd tell her that her smile was as radiant as rays of sunshine reflecting off the sparkling lake in July. That the vastness of his love for her would overflow the depths of the Grand Canyon. But those words would sound corny if he spoke them, so instead he sat beside her and dropped a tender kiss on her curved, sweet lips.

"I love you." He let the emotion in his eyes convey all he meant.

Her sweet smile changed, became impudent. "I should hope so. Because we went through quite a bit to get here, you know." She stretched toward him and grazed his cheek with her knuckles, stroked his temples. "So, are we doing this?"

He rose and took her hand, then rushed her to the clerk's counter. He'd do whatever it took to make her his wife.

Jake's week rushed by with the swiftness of a cheetah on speed. The lull of activity and the lack of office staff during the holiday season normally had him on edge. But it was Thursday and today his nerves screamed and his insides were twisted like the roots beneath Allie's favorite rose bush.

The shrill ring of the office phone went unanswered for what must be the fourteenth time. "Damn it!" He had to get out of there. The piles on his desk weren't going anywhere. He stomped through the entrance door and locked it behind him, his mood both as edgy and as capricious as the skies above.

Tomorrow. By this time tomorrow he would be a married man. Lawfully wedded. Something he definitely looked forward to, so why was he nervous? He climbed into his truck and started it up, then turned the knob for the wipers, removing the moisture that remained from an earlier thundershower.

Allie trusted him, trusted he would never betray her, never hurt her. She had no doubts. And he didn't have a single doubt about her, either. On the contrary, she was the answer to his whispered prayers. He was eager, giddier than the grand prize winner on a daytime game show. Suddenly his irritability evaporated. His eyes danced as he steered his vehicle toward the dry cleaners. Him, a nervous bridegroom? He never would have guessed.

Trey spent his days shadowing both he and Nick around the office and out at job sites. He made notes of headway on all their projects, and helped out where needed. He commuted to and from work with Jake, and that was just fine. He loved the kid as if he was his own son. It was convenient to use the time spent stuck in freeway traffic to review the plans and progress of current jobs. Sometimes they merely discussed sports or the hot topic of the day.

Jake set the alarm code and locked the office door. His final errand of the day had been to pick up Allie's wedding gift. He patted the inside pocket of his jacket as he sauntered toward the parking lot. Still there. The knots he spent the afternoon slowly untangling tried to regain their hold. He took a deep breath. He'd rather not go through that again.

He neared his truck. Trey was talking on his cell in the cab, gesturing with tense, agitated movements. He ended his call and tossed the phone onto the dash as Jake swung open the door, illuminating the interior with a bright glow. Trey's face was clearly miserable.

"Nick says you're doing a great job helping him out." Bouncing and splashing through puddles, he swung the truck onto the main road and flicked his eyes toward Trey. His attention was caught somewhere in the lights on the horizon. Several quiet minutes later he turned onto the freeway. "You have a natural talent for this work, and you seem to enjoy it."

"Hmm. Yeah."

Jake frowned. What would it take to get a reaction? "Nick and I were talking about putting you in charge of the company this summer."

"Sure. Okay." Well, that wasn't it.

"Your mom and I are moving to Tahiti next week."

"That's fine." The kid was a million miles away.

"We plan to live in a tree house." Now, that was funny. He had no defense against his stupid grin.

Trey's head snapped around. "What? *What*? Moving *where*?"

Finally. He gave Trey a long look. "What's up, Trey?"

Trey frowned. "Um. Nothing. Just . . . nothing."

"*Nothing* seems to have you a little preoccupied tonight." He adjusted the rearview and darted his eyes to the speedometer when a cop pulled in behind him. Yeah, he was safe. His eyes landed on Trey again. "Sure you don't want to talk about it?"

Trey sank further into the contoured leather seat and sighed like the weight of the entire world rested solely on his shoulders, Atlas-style. A sigh dredged all the way up from the soles of his muddy work boots. "Yeah, maybe I need to talk about it." Trey turned toward him, his eyes pleading. "But you can't tell my mom. She won't understand."

He may be a rookie, but he knew better than to promise that. "Maybe. Maybe not. I need to know what you're up against first."

Trey took in a deep breath, then let it out on a long sigh. "There's a girl."

Jake smirked, then let his tone go dry. "Trey, when a guy's this jacked up, there's usually a girl."

"This girl's different. She's special."

"No need to get defensive."

Trey's face whipped his way. "Sorry."

"We're good. Go on."

"She's in one of my study groups. We started hanging out last month."

"That sounds normal, nothing your mom wouldn't understand. I still don't get the problem."

Trey's sigh carried relief as well as worry. "It's sex."

Oh, crap. Now he was ready to slink down in *his* seat. "So the problem is she won't let you in her pants?" And was there, please God, any way to sound a little less lame?

Uh oh. He could read those squinty eyes. He'd missed the point again.

"The *problem* is I don't love her. She's cool and all, and we have fun. Fool around a little sometimes. But that's as far as I want to go right now. We've only had four dates—I don't even know her—and I'm not all over her shit so she thinks I'm hooking up with someone else." Trey punched the dashboard. *What the hell?* Now the kid was pissed. "She's blowing up my phone, acting all crazy jealous."

Jake slid eyes right to the abused dash. Kid better not have cracked it. "You've talked to her about this, I imagine."

"She doesn't get it. All she sees is she's not getting any."

He choked out a cough. Good thing it was dark out. He'd never be able to have this conversation in the light of day. "Talk to Jax?"

Trey snorted. "She's a straight-up bitch to him. Guess what he says." He stared through the windshield, at the wipers steadily slapping the raindrops away. "I'm trying to decide if I should cave or ditch her." Jesus. Back to miserable. Good times.

He exited the freeway, nearly home. Time to wrap this up. "Got to remind you, Trey. There are a whole lot of hot girls out there. And you don't want to hear it, but you're young yet. Remember to let your intellect keep instinct firmly in check."

Trey turned from staring through the windshield. Looked at him in confusion. "Huh?"

Allie was definitely cooler than her son realized. He grinned. "Make sure the big head's doing the thinking for the little head."

Trey smirked. "Yeah." The word escaped his mouth slowly, like resin seeping through new pine. "But she really knows which buttons to push."

It probably wasn't Trey's buttons they should be concerned about. More like his zipper. "If she doesn't respect the way you feel, if she doesn't respect *you* . . . I'd say she's really not that special."

Again a long, slow breath. "Yeah."

Jake's finger tapped the wheel as he steered through traffic. It was time to raise the stakes. "Trey, can I ask you something? It's kind of personal."

Trey's lips curved. "What have we been talking about that wasn't personal?"

He blew out a huffing laugh. "You got me there. But seriously, is this the first girl? I mean . . . have you ever . . . um . . . *been* with a girl?" Oh my God, how *ever* did fathers do this?

The little shit had the nerve to laugh at him. "Are you asking if I'm still a virgin?"

He tightened his hands on the steering wheel. He was all in now. "Yeah, I am."

"Not really."

Well, what the hell did that mean?

Then again, did he really want to know? He needed out of this conversation before he died of mortification. He pointed his eyes forward as he turned onto their street. "Well, remember . . . in this day and age . . . if you're going to play the game you've got to suit up. There's more at stake than just an unwanted pregnancy."

"I've got it covered."

His eyes flew to Trey. "Yeah?"

Trey smirked. "Yeah."

Oh, thank God. "All right then." He pulled into the driveway and killed the engine. Pushed the button to open the garage. "And you're wrong about your mom. She's a pretty amazing lady."

Trey stilled with his hand on the door pull. "You're right. She is." He looked like he might say something else as he met Jake at the front of the truck, but then halted. "Thanks for talking to me tonight, Jake. Sometimes I really miss my dad."

Jake dropped an arm around his shoulder and headed toward the house. "Yeah kid, so do I."

"So . . . looks like the Cardinals are gonna make the playoffs, huh?"

Jake padded into the kitchen in his socks and leaned against the counter. Allie lowered the knife she was using to chop tomatoes for salad. "Everything okay?"

Yeah, it really was. Her arms wrapped around him as he pulled her against him, burying his face in her sweet-smelling hair. "I think I grew up tonight."

She nestled against him. The motion of her smile tickled his chest. "Care to tell me about it?"

He smiled into the soft silk floating around him. "Not this time, babe. But I *can* tell you, Trey is one great kid. You did a helluva job raising him."

She lifted her face and beamed. "Thank you, sweetheart. I didn't do it alone, you know."

He pulled back and looked into her eyes. "No, everything else aside, Ben was a damn good dad."

"He was, but I was talking about you. I couldn't have made it through those first years alone without you. You've always been there for Trey. He looks up to you."

She'd told him that many times over the years, but tonight it really hit home. "I never realized what a responsibility that was. It's rather awe-inspiring." And more than a little scary.

Grinning, she smacked her lips against his and patted his chest. "There's nothing to be frightened of. You're a natural."

Dinnertime with his ready-made family was his favorite time of the day. After spending most of his adult life eating solitary meals, this interaction at the end of a good day was peacefully satisfying. Trey's presence was an advantage he hadn't foreseen. He would miss him as much as Allie did when he returned to school.

Seated at the dinner table, Trey's phone buzzed and he glanced at the screen. Shooting a wretched look toward Jake he put the phone to his ear and left for the privacy of his room. Thirty minutes later the dishwasher was busy whirring and sloshing. Allie relaxed against him on the sofa, flipping through television stations.

She clicked off the television and tossed the remote onto the table. "This is silly. It's the night before our wedding. There must be something better to do."

He straightened when she stood. "You want to play cards? Maybe a little strip poker?" He easily dodged the throw pillow she threw at his head—a typical female response to his wolfish smile.

She rolled her eyes. "How about Monopoly?"

"Yeah. That's what I meant to say." He stood. Got the board game from the closet shelf. "I get to be the dog."

She lifted a brow and followed him to the table. "You don't say."

Perusing the game board, Allie held the dice in her hand, cocking her fist to make her first roll when Trey ambled in and plopped onto an empty chair.

"Can I play too?"

"Of course. What piece do you want?" She lowered the dice to the table and passed him a stack of play money.

He grinned. "The wheelbarrow. I've gotten quite familiar with those lately."

She placed his token on the board, picked up the dice again and rolled a six. She paid the bank and scooped up the card for her new property.

Jake raised the dice and rolled double fives. He slid into the *Just Visiting* space as Allie turned her attention to Trey. "So, are you going to tell us who you've been talking to on your phone?"

Trey's eyes flew to him.

He shrugged. "I didn't say anything." He made his play and nudged the dice toward Trey.

Trey rolled then turned to Allie. "I had a girlfriend. Dylan."

"Had?"

"Yeah. It's over now."

Looked like the kid made a decision. He arched his eyebrows, got Trey's attention. "Everything okay?"

Trey smirked. "Sure. Just had to get my head on straight."

Chapter Twenty Nine

She'd been watching him for nearly an hour already, afraid to touch for fear she'd wake him. She smiled and let her gaze follow the fluid motion of his bare chest as it lifted and fell in breaths as steady and sure as the man himself. Jake was every woman's dream, tender and devoted, passionate and determined. And today he would become her husband. The idea coursed through her, lighting every dim corner of her soul.

From time to time he snorted, and the slow, even breaths were replaced with a snuffle and a sort of stuttering movement that interestingly enough caused his work-chiseled abs to ripple clear down his front.

Propped on an elbow, she hadn't taken her eyes from him just to see it happen again.

She'd never before had an opportunity to explore him fully as he slept. Temptation finally won and she let her free hand wander. His firm skin was sleep-warmed under her meandering fingers as she mapped the smooth ridge of his collar bone. Starting at his near shoulder, she worked her way across the hollow of his throat, stretching to reach his far side. She smiled as a lone finger traced the misshapen angle of the bone there. He'd broken it in high school. A bad slide to second, if she remembered the story correctly.

He snuffled again, his breath catching before smoothing out again, a rolling wave of muscle fading into the covers. Remarkable. Raising to her knees she hovered over him and captured his wide jaw in her hands. Captivated, she studied her movements as the pads of her thumbs smoothed the softness of the cultivated stubble masking the lower portion of his face. The same smooth rasp he brushed across her sensitive skin until she exploded in ecstasy. A shiver of anticipation chased up her spine.

Following instinct, she used the tips of her fingers to outline his full, sensuous lips. They parted at her touch and his tongue peeked through the gap. Her face warmed. Jake was amazingly adept at causing her to moan— both shamelessly and with great regularity—using only that tongue.

Lifting her hands, she followed the slope of his nose and then let the range of her exploration widen until the blades of his cheek bones were hidden beneath her fingertips. His eyelids fluttered and she stilled. The etched corners of his eyes creased as his face scrunched, and then smoothed out as he yawned and his ebony eyes opened fully.

He yawned again. "Good morning." Every muscle in his arms bunched and then lengthened as he stretched. *Fascinating.*

She tore her eyes away to meet his gaze. "I woke you."

"Yes you did. And thank you."

A grin stretched across her face. "We're getting married today."

"And it's about time."

That sexy smile melted her every time. She pushed her nest of hair off her face and rocked back until she sat on her heels. "Did you know you snore? Well, it's actually more like heavy breathing, but it's kind of cute and your abs do this really sexy rolling flex thi—"

"Do you know how beautiful you are?"

Her breath trapped in her chest, then rushed out. "But's still so early and I probably have yesterday's mascara smeared under my—"

"And you're still beautiful." Raising a hand, he captured her neck and held her. His abs clenched as he lifted his head to nip at the slope of her breast through her thin nightgown, the abrasion of his beard causing her nipples to bead and pucker, and overwhelming fire rushed to her core. He tugged her down until she lay against him. "Now come here."

Jake wandered into the living room from the bathroom after Allie asked him to leave. Well, kicked him out, really—but hell, she was parading around in nothing but scraps of silk and dental floss and had those sheer stockings that . . . yeah. The joke was on him that the private showing she promised wouldn't actually happen until much later than she realized.

He paced as he waited for her, in steps measuring the length of the room, around the expanse of leather sofa and to the table on the other side The photographs Allie kept on display were a chronicle of the family inhabiting the home.

Trey at Christmas, about four years old. Trey with Allie and Maddie on some kind of school field trip. He picked up a small snapshot in a simple frame, a young Ben and Allie cradling a sleeping Trey, probably taken the day he was born. Their goofy grins had him smiling. The possibility of him featuring in a shot like that was gone now, but with Allie as the prize he was more than satisfied.

Here was one he didn't remember—him standing between both of his parents, saluting the photographer with a bottle of beer. His father had apparently arrived late from the hospital; he still wore scrubs. His mom was wearing a cocktail dress and making bunny ears behind his head. He replaced the photo. It didn't do any good to wish they were here today, but he liked to think they would have become friends with Allie.

Trey, dressed in a classic navy suit similar to his own entered from the hallway, his finger digging into the collar of crisp white shirt. "My mom went through a few of the boxes you brought over. She thought you might like to have that out." He peered closer. "It's a good picture of you, but I don't remember meeting your parents."

"It was my twenty-first birthday." He studied the picture again. "My dad died the next month—heart attack. My mom died a few years ago."

"Oh man, I'm sorry. Mom moved the pictures of my dad into my room. All except that one." He pointed to the silver frame on the table. "She didn't think you'd mind if we kept it out."

Jake had to clear his throat to speak. "Of course not. I remember that day like yesterday. They were so happy."

He turned as heels clicked across the tile floor. The breath he suddenly couldn't control caught in his chest as Allie glided into the room to stand beside him. He caught a hint of her subtle perfume and dove his face into her neck. "You're stunning."

Her hair was pulled into a fancy knot at the back of her head. He had hours to imagine yanking those pins out and letting it sift through his fingers.

Allie grinned and raked him over him until he arched a brow, settled his jacket on his shoulders and yanked his tie loose. "Thank you for not making us wear monkey suits today.

With an exasperated smirk she lifted her hands to his shoulders and pressed a kiss to his lips. "You look fabulous, too. You're both very handsome." She turned to Trey and adjusted his loosened tie. "After today we'll have a few more photos to set out."

"I remembered my homework, teach." Jake unfolded a paper he had in his jacket pocket and handed it to her.

Her head snapped up when she finished reading. "Wow." His chest puffed at her whispered word. "This is really good."

Allie folded herself into his car, adjusting her skirt and fastening the safety harness. Her startled gaze whipped to him when he started the car and pulled out of the driveway. "Trey's not following us?"

He shook his head. "He had something to do first. He'll meet us there." He allowed his eyes to skim over her from eyebrows to peep toes, then settle on her smile. "By the way, have I told you how much I love you?"

When they arrived he led her to join their crowd bunched into the courthouse lobby. Trey arrived within minutes, gave him a nod and made a beeline to stand beside Jax. Maddie produced a cellophane box, enlisting her daughters to pass out perfect white calla lilies.

Jake somehow got separated from Allie. He glanced around until he found her and stilled. She mesmerized him, standing in her soft white dress and shimmery silver shoes, holding a white bouquet that was nowhere near as silky smooth nor as fragrant as she was. He worked his way closer to her and snaked his arm around her waist, tucking her against him.

"Ready?" He glanced at his watch. Ten fifty; their appointment was for eleven. "It should only be a few more minutes."

She flashed him a nervous smile as a clerk bellowed their names into the noisy room. "Looks like we're up."

They filed into a vacant courtroom. Moments later a judge swept through a discreet door at the rear and shook his hand. "Mr. Taylor, is everybody here?"

He ignored the jitters rolling in waves through his body. They'd calm down as soon as Allie was beside him. "We're ready, sir."

"Then please take your places at the front of the room."

He motioned Trey and Nick to his side while Reese and Maddie stepped forward to join Allie. The judge moved before them. This was it. Allie's hand slid into his and his eyelids lowered. Yep. All smoothed out. He met her gaze and smiled.

"We are gathered here today in the presence of these witnesses—"

Eager anticipation rushed through him as the judge recited the generic ceremony. When it came time for the vows the judge opened the paper he passed him during their introductions.

He turned to face Allie and took her hands as she spoke.

"I, Allie Harper Tate, love you. You are my best friend. Today I gladly and without reservation join you in marriage, pledging my faith and my heart for the last time."

They were simple promises, but she made them to him. All traces of nerves were gone. He couldn't wait to swear his to her. "I, Jake Taylor, love you. You are my best friend. Today I joyfully and with great anticipation join you in marriage, pledging my faith and my heart for the first and last time." Suddenly the weight of what he just did pressed against his heart and he grinned.

As one they turned to face the judge as he spoke. "Do you promise to laugh together when life seems easy? To comfort each other when life seems hard? To cherish each other when love is simple and more importantly, when it requires effort? To honor and respect each other, all the days of your life?"

"We do."

The band he selected for her was simple yet elegant. He slipped it on with traditional vows. Then grinned in surprise when she reached for his hand.

With a smile as brilliant as the Arizona summer sun, Allie slipped a matching band on his finger. "I love you."

Allie passed through the bustling restaurant beside Jake and entered a small, private dining room where eleven chairs were crowded around a table meant for ten. She turned to Trey and pointed toward a square table set for four nearby. "Looks like they set that up for you, Jax and the girls."

After Jake seated her, her eyes darted around the room. There were two unoccupied chairs. "Maddie and Michael aren't here yet."

The waitress set a pitcher of margaritas on the table before them. Jake patted her hand then poured them each a glass of the slushy concoction. "They're fine. Maddie forgot her camera so they ran home. They should be here any minute."

She turned as Reese asked her a question. "I'm sorry Reese, what did you say?"

"I asked if you'll be staying at your school next year. Maddie told me you're getting a new principal." Reese made a snarly face, indicating her opinion of a change in administration.

Amusement bubbled at the expression on her friend's face. "I never really thought of leaving." She delivered the confession along with another rumor. "I heard the assistant principal is getting promoted. I'll admit she can be callous and snarky, but I'm not familiar with the other principals in the district." She shrugged. "Sometimes the devil you know is better than the devil you don't."

"It would be easier to stay where you are, that's for certain."

Maddie and Michael hurried in. There was the unmistakable jingle of keys as Maddie she leaned over and gave her and then Jake a quick hug. "So sorry we're late." With a bland expression, she held up her camera and moved to the other side of the table. "Sit together you two. Let me get a few good shots."

She grabbed Jake and posed for picture after picture, then sicced Maddie on the rest of the wedding guests.

The room grew louder, voices raising and lowering as lunch orders were taken and food delivered. On mother's instinct she checked on the teenagers sitting quietly at their own table. Their water glasses were all filled with icy margaritas.

It was her wedding day; she wouldn't be the bad guy today. She nudged Maddie to get her attention, cocking her head their way.

In her periphery Jake checked his watch. He'd been doing that since they sat. He couldn't be in that big a hurry to leave could he? She chuckled to herself. Maybe he really was.

"Oh, for goodness sake." Maddie blustered as she marched over and removed the glasses, placing three of them in the center of the round table. The fourth she set before her own plate and laughed. "If you guys drink these there won't be enough for us."

"But they're good." Emily whined after being relieved of what was probably her first taste of illicit alcohol.

"Fine, I'll order you drinks without tequila."

After a quick perusal of the table Jake stood and cleared his throat, raising his margarita, clinking the glass with his knife. The table went silent.

"We want to thank you all for joining us today." Every face at the table wore a rapt expression. "You all mean a lot to Allie, and to me."

Her gaze scanned the table, landing on everyone who was important in her life. Her mother and father were there, and Bentley, whom she'd loved as a father for many years.

"I promise to take good care of her, to make her as happy as she's made me." He smiled and reached for her hand to pull her up beside him. "I plan to spoil her every chance I get, the way she spoils me every day, with every gesture. And I plan to start today, with this."

She opened the brown leather case he handed her. Cancun! "*Cancun?*"

He grinned and nodded. "Our flight's in three hours."

Her heart raced. "But Jake, we can't go that soon! I'm not packed, and I have to find my passport—"

The light danced in the triumphant caress of his gaze. "Handled, and handled. Our suitcases are in the car, all ready for a week at the beach. And your passport is right here." He pointed it out, hiding behind the airline tickets. "Do you want to tell everyone good-bye so we don't miss our flight?"

Oh, how exciting! She threw her arms around him and rained kisses on his chin. "Who? . . . How?" Her words wouldn't come. He lowered his head so she could reach his lips.

"I picked up the tickets from the travel agent yesterday. Trey dug your passport out of your desk. And Maddie packed your suitcase. If she forgot anything we can get it there." He nudged her into gear. "Now, grab your purse, please."

She quickly made the rounds, tugging Jake along behind, hugging and kissing everyone good-bye, saving Trey for last. He walked out with them.

"You'll be all right until we get back?" She stood in the parking lot with the car door open.

"Mom, I live by myself at school. Don't call."

She reached up and pressed her palm to his cheek. "Thank you so much. I love you."

"Adios, *mamacita*. Love you, too." He took the hand Jake offered and shook it firmly, then reached in for a hard man hug. His voice was rough when he turned to his new stepfather. "Love you too, Jake."

She kept her eyes on him as they backed out of their parking space. He yelled out as they pulled away, thrashing his arm in the air.

"You guys have fun. And don't let her call!"

Jake hurried her through the airport terminal to check-in and handed the clerk their boarding passes.

Allie stretched to examine the papers with interest. "Where did you get those?"

He heaved the first suitcase on the scale.

"ID please." The grumpy ticket clerk held his hand out.

"I checked us in online." He fished out his wallet. "Thought we might be pressed for time today."

"Very shrewd." She passed her driver's license across the counter.

"No, but I know you." The clerk fastened a tag on the first bag and tossed it to the conveyer belt behind him. Jake dropped the second bag on the scale and passed the attendant his license.

"One of these days you won't be so smart, Mr. Taylor."

"Will you still love me?"

"I'll always love you."

"Let me guess, honeymoon?" The grumpy ticket clerk returned slid their boarding passes across the counter.

"Yep.

"Hmph. Don't drink the water."

Following signs, Jake led the way to the correct gate and then through the creeping serpentine line of security. As the line stalled, Allie struggled to shift her heavy tote to her other shoulder and he took it from her, then checked his watch. He shuffled forward three feet and checked it again.

"Relax. There's plenty of time to make the flight."

"I'll relax when we're on the plane."

"Come on, you're standing here with the woman you love most in the world and we're all dressed up in the pretty clothes we got married in. You'd rather be sitting on a stuffy airplane?"

"No, I'd rather be lying on a beach in Cancun with the woman I love most in the world wearing that string bikini you thought you were hiding." He kissed her lightly on her nose. "Or not."

Allie waited for him to tie his shoes after finally being screened. Their gate was only a short way down the walkway. Passengers milled about, unconcerned. "You want a magazine?"

She nodded and wandered to the newsstand. Over a PA the gate attendant call first class passengers to board.

"Hurry Allie, they're calling us."

"That's first class. We have a good twenty minutes before the plane finishes boarding."

He rolled his eyes. "Did you *look* at the tickets, Allie? We're first class."

She gaped. "I haven't ever sat in first class before."

"Neither have I. I thought it might be fun." He grabbed their magazines and stepped to checkout. "You want gum?"

"Thanks. I've never been to Mexico before either."

He grinned. "I thought that might be fun, too." He took his purchases and change from the clerk and steered her toward their gate.

Jake finished stowing his bag and sat beside her in the roomy leather seat. Her bag and purse were safely tucked under the seat before her. "This is wonderful."

She took a glass of champagne from a passing attendant and raised it for a toast. "To surprises."

His echo mingled with the clink of glasses. "To surprises."

She breathed a relieved sigh after the smooth take-off, turned on her reading lamp and lifted the arm rest between their seats. Jake stole one of her new magazines and leafed through it until he came to an article that seemed to interest him.

"Here, look at this." His finger pointed out a passage. "I want to try this."

Did he just *leer* at her? She scanned the article he was reading and choked on her champagne. "Sure you can handle that?"

"I haven't had any complaints so far."

Okay, now *that* was definitely a leer. She choked again, this time on a laugh. "You're right, sweetheart. Absolutely no complaints."

Her dress rode up as she laid her head in Jake's lap and tucked her legs beneath her. So far it had been a long and nerve-racking day, but all her tension rolled away with his steady, calming heartbeat at her back and the crisp, bubbly champagne streaming through her system. Jake draped a thin blanket over her and her weighted eyelids closed.

She lurched and her eyes flew open as the plane suddenly lost altitude. Jake tightened his hold on her. "Hush, baby. Go back to sleep. We'll be there soon."

Soon? She pushed herself upright and stretched. She peeked at his watch and mentally computed the time change. "Thirty more minutes?"

He nodded. "Give or take."

Good. She had time for repairs. She took her makeup bag from her carry on and made her way precariously toward the restroom.

Jake's face held an obvious look of relief as she climbed over him on the way to her seat.

"What?"

"I was afraid you would take the pins out of your hair." He shrugged at her grin. "I've had a fantasy about it all day."

She laughed and cupped her hand around his ear, leaning in to whisper. "So have I."

Chapter Thirty

The elegance of the extravagant marble lobby impressed her, but the sheer opulence of their suite on the top floor of the hotel had her grasping for words. Wide marble expanses, sophisticated upholsteries, deep cushions—she oohed and aahed as they meandered through a doorway and into the bedroom to discover a king-sized bed covered in rose silk.

She peeked through another doorway and then stepped in as if drawn by an invisible force. Spinning slowly to take in the jetted soaking tub and the inviting glass-encased shower, she scooped up a plush robe and brushed its velvety softness against her cheek. She could live in here all week! Laying the robe across more of that elegant marble, she grasped Jake's hand and pulled him back through the lavish rooms and onto the balcony.

The sound of the ocean surf was soothing, almost hypnotizing, and Allie fell into her thoughts. It was impossible for any other woman to be as happy as she was tonight. She sighed as he drew her to him, facing the darkened horizon. Today she married the man she loved. While she looked for companionship, someone to have a little fun with, Jake's steady presence stole her heart. Maybe she couldn't offer him everything he dreamed of, but she could offer him love. He loved her so well, so thoroughly, swore that her love was all he needed. She tightened his arms around her. She would make sure that it was enough.

"The moon's shining on the water. It looks like a great night for a walk on the beach."

Did they make them any better than that?

One after the other she slipped out of her heels and handed them to Jake to stuff in his jacket pockets. "You have that romantic, sappy look again." His teasing didn't bother her tonight.

"This is actually my *I'm exquisitely happy* look." she corrected him with a prim smile. "I'm here on this beautiful beach." She swept her hands before her. "At a stunning hotel with a really great guy . . . who went above and beyond in the accommodations department, by the way. And . . . as it happens, he's my husband. What more could I ask?"

With tug he pulled her closer and slowed their steps. He leaned just a little and whispered into her lips. "Thank you."

On her tip toes in the sand, she nuzzled her mouth against his. "You're welcome. What did I do?"

His lips kissed their way to her ear. "You married me. You make me happier than I could ever imagine. You make me want to be . . . more."

She turned in his arms, her back to him. Placing her hands on his forearms, she leaned into him, the warm Caribbean breeze soothing them, the slow lapping of moon washed waves peaceful. "If someone said to me six months ago that I would be here with you today—that we would be married—I would have thought they were insane." She shook her head ruefully. "But now, now I can't picture my life any other way." She turned and stretched to meet his waiting lips. "Thank *you*, sweetheart."

They wandered their way back upstairs. Jake began undressing while she unpacked. Shouldn't take long. Knowing Maddie, it was filled with nothing but bikinis and lingerie. Laying her suitcase open on the luggage rack she picked up the package lying on top and smiled. Yep, lingerie, she recognized the gift wrap. She rifled through the rest of the contents. Phew, Maddie did her proud. She had plenty of real clothes. And running shoes.

Jake finished pulling off his socks and stood. "I'm going to take a quick shower." He cocked his head to the side. "Care to join me?"

On their wedding night? "Absolutely."

Box in hand, she trailed him into that little slice of marble heaven. He closed the door behind them and nodded at the box. "What's that?"

With a secretive smile she set the package on the vanity. "A little gift from the girls."

He tugged her close. "What's in it?"

From Maddie the Romantic? Something to knock his socks off, undoubtedly. Or his pants. "I don't know yet. It's still wrapped."

Jake adjusted the water spray. "Don't you want to open it?"

"I will."

Thoroughly scrubbed and wearing a satisfied smile, Jake stepped through the glass door and wrapped a towel around his waist. "Are you coming out?"

She tiptoed across hairpins and let her eyes follow him as he tossed the comforter to the end of the bed. "I'll only be a minute."

Paper ripped and tissue rustled as she tore into her present and uncovered handsful of delicate, foamy froth. *Oh, bless you, Maddie!*

There was nothing like sheer white silk slithering and sliding over female curves to make a girl feel sexy. But, uh oh. She gave the satin ribbons at her shoulders a tug. Nope. There was no way those tiny lace triangles would hold all her breasts. Oh well, Jake was sure to enjoy the show.

In was new to waken in degrees, awareness filtering into his brain one step at a time as first his eyelids cracked open and then his body roused bit by bit. His hand automatically reached out, stroking the smooth skin of Allie's hip as he spooned her. This was new, too.

Leaving her warmth he rolled out of bed, stripping of his T-shirt as he padded to the shower. How did he ever live without her? Answer was easy: pretty sure he didn't. He went through the motions from one day to the next, always searching for ... something. But that wasn't really living. Allie brought light. Sounds and aromas became more distinct. He let his eyes land on her as he turned to close the bathroom door. It was her love that made him alive.

Allie sailed across the front porch and through the doorway. Reaching up, she released her hair and let it fall. She removed her running shoes and carried them with her into the kitchen. The house was quiet, She probably had time for a shower before Trey woke. It would be nice to shower in her own bathroom again. But then again, the glass *room* they used for the past week was a tough act to follow. Allie pulled a bottle of water from the fridge and set it on the counter as Trey careened through the house.

He skidded to a stop at her feet, panting, looking for all the world like a puppy happy to see his master. "Mom, you're home! Did you have a good trip?"

Early morning runs on a deserted beach. Snorkeling in waters teeming with vivid tropical fish. Romantic moonlit walks under a star draped sky. And sex. Hours and hours of passionate sex. She couldn't imagine anything better. "We had a great trip! But I missed you!" She opened her arms to hug him with abandon. "We'll tell you all about it at dinner." She glanced around. "Where's Jake?"

"Nick called early this morning. He needed him to check a job site." Trey got down two big glasses as he spoke, then pulled the orange juice from the refrigerator. "Jake said to tell you he was sorry he had to rush out on your first day back." He poured out the juice, shoved one glass toward her."

"Are you tired? You guys got home really late last night."

She shook her head. "Not tired at all. I need to get dressed and go to my classroom. I still have to take down all the holiday stuff."

He chugged his juice and put the empty glass on the sink counter. "I don't have anything planned. I can help."

She'd be a fool to turn down an offer of free labor. "Thanks. Now rinse the glass."

"Aw, c'mon, Mom." He rolled his eyes.

Some things never changed.

It was going to be a while yet before the unexpected sight of Jake sprawled across her sofa didn't cause her heart to bump. And when warmth blossomed in her belly and spread to, well, *south*? That was good, too. "Hi sweetheart, how's work?"

"Under control. How was your run?" He tossed the remote and made room for her to sit.

She sat. "Cold. I could seriously get used to running on the beach in warm weather."

"As long as I can watch from the sidelines."

"Whiner." She'd bribed him into joining her for a three-mile jog. And ended up babying him for the next two days while his legs recovered.

Which was actually kind of fun.

He grinned like he could read her mind. And then was kind enough to change the subject. "Feel like doing something today?"

"Trey said he'd help me reset my classroom when I'm done here. We'll get done faster if you come along.

"Sounds good. I'm in."

Allie stood in the center of her classroom. They'd converted it from Merry Christmas to Winter Wonderland in record time, and now she was ready for Monday morning. Having her guys along made a big difference. *Her guys.* It sounded good.

Oh, she didn't want to forget this one last thing. Picking up the chalk she wrote her name on the blackboard. *Mrs. Taylor.* She nodded in satisfaction. Now she was ready.

She'd been back at school for forty-five minutes and already she was ready for a vacation. In that short amount of time she was forced to send one girl to the nurse—a sobbing sixth grader who was on the wrong playground and had either a hornet sting or a zit, two boys to time out for staging a spitting contest—the criteria being both volume and distance, and the principal's grandson of all people to the safety officer for collecting quarters from children standing in line for the slide. One father had already called the school and threatened to sue for extortion.

Never a dull moment in primary.

But finally—finally she stood at the front of her drama-free classroom, ready to make her big announcement.

"Mrs. Tate? Mrs. Tate! Who's Mrs. Taylor?" Amy Johnson was such a good little reader. "Good job, Amy."

"Is she a sub? We aren't we gonna have a sub, are we?" Aaron Phillips had separation anxiety.

She shook her head. "No, Aaron, there's no sub."

"Then who is she?" One at a time, she may have stood a chance at control. When they all started in, she didn't have a shot. She looked around the room at her entire class and grinned. Better to roll with it.

"Mrs. Taylor is me. I got married right after Christmas." Before she could get the final words out she was surrounded by students, all jabbering at once. Yep. Not a shot.

"But you're old, Mrs. Tate. I mean, Mrs. Taylor. Are you allowed to get married when you're old?"

"I'm not *that* old, Billy."

"Are you gonna have a baby, Mrs. Taylor? My sister got married 'cause she was gonna have a baby."

"No, Jennifer, I'm not having a baby."

She studied the magpies chirping her name as they swarmed. One was missing. When her gaze landed at his seat, her shoulders sagged. She picked up the tissues from her desk and walked over. Squatting beside him, she laid a hand on the back of his chair. If only she could break policy and drag the boy into her arms. His silent tears broke her heart. "Jason, why are you so upset?" She held out the tissue box and he pulled out a couple.

He scrubbed his eyes and blew. "Are you gonna move away?"

"Oh, Jason. No. I have a house here and all you children. I'm not going anywhere."

"Are you sure, um, Mrs. Taylor?" He sniffed. "Really, really sure? 'Cause my mom got married and she moved away. Now I live with just my dad."

Her heart melted. "Promise. I'm staying right here."

He managed a watery smile. "Okay, Mrs. Taylor.

Time to wrap up this carnival. She stood and addressed the entire classroom. "Listen up. I need you all to find your seats so we can get started on the day." After the morning they had, she wouldn't be surprised if they whined and dawdled.

"Now, please." Nope. Not surprised at all.

But she was Mrs. Taylor.

She'd tried to avoid thinking of this day since they returned from their honeymoon. But now that it was the third week of January, it was time for Trey to head north again. Allie lifted her head from her pillow to check the clock. Three thirty. She would fall asleep at her desk if she didn't fall asleep soon. Rolling to her side, she yanked the covers and forced her eyes to close.

"Allie, what's up? Go to sleep, would you? You've been tossing around all night." Jake's words were laced with impatience, but it was the third time she'd woken him.

"Yes, Jake. I know I have. I'm the one doing the tossing. Don't you think I'd sleep if I could? I'm going to be a wreck tomorrow." Each word was delivered like icy hail spit from the sky. *Darn it.* He didn't deserve that.

He laced his fingers behind his head and stared at the ceiling.

"I'm sorry. I shouldn't have said that." Tears gathered at the back of her throat. Her voice was thick with it when she spoke. "I'll go lay on the sofa."

He unthreaded his hands and rolled to face her. "You're not going anywhere. Come closer." He pulled her to him, against his warmth. "There, that's better. Now, tell me what's wrong."

"Everything's wrong." Her words fell as freely as the fresh batch of tears. "Everything's changing so fast and I'm tired and I'm bitchy. The race we worked so hard for is over and Trey's leaving tomorrow. And I can't have a baby." The last came out on a loud, keening wail.

Shifting his weight, Jake gathered her closer still and tightened the arm covering her waist. "Well, hell, Allie. *This* marathon is over, but you and Maddie can start planning for the next one." He smoothed her hair back and kissed her forehead. "And Trey was always going back to school. You're just used to having him home, but in a week you'll be used to having him gone again."

Yeah, that was sensible. She sniffled. "I guess it all kind of hit me."

"I know, babe." Jake ran his palm along the ball of her shoulder and down her arm. It was soothing. "Now tell me this thing about a baby. Is this something new?"

She hiccupped. "I don't know where that came from."

"Well, it seems this is something we're not done dealing with."

It was much easier to talk in the dark, tucked against his belly. "I can't get it out of my mind. Everywhere I go I see babies in strollers, babies in car seats, pregnant women." Those damn tears were starting again.

"Okay, hush, hush now." His hands circled her back in slow, deliberate movements. She pushed herself to a sit.

"It's not fair, Jake. I'm only forty-one and I feel betrayed by my body." The edge of the sheet worked well to dry her eyes. Her voice lowered to a tortured whisper. "I love you. I want to have a baby with you."

She let him drag her into his arms, then lay there sniffling. "Allie, baby, I've got you. But life is not always fair. As much as I want a little girl with pretty curls running around our house—" He rubbed his cheek against her hair. "As much as the idea appeals to me, I didn't marry you thinking it may happen."

She turned her head to face him. "But wouldn't it—"

Angling over her, he tipped her chin and cut her off with his mouth. Then murmured into her ear. "Yes, it would. But I love you even if it's not happening."

The anxiety she hadn't been able to control faded like thunder moving on after a storm. "Why are you so good to me?" She wiggled until she lay flat again, pulling him with her. His warm breath caused familiar needs to stir low in her belly. "Are you ready to sleep now?" She turned into him, nibbling his chin until he lowered his head.

She cooled when he lifted away, then warmed again when he covered her.

"Not quite yet."

Chapter Thirty One

Trey was making the last noises he'd make at her house for months. A *thud* when his final duffle bag hit the bed of his truck, a *slam* when he shoved the tailgate back in place, and a *slap* when his palms struck his thighs as he returned to say good-bye.

"All loaded. Just need my backpack from inside."

How long until the quiet was normal again?

He opened the door and beckoned her to enter. "Come inside, Mom. It's too cold to be out here in your pajamas."

She followed him in. "Did you say good-bye to Jake?"

"Not yet. He was already gone when I got up." His voice faded as he disappeared down the hallway.

"Maybe you could give him a call," she called after him. She was stalling.

He probably knew she was stalling.

He returned with his backpack slung over his shoulder. "I need to stop by the office to pick up my last paycheck. I'll see him then."

She nodded. "So, you're ready?"

"Good to go."

She tried to smile. "Well . . . drive safe. Don't speed. Call me when you get there."

"You'll be in school. I'll call you tonight."

"Okay, I'll talk to you tonight, then."

"Oh, Mama. Stop crying."

She swiped at her cheek. "I miss you when you're gone."

"I'll be back soon."

"I know you will." He let her wrap her arms around him, but she'd embarrass him if she started sobbing. "Go now. And don't forget to call."

From the front porch she allowed herself to follow his taillights until they were no longer visible. Would she ever get used to this? She walked back into the house, veering toward her bedroom. Maybe a long run in the cold morning air would make her feel better. As she passed the sofa she plopped into the corner. First she would have a little cry.

Allie leaned into the last turn of her first lap. Maddie kept pace beside her. "Hard to imagine this school year will be over in only three months. Next thing we know, the new year will be starting."

"Speaking of time, you've been married two months already."

She grinned. Couldn't help it. "After my meltdown last month the poor guy probably regrets ever meeting me." She could laugh about it now. "But he was great, even after I was mean to him."

"You've had a lot of changes in your life lately. It would make any woman moody."

Trey leaving home. Her drama with Jake. Their sudden marriage. "I think I'm starting menopause."

Maddie's head whipped her way. "Are you kidding?"

"I have all the classic symptoms. I'm moody and achy, I've put on a few pounds, I'm tired all the time but I can't sleep. And then there's the big one.

No period for months now." She rounded the next bend, starting mile four.

"I wondered where you got those."

Her brand new thirty-four D's had caused Jake to snarl at more than one teenage boy during their week at the beach. "A little gift from Mother Nature."

Crossing the white finish line for the last time they turned and ambled toward their cars.

"Has the doctor given you anything yet? You know, for the symptoms?"

There was that niggle of guilt again. She really should take better care of her body. "Not yet, but her office called last week to schedule my annual. I have an appointment later today after school."

No way! Not today! Allie tried the ignition one more time. Nothing but that annoying metallic gnashing. "Damn!" She thumped the steering wheel in frustration. Now she'd be late for the doctor. She pushed open the door and climbed out. It would be nice if she had time to enjoy the warm sun beating on her or the new buds sprouting on the trees. Instead she pulled out her cell phone and punched the speed dial.

"Hey, babe. How was school today?" He sounded distracted. And someone was talking in the background.

"It's Friday. Whole school assembly." In other words, controlled chaos. "And that was the good part of my day."

"Uh oh. What happened?"

"My car died again. There's nothing but a loud grinding."

Of course he asked the logical question. "Did you call Triple A?"

"I have a doctor's appointment in thirty minutes and Maddie already left." She crossed her fingers. "Can you get away?"

She probably wasn't meant to hear that growl. "Give me a few minutes to tie up loose ends."

Jake had repeatedly suggested she retire her clunker and drive his much newer sports car. Maybe it was time to take up his offer. She circled her aging sedan, kicked its balding tires. Oh, the vehicle had served her well for several years, no need to abuse it. She rubbed its sun-faded hood as though she were comforting a child to sleep.

Chapter Thirty Two

Thirty-five minutes after her call for help, Jake had Allie at the women's clinic. Not bad, considering everything he had to blow off. She signed in and took the padded seat beside him.

Could she tell he was uneasy? A quick glance confirmed there were enough pregnant women in the waiting room to make any warm-blooded male nervous. Only a few sat alone. Some seemed to have their entire family in tow; others sat quietly beside a man. Husband? Significant other? He could only speculate. Had those women's cars broken down, too, or were those poor suckers here of their own free will?

When Allie passed him a *Sports Illustrated* he grabbed it like a lifeline. Guys in the waiting room must be commonplace. He cracked his fingers, crossed his legs, drew three deep breaths, but it was no use. The butterflies were dug in.

The magazine did a lousy job of holding his attention, and he startled when a nurse read Allie's name from a chart and she popped up. "Do you want to come in with me?"

That brought him up straight in his seat. *Oh, hell, no.* He knew what happened in there. He was flipping channels one night and came across a show on cable. Thought it might be something it most definitely wasn't. He had weird dreams for a week.

He cleared his throat and pointed to the magazine in his lap. "I think I'll finish this article about the Suns."

"I won't be long, dear. Don't go away." She gave him a little pat on his cheek.

And grinned. Damn her, she knew he was scared and she was laughing.

Allie sat on the edge of the exam table wearing a flimsy cotton gown when the doctor gave a brief rap and entered the room. She rubbed to quell the nerves fluttering in her stomach. "Hi, Doctor Quinn."

Emma Quinn, a woman in her early forties with streaked blond hair caught back in a tail and purple print scrubs, took her time examining her chart. "It's good to see you again, Allie." Continuing to read the chart, she smiled and lifted her eyes. "I see you got remarried, congratulations."

"Yes, thank you. He actually brought me today."

"Hmm . . ." The doctor made a distracted noise. "So, tell me how you've been feeling. How's your health?"

"Well, a few things have been bothering me lately." She went on to explain about the stomach flu she'd suffered last fall. About the achiness and fatigue. And her moodiness. Doctor Quinn clicked her pen and made a note on the chart. "And when was your last period?"

"Back in May. I spotted for a few months, then nothing at all. I think I'm starting menopause."

Doctor Quinn made a few more notes. "Why don't we have a look?" She laid the chart on a nearby desk and helped Allie lay back on the table. "You were preparing to run in your first marathon. How did that go?"

Doctor Quinn had an easy manner, but the flutters in her stomach wouldn't stop. God, she hated these appointments. "It was a half-marathon, actually, and it went well. She lay her hand on her belly as the doctor checked her breasts. Then she lifted each foot into a padded stirrup. The good doctor was kind enough to provide sheepskin coverings over the cold metal. She studied Doctor Quinn closely, but her face gave nothing away.

"Has your stomach been bothering you?"

Allie's hand stopped. She hadn't even realized she was rubbing. "For a few days now. At first I thought it was gas, but it must be anxiety." She let out a meager laugh, gesturing to the room. "Who actually *likes* this, anyway?"

Doctor Quinn took a seat on her rolling stool, donned latex gloves and began the dreaded exam. "Tell me about any other symptoms you may have."

"What? What do you mean?"

"Weight gain, bloating, night sweats, dizziness, changes in your libido. Are you experiencing any of this? Doctor Quinn finished the exam and helped her sit, leaving her feet to dangle over the edge of the exam table.

Her eyebrows tilted down as she gave the question serious thought. "I've gained a few pounds and my feet sometimes swell if I've been on them all day, but nothing too weird." The butterflies were active again, each one banging away with a sledgehammer. "Why?"

"Allie, did you ever talk to anyone—a friend or a professional—about the physical ramifications of such a grueling exercise schedule?"

She shook her head slowly. "Nooo. Why?

"Running as much as you do can bring on a condition that affects your cycle. And as long as you were at least spotting, you would have been ovulating."

Doctor Quinn lifted the chart from the desk and flipped through the pages. "You had a child once before, is that right?" At Allie's hesitant nod she continued. "Do any of your symptoms seem familiar?"

Suddenly it all came together and she couldn't catch her breath. The crying jags, the constant drowsiness, her breasts, *everything*. A fifteen-year-old would have recognized what she had rationalized away.

Shock. She was in shock. But as the realization resonated throughout her, she turned to Doctor Quinn with joy spilling from her eyes. And whispered a single word.

"When?"

Doctor Quinn answered her with amused indulgence. "Since you're obviously not eight months along, I suggest we do a sonogram to measure the baby, okay?"

Allie nodded dumbly, placing her hands over her flutters.

"My guess is those little nervous butterflies you feel is the baby moving, not a reaction to our little tea party here."

A baby? A *baby*. Allie massaged her belly with a new reverence.

"Would you like to bring your husband in for the sonogram?"

Allie nodded again. There was nothing to compare to the news he was about to receive. "Jake. His name's Jake." Her voice seemed to come from very far away.

The doctor stepped into the hallway but returned in a few seconds. "The nurse will bring him right in."

Jake flipped through an outdated issue of *Newsweek*, checked his watch again. She'd been gone an hour already. Where was she? He didn't realize how worried he was until she stepped through that doorway with the nurse.

She'd better tell the doctor every damn thing that was going on, too. He wanted to know what the hell was wrong.

"Jake Taylor?"

He sprang from his seat. It was the same nurse who took Allie back. He *knew* it. Something was wrong. "Is everything all right?"

She shared a guarded smile that told him nothing. They must practice those smiles in nursing school.

"The doctor asked for you. Would you mind following me?"

Oh, God, he should have dragged her in here months ago. Hauled her through the door and down the hallway and plopped her cute little ass in one of those rooms hidden back there. He was an idiot. He didn't deserve her if he couldn't take better care of her than this. He would never forgive himself if something happened to her.

The nurse edged open a door and motioned him through. He stepped over the threshold. Where was his wife? There she was, lying flat on the exam table with tearstains on her face. He hurried over.

A woman in funny purple pajamas drew an intimidating piece of equipment alongside the table so he stepped around it to bend and kiss her. "Everything will be fine, baby, you'll see. Whatever's wrong, we can fight it together.

"Sweetheart, this is Doctor Quinn."

He grabbed Allie's hand and held tight, willing his strength into her. What the hell was wrong with her? Was she in shock? Did she realize she was smiling? That her dimple was winking?

Whoa. What was that slimy goop the doctor was squirting on her stomach? Since Allie's eyes were glued to the TV screen on the large contraption, he looked there, too. Black and white, squiggly lines and bumps. Something throbbing in the middle of the screen. They really needed to fix that. It was distracting.

"Do you see it?" Doctor Quinn's hand deftly guided a wand over Allie's belly.

"I see it."

See what? The squiggly blob kept moving, weaving in and out of the picture. And now two damn blips pulsed away. Was it a tumor?

"Two?" The disbelief in Allie's voice penetrated his conscience.

Two what? Two tumors? Oh, Jesus.

"Two." Doctor Quinn's nod seemed to confirm the diagnosis. She reached with her free hand and flipped a switch.

What the hell was that noise? The rapid tempo pulsed quickly, reverberating throughout the room like the soundtrack of an alien space invader movie. She should flip the switch back off. "You'll be fine, baby, I promise." He patted Allie's arm. "I'll take care of you." No need to tell her his heart was ready to beat out of his chest. The doctor was certainly taking this calmly. "What can we do about this?"

Allie finally peeled her face away and back to him. He must be a sight with his sweaty forehead, his shaking hands, because she laughed.

The doctor lost her own battle with mirth. "I'd recommend car seats."

"Car seats?" They were both mad.

"Jake, listen. Look closely." Allie peeled her hand out of his death grip and pointed to the screen.

He focused on the screen and all of a sudden the blob was familiar. Allie had a Polaroid similar to that hanging on her refrigerator for a while. A hundred years ago.

Or nineteen.

Oh, my God!

Now that he really concentrated, that alien noise took on a familiar rhythmic cadence.

Oh, my God!

His eyes darted around the room.

Doctor Quinn gave her rolling stool a shove. He dropped onto it, gaping at a beaming Allie. His mouth opened and then closed several times before he finally croaked, "A baby?"

"Almost right. Twins."

His eyes flew to the doctor. Then volleyed back and forth between Allie and the screen. "Twins? Oh, my God, Allie . . . babies?"

Doctor Quinn finished making her marks on the monitor and did a little calculating. "I'd say they'll be along around the middle of July."

July? Shit, that was right around the corner. They had things to do.

Doctor Quinn wiped the gel from Allie's belly. "You can get dressed now." Then she pressed a few more buttons and a photo spit out. She handed it to Jake, then rolled that magical piece of medical equipment to the far side of the room.

Allie wiggled to rise and he rushed to help her up and off the table. "Can you believe it, Jake? I'm so happy."

He bound her to him in an unyielding embrace. He couldn't get close enough to this woman. Get enough of her. "You always make me happy, Allie. But this is amazing. A gift."

Visions danced in his head as he waited for her to dress. His life was bound to have significant changes in the coming years. The doctor wrote a prescription for prenatal vitamins and he tried to pay attention as she instructed Allie about diet and what changes to expect in the near future. When she was finally released, he escorted her back through the lobby. A stupid, silly grin was plastered to his face and he didn't even care. He planned to leave it there for years.

He pulled the truck out of the parking lot and turned left.

"Jake, sweetheart, the house is that way." She pointed over her shoulder, looking out her window.

"Taking a little side trip. This is big news." He took her hand, glanced at the diamond ring he finally was allowed to put on her finger not so long ago. Pretty sure his smile was nearly that bright today. His words rang with laughter as he took his eyes off the road and leveled his gaze on her. "Boy, Allie, your definition of *change of life* is sure different than mine."

She frowned, then squirmed in her seat. "You know, Jake. I'm an educated woman. I am not stupid. But there were a few important details about my body that weren't included in the user's manual."

Yeah, he was still grinning. "You don't hear me complaining."

"Oh. We have to call Trey." She dropped his hand and dug through her purse for her cell phone. There was no answer so she left a message for him to call.

He directed the truck onto the freeway. "I was thinking . . . we can set up the babies' stuff in the spare bedroom. Or we can get those little rocking cradles for our room."

He was so adorable, and already putting a lot of thought into this. "Babies. I like the sound of that." She savored the sound of the word on her tongue. "Jake, pinch me. It still seems so unreal."

He reached for her hand instead.

She placed both their hands low on her abdomen. "I wonder if they're girls or boys." The wheels would be turning in his head, planning for the future.

"I can picture them clearly." His eyes were shining with anticipation. "Little girls with curly red hair and dimples like their mommy. Their dolls scattered all over the house."

"What if they're boys? You could play ball with them and teach them not to pound each other with hammers."

"Sons." He considered this seriously, almost reverently, and nodded. "Yeah, I'd like that, too."

"I'm scheduled to have an amnio next week. Doctor Quinn said we can find out what sex they are if we want."

"What's that . . . Amnio?"

What was she thinking, even mentioning the word? "They take a little fluid from around the babies and send it to the lab. Just to make sure there's nothing wrong."

Jake took his eyes off the road and stole a glance at her still flat stomach. Did he realize his hands trembled on the steering wheel? He cleared his throat. "Exactly *how* do they get the fluid, Alexandra?"

Yeah, he wasn't letting that one go, was he? This would be a good time to have an aptitude for poker. "It's no big deal. They simply insert a little needle into my stomach." She was lying through her teeth. From what she heard it was a damn big needle. And scary as all hell.

"Jake, get back on the road!"

He jerked the swerving truck back into his own lane. "When is your appointment?" He bit out each word nervously.

"Tuesday afternoon. Why? Do you want to come along?"

His expression was pained. And he seemed to have turned pale. "Of course."

She knew from the beginning where they were headed. Jake slowed the truck to made the turn.

"Jake, do you want to know the sex of the babies?"

He turned to her with a shy smile. "Is it okay if it's a surprise?"

She smiled back at him. "I was hoping you'd say that. Surprises have worked out well for us so far."

Jake drove to the end of the lane and parked beneath a jacaranda laden with fragrant purple blossoms. His expression was thoughtful as he stared into middle space. "We have a lot to do in the next few months, don't we?"

Yes, they did. Better to not overwhelm him. She nodded. "We do. But we don't need to do everything at once. We only need to clean out the spare bedroom and buy cribs."

"And diapers. That's a fucking lot of diapers."

"And don't forget the car seats"

"Jesus." Two of them. Would they even fit in her car? He climbed out of the truck. Walking around to the other side, he opened Allie's door and helped her down. "The babies will be crowded with two cribs in the spare room. What if we look for a new house—something bigger. Or we can build one."

"We can do that?"

"Sure, I know a great general contractor."

"Hey, Ben." Allie spoke easily as they approached, as if he were there beside them. They crossed to the bench and took a seat, holding hands. She took a moment to collect her thoughts. Gave Jake time to do the same. These meetings usually ended up as a series of disjointed ramblings, but it felt natural for Ben to remain a part of their lives.

It took time, and their love for each other, but together she and Jake had moved on. Fond memories of their earlier years with Ben were tucked safe and warm in the precious corners of their hearts. Ben was an idiot; a selfish, lying, cheating bastard. But he loved them. And they loved him. There was still much to resolve—her son and Ben's family would need to be told about Meredith—but life went on. And they would handle whatever it threw at them . . . together.

She let a private smile tip the corners of her mouth. Trey was a prime example. On the verge of manhood, he was a mature adult one minute and an awkward adolescent the next.

She stood and wandered the area, kicking up fallen flowers. Trey's back at school now. He's doing well. He and Jax have decided they like snowboarding. What do you think, huh?" She paused as if allowing him time to respond. "Our little desert rat is now a snow bum."

Jake popped up. Kicked at a weed with the toe of his work boot. "Hey B, the Sox got a new pitcher. Maybe this year they'll get their shit together. Last season they imploded after the all-star break. You would have cried."

A few bits of paper lodged up against Ben's headstone, remnants of the last breezy day. Allie strolled over to retrieve them. "I forgot to tell you when I was here before, but your dad and Nick came for Christmas dinner." She laughed because he always teased her about meddling. "Your dad looks good but it seems like he must be lonely all alone in that big house. I wish he'd find someone."

"Trey worked for us over Christmas break again." Jake stopped pacing, sat back down on the bench with a proud smile. "Kid's smart as a whip. Nick says he's good with the subs, too. He'll probably be in charge of one of the crews this summer."

Standing idly with her hand full, Allie went to drop her litter in a nearby trash can. She continued as she walked back. "Maddie and I both finished our race with respectable times. Since our goal was just to finish, we're planning to run it again next year. Maybe a couple of other races, too."

Jake stood and held Allie's hand. "I signed on another block of land in the East Valley. A hundred eighty-seven houses. Business is good, partner, like we always planned. But damn, I sure miss you there."

Allie let her gaze focus on a crowd across the cemetery. Who did they lose?

"Trey had his first girlfriend this winter. She lasted about a minute." A curious smirk bloomed on his face. "The kid's got a good head on his shoulders."

Afternoon stretched into early evening. She shivered and Jake wrapped his arms around her. She tipped her face up to him. He nodded encouragement. This was her story to tell.

"Life doesn't always work out the way we plan, does it, Ben? Sometimes things go sideways and we have to make a new start. I'm making a new start with Jake now. I know you understand, because it was your idea, wasn't it?"

She tucked further into Jake's shoulder and brought his hands around her stomach. "Jake gets to be a daddy now, too. He and I will love our children the same way we love Trey."

She took a deep breath. Tears flooded her eyes, but these were good tears. Happy tears. "Life changes, Ben. Thank you for showing us that."

Facing west with the twilight horizon painted in unusual vivid hues of purple and pink, with her husband's arms warm around her and his gentle calloused hands laid over his children, Jake spoke up.

"Hey buddy, you were my best friend from the time we still peed sitting down. I promised you I'd take care of our girl here and you can count on me to do that.

Allie let her gaze follow his as he studied the engraving on the granite headstone. *Bentley Logan Tate, Junior. Beloved Son. Husband. Father. Friend.*

"You were always such a great dad. You let me tag along and play favorite uncle. Well, I'm counting on you now. I'll need help from my friend."

Her heart tugged as Jake stood there, talking to his friend with the blossoms a profusion of color in the brick-lined beds and the sweet scent of jasmine hovering in the air around him. She grinned as a smile took over his face. A smile that was mostly a smirk.

"Besides, you got me into this."

Epilogue

"Hey champ." The little guy is awake and standing in his crib. I sidestep a pile of blocks and almost trip over a big yellow dump truck to reach him. "You ready to get up now?" He stares up at me with his funny colored eyes. Gray and green, same color as our mom's. His eyelashes are still wet and spiky, but at least he stopped crying. He shakes his head from side to side, obviously misunderstanding the question.

I chuckle and nod my head up and down. "Yes," I tell him. "Up." He just grins that dimply grin of his and shakes his head from side to side again, and again I laugh. "Okay then, now that we have that settled, let's get you dry so you're fit for company."

The little guy raises his arms, waiting to be picked up. I, experienced brother that I am, lift him from his crib and bounce the kid to the changing table. Once he smells human again I rearrange the pint-sized overalls and attempt the impossible task of taming those ridiculous curls. Kind of reddish, but mostly brown. Again, like Mom's. After strapping on his brown leather sandals, I pick him back up and take the wiggle monster to join the party.

The sliding door opens and noise from the backyard pours into the house as I descend the stairs. It's kind of weird, being in this new house when I only ever remember living in the other one. But Mom and Jake made sure I have my own room and I guess by now it kind of feels like home, even though I'm only there during school breaks.

I set the boy down on all fours in the carpeted living room. "Off you go, Aiden," I tell him. "You're a free man now." He speeds away, crawling toward the kitchen and the sound of our mom's voice. He's making this funny giggly noise and his dimple's showing. I always secretly wished I had dimples, too, but I never did. One day when he's older I'll have to explain to him how to use it to get what he wants.

I stop to say hello to Gramps, and look around for Uncle Nick, but he's off in the corner with his date. Apparently, some girl he used to go with in high school. Things seem to be a little heated over there so I follow Aiden into the kitchen.

My sister is there with Mom, putting candles on the fancy cupcakes. I guess I should say my bigger sister, even though she's not bigger than me, just bigger than my other sister. She was a surprise, let me tell you. Yeah, still getting over that one.

But Mom and Jake and I talked and talked until I was all talked out and in the end I figure my dad was a dumbshit who screwed up his life. Sort of screwed up a couple other lives in the process. But he was still my dad and I guess everything I knew about him was true, there was just a whole lot of other shit I didn't know, too. Sometimes I wish I still didn't, but then I wouldn't know Merrie either, and she's a sweet kid. She has blonde hair too, and kind of looks like me, but her eyes are brown, not blue. She's gonna start junior high next month, the same place I went. Kinda weird.

Mom's dealing with my little sister, the littler one. She's crying, and these big crocodile tears are in her dark eyes, and she's sticking her bottom lip out. She learned a long time ago that that's pretty much all she has to do to get her way. She's a brat, and more than a little spoiled, but she's stinkin' cute, so what's a guy gonna do? She's got those ridiculous curls too. Thank God

I didn't get *those* from Mom, but her hair is black and my mom always puts these ruffly hairbands on her head. Which I find laying all over the house when she yanks them off. But Mom quit teaching after she found out about the twins so I figure she has plenty of time to pick up after them.

My little sister can be pretty demanding, exactly the opposite of my brother, who is really pretty mellow. Right now he's sitting there quietly, just chillin' with his chubby little thumb in his mouth. Yeah, he's stinkin' cute too. But my sister, the littler one, just took a deep breath and is screwing up her face, ready and willing to start a hair-raising wail. Situation normal around here. But I try to distract her anyway by lifting her up and plopping her pink ruffles onto the edge of the counter, where she proceeds to kick the cabinet with her little white sandals. Finally she starts giggling when Mom scoops a fingertip of icing off one of the cupcakes and pokes it into her mouth. Everything seems to be under control, so I leave her to our mom and stand back to watch the show.

"There you go, Little Miss Crabbypants." Mom has a whole shitload of funny names for them. Sometimes, like an idiot, I catch myself using them too. I wonder if she called me those stupid names when I was little too. Who knows? Probably.

"Mo!" Like I said, she can be stinkin' cute.

"No more, Princess." Mom hugs her tight and sets her on her feet. "Down you go, Addison."

Oh yeah, her name's Addison. Mom fixes the flower on her stretchy hairband before she escapes just as Jake comes in from the back yard.

"Dada!" Addison giggles again and toddles to Jake, who obediently picks her up.

"Hello, Princess Addie."

He's a sucker. And he gets the funniest look on his face when he watches her. Aiden too. But right now he's smiling pretty normal and smoothing her dress that hiked up when he lifted her.

"Isn't Addison pretty today." She shows him her dimple and there's that dumbass look on his face again. A sucker.

"Addie." She shoves her stubby little finger into her chest, pointing to herself. Again, cute.

Jake walks over to Mom and licks icing off her lip. Pretends he's all stealthy or something and steals a kiss, like Addison's not getting squished.

"How are you doing in here?" he asks Mom.

Mom traps his hand and places it low on her stomach and tells him, "We're good," and all of a sudden her face shines. I read that expression in a magazine once—*Cosmo,* I think—and thought it was a little over the top dramatic at the time. But it really does; it just shines.

Mom already dropped this little bomb on me earlier in the day, and told me it was a secret. But now Jake's face is shining too as it dawns on him what she's saying and he kisses her for so long I'm beginning to wonder if I should get the kids out of the room. Finally they stop and just sort of stand there looking at each other, both of them with goofy grins.

Aiden apparently decides it's been far too long since he was the center of attention, so he takes a page out of Addie's book and starts crying. Jake pulls himself away from my mom and walks over to him. Smoothly executes a one-handed scoop, which brings an immediate stop to the waterworks. He's really got this dad shit down. And not just with the babies, either. I guess I have to admit that I think of him as a father too. But sometimes I call him Uncle Jake, just as a joke. But once I did it to piss him off.

From her perch in Jake's arm Addie can see the platter of yellow frosted cupcakes. They're really fancy; Aunt Tess made them for the party, and Addie reaches out like she's gonna grab one. As if. Jake notices, and starts playing airplane with the kids. He might be a sucker, but it actually is kind of fun to play airplane with them.

For someone who's been an only child practically his whole life, I'm kind of liking this big-brother thing. But sometimes I wonder if I'm gonna have to kick some guy's ass if he tries to get too friendly with Meredith. Addie too, but that's still a long way off. Better talk to Jax about that; he's the one with all the big brother experience. Then again, I won't be the only big brother now. Looks like Aiden will be one, too. Isn't that something?

Meredith's put candles that look like the number *one* into two of the cupcakes and Mom picks up the tray.

Jake calls everybody in, and, sap that he is, winks at Mom, who he calls the love of his lifetime, and kisses the kids, ready to go.

Addie and Aiden squirm in Jake's arms but he holds on tight and steps into the dining room right behind my mom, with Merrie right behind them.

There are still quite a few people standing around outside, but everyone else is in here.

Jake makes a little speech—like he always does whenever there's a big group of people—and everyone gathers close. A minute later everyone is singing loud enough to wake the dead. "Happy Birthday to you—"

THE END

Acknowledgements

The process of writing this book was a thrilling ride. It started off fun and exciting. Eventually became frustrating and maddening. Was often lonely and exhausting, and even frightening . . . and then it was back again to exhilarating and fulfilling. If you knew me during that period of time, you got to witness that. Lucky you!

There were a couple of special women along with me on that roller coaster, both wonderful authors who understood exactly what I was going through—Jes and Carol, you saved my sanity and my book more times than you know. Are you ready to do it again?

It takes a village to get a book from rough draft to publication and if I attempt to thank everyone I will fail miserably. But for my family and friends who jumped on board and encouraged me from Day One, I love you all. Everyone's support is truly inspiring. Mark, I'm sorry but I will probably never write a thriller. Bobby, you can relax, I promise to never try to be the next E.L. James. And Jo, you have the nicest way of telling me my character needs work. Thank you!

For the handful who offered themselves up as beta readers, Allie, Ben, and Jake are better for you. For the bloggers and reviewers who tirelessly promote indie authors and their books, you guys are seriously awesome! And for Indie Chicks Rock, our little group of indie authors scattered all across the country and even a little further . . . sister chicks rock!

About the Author

Hello! Thanks for picking up *Twice in a Lifetime!* I'm an Arizona girl, and I write contemporary romance with heroes who make you swoon yet might live right next door. I'm a true romance junkie and a lifetime avid reader who spent far too much time shushing the voices in my head—until the day I decided to sit down at my keyboard and see what all those voices had to say.

I love music, especially country music, and that's generally the soundtrack to whatever I have going on. At work, doing housework, in the car—the music is always on. Except when I write— that I do in silence.

I also love chatting with other readers, sharing my favorite books and authors, and discovering those new to me. Come by and hang out with me on any of my social media!

www.ingramcontent.com/pod-product-compliance
Lightning Source LLC
Chambersburg PA
CBHW072130250626
47159CB00007B/2630